*Ne*[illegible] has had over t[illegible] novels published and has thrilled leg[illegible] of fans with her seductive Dark Carpathian tales. She has received numerous honours throughout her career, including being a nominee for the Romance Writers of America RITA and receiving a Career Achievement Award from *Romantic Times*, and has been published in multiple languages and in many formats, including audio book, ebook and large print.

Visit Christine Feehan online:

www.christinefeehan.com
www.facebook.com/christinefeehanauthor
@AuthorCFeehan

***Praise for Christine Feehan*:**

'After Bram Stoker, Anne Rice and Joss Whedon,
Feehan is the person most credited with
popularizing the neck gripper'
*Time* magazine

'The queen of paranormal romance'
*USA Today*

'Feehan has a knack for bringing vampiric
Carpathians to vivid, virile life in her
Dark Carpathian novels'
*Publishers Weekly*

'The amazingly prolific author's ability to
create captivating and adrenaline-raising

*By Christine Feehan*

*Torpedo Ink* series:

Judgment Road

*Shadow* series:

Shadow Rider
Shadow Reaper
Shadow Keeper

Christine Feehan's
*'Dark' Carpathian* series:

Dark Prince
Dark Desire
Dark Gold
Dark Magic
Dark Challenge
Dark Fire
Dark Legend
Dark Guardian
Dark Symphony
Dark Melody
Dark Destiny
Dark Secret
Dark Demon
Dark Celebration
Dark Possession
Dark Curse
Dark Slayer
Dark Peril
Dark Predator
Dark Storm
Dark Lycan
Dark Wolf
Dark Blood
Dark Ghost
Dark Promises
Dark Carousel
Dark Legacy

Dark Nights
Darkest at Dawn (omnibus)

*Sea Haven* series:

Water Bound
Spirit Bound
Air Bound
Earth Bound
Fire Bound
Bound Together

*GhostWalker* series:

Shadow Game
Mind Game
Night Game
Conspiracy Game
Deadly Game
Predatory Game
Murder Game
Street Game
Ruthless Game
Samurai Game
Viper Game
Spider Game
Power Game
Covert Game

*Drake Sisters* series:

Oceans of Fire
Dangerous Tides
Safe Harbour
Turbulent Sea
Hidden Currents
Magic Before Christmas

*Leopard People* series:

Fever
Burning Wild
Wild Fire
Savage Nature
Leopard's Prey
Cat's Lair
Wild Cat
Leopard's Fury
Leopard's Blood

The Scarletti Curse

Lair of the Lion

# SHADOW KEEPER

CHRISTINE FEEHAN

piatkus

PIATKUS

First published in the US in 2018 by Jove
An imprint of Penguin Random House LLC
First published in Great Britain in 2018 by Piatkus

1 3 5 7 9 10 8 6 4 2



A CIP catalogue record for this book is available from the British Library.

ISBN: 978-0-349-41975-6

Printed and bound in Great Britain by
Clays Ltd, St Ives plc

Papers used by Piatkus are from well-managed forests and other responsible sources.

Piatkus
An imprint of
Little, Brown Book Group
Carmelite House
50 Victoria Embankment
London EC4Y 0DZ

An Hachette UK Company
www.hachette.co.uk

www.littlebrown.co.uk

*For all my sisters of the heart.*
*This one is for you.*

## FOR MY READERS

Be sure to go to christinefeehan.com/members/ to sign up for my PRIVATE book announcement list and download the FREE ebook of *Dark Desserts*. Join my community and get firsthand news, enter the book discussions, ask your questions and chat with me. Please feel free to email me at Christine @christinefeehan.com. I would love to hear from you.

# ACKNOWLEDGMENTS

As always, I need to thank people for their help. Writing is a solitary business, but it helps when others take care of so many other details of my life in order to give me the opportunity to write when I need to. Special thanks to Domini Walker and Denise Feehan for their continued support. To Sheila English for helping with extra proofing. And also to Brian Feehan for competing with me. You know how that makes me write faster!

# CHAPTER ONE

"Did you really think you were falling in love with her?" Giovanni Ferraro asked his cousin. "Seriously, Salvatore?" He pulled his gaze from the little cocktail waitress winding her way through the VIP tables on the second tier. He'd been watching her for most of the night. Each time something captured his attention, he found his gaze straying back to her.

It was her smile. She could light up the room despite the darkness of the nightclub. There was something innocent and wholesome about her, even wearing the club uniform. She was just the type of woman he would never ever get near, but he couldn't stop watching her until the hurt in his cousin's voice dragged his attention back to those around the table.

Salvatore Ferraro shrugged. He was from New York and had a slight accent his Chicago cousin didn't have. "I wanted the chance at least. I've given up thinking I'm going to find the perfect one, the one my family wants."

There was an edge of bitterness in his voice Giovanni had never heard before, but he understood it. They were shadow riders, and unlike anyone else in their families, their lives were not their own. They meted out justice and protected their people. They were required to begin training at the age of two, so they didn't have childhoods or friendships outside their families. They were assigned bodyguards because, although they were lethal by the time they were in their teens, they were considered too valuable to their families to risk. They also weren't allowed to fall in love with just anyone.

"We don't have that luxury and you know it," Geno, Salvatore's brother, pointed out.

"She was just like every other woman I've met," Salvatore said.

Giovanni hated the underlying hurt in his voice. "What happened?" He already knew because it had happened to all of them. A woman professed undying love when in reality she was after their money. The Ferraros owned international banks, hotels, nightclubs and casinos as well as many other businesses. They lived life in the fast lane, and that drew a certain type of woman.

"She used the 'I'll take the condom to the bathroom for you' ploy. Of course, she had a syringe. Then it was she loved me so much she would do anything for a baby." Salvatore pushed the heel of his hand against his forehead. "*Dio*, this life is fucked."

"Stefano found someone," Taviano, Giovanni's youngest brother, pointed out. "It could happen. Francesca just walked into his life, right there off the street. You never know."

"I know I won't find her here," Salvatore said bitterly, looking around the club at the women flashing smiles at them and trying to get their attention by shifting in their seats and opening their legs to show they wore no panties under their club clothing.

"I've got something that might cheer you up," Giovanni said. "*And* you could make a little money. We all have to agree to the payout."

Salvatore looked up, interested. Vittorio, Giovanni's brother, groaned. "Not again."

"We need to cheer him up," Giovanni insisted.

"I'm all for getting drunk if we're betting on shots," Salvatore said.

"Something a little more interesting," Taviano said. "It's

a game with a point system. Each point is worth a thousand dollars from each of us. Well, not the first point, that's only worth a hundred just to make life better."

"I have to keep track of points?" Salvatore asked, groaning.

"A thousand dollars from each of you?" Geno grinned at them. "I'm in."

"The point system is easy, Salvatore," Giovanni said, leaning across the table toward his cousin. He had to raise his voice a little to be heard above the music. "It's an honor system. One point when a woman asks to dance with you. You can't ask her, she has to ask you. Every single thing has to be the woman's idea. Two points if she lets you feel her breasts on the dance floor. She has to initiate it by giving you the signal, rubbing herself all over you or guiding your hands to her. Three for feeling her breasts under her clothes, skin to skin. Again, she has to be the one to expose herself to you. Undo her buttons, take your hand and put it on her, anything like that. Four is hands on her ass or pussy over panties. Five, the goal is under the panties. It has to be on the dance floor or it doesn't count. She absolutely has to initiate every step at all times. There's no going into the dark, because just about any little fortune hunter will let you feel her up if she knows who you are."

Salvatore sank back in his chair, shaking his head, his white teeth flashing as he grinned at Giovanni, Vittorio, Taviano, and his brother. "I should have known you'd invent a game out of this. You're so competitive."

"Had to do something or I would have gone out of my mind." Giovanni looked around him at the crowd of writhing bodies. "Easy pickings. They're all out to trap you, so have fun turning the tables."

"What if we manage a blow job?" Salvatore asked.

"Seven points," Giovanni said.

"Only seven?" Geno asked. "I'm guessing she still has to initiate."

"It has to be her idea. You're getting a blow job, *and* the possibility of a whole hell of a lot of money from the rest of us," Giovanni said. "It's ten if you manage to nab one that will go all the way, but you have to be willing to be out in the open. No bathroom stalls. A thousand a point from everyone playing. Put your names in the pot, and happy hunting because I assure you, gentlemen, you are being hunted right now." Giovanni leaned back in his chair, smirking.

"Should be easy enough," Geno said. "There's a lot of women who are on the hunt to land a big fish and I'm always willing to oblige them, but somehow they slip right off that hook."

Another round of laughter went up. Giovanni felt eyes on him and glanced up, across the table, to the waitress standing there with her tray of drinks. It was the one he'd been watching all night. She didn't blush when he winked at her, if anything she gave him a look of pure disgust. She'd heard every word. He didn't change expression. Who cared if she heard? She worked for him. He stared her right in the eye.

She had gorgeous eyes. Blue. Not just any blue, but sapphire blue. Like the gems. Her eyes were framed with impossibly long lashes, and right now the contempt in them wasn't working for him at all. She lowered her gaze to the table as she put the drinks there. She turned away without picking up the money for her tip. All five men at the table had thrown in bills, so it was a fair amount of money. There was no running tab at their table, so the tips for their server had to be cash.

She felt so much contempt for them she walked away from her tip—one Giovanni instinctively knew she needed. Who the hell was she to judge him? She didn't know the first thing about his life. And why did he care what she thought? What did he care that she didn't know why he was sent over and over into the clubs so he could cause enough of a thrill ride for the paparazzi to photograph his cousins with him. None knew that the third cousin, Salvatore and Geno's brother, had also come. Lucca was riding the shadows there in Chicago, meting out justice. They were the alibis.

"Fuck," he hissed under his breath, and then he raised his voice, not loud, just pitched to carry. "Stop." He made it an order. A command in a low tone.

She had her back to them, and he watched her stiffen. She had a fantastic ass. Exceptional. Giovanni sat up straighter. The table went quiet as his brothers and cousins realized Giovanni was doing something completely out of character.

She turned slowly back to them. She was wearing the standard uniform of the waitresses at his nightclub. They were all required to wear them. Hers fit her body like a glove. The swell of her breasts could barely be contained in the tight corset. The skirt was short, a little black swingy thing, the corset red, laced up the front. She wore the fishnet stockings, black, of course, held up by a red garter. The heels were red. He'd always liked the uniform, somewhere between classy and sexy, but on her . . .

He pointed to his left side, forcing her to walk around the table to him. He was being a first-class dick. He knew it, too, but that look of contempt on her face, all that soft skin and the wealth of blond curls just barely contained by something red, made him lose all sense of propriety. He wanted to jerk that red thing right out of her hair to send it tumbling down so he could bury his fingers in all those curls. Or maybe it was her mouth. Fuck. That mouth. She wore red lipstick, and she had a perfect mouth. Full lower lip. Full upper lip.

His cock reacted, and there was no stopping it once she stood close and he caught a whiff of her scent. She smelled like cinnamon candy. A cinnamon candy-covered apple. Hot and sweet. Her lashes really were her own, and so were those luscious breasts. He hadn't been so aroused by a woman in a very long time.

She was angry, holding her temper by a thread. She looked straight through him. He didn't say a word. If she had been one of the servers trained to deal with the top two tiers, celebrities who often had a sense of entitlement, she would have known exactly what to do. And where the hell was security? The moment she looked uncomfortable, they should have been at the table regardless of who he was. The rule was absolute. No woman—or man for that matter—was sexually or otherwise harassed in their club. He was going to go on the warpath over this incident.

Still, he couldn't exactly pretend to himself that he was testing their policies, as much as he wanted to. He didn't understand his own feelings. It had never mattered to him what others thought. His family was secretive, and they only had one another. They all knew it from the time they were toddlers and had already begun preparing for their lives. Others thought they were a crime family, criminals, maybe mafia, but no one could prove anything because they were too careful. There was no way for investigators to find the money they laundered through their many businesses.

Playing a game with the women in the club was a dick move, pure and simple, even if they deserved it. She had every right to feel contempt. He was in every gossip rag there was, purposefully. He courted the paparazzi, and he was a favorite. Any member of his famous family was sought after. Everything they did was photographed. They often partied with their cousins out of town or when their cousins flew in to see them. Everything they did had a purpose.

They were handsome men with too much money and far too much charm. They liked to live dangerously and thought nothing of gambling insane amounts of money. They had different women on their arms every night, and the stories of their exploits were in every tabloid. She might blame him all she wanted, but it was the women who threw themselves at the Ferraro brothers and cousins. Not because they cared. Not even for the sex, and if he did say so himself, it was exceptional. Women threw themselves at them for the money.

Should he respect women like that? Essentially, they were trading their bodies for money. They didn't care which brother or cousin they got, they cared about what they could get out of them at the end of their journey. It was like that day after day, year after year.

The waitress held out a long time, but finally—*finally*—she shifted her gaze to his. The jolt hit him right in his cock. It jerked. Pulsed. It was so hard it hurt. He was grateful the table hid the thick length straining against the material of his suit. It felt as though nothing could contain that very healthy erection. He knew better than to continue with what he was doing, but he couldn't stop himself. By now, he should have called security himself and demanded to know why they weren't there, pulling a Ferraro server out of the situation if she couldn't get out herself.

"What is it I can do for you?" She waited a heartbeat. Two. "Sir."

The tone, sweet, musical, pushed right through his chest, shifting something hard and tight inside of him. That note in her voice spoke to something in him, a key to unlock a part of him that was protecting his true identity. He felt as if something inside him ripped apart, leaving him exposed and vulnerable. The feeling was so acute he put his hand over his chest to try to stop the persistent ache.

"I'm Giovanni Ferraro, and you are?"

Like all the waitresses, she wore her name tag on her waistband, right side, but he didn't drop his gaze to look. He forced her to stare right into his eyes. It was like looking at two blue flames, she was that angry—and that beautiful.

She narrowed her eyes at him, and he almost pulled her into his lap. Almost. He had some discipline left. What the hell was wrong with him? He was intentionally taunting his own employee. There was just something about her little flair of temper that got to him right in his gut—or maybe it was his cock again.

"Sasha." Deliberately she didn't give him her last name. "Would you like something else, Mr. Ferraro?"

"Sasha what?" he insisted.

He loved that little snippy voice. Princess reprimanding the peasant. It didn't matter to her that he was the richest man in the room, good-looking and owned the nightclub where she worked; she lifted her chin and gave him a superior you're-a-jerk look. And he was. His brothers and cousins seated at the table with him were utterly silent. He was certain at any moment she would throw a punch at him—and he wanted her to. No one had the right to treat her the way he was treating her. Damn it all to hell. She should have had their security training. If she'd had it, something was really wrong and they needed something better for their servers in place.

"Provis." That was almost a hiss.

"Dance with me, Sasha." Whatever possessed him to ask her to dance? He was really stepping over the line. He hadn't intended to ask her. He wanted her to pick up her tip. He wanted her anger with him to boil over so that she simply walked away and asked another server or the manager to take over.

"I'm working, Mr. Ferraro, and according to the employee manual, we are not allowed to fraternize with the owners. If this is a test to see if I read the rules, I can assure you, I have." She tugged to get her wrist loose, but his fingers tightened, preventing her from leaving.

His conscience was screaming at him, but Giovanni couldn't let her go. "I could fire you. Dance with you and then rehire you," he offered. And the offer was more sincere than he wanted to believe.

"I see. Part of your little game where you win money for treating women with disrespect? I don't think so, Mr. Ferraro. You're not that charming." She leaned down, very close to his ear. "This is called sexual harassment."

Before she could straighten, he caught her by the nape of her neck and turned his head to bring his mouth against her ear. "Baby," he whispered, "clearly, you don't know the first thing about sexual harassment, but I'd be more than happy to teach you." Every word he formed had his lips brushing over her ear. So delicate. Her scent enveloped him, drove him wild. Temptation and sin were wrapped around this exotic creature, and he was falling over the edge fast. Where the *fuck* was security?

She straightened abruptly, quickly, as if he'd bit her, which he considered doing. The enticement had been so strong his teeth had snapped together, just missing her earlobe. A little shiver went through her body, telling him she was far from unaffected.

"Your tip, Sasha," he forced himself to say. "You forgot it." He released her, his fingers sliding over the pulse beating frantically in her wrist. He sat back in his chair, looking as bored as he was capable of—and he'd perfected that look when he was a teen.

Taviano gathered the bills into a pile and handed them to her. She sent him a smile, and Giovanni wanted to slam his fist right into his brother's face. He was playing the game, too. Why didn't she give him a lecture? She didn't look at Giovanni as she walked away. He knew, because he watched her the entire time, or maybe she did, because more precisely, he watched her sweet ass walk away.

He became aware of the silence at the table and eyes on him. He looked around at his family, keeping his expression carefully blank. "What?"

"What the hell was that, Gee?" Taviano demanded. "You were acting the Big Bad Wolf to that girl's Red Riding Hood."

"Just fuckin' bored," he lied, rubbing his chest where it felt as if she'd ripped it open. "One more nightclub and I'm going to shoot myself."

It took discipline not to watch her as she went to two more tables to collect glasses and ask if the occupants wanted more drinks—and apparently, he didn't have any discipline because he watched her the entire time.

"She's gorgeous," Salvatore said. "Wouldn't mind getting to know that woman."

Giovanni's head snapped up and he glared at his cousin. "You touch that and you're a dead man. Or at least maimed."

A roar of laughter went up, but he could feel Taviano's eyes on him. His brother saw too much and Giovanni didn't like it. Until he knew why he was so drawn in by Sasha Provis, he didn't want to discuss it with anyone.

"So, your little waitress is off-limits," Geno said. Salvatore's brother was every bit as good-looking and reputed to be the playboy of New York.

"*All* our waitresses are off-limits," Giovanni said, knowing he was trying to deflect.

"I'm going to make some money tonight," Geno stated. "You all will be paying me a fortune before the night is through." He stood up.

Salvatore and Vittorio stood up with him. Taviano remained seated with Giovanni. When they looked at him expectantly, Giovanni gestured toward the dance floor. "Go have some fun. My leg's aching tonight. I'll wait awhile, see if it's going to get better and then join you. You're going to need the head start."

"You've got it bad, bro," Vittorio said and started down the stairs.

Salvatore and Geno followed their cousin, leaving Giovanni and Taviano alone. Giovanni tried to look like he didn't have a care in the world, but the problem was, he couldn't stop watching Sasha as she moved from table to table and he was furious that no one had stepped forward to protect her.

Sasha wasn't even that good of a waitress. She was pleasant, and it was her smile that drew him from the beginning. She seemed to remember drinks, but she occasionally tipped the glass slightly as she put it down. No one seemed to care because they were too busy looking at her, but one of the women might get jealous and object. He had to guess that she had no training whatsoever dealing with sharks like him.

She had no business serving the VIP customers. Usually

their most experienced waitresses or waiters were given the two top tiers to attend. New servers were given the floor. Spilled drinks weren't noticed as much there. Not only hadn't he seen Sasha before, but it was clear from the way she fumbled several glasses that she was relatively new.

VIPs could be pains in the ass. Right now, there were two tables he was keeping an eye on. One was the mixed martial arts fighters, gathered to celebrate a major win by Aaron Anderson. He was a star in that community and garnered a lot of tabloid attention. He was good-looking and had come up out of the streets, always a great story. At this very moment, he had three women fawning all over him, and he was making out with all three very publicly. The other men at his table were getting similar notice, due to the fact that they were champions in other weight divisions or up-and-coming fighters on their way to stardom in Aaron's division.

Twice, Giovanni saw Aaron put his hand on Sasha's ass. Both times he'd nearly risen, clenching his teeth, furious that anyone would touch her like that. She moved the first time, a subtle hint to stop, and one of the other women moved into position quickly, afraid of losing her place with the fighter.

The second time Aaron grabbed Sasha, she moved back quickly. That put her directly in the path of James Corlege, a fighter on his way up. The man was a friend of Aaron's and running right behind him in rank. Corlege tried pulling her onto his lap. Next to him was Tom Mariland, another fighter in Aaron's division working his way up. He grabbed at Sasha as well, laughing at her struggles to get away.

That brought Giovanni to his feet, but security was already there. They didn't have to intervene because Aaron immediately said something to Corlege and he let her go. Aaron clearly apologized and Sasha nodded and moved away to the next table, the other one causing Giovanni concern.

"Taviano, who's managing tonight?"

"Gee . . ." Taviano's voice held a warning. "We don't interfere with management. What's going on with you tonight?"

"She shouldn't be trying to serve drinks to those assholes, let alone us," Giovanni snapped. "And you know it. It takes specialized training, which she clearly hasn't had. Even coming to our table and putting up with my bullshit. She should have told me to go to hell, or laughed it off. At the very least she should have called security to help her. She didn't know what to do. Who's on?"

"West. He knows what he's doing, and it's obvious he has security watching closely for her safety."

"It's not obvious to me. They didn't come to her rescue when I was harassing her."

"Come on, Gee. You own the fucking place."

"It doesn't give me the right to harass a woman. Especially one in my employ. Which means security needs more training as well. They should have been all over our table, owners or not. What I did was pure bullshit, and no server should have to put up with it. They know that. It's supposed to be part of their training. We made that clear to our managers. We got the best training possible to spot harassment. Where the fuck were they if West has them watching her?"

Giovanni pulled out his phone, slid his thumb down the list of contacts and tapped a curt demand of West, summoning him to their table. He put the phone away and met his brother's eyes. "I've had it with this job," he said. "I belong out there working, not pretending to be the world's biggest playboy."

"We all have to play that role when it's needed, Gee, you know that."

"I know—I've done it longer than any of the rest of you. I *have* to get this hardware out of my leg so I can work again."

Being shot was no fun. He'd taken two bullets in his left leg, one in the thigh and one in the calf. Extensive surgery had saved his life, but had left him with metal in his leg—

and that meant he couldn't do his job. He couldn't go into the shadows as he was born to do. He'd trained his entire life. It didn't matter all the training he had, he'd been reduced to the resident playboy.

He was the decoy. His cousins had flown into town, using their private jet. They were splashy as hell, and he was showing them a good time. The best restaurants, the hottest nightclub, which just happened to be the one the Ferraros owned. No one saw the third cousin, Lucca, who had also come in on that jet. He was out doing his job, meting out justice to someone who thought he'd escaped it. No one would ever see him or know that he'd made the trip from New York to Chicago. The paparazzi made certain to keep that glaring spotlight on the ones in the club, never realizing they saw only what the Ferraros wanted them to see.

"The doctor said a year to eighteen months, Giovanni," Taviano cautioned.

"It won't do any good waiting if I lose my mind."

God, he was in a foul mood. Worse, he couldn't stop watching the waitress. She was at the second table now. John Darby was hosting his friends as he often did. He liked the cameras on him and didn't mind a scene in the least. They tore up hotel rooms and started fights in bars. His reality television program was a number-one hit because the man was willing to do almost anything to get eyes on him. No way should Sasha be waiting on those tables without the specialized training given to the servers dealing with celebrities.

"Mr. Ferraro." West arrived in his immaculate suit, looking every inch the man in charge.

"What's that, West?" Giovanni swept his hand toward Sasha. "She's totally green and you've got her waiting tables she can't possibly handle." He was pissed and it showed in his voice. He let his expression show it as well.

"She has a good memory," West defended. "Better, even, than the experienced girls. There was an emergency tonight. Nancy called in sick at the last minute, and even though some of the others have more experience, they don't have the memory like she does. You know we can't have someone trying to write down the orders. Not for those tables. She's our best for the job tonight."

It made sense. They didn't move anyone up to the first and second tier unless they could memorize orders, keep them straight and were fast. Sasha, apparently, was all three.

"She's not experienced enough to handle the drunks and the attention they're going to give to someone looking like she does." He made it a statement. He couldn't come out and say he didn't want anyone close to her, not while they were drunk. Who was he kidding? He didn't want anyone close to her, drunk or sober.

"Do you want her replaced? Did she do something that upset you?" West persisted.

"No. Just bring me whatever you have on her." They didn't hire without background checks. West and two others were responsible for the hiring.

West frowned. "You mean you want to see the file we have on her?"

"Yeah, West, that's exactly what I want to see." Giovanni couldn't help the sarcasm. What did West *think* he meant?

West's lips tightened, but he nodded and turned away, striding through the tables to the wide stairs leading down to the second tier. Giovanni watched him go down the carpeted steps before turning to his brother. "Don't say it."

"You're out of control."

"Do you think I don't know that?"

"Over having to play the part of a playboy, which all of us have done since puberty, or because of that waitress?"

Giovanni wished he knew the answer to that. He'd made an ass of himself in front of her, that much was certain. His gaze kept straying to her, watching her as she moved through the tables, doing her job. He wasn't doing his, but she was doing hers. For some reason, his job suddenly seemed abhorrent. He didn't want to dance with another woman. He didn't want to touch one or kiss one. He had no interest in a blow job by anyone—unless it was from those red lips and that mouth.

He pressed the heel of his hand against his temple, right where the nagging headache persisted. The loud music wasn't helping, and the fact that he was acting so out of character in front of his family made it worse.

"It might be the waitress," he conceded. He looked at his brother, his hand dropping down to his chest to rub there, right over his heart. "I don't know what it is about her, but she got to me. I've never been this interested in just one. Not like this."

"Asking her out isn't going to be easy after that, bro," Taviano said. "She'll think everything you say or do is part of our game. Thinking about it, it's a shit game anyway."

Giovanni nodded, because it was. His gaze followed Sasha as she once again started up the stairs toward their tier. The more he looked at her, the more beautiful he thought her. Not in a conventional way, it was more than that. Her skin glowed under the lights. There was a softness to her face, as if she didn't wear much makeup and it was her natural skin he was seeing. She had full breasts and a narrow waist, which only served to emphasize her hips.

He glanced over to the table of MMA fighters. Aaron had a woman in his lap, kissing his throat, while another whispered in his ear. Another one appeared to be trying to put his hand on her breast. In spite of all the attention, the champion had moved his head to the side in order to see around the girl in his lap, his gaze on Sasha as she came up the stairs. Giovanni's breath hissed out in a rush.

"Here's her file, Mr. Ferraro," West said, putting a folder on the table. "I printed out everything for you." His voice was stiff and very businesslike. "Will that be all?"

"I've been acting like an ass all evening," Giovanni said immediately. Deliberately, he rubbed his temples. "Unfortunately, you got caught up in my protest. You certainly run this place without any hitches, or if there are, like tonight, you find a way to smooth them over. I appreciate that, as do the other family members." As Giovanni apologized, the tension receded from the manager's face.

"No problem, Mr. Ferraro. I was worried about Sasha as well. I'll pull her off if you'd prefer," he added.

"No." Giovanni shook his head. He was already in her bad graces enough as it was. The top tier of tables earned the most tips. By now, Sasha was aware her take-home could be several thousand dollars. He wasn't about to lose her that, although he'd give her the money to keep her out of harm's way. He kept his hand on the file to prevent West from taking it away with him.

"I do want more training for security, and if she continues to be a fill-in, have her given the training for working a tier like this." He sighed. "I'll shoot you an email."

West nodded. "Of course, Mr. Ferraro. If that's all?"

Giovanni nodded and turned to watch his favorite waitress. Sasha served John Darby's table first, putting the drinks down in front of each of his guests, mostly out-of-control college students. Darby's family was wealthy by most people's standards and getting wealthier through John's celebrity. He'd dropped out of college and become the star of his own reality show, bringing his former frat boys with him on all his excursions. The fines he incurred from hotels and restaurants his friends and he tore up were nothing in comparison to the money pouring in for his show. People seemed to love watching a train wreck in action.

Giovanni knew that Darby had been taken aside, away from the cameras, and warned not to make trouble in the nightclub. Stefano, Giovanni's oldest brother, was a very scary—and dangerous—man. Darby might think he was protected by those cameras, but he wasn't. There would be retaliation if he dared to cause a scene in any business owned by the Ferraro family.

Still, it was important to Giovanni that his family not

find out that the warning wasn't enough by Darby doing something to Sasha to increase his television ratings. Darby was getting too much attention and wasn't taking responsibility for any of his actions. When that happened, Giovanni knew, bad behavior only escalated.

He watched as Sasha shook her head, smiled and stepped back when Darby tried to stuff the wad of bills down her top. He was half out of his seat when Darby laughed and handed her the money. She nodded and moved away, back down the stairs to get her next round of drinks. She only had to go down to the bar that served the two VIP tiers. It made it easier for the waitresses, not having to carry drinks up or down two flights of stairs.

Seeing she was safe for the moment, Giovanni flipped open the folder and began to read the pertinent facts. She was single, no committed relationship. That was always asked casually in conversation. It helped to determine whether or not the potential server was available in the night hours. No husband, boyfriend or child calling them back home before closing, although many of their servers were married.

She was twenty-two. There was no one listed for an emergency call. She lived in one of the apartments over Masci's deli, so in the heart of Ferraro territory. The family, in fact, owned the building and the apartment she rented. They had a property manager, of course, but there was satisfaction in knowing she was protected.

"Giovanni." Taviano's voice was low. A warning.

He lifted his gaze to the stairs. Sasha was just a few feet from the MMA champion's table. All eyes were on her. The way several of the men, including Aaron, were staring at her in such a predatory way had him on his feet. Sasha set the drinks on the table, each one in front of the men and women. James Corlege's hand disappeared under her skirt, and Sasha leapt back, half turning, dropping the tray. Aaron steadied her with his hands on her waist. He pulled her back onto his lap and nuzzled her throat.

Giovanni and Taviano both were on their feet and moving fast. The MMA table was only a few feet away, and Giovanni tossed men out of the way as if they were dolls, got to Sasha, pulled her off Aaron and pushed her behind him. Taviano caught her and handed her off to Emilio and Enzo, two of their private bodyguards, who had followed them.

Corlege took a swing at Giovanni as Aaron stood up. Giovanni ducked the punch and landed three on Corlege so fast his hands appeared a blur. The first punch doubled Corlege over, the second straightened him up and the third knocked him out. Giovanni turned toward Aaron, who backed up, hands in the air. The rest of the fighters were up as well, looking to spring into action. One, Tom Mariland, snapped a roundhouse kick at Giovanni's head. Giovanni blocked it so hard, the leg slammed down, dead. Giovanni followed the block with a sweep, taking both legs out from under the man and sending him crashing to the floor.

"Wait, wait," Aaron said. "Everyone stop. Giovanni, man, we've been friends for years. We were just celebrating. I'm a little drunk and things got out of hand. Let me apologize to your waitress. It won't happen again. I swear it won't."

Giovanni wanted to deck him on principle, but truthfully, he'd acted nearly as bad. Aaron was a good man and a friend he'd known since childhood. He didn't know much about James Corlege, or Tom Mariland, but they'd been drinking heavily as well.

"You can leave her a good tip," Giovanni decreed. "And Aaron, you know me. Your friends don't." It was a warning that despite the training, Giovanni could take them. Aaron had come to his house a few times to train. He knew Giovanni could wipe up the floor with any of the fighters. "No more problems tonight. I'm not going to have my waitress lose out on her tips on this tier by sending her somewhere else. Keep your hands off her. You'll go, not her."

Aaron nodded. "You got it. Again, I'm really sorry."

Giovanni bent down and picked up the tray. The fighters were pulling Corlege off the floor and getting him into a chair. Corlege, looking a little groggy, glared up at Giovanni. "That felt like I ran into a fucking freight train. I've taken a lot of hard hits, but never felt anything like that."

A few others helped Tom Mariland up. He didn't say anything, but he did eye Giovanni warily.

Giovanni ignored the man and turned back to the waitress. Emilio and Enzo made a solid wall on either side of Sasha. Giovanni went right up to her.

"Are you all right?"

She nodded. He could see the pulse pounding frantically in her throat. He reached for her, taking her out of his bodyguards' hands. Pulling her in close, until he felt her body pressed to his, he hugged her gently. "I'm sorry this happened. We're protective of our servers and we definitely should have gotten here faster. Were you hurt?"

She shook her head. He could feel the fine tremors running through her body. He knew he couldn't hold her forever or she would think he was just as bad as Aaron. Also, the paparazzi were out in force. Flashes had been going off everywhere during the brief exchange. He angled them so his body prevented pictures of her. Very reluctantly he let go of her.

"Take a fifteen-minute break and then come back. No one is going to put their hands on you again. Anyone tries it, you tell me or security immediately and they're gone."

"I'll be fine," she said, her voice steady. She took the tray. "Thank you. I wasn't certain what to do. I know they're regulars and pay a good deal of money for having those tables."

"That's *all* they're paying for. They don't get to touch you or any other server. They want that kind of service they can go to a strip joint." He knew, after overhearing the rules of his ridiculous game, he sounded like a hypocrite, but he had to make her understand. "You're under our family's protection, Sasha. The nonsense I was spouting was a load of crap. No one touches you without your consent. Not ever. You understand? Security should have come to our table when it was clear you were uncomfortable with what I was saying to you. You understand? You don't have to put up with *anything*."

She nodded. "Thank you." She turned away, and he nodded to his bodyguards.

Emilio stepped in front of her. "I'll take you down so the cameras stay out of your face."

She flashed Emilio the smile Giovanni wished was for him alone. Up close to her, his body reacted. Not just his cock, his entire body. She did something to him he didn't understand or necessarily want, but it wasn't going away. It was getting stronger. He went back to his table where West was waiting again.

"You were right. She shouldn't have been up there."

"No, that wasn't her fault. They've had a lot to drink. She's gorgeous though. Let her finish out the night. They're ordering more drinks because of her. She's an asset. Just give her the training in what to do if she's in trouble. Taviano spotted the trouble before it really got off the ground. But, West, you go look at the security tapes. I was harassing her big-time. I put my hands on her. Where the fuck was security? They should have been all over that."

West nodded. He held out his hand for the folder on his employee, and Giovanni put it in his hands, detesting giving it up. He hoped he'd made a little headway with her, but he doubted it, not if the smile she'd given Emilio was anything to go by—she hadn't given him one.

The rest of the night slipped away. He danced because he was supposed to, but he didn't play the game and he knew he would owe the winner thousands of dollars. It didn't matter. His gaze followed the waitress until he felt like a creepy stalker. There was nothing he could think of to make things better between them.

She served the drinks to his table every time they sank

into their seats, making eye contact with all of them, Taviano, Vittorio, Salvatore and Geno. It was only Giovanni she didn't really look at. She remembered every drink and who it belonged to. He switched to coffee and water abruptly right after midnight. They'd learned the trick of appearing to drink a lot, and then hydrating. All riders had to be sharp at all times, and that meant not getting plastered. Only Taviano didn't have to stay sober because he'd just come off a job. They could drink after a mission or on special occasions, but not now, while they were working, and technically, Giovanni and the others were working.

The group at Darby's table was beginning to get more than rowdy. They had become obnoxious, taunting the MMA fighters, but Aaron, true to his promise, was keeping those at his table under control. On the dance floor, two of the college boys ended up being thrown out for pushing a woman against the wall and putting their hands on her. Twice, West talked to Darby and security moved a little closer to the table.

"Can't believe that little bastard is going to risk Stefano coming to see him," Vittorio said. "He wants the attention, creating a problem in the Ferraro nightclub."

Giovanni had to agree. He had turned his chair so it put him in a direct line with the Darby table. Only the MMA table was between them. His gut tightened when he saw John whispering to Jerry Higgens, the single cameraman the club had allowed in with them. Around thc table, Darby's frat brothers were grinning, turning their heads toward the stairway and Sasha as she made another trip toward the group. Higgens swung the camera in her direction.

"Fuck," Giovanni whispered. "They're planning something."

He was up and moving, but he knew it was too late. Even if he called out to warn her, it was going to be too late. She was there, bending to put the drinks in front of John. He caught the front of her corset with all the red laces and jerked. She cried out, pulling back instinctively, and the laces gave way. A roar of approval went up as she stumbled back into the college boys with their outstretched, greedy hands. Several grabbed for her naked breasts, wanting to play to the camera. The tray went to the floor, drinks spilling everywhere.

Giovanni waded in, decking John as he passed, ripping Sasha out of their hands, already pulling his coat off to wrap her in. Emilio and Enzo went for the cameraman, removing it from his hands, while Salvatore, Geno, Vittorio and Taviano laid waste to those at the table. It didn't take much, about four seconds, and it was over.

The entire time, the bodyguards for the New York riders stood shoulder to shoulder, preventing anyone from below them seeing Sasha or what was happening at Darby's table.

"Get them out of here," Giovanni said as the club's security swarmed. He didn't bother to listen to Jerry Higgens's threats as the man was escorted out without his camera. It would be returned to him without a single documentation of the night's activities. The paparazzi might have photographs of Darby's party in the club, but not of this incident; it had been contained too fast.

He kept his arm around Sasha, keeping her under the protection of his shoulder. "No one saw that," he assured.

"*You* did," she pointed out.

"One second of it," he admitted. "I'm taking you out of here. Keep your head down and I'll shield you with my hand from any other cameras. Emilio and Enzo will clear us a path to the back office. My brothers and cousins will make certain no one gets near us. Got that?"

Her blue eyes looked a little shocked. Her body was trembling again, and he had the strange desire to pick her up in his arms and carry her from all danger. The music was going strong and most people hadn't even been aware that there was drama. Darby's nasty assault for the cameras hadn't worked out this time. It was business as usual in the nightclub and one more place John Darby would never be welcome again.

"He's a horrible little toad," Sasha burst out.

He glanced down at her. He was a big man, wide shoulders and a strong chest. She was petite, but he could see she was angry as hell. He liked that she was angry instead of wanting to burst into tears.

"It's called sexual assault, Sasha, and you should press charges."

She didn't respond, and he wanted to tip her face up to see her expression so he could tell what she was thinking.

"You're not crying."

"Not yet. I will. Tonight, when I'm in my apartment and no one can see, especially that nasty little weasel. I'd like to meet him in my hometown. I wanted to punch him right in the face. Hard."

"You work those tables, they don't have the right to touch you. I didn't have the right to touch you. Had you been trained properly, you would have signaled security. But they should have seen you were in trouble. I gave them every chance, and they didn't help you out. There's going to be hell to pay for that. Next time, Sasha, walk away. The hell with giving them drinks if they're acting like assholes."

He kept her walking, aware of a few cameras. The cameramen knew him. He was generally easy to get photographs of. He shook his head at them indicating they should back off, and all but one did. He noted that man. Chesney Reynolds. They'd never gotten along, but in the club, he'd always cooperated. Why wouldn't he back off now? Unless?

"Emilio, find Reynolds and talk to him. Money works. A lot of it. If he has footage because Darby paid him, get him to turn it over. Pay him whatever Darby did, the cost of that for a magazine and a bonus."

Emilio nodded. Sasha looked up at him. "Why would you do that? It could be thousands of dollars."

"You're under my family's protection. You work for us,

and that should never have happened. We agreed to take the chance with John Darby because our mothers go way back and they asked us, but we were all worried he might try something. It never occurred to us he might assault one of our servers."

He pulled open the door and found himself alone in an office with her. His brothers and cousins had gone with the bodyguards to make certain there was no film of Sasha anywhere.

Sasha moved away from him immediately, wrapping her arms around her middle. His jacket was huge on her, reaching down to her knees. It made her look smaller, more delicate than ever.

"I don't think I'm cut out for this environment," she said. "I don't understand men like that." *Or you.* It was unspoken, but it was there between them. "I made a lot of money tonight, but I don't think it was worth it. I need it, or I would quit. Which," she said, "I'm not about to do. I still wish I'd punched that asshole."

He sure as hell didn't want her working there, but if she left, she might very well think she had to leave his territory. That wasn't going to happen, so he was glad she needed the money enough to stay.

"I don't understand men like Darby, either. I'm sorry about what you overheard at my table. I can see why you would think the worst of me and lump me in with him." It was frustrating. He couldn't tell her he had no choice but to go to nightclubs in New York, San Francisco, Los Angeles and his hometown, Chicago, and play the part of a playboy—that it was his job. They used the women who would use them as tools, just as they did the paparazzi.

"You're done for the night," Giovanni said. "Go change, and I'll take you out for something to eat and we can sort this out."

"You don't have to do that."

"This happened to you in my establishment. You're

shaken up, which is understandable when someone put their hands on you yet again." He scrubbed his hand down his face, wishing he could take back the rules of that stupid, insane game he'd made up. He wasn't about to let her go; he'd have to switch tactics.

# CHAPTER TWO

Sasha stared up at Giovanni Ferraro for a long time. He was the most gorgeous, dangerous man she'd ever laid eyes on, and he scared her to death when she'd never been afraid of anything human. She came from the country—a very small town, mostly open country, in Wyoming. Men like Giovanni Ferraro didn't exist there. She wasn't a shy, retiring sort of girl. She'd hunted with her father and brother from the time she was about five, although she'd been taught to shoot even younger than that.

Her father believed in teaching his children how to handle and respect firearms. They shot ground squirrels that made holes for the cattle to step in and break legs. The squirrels also attracted snakes that injected venom in the cattle, sometimes killing them. She learned to hunt any predator that might kill and eat their cattle. She had done those things from a very early age.

She had been surrounded by men as she grew up. They were hard-working, good men, all of whom respected women—or at least seemed to. Men who assaulted women to play to cameras or played games for money, she just didn't get. Giovanni certainly was terrifying in that he was very intimidating, and for the first time in her life she wondered what she'd gotten herself into.

"Do you have a change of clothes here?" Giovanni asked, his voice gentle.

She had almost forgotten her corset was ripped. Both

hands flew up to cover her breasts. His jacket was huge on her and she had to hold the lapels closed with one hand. "Yes." Thankfully she'd arrived in her jeans and T-shirt and changed there. She had done that since she'd gotten the job, still too uncomfortable to come to work in the uniform.

"Go change." Again, his voice was very gentle, yet there was a soft note of command. "I'm waiting here for you, so don't think about running off."

Sasha nodded and hurried down the hall to the women's employee restroom where she'd left her clothes. It was a relief to get out of his company. There were rumors about the Ferraros. She saw them come and go from her apartment over Masci's deli. She loved her new home. She especially loved the location. On the ranch, she'd dreamt of living in the city, as teens often did, but she thought she'd never leave Wyoming. She had been certain she would marry a rancher and live close to her parents for the rest of her life.

"Are you all right?" Mary Braiton asked. She was another server and had hired on around the same time Sasha had. She was renewing her lipstick as Sasha hastily took off the torn corset and pulled on her T-shirt.

"Yes." She wasn't certain that was the truth. "What is wrong with these people?"

"I have no idea. They're a different breed, that's for sure. I totally envied you when Mr. West said you could work that VIP tier. All those hot millionaires sitting up there, just waiting to find a girl like me. All that money to be had. Maybe it would have been worth it to have John Darby and his crew take notice."

"For money?" Sasha asked, looking at the other woman through the mirror as she tugged on jeans. "You think it would be worth being assaulted, having your breasts exposed to cameras and letting them touch you, for money?"

"Just think about how much you could have if you were his girlfriend, let alone his wife. And Giovanni Ferraro coming to your rescue? That's the mother lode right there,

Sasha. Sleep with him. Get pregnant. Do whatever you have to do to snag him. If you miss, you can always sell your story."

Sasha slowly straightened. "For money?" She knew she sounded like a parrot, but she couldn't stop.

"Of course, for money. Why else are you working here? Why do you think most of these women come here? They want a chance at the big payoff, one of the Ferraros noticing them. Don't you get it, sweetie? *Millionaires* come here. Celebrities. This is like a huge lottery and you're throwing your ticket in when you come here. It's the best place for people like you and me to meet them. If having John Darby rip my top and feel me up in front of a camera gets me noticed, especially by Giovanni Ferraro or one of his brothers or cousins, believe me, I'd pay him to do it."

Sasha tugged on her shoes. "If one of them asked you to dance, would you try to get him to touch you? Under your clothes?"

"Hell yes," Mary said. "Honey, you've got to get in the game somehow."

"So, giving him a blow job would be acceptable?"

"Anytime, anywhere," Mary said. "That's one step closer to the goal. You want the sex, and hopefully he'll forget to use a condom, or you can at least pretend the condom broke."

"That's horrible, Mary."

Mary shrugged. "It's just as easy to fuck a millionaire as some poor guy, right?"

Sasha shook her head because she couldn't think of anything to say. Maybe there was a reason Giovanni and his brothers played their stupid game. If they knew women came to the club to hunt them, they had every reason to feel jaded. Now, she was kind of embarrassed to join Giovanni. If women worked in the club in order to meet the Ferraros, he probably thought she'd gotten work there for the same reason.

Muttering curses, she stomped down the hall to the office where he waited. He was pacing, but stopped the moment she returned. Chin up, she handed him his jacket. His gaze had jumped immediately to her face when she entered the room. Focused. Intense. Who could look like that? She blushed. She detested blushing, but nothing controlled her color when she was embarrassed.

He slipped into his jacket and gestured toward the door. “Let’s go.”

Sasha stepped back and shook her head. “I’m good now. It just shook me up momentarily, but seriously, I’m all right. I’ll just head home and go to bed.”

There was a small silence. He didn’t move. He just stared at her. Why in the world had she said “go to bed”? Now she couldn’t get the picture of Giovanni naked in her bed out of her mind. Her color deepened. Worse, he looked like a predator about to leap on his prey and devour it—her. She was his prey. A little shiver crept down her spine.

“Sasha, you agreed to go out to eat with me. I’m hungry and want to talk to you about this incident. It was sexual assault. The kind that needs to be addressed. More, security should have come to my table the moment you were uncomfortable. The same with Aaron’s table. We need to have that discussion. I want you to feel safe in your work environment. We may as well do both at the same time.” Again, he gestured toward the door. “Let’s go.”

Had she agreed? She honestly didn’t know. In the restroom, she’d counted up her tips for the night and she’d made a small fortune. It was more than she’d ever considered she could make in a month, let alone in a single night. She needed the money desperately and hated that she did. She didn’t want to work there, surrounded by people she didn’t understand. Nor did she want anyone to think she was after the owners of the club. Still, she had no choice. That money was everything right now.

He’d also mentioned security coming to his table twice, as if he was angry that they hadn’t. Maybe she really did need to know more. If they tested their employees by acting a certain way to see if they did their jobs, she needed to know that to keep working there.

She went out the door ahead of Giovanni, going toward the back exit that led into the employee parking lot. She wished she had a car so that she could just drive away, but she'd taken the bus because she couldn't afford a car. She kept her head down, even when he rested his palm against the small of her back. She felt the heat right through her thin tee. That heat radiated out from his hand and spread through her body, moving like slow molasses, heating her blood until it sang with need.

She tried to outwalk his touch, but he had much longer strides than she did. Overhead lights cast numerous shadows around the lot while illuminating the cars. She stopped, uncertain of where she was going. That was a terrible mistake. He curled his arm around her waist and guided her toward the low-slung Aston Martin in the VIP-only section for family right in front.

The moment his arm was around her, heat went up a thousand degrees in her deepest core. Maybe other women wanted him for his money, but they were crazy if that's what they were thinking about. Her body went into total meltdown. There was no controlling her reaction to him. It was as if two sticks of dynamite collided and detonated together. The rush was almost beyond her ability to control.

She felt his breath hitch in his lungs, just for a moment. His arm tightened around her and he kept walking, holding her upright. Her knees weakened, so she was grateful for his strength. On the asphalt, she could see their shadows had come together, connecting with all the other shadows in the parking lot.

Giovanni opened the door for her, and she slid in without a murmur. She couldn't trust herself to speak, and she was very happy he had to let her go in order for her to get inside the car. The leather felt like soft butter against her arms and, when she sank back into it, felt as if it molded around her yet was firm enough on her back. She concentrated on doing up the seat belt while he slipped into the car, to keep from having to look at him. She was still trying to control her breathing and the scorching need that wasn't letting up.

"You live above Masci's deli, right?"

How did he know that? Yeah, she worked for him, but did the Ferraros vet every employee of each of their many businesses? The manager had been talking to him, so maybe he'd said something. Did it matter? "Yes." She sounded a little curt and tried to soften it with a small smile.

"Petrov's is still open. It's pizza, but in my defense, it's very good pizza. I'm not being cheap. If you'd rather go somewhere else, we can."

"Every single person I've talked to since I moved into my apartment has mentioned Petrov's Pizzeria. I haven't been there yet, but it's on my list," she admitted.

"Your list?"

"I make lists." Her mother had made lists. She couldn't help smiling at the memory. The lists had been everywhere in their house as she grew up. Now, they were everywhere in her house.

"Lists? As in plural?" There was a tinge of amusement in his voice.

She glanced at him, but he didn't look like he was making fun of her. "I make lists about everything. It keeps me on track, although I have to admit, I ignore the lists I don't want to do until it's almost too late."

"Such as . . ." he prompted.

"Buying a car. I'm not wild about the idea of driving in the city. I'm a country girl. I grew up on a ranch, and we didn't have traffic jams. If we actually stopped at a stop sign, we complained about it." And she didn't want to spend the money. She didn't want to have to take a single cent and put it aside to buy a car. She was grateful Chicago had buses.

"What kind of ranch?"

"Cattle. We had a big spread and all of us worked, Mom,

Dad, my older brother and me. We had a couple of seasonal hands, but for the most part, it was just the four of us. Sometimes only three if Sandlin had to work away from home to bring in cash for the ranch. That happened some years, then it was essentially my dad and me working the cattle by ourselves."

"Sounds nice," Giovanni said. "My family works closely together, and we like it that way. My sister-in-law, Francesca, is a wonderful cook. So is Taviano, my youngest brother. He was there tonight with me. One of my favorite things to do is to get together with my brothers and sisters—meaning Emmanuelle, my sister, and Francesca and Mariko, my two sisters-in-law—and have dinner together. It's loud and crazy, but it's always fun."

She couldn't help but be surprised. She pictured him in five-star restaurants every night. "I only have the one sibling. Sandlin. He's eight years older than me, but we were always really close. My dad doted on me, but Sandlin did as well. I think they spoiled me rotten. I went hunting and fishing with them, out with the cattle, camping at night, just about everything. When I had school dances, my dad and mother chaperoned every single one." She laughed at the memory. "It wasn't like I was ever going to get any action with the two of them breathing down my neck. If a boy did ask me out, my dad was like one of those old-school fathers you hear about, he'd take out his guns and clean them in front of my date. If it wasn't them, it was my older, very scary big brother."

"What happened to them?"

She looked at him sharply, the smile fading from her face. "How do you know something happened to them?"

"You're here, not there. There's so much love in your voice, I can't imagine you moving away from them and the ranch. You wouldn't leave them when you would think they needed you the most." His tone was very matter-of-fact.

She was *such* an idiot. Why would she think Giovanni Ferraro was interested in her just because he knew where she lived and now this? "My father got cancer. It was a long road."

With only Sandlin and Sasha to do the work on the ranch, the bills piled up so fast they couldn't pay them all. There was no way to sell off enough land or cattle to pay those bills.

"Just when the doctors told us Dad was in remission, he and Mom were killed in a car accident on the way home from their first dinner out in over a year." She swallowed hard. "Sandlin was driving, but he wasn't at fault. The other driver was drunk. She claimed she swerved to avoid deer, sideswiped them and sent them careening off the road into rock."

"I'm so sorry, Sasha. It's strange to say those words to anyone who suffered loss. They're meant, and yet they don't convey what's really heartfelt. I lost my father a few months ago. We weren't close the way you and your parents and brother were, but it still hurt. I think about all the things I didn't say to him, or he didn't say to me, and there are so many regrets. I hope you don't have those. I hope your times with your parents and brother were good and the memories are beautiful ones."

"They are. I'm sorry about your father." She was learning quite a bit about him in the short ride to Petrov's. She should tell him Sandlin was still alive, but she didn't want to talk about her brother. In spite of the strange connection she felt with Giovanni, she really didn't know him that well, and that was a long, sad story.

He pulled the Aston Martin into a parking slot and turned off the engine. She realized she thought of the sound as purring. The engine purred right before it went off. She couldn't afford one, but she was a little in love with the car. By the time she had the seat belt off, he was around the car, her door opened and his hand was extended. How did he do that? She'd looked down for one or two seconds and then up and he was standing there. He was fast, or she was slow. Either way, she had to take his hand or look churlish.

Giovanni closed the door behind her and, retaining possession of her hand, walked her through a back entrance provided for locals. She didn't want to make a scene by pulling her hand away, so she walked with him, trying to keep space between them. Even this late at night, and it was late, nearly two in the morning, Petrov's was crowded. Heads turned toward them, and she found herself the center of attention.

"Why is everyone staring at us?" she asked. She was fairly certain she knew. Giovanni Ferraro was a big deal. He was gorgeous. Wealthy beyond most people's dreams. He was probably part of some dangerous underground crime syndicate, or maybe an aboveground one. He owned their part of the city for blocks and blocks. For all she knew, he owned the building they were in as well as the apartment she rented.

"I've never brought a woman here before," he said.

She stared up at him, shocked. He'd been with countless women. She just had to go to a supermarket to see his face plastered on all the magazines. He always had a woman on his arm. Usually it was a movie star or model. Sometimes an heiress. Always someone. She'd read the articles and looked at all the pictures. She even had a few magazines stashed in her home, just because she liked to look at his picture. That was before tonight, when she'd discovered the little game he played when he was out with his brothers and cousins. She was certain she'd throw those pictures away.

"Mr. Ferraro." A woman came right up to him, in spite of the fact that there were two couples waiting to be seated. "We have your table waiting."

"I texted them," he said, by way of explaining to Sasha. "Thanks, Berta," he added.

Keeping Sasha's hand, he followed the hostess to a large, curved booth set in the shadows of the restaurant. He stepped aside and allowed her to slide in first and then he slid in beside her. Close. Thighs touching. She didn't think she could handle touching any part of him without having a reaction. Butterflies were having a field day in her stomach and her heart was racing. She knew it was silly to have any reaction at all. Giovanni wasn't for her.

Berta handed them menus. "Wine?"

He nodded. "Ours, you know what I like. Sasha? Do you drink wine?"

She mostly drank beer or a mixed drink, but she was game to try. She shrugged. "I've not had a lot of wine. I don't like white, but I've tried a couple of reds I enjoyed." She was going to be absolutely honest with him. She didn't want him to think she was trying to be something she wasn't. Or after him. She wasn't chasing after him *at all*. She was going to spend a few nights thinking about him, but she wasn't going to pretend. "Back home, there wasn't much opportunity to drink wine. It was mostly beer or hard liquor."

"If she doesn't like it, Berta, bring her a beer," Giovanni ordered. "And bring the antipasto and breadsticks while we're deciding. Who's working tonight?"

There was something in his voice that had Sasha observing him carefully. She couldn't tell from his voice why, but it mattered to him who was making their pizza.

"Benito is on until closing." Berta glanced at her watch. "He closes right at three. Tito will open for lunch."

"Thanks. How's your mother doing?"

Giovanni asking after the hostess's mother shocked Sasha. The fact that he knew she had a mother, or that he cared, shocked her.

"She's much better, Mr. Ferraro. She's out of the hospital and is doing physical therapy. We really appreciate your family helping us when we needed it."

He waved that away. "Emme and Francesca said they thought she'd be able to walk without crutches soon. Anything else she needs, you let one of us know."

"They came twice a week to check on her," Berta said. "It really cheered her up, and they always brought her some little gift. That sister of yours is so sweet. And Francesca, she knew exactly what to bring *mia madre*. I truly don't know what we would have done without all of you. I was so worried about the bills . . ." Tears swam in her eyes.

"Berta." Giovanni's voice was so gentle it turned Sasha's heart over. "The only thing that matters is your mother's recovery."

He glanced down at Sasha and smiled. That smile nearly robbed her of breath. The man was lethal.

"You want to try their meat pie? No one makes it better than Benito. There's black olives on it as well."

"With mushrooms," she supplied when she could quit staring at his mouth.

"There you go, Berta. House meat pie with mushrooms."

The hostess nodded her head and hurried away, leaving Sasha alone with him. She rested her elbow on the table, put her chin in her hand and stared at him. "How well do you know her?"

"Berta? Her parents have been here as long as mine have. She graduated a couple of years ago from high school, was going to college and then her dad was in an accident. It was industrial. He worked away from home and there was some kind of explosion. He lived about eighteen months and Berta and her mother took excellent care of him. He was a good man, and they were very devoted to him. She didn't want to go back to college and leave her mother, so she stayed home with her."

"She's around my age then," Sasha said. "Were you close to her family?" She didn't know why she had to press, but she did. She needed to understand the dynamic going on. He didn't seem the same man as the one she'd met in the nightclub.

"Not particularly, but she's from the neighborhood."

That didn't answer why his family had helped out with bills and care for Berta's mother. "Why don't you take other women here?" She felt silly calling him Mr. Ferraro when they were having dinner together, but he was technically her boss and she wasn't about to call him Giovanni. She had no idea how to address him, so she didn't call him anything.

"It's home. On my home turf, I don't have to be that man."

She wasn't about to let him get away with that. "That man?" She kept pushing because she really wanted to understand—she liked this Giovanni Ferraro.

"You saw him. The playboy. The man partying it up every night. My cousins come into town and what else would we do but go clubbing? Fly to New York, or San Francisco, or anywhere in the world, what's expected of me? Of us?"

There was the slightest hint of bitterness in his voice. That didn't make sense, either. "Can't you do the unexpected?"

"For the outside world? No." That was adamant. "Here? Where I live? Where I count the people mine? Yes. I'm doing it right now."

He fascinated her, when nothing had for a long time. She was beginning to relax in his company, even with his thigh pressed tight against hers. She'd turned toward him, angling in her seat, one leg drawn up. Her denim-clad thigh rubbed against his immaculate suit. She was becoming a little fixated on his eyelashes. They were unexpectedly long and thick and even curved up on the ends. That should have softened his features, but it didn't. It only made him look more intense and compelling. Then there was his mouth . . .

"You sounded as if you really liked Berta and her family, as if you were close friends." She knew she should quit pursuing it, but Giovanni Ferraro had secrets, and for some insane reason, she wanted to know every one of them.

She leaned closer to him, her eyes on his face. When he talked about Berta and her family, he was different—animated. Most of the time, his handsome features were set in stone, those angles and planes unreadable, but she was certain Berta's family was something very important to him because his entire demeanor lit up when he talked about them.

"I do like them," he admitted. "They're hardworking. Honest. Loyal. You can't ask for better people."

She bit back her surprise, knowing if she blurted out how shocking his statement was to her, it would tell him that she thought he was shallow—which she had. Berta arrived with the antipasto, breadsticks and wine. Expertly she took out the cork and then grinned at Giovanni, her eyes laughing.

"Nice job," he commented, a teasing note in his voice.

Sasha had to change everything she'd thought about him. She couldn't equate this man with the one in the club, hunting women for a game and money. She detested that he had been so demeaning toward women, although after listening to Mary in the employee restroom go on about how to trap one of the Ferraros, she had a better understanding of his life.

"Right?" Berta said. She poured a small amount into Giovanni's wineglass. "Do you have any idea how many corks I ruined learning to do this? Benito told me he was taking the wine bottles out of my paycheck."

The hostess was laughing, but the gorgeous smile on Giovanni's face faded. "He what?"

Sasha shivered in spite of herself. At once that got his attention. His focus had been on Berta, but he immediately put his jacket around Sasha, and then his arm, drawing her beneath his shoulder, one hand rubbing up and down her arm. He did it smoothly, accomplishing all of it in seconds, with the minimum amount of fuss, so it was done before Sasha realized what was happening.

"No, no, Mr. Ferraro," Berta hastened to explain. "He was only teasing me. Benito would never dock my pay while I was learning something."

Giovanni took a sip of the wine and nodded. She poured more into his glass and then into Sasha's. The room fell into a hush again. Sasha looked up and Berta hurried away, back toward the newcomers. His brothers had arrived with the cousins. Sasha sat up straighter and tried to pull away from him.

"What are they doing here?" There was no keeping the suspicion out of her voice. If they got one point for getting a woman to dance, what would it be for coaxing a woman to go out when she'd overheard the rules of their stupid, childish game? How could she have been so stupid?

"Relax, Sasha."

His voice was mesmerizing. Gentle. Caring. How could he sound like that when he wasn't that way? She hated that she was so susceptible to him. She'd been alone since her parents had died, and she was starved for affection and company. That was all. Simple human needs. But she wasn't going to be the butt of a wealthy man's joke.

"I'm leaving. I can walk home." She was more shaken than she realized. She actually felt the burn of tears behind her eyes and that added to her anger. She didn't cry easily and certainly not over a man. She pushed at his rib cage.

His arm didn't budge. "Sasha, just take a breath and give me a minute. You aren't being fair to me. I fucked up big-time with that ridiculous game. It was wrong, and I apologize for it. My family comes here often. Most likely, some of the others will show up as well. Don't leave because the pizzeria is a popular spot with us. I've known Benito since I was a boy, as have my sister and brothers. Of course, we would give him our business rather than take it elsewhere. And he'd be hurt if we did."

He sounded so sincere. His family was on their way over to their booth. She told herself she stopped struggling to get out of the booth because she didn't want to look like it mattered one way or the other. She refused to look at Giovanni. If he was making her the butt of a family joke, she despised him. If he wasn't, and she'd accused him, she would be ashamed of herself.

He might play games in his nightclub, but she wouldn't stoop to his level and be someone her parents would be ashamed of. They wouldn't want her jumping to conclusions because she'd overheard something she knew to be wrong.

"I don't know how I can change your opinion of me, Sasha," Giovanni said. "I don't like that you keep thinking I'm making fun of you, or whatever it is you're thinking of me."

"That you're an ass for making up such a mean, spiteful, hurtful game," she said and picked up the wineglass. She needed something to fortify her. What was she doing, sitting in the Ferraro booth with Giovanni Ferraro? She didn't belong there. She didn't even want to be there.

"That much is true," he admitted. "I hope you like the wine. We have vineyards and a winery in Italy. My family runs it. Cousins."

"You have a huge family. So many cousins." She took a cautious sip of the wine. She didn't know much about wine, but it was good.

"It's rich. Full-bodied," Giovanni said. "It's said that when you open a bottle of this wine, with each sip you get unique sensations and taste. Even emotion." His smile took her breath. "Keep sipping. Right now, you're angry with me, justifiably so, but perhaps another sip will make you like me a little better."

"Giovanni, Sasha." Taviano slid into the booth on the other side of Sasha, hemming her in. "We couldn't get out of there. Believe it or not, Sid Larsen refused to give up his film, and he's always been cooperative with us. The cameraman Darby hired, Jerry Higgens, got nasty, although all he did was make threats. What an asshole." He glanced down at Sasha. "Sorry, didn't mean to talk crap in front of you. Men like Larsen and Higgens get to me. They make a living out of taking photographs of other people's private moments."

"Don't forget that little runt, Chesney Reynolds," Vittorio said. "He wanted to fight us. I think he had someone in the bushes trying to film us with their cell."

Vittorio slid into the booth beside Taviano, and Geno pushed in beside Giovanni. Now she was in a booth surrounded by Ferraros. They were big men, and she felt a little dwarfed in comparison. Salvatore took the last option, a seat by his brother. Berta put more wineglasses on the table as well as two more bottles of wine.

"I sent the names of all the cameramen to the aunt and uncle," Taviano said.

Sasha had no idea what that meant and she wasn't going to ask. "Why would they want to fight you?" she asked.

"Darby makes his living on his reality television show," Giovanni explained. "The show gets high ratings because they cause problems. Darby wanted to make a scene, and that's why he ripped your clothes. He doesn't care who he hurts in the process, it's all a—" He broke off.

Sasha knew he'd been about to say *game* and thought better of it.

The antipasto was gone in seconds as well as all the breadsticks. Giovanni grabbed the last one right out of Vittorio's hand and gave it to her. "Thief. What the hell are you all doing?"

"Saving little Sasha, of course," Vittorio said placidly. He leaned back and flashed her a smile. "Giovanni has a tendency to give us all a bad name. We're not anything like him."

"You were pretty eager to play your little game," she pointed out, leveling her gaze at him. Giovanni might not want to bring it up but she wasn't going to let the opportunity pass. "In fact, you were the first one leaving the table. Your two brothers remained behind."

A roar of laughter went up at Vittorio's expense. He put his hand over his heart. "You've crushed me, *bella*. *Crushed* me."

He was so dramatic she couldn't help but laugh with them. "I don't think I believe a word of it. Who was the big winner tonight?"

There was a sudden, sobering silence. She looked

around the table. "Someone had to have won." She wasn't letting it go. They could kick her out of their little circle for all she cared. If they could play their game, the least they could do was own up to it.

"I did," Geno admitted. "Had four different women want to marry me on the spot."

"That must be distressing." Her tone was sarcastic. "Women liking you."

"It is, *tesoro*," Giovanni said. "It sounds wonderful to someone who doesn't have this kind of problem everywhere they go. How could any of those women possibly love him enough to marry him? Or even like him? They don't know him. They aren't trying to get to know him. If they sleep with him, it isn't for a hookup or because they're so wildly attracted to him. It's because of money. Pure and simple. They want money, and we've got it."

She lifted her gaze to his face. "So, you're saying, if I'm at a nightclub and a wealthy man comes up to ask me to dance, I should say no, because if I don't, he thinks I'm after his money? That's ridiculous. I don't know what he's thinking any more than he knows what I am. I want to dance. I'm thinking he wants to dance. You all started your game with that premise—anyone asking you or agreeing to dance wants your money."

"Because they do, *cara*," Vittorio said. "It's the sad truth. We go to a lot of nightclubs, and it's the same night after night."

"I love to dance. My guess is, at least half the women in the nightclub, maybe a much larger percentage, are there just to dance and have fun. It would be such a shame for you to miss out on getting to know someone nice because you're so busy trying to win your game."

"It's easy enough to find out," Salvatore said. "What woman, just wanting to dance, allows a man to put his hands all over her, or initiates giving him a blow job? *Initiates* it?"

"Well, obviously, then you would be right about her, but

if I agreed to dance with a man and he tried putting his hands on me, I'd make it very clear he was out of line. If he did it a second time, I'd probably deck him."

That made them all laugh again. Taviano poked Giovanni. "Your little kitten has claws."

*"Or,"* Sasha continued because Giovanni had put his hands on her and she hadn't really objected because she was attracted to him, "she might be physically attracted, because, let's face it, all of you are rather good-looking, although I don't want that to go to your heads. If she was drinking and wanted to have a good time and maybe find a partner for the night, or hope she's finding a man interested in her, she might let him touch her that way."

Giovanni's arm had settled back around her shoulders and he ran his finger along her arm. Even under his coat, she felt the impact and another little frisson of heat moved down her spine to settle low. He was definitely lethal to women, and to her in particular.

Taviano suddenly narrowed his eyes. "Damn it. Just fucking damn it. What is she doing here this time of night?"

They all followed his gaze to the entrance. Two girls and three boys were waiting to be seated. One of the girls stumbled and giggled as a boy caught her around the waist, and all five laughed. The girl that had stumbled was beautiful, with long, dark hair falling almost to her waist. She looked like Sasha imagined an angel might, too beautiful to be of this earth.

"She's drunk," Taviano said. "I'm getting tired of having to pull her ass out of parties and get her home. That fucking Bruno Vitale has her going out with boys out of the neighborhood and way too old for her. I told Stefano to talk to her. If I have to do it, I'm going to lose my mind and do something crazy like put her over my knee." He took another sip of wine and slid out of the booth, storming over to the group.

"Who is she?" Sasha said. "They look harmless enough." The girls looked young, the boys college age, a little older.

"Nicoletta," Giovanni answered, his voice tight. "Vittorio, how much has Taviano had to drink tonight?" He glanced down at Sasha. "He doesn't usually drink, but he had the night off, the first in a long time. He's been covering my shifts after my accident." He hadn't been paying attention because he was watching Sasha.

Sasha wanted to know what accident he'd been in.

"Taviano *has* been drinking a lot. More than I've ever seen him. He seemed upset about something tonight," Vittorio said.

"Should we call Emme to escort Nicoletta home?" Giovanni asked.

It was too late. Taviano was in a heated argument with her. She backed away, shaking her head. He caught her around her waist and slung her over his shoulder and marched out. The others in her group stood at the entrance, stunned, staring after Taviano and the struggling girl uneasily. Everyone saw him reach up and smack her bottom hard as he went through the door.

"He didn't just remind her in that very loud voice, in front of her friends and everyone in here, that it's past her curfew, did he? Or *spank* her?" Sasha was outraged.

Giovanni wiped the smirk off his face instantly. "Nicoletta is the epitome of a pain in the ass," he explained. "You have no idea how many times a member of my family has been called to find her and escort her home. I'm talking called out of important meetings, dinners, our beds. If we happen to be on a date. Major charity events. You name practically any circumstance and we've had to leave to find that little hellion. I don't envy the man who ends up with her."

"Is she related to you?" Underneath Giovanni's humor, she heard worry.

"Not by blood, but we look out for her. She's Lucia and Amo's foster daughter. She's had it rough, I'm not going to lie, but she's wild and they worry. Stefano needs to step in."

Stefano Ferraro was the head of the Ferraro family in

Chicago. She knew that much. Everyone knew it. "What could Stefano possibly do to change a wild teen? Weren't all of you a little wild? Didn't you sneak out of the house and party?"

The men looked at one another and she could see something secretive pass between them, but no one answered her. More antipasto and breadsticks were ordered along with several large pizzas. She felt a little funny being the only woman in the booth with the powerful Ferraro family, but she had to admit, they treated her with the utmost respect.

She found herself laughing more than she had the entire time since her parents died. They seemed to know everyone. They weren't in the least patronizing and included her in the conversation, asking her opinion and sometimes debating a point with her. Through it all, Giovanni kept his arm around her. He was warm and solid. He felt protective, and that was something she hadn't known in a long while, either. Sasha gave herself permission to enjoy the rest of the early morning hours with them. Once she did that, she had fun because they were that—just plain fun.

# CHAPTER THREE

"Sasha Provis is a shadow rider. At least, she's capable of being one," Giovanni announced to his family. "She's definitely mine. I was attracted to her before our shadows ever connected. In the club, when she spoke for the first time something in me opened up and she just poured inside." He didn't know any other way to describe it.

Stefano glanced up at him from where he was carrying Francesca's famous avocado pasta to the table. It was a huge bowl, one, Giovanni noted, that was getting larger and larger. "You didn't call me?"

Giovanni concentrated on putting silverware on the table, not looking at his older brother. He could barely breathe thinking about Sasha sitting up in her apartment alone, or maybe getting phone calls from other men asking her out. She had said no when he asked her out the next night, although she softened the blow by telling him she was scheduled to work at her second job. Who knew she had a second job? Why didn't he know? He'd put the investigators on her. By the end of the night, he hoped to know everything there was to know about her.

"You and Francesca had the night off together for a change. No one was going to interrupt you."

Stefano looked around at his brothers, sister and sister-in-law, all gathered together for a meal. The sourdough bread was fresh and hot. The pasta and a giant salad were already on the table. They all pulled out chairs. No one had assigned them individual seats, but they tended to choose the same ones all the time.

"We're looking for nieces and nephews," Vittorio said. "Looking to you to get it done, Stefano. Giving you as much time alone with your woman as possible."

"It's not easy when we're one rider down," Ricco said. "I told you I'd give you a few lessons with the rope. Tie her down and get it done."

Francesca turned a fiery shade of red. "You are *not* discussing our sex life." She made it a statement as she glared at them all, one hand poised above her water glass.

"Of course we are," Giovanni said. "Why wouldn't we? It's important he keeps you happy, satisfied, and knocks you up. You ever heard of barefoot and pregnant? Stefano is so damned bossy he's going to piss you off a lot. We're not losing you, so that means we need a lot of *bambinos* running around, keeping you too busy to run off."

A look passed between Francesca and Stefano. She shook her head slightly and then rolled her eyes while the others laughed, but nodded as if in complete agreement. "See, Mariko?" She turned to her sister-in-law. "They're taking it easy on you, but this is going to be your life soon. They interfere with everything. I can't turn around without one of them underfoot, or one or more of their cousins. Emilio, Enzo and the others. Try planning surprises for your husband."

Mariko smiled. "You're the one we all look to, Francesca," she explained gently. "Of course, we're going to look out for you."

Giovanni noted that Mariko, Ricco's wife, used *we* instead of *they*. She'd included herself in looking after Francesca. Mariko was a huge asset to the family, a trained shadow rider, very fast and efficient. Without Giovanni's ability to ride, she was taking jobs as well.

They rarely worked in Chicago. They were called in to work in New York, San Francisco and Los Angeles. Their work took them all over, but those were the main places they traveled. Salvatore, Lucca and Geno, three brothers and their cousins, were called in from New York if there was a job to be done in Chicago, as they had been the other night.

"Who looks after you, Mariko?" Francesca asked. "And Emme?" She looked down the table to Emmanuelle, Giovanni's sister.

"We're riders, honey, so they do put bodyguards on us, but it isn't the same," Emmanuelle said. "We were trained from a young age to fight in just about every style imaginable. You are the center of our world. You know that, Francesca."

"What's wrong, baby?" Stefano's voice was soft. Loving.

There was silence at the table. All forks went down as they collectively looked at her. Her hand trembled as she took a sip of water. A distraction, Giovanni knew. She was being cautious. She shook her head and carefully placed the glass back on the table.

"Nothing. Really."

"Francesca."

That was all Stefano said, but they all knew that voice. When he used it, the tone was pure command and there was no getting around it. They were all capable of using that voice. They had to be, but Stefano was different. No one argued much with him. His hand went to the back of his wife's head, stroking a caress down that length of gleaming hair.

She shrugged. "It's just silly really. I'd like to do a few things outside of my home sometimes. Have a girlfriend to go shopping with. Go out to lunch. Work again." She lifted her lashes just enough to see Stefano's face. His features were expressionless.

Giovanni found his own body tensing up. Francesca had worked at Masci's when she'd first arrived in Ferraro territory, but she had quit just before her wedding. The paparazzi had bothered her nonstop, and she'd had enemies. Stefano had orchestrated her quitting the job in order to better protect her. Giovanni looked at Stefano, waiting for his reaction.

"Baby, you know if you want to work, I'm going to be

supportive of that, unless of course you were pregnant, and then standing on your feet all day wouldn't be good."

Giovanni snapped his head around, looking at Vittorio and Taviano. Then Ricco and Mariko. Lastly Emme. No one moved. No one ate. They waited.

"I don't want you ever to feel like a prisoner in our home. Or with me or your family. I know sometimes it has to feel like we're smothering you with our protection. What would you like to do, Francesca? I know Pietro has hired another woman, but he'd give you your job back the moment you asked for it. He can lower her hours and give you whatever hours you want to work." It was a subtle reminder she would be taking a job someone else really needed.

Stefano's gaze shifted toward Ricco just for a moment, but he took the cue. He leaned across the table toward his sister-in-law. "I thought you were doing tons of charity work and handling all the people in our territory. Are you tired of that?"

She was doing far more than her share in that field. Sometimes Emmanuelle could go with her, other times not.

Francesca shook her head. "No, it's interesting work. I'm on a few committees and the board for raising funds for the local cancer fund. The one that helps the families through it. I think it's important work. And I do love visiting with all the families . . ." Her voice trailed off.

"Honey." Emmanuelle's voice was very low. "What is it that's making you upset? You told me the other day that you loved what you did. It *is* important work."

"I was talking with Eloisa the other day . . ."

There was a swift intake of breath. Giovanni felt his stomach start to burn. Stefano's features darkened, but he remained silent. All of them did. Waiting. Their mother could wreak havoc as no other woman could.

"No one is eating," Francesca said rather desperately. "The food's going to get cold. This isn't important enough that you're all getting upset."

"Of course it is, Francesca," Vittorio said. He was gentle

with his sister-in-law, his voice almost mesmerizing. He didn't raise his voice, but then Vittorio never did. He kept that velvet soft tone that stroked inside a person and made them want to comply. "Anything that makes you upset is important to all of us, let alone Stefano."

"Enlighten us to what wisdom our parent passed on to you," Stefano said.

Francesca's gaze shifted to his face. "Don't be like that. Eloisa is trying."

"Bullshit, she's trying," he snapped. "Damn it, Francesca, when are you going to learn our mother is a first-class bitch?" His breath hissed out between his teeth.

Giovanni understood. They all did, all of them with the exception of Francesca. Even Mariko knew Eloisa took great pleasure in shredding others. She enjoyed ripping people into little pieces, making them cry and then walking away, superior and happy that she'd accomplished her mission.

"That's not nice, Stefano," Francesca said. "She's your mother."

"Baby." His voice softened. "You had a wonderful mother and you're going to be one. Our mother was never that. Never. She didn't hold newborn babies and look down at them with love. She handed them off and stayed away until they were two and she could start their training. She didn't cuddle them when they got hurt. Or get up with them in the middle of the night if they had a nightmare. I know Eloisa and what she's like."

"She loves all of you."

"In her way, yes, she does. I won't argue with that. But she isn't compassionate or caring, at least not to us. For whatever reason, Eloisa chose to ignore that she had children. We're all past that. We don't have mommy issues. You keep trying to mend those fences, and I love you for it. We all do, but she's going to eat you alive, and I can't allow that." Stefano's voice changed completely. He used his commanding don't-fuck-with-me-or-else voice. Giovanni couldn't help wincing. "Tell me what she said to you."

Francesca sighed. "She said I was rather worthless sitting on my barren ass at home all day. She asked me point-blank if I had been tested and was I able to produce children. She made it very clear that I better be able to at least have children or I was useless to you and the family."

Giovanni gasped, and he wasn't alone. Francesca was the center of their lives. She mellowed Stefano, the head of their family. More, she brought him joy and fun, things he'd never had. He couldn't imagine what they'd do without her now that she was with them.

Stefano studied his wife's face for a long time. The clock ticked. Breath moved in and out of lungs. Silence stretched to a screaming point. He caught Francesca's chin and turned her face fully to his. "I never, in my life, heard the kind of fucked-up bullshit my mother manages to spout. I often wonder if she's in her room all night just thinking shit up. You don't sit on your ass. You go out in the neighborhood and visit the elderly. Men and women we've known our entire lives, but you just met. You do that. You bring them groceries and make certain they have what they need to be comfortable. I heard you helped old man Lozzi pay his bills when he was confused. You took him to the doctor, didn't you?"

Francesca frowned at him, nodding. "His diabetes was out of control."

"The doctor told me you saved his life. Then you went back to his home, paid his bills, cleaned his house, which by the way next time you bring in the cleaning crews. You also stocked his home with the kind of food he needed. He isn't the only one. You visit the residents who are sick. I tried to do that in my spare time, but never could fit it all in. We all did. Even dividing the work between us, we couldn't get it done. You took that off of all of us."

"Emme goes with me."

"When I can," Emmanuelle said. "But it isn't that often."

"And all the committees and boards you're on, Francesca," Stefano continued. "Each of them needs a Ferraro on them. You took that off of us as well. More importantly, baby, you are my entire world."

"*Our* world," Giovanni said. "You, Mariko and Emmanuelle are important to us, and not because you can give the family babies."

"If we never have a child, I would go through my life happy," Stefano assured. "The doctor said there was no problem and we can have children." He reached out his hand to her, threading his fingers through hers, his eyes on hers. "Just relax, baby, we're going to be fine. *You're* going to be fine. Just stay the hell away from Eloisa. I'm going to make it very clear to her that she doesn't come here unless I'm home."

"Don't do that, Stefano," Francesca said. "It was silly of me to let her upset me."

"I'm going to make it *very* clear to my mother that she isn't allowed to come near you unless I'm with you," he reiterated, making it a decree. "Dinner is getting cold."

That was the end of the discussion, and they turned back to their food. Giovanni felt relief that Stefano had handled the situation the way he had. It was a learning experience. He'd need a few lessons, especially after blowing it with Sasha.

"How the hell do you keep your temper in check?" he asked Stefano.

Stefano's gaze swept over him. "You've always been cool and then your temper burns so hot and out of control, it takes down everything in its path. You just have to acknowledge to yourself that that cool is all a façade. Know what triggers it and be very careful. You're going to need to be calm and rational to reel this girl in."

"She isn't a fish," Francesca objected.

"She's not even on the hook," Giovanni said, annoyed. "I can get every woman I *don't* want, but not the one I do. She's attracted, but running in the opposite direction very fast."

Ordinarily, his family would have been teasing the hell

out of him, but Sasha was the *one*. He'd made that clear. Their shadows had connected, and already that pull was being felt. She'd unlocked that vulnerable place inside of him and now he had no choice but to actively pursue her. There could be no mistakes. She was that woman, the one destined to be the center of his world in the way Francesca was for Stefano and Mariko was for Ricco.

"Why?" Stefano asked.

Giovanni stiffened. "Why what?"

"Why isn't she on the hook? She's a server in our nightclub. You had dinner with her after hours. From what I was told, there were two incidents at the club and both times you stepped in and took care of it before security. Why isn't she on the hook?"

"Stefano," Francesca said gently.

Giovanni knew he wasn't going to drop it. He was ashamed to tell Stefano in front of Francesca and Mariko about the game he'd made up.

Stefano watched him eat his pasta. Giovanni took a sip of wine to wash the pasta down and then made his confession. "She overheard me telling Salvatore and Geno about this stupid game we sometimes play when we're bored."

Stefano's face darkened. "Game?"

"For money. We bet on women." Giovanni glanced at Francesca's face. She looked at him under her long lashes, her face soft and compassionate. He hated that she was going to be disappointed in him. "I get so fucking sick of women throwing themselves at us because we're Ferraros."

"The point is, Giovanni, to use that to our advantage. We need to be seen in public while one of us is dispensing justice," Stefano said mildly. "What did she overhear?"

"Nothing that could compromise us," Giovanni said. "You know I would never talk about our work." Although he would have liked to do just that with her. He wanted to explain to Sasha why he was upset and tired of the nightclubs. Why he had to appear to be a playboy when he wasn't. Okay, maybe he was. God. He scrubbed a hand down his face. He didn't even know anymore. He wanted to go up to her apartment and just sit with her. See her face. Watch her smile light up her eyes. All this time, and he hadn't made any headway.

"What did she overhear?" Stefano repeated.

"The game. It's a point system, Stefano. A woman asks us to dance is one point. She initiates certain things on the dance floor, more points. She offers to do certain things, more points. That sort of thing. Sasha overheard and was rightfully disgusted and now has a very bad opinion of me."

"The woman has to initiate the contact?" Francesca asked, leveling her gaze at him.

She understood all right. There was nothing slow about Francesca. He glanced at Mariko. She had been raised in Japan, and English wasn't her first language, but she understood as well.

"This is a game you played, Ricco?" she asked her husband.

Ricco took her hand. "You know I did all sorts of things I shouldn't have done, *farfallina mia*. I'm not that man now."

"Perhaps it would be good to retire this game," Francesca said and looked pointedly at Vittorio and Taviano. "And if there is a female version of the game, Emme, you need to opt out of that as well."

Taviano and Vittorio concentrated on their food. Emme glared at Giovanni. "There is definitely no female version of the game, nor have they played it around me." Her tone indicated she would have shut it down, which they knew, so they'd never allowed her to overhear the bets between them.

Giovanni wanted to kick his brothers under the table for leaving him hanging out there. "Taviano had to take Nicoletta home last night, Stefano. She was drunk again and out far past her curfew. She's out of hand."

"She's a hellion," Vittorio said. "You *have* to talk to her, Stefano."

"I talked to her last night," Taviano said. He looked

around the table. He hadn't touched his wine and he looked very serious. "Someone had to, Stefano. She was out of control. I don't care if she's eighteen, twenty or older. She has no business getting drunk and missing her curfew or putting herself in danger like that. Lucia and Amo are good people. They took her in and gave her a good home. They deserve respect at the very least."

"Taviano"—Francesca's voice was gentle—"she doesn't respect herself yet. She needs direction."

"I gave her direction," he snapped and then shook his head. *"Mi dispiace,"* he apologized. "I might have been too hard on her." He pushed the heel of his hand against his forehead, rubbed as if he had a headache and then took a deep breath and looked around. "I was hard on her. Deliberately. I wanted her to think about the chances she's throwing away. I was fucking drunk myself, and when she fought me . . ." He shook his head. "Let's just say, I wasn't gentle."

"Taviano." Francesca's voice was soothing.

Giovanni felt guilt. He knew Taviano was getting fed up with Nicoletta's late nights, her escapes out the window and the incessant partying. All of them were, being called away when they were busy. He also knew Taviano didn't drink much. It made him belligerent. Giovanni knew he should have escorted Nicoletta home instead, but he hadn't wanted to leave Sasha.

"We'll start her self-defense training," Stefano decided. "That will at least make her so tired she won't be looking to crawl out her window. She'll never be fast enough to ride the shadows, but she'll know how to defend herself and she'll be able to get into the shadows if there's a need to escape fast. I've been working with Francesca. No matter what, our women need to know how to use the shadows to escape if we're ever under attack again."

"I don't know if training her to beat the hell out of us is the right thing to do," Taviano said. "I've got a few bruises."

"We'll make it clear she isn't to use her knowledge on any family member," Stefano said. "Taviano, you can tell her—"

Taviano shook his head, throwing his hands into the air. "Not me. I'm done with her for a while. One of you can talk to her."

"I will," Francesca said. "I want to meet Giovanni's Sasha anyway. I heard she was the one working my old job at the deli. Pietro hired her full-time. Most of the other workers are part-time. Nicoletta works with Lucia at Lucia's Treasures and then she goes to the flower shop. I can time it so I can see both of them."

"That fucking Bruno at the flower shop needs to have the shit kicked out of him," Taviano snapped. "He's the one that's been dragging Nicoletta to these parties."

"He'll be taken care of," Stefano said.

"I want to be there," Taviano insisted, looking straight at his brother, waiting for the nod.

"Wait a minute. Are you telling me Sasha works full-time at the deli and full-time at the nightclub?" Giovanni was outraged. "That's *sixteen* hours of work. Is she crazy?" He started to get up, as if he might rush right over to her apartment and confront her—and he might have.

"My advice, Giovanni," Stefano said, "is to keep her from seeing that temper of yours as long as possible. Reel her in and make her fall madly in love before she finds out you're a bossy, paranoid, overprotective beast and you're going to do everything you can to clip her wings. That's what I did."

Everyone burst out laughing. He frowned at them. "Francesca is sitting right there." He held out a few seconds and then grinned at his wife. She'd known all about his temper, his bossy ways, his jealousy and every other difficult trait he had before she married him. He knew it, too.

Giovanni was fairly certain Sasha had already condemned him for the game he played with his brothers and cousins. She'd be really upset that he'd invented it. What she hadn't heard, because they all knew the rule, it was one they lived by, was they didn't ever include innocents, only women who knew the score—women propositioning them because they had money.

"Aaron Anderson ordered your woman a huge bouquet of flowers," Emmanuelle announced.

"What?" Hot rage rushed through Giovanni's veins. He could barely breathe. "That bastard. I should have known he'd pull something like that."

"It isn't as if you made a claim on her publicly," Vittorio pointed out. "We knew because you were acting completely out of character with her."

"How was he acting?" Stefano asked.

"Forget that," Giovanni snapped, glaring at Vittorio and Taviano.

"Like a complete ass," Taviano said.

"Is that unusual?" Ricco asked.

"Shut the fuck up, all of you," Giovanni ordered. He pinned his sister with a steely gaze. "This is important. Are you sure, Emme?"

She nodded. "I was in the flower shop when Aaron came in. He trained on and off with you, Giovanni, so I thought you were friends. We struck up a conversation, and he told me he was ordering flowers for a woman. He wanted to pick them out personally, not have someone order over the phone for him. I didn't know she was yours, so I just thought it was sweet."

"It's not sweet," Giovanni bit out. "He's making his move. I knew he was interested. The bastard had women hanging all over him, practically blowing him right there at the table; in fact, he probably did. He acts like an asshole to her, and she's going to forgive him because he sends flowers. Women. Shit."

"Women don't forgive a man just because he sends her a bouquet of flowers," Emmanuelle said, lifting her chin and leveling her gaze at him. "Sometimes the flowers end up cut to pieces in the garbage can."

There was a sudden silence. Emmanuelle looked around

the table and the half-raised forks. "What? It happens. Am I wrong, Francesca? Mariko?"

"You are not wrong," Francesca said.

Stefano narrowed his gaze at her. "Have you ever cut up flowers I brought home to you?"

"You know very well I have. I did it right in front of you. You were being a bossy jackass, driving me crazy with your paranoid delusions that every person in the world is out to take me from you," Francesca said firmly.

Stefano brought her hand to his mouth, kissed her knuckles and then ran his thumb over them gently, stroking back and forth. "Aren't they?"

His family erupted into laughter. Even Giovanni had to laugh.

"I've only received flowers from Ricco," Mariko said. "I would never cut them up and put them in the garbage, even if he made me very, very angry, which he never has." She sent him a sweet, intimate smile.

Ricco reached for her hand and brought it to his chest, over his heart.

"Emmanuelle." Stefano continued to look at his sister. Instantly the forks stopped moving again. "What were you doing at the flower shop?"

She was the only one to continue to eat. She took a bite of pasta and delicately chewed it before taking a sip of wine. When Stefano kept looking at her, she shrugged. "I visit Signora Vitale often."

Shadow riders could hear truth, and Emmanuelle's voice righteously rang with honesty. Stefano continued to look at her. "I'm well aware you visit Signora Vitale on a regular basis. I also know she doesn't go to the flower shop. Her grandson, Bruno, runs it now. I check on him regularly. If I didn't, he would probably be sending drugs out with every order."

Taviano sighed. "I check on him, too. Just in case. Nicoletta works for the Vitales, so I want to make certain Bruno toes the line. Which he doesn't and has no business pulling

Nicoletta into his shit." He looked at his sister. "Stefano's right, Signora Vitale doesn't frequent the flower shop."

Emmanuelle glared at him and mouthed "traitor" over her wineglass. She was the youngest of the Ferraros and strikingly beautiful with her long dark hair and curvy body.

"Emme?" Ricco pushed.

"It isn't anyone's business," she snapped. "I'm over twenty-one. You can all stay the hell out of my business."

"Emmanuelle," Stefano cautioned. He sat up straight. "Damn it. That fucking Valentino Saldi has been coming around again, hasn't he? Are you seeing him?"

There was a small telling silence. Every fork and wineglass went on the table and once again only the ticking of the clock and the breath rushing in and out of their lungs could be heard.

"It isn't your business."

"It *is* my business. It's the entire family's business. The Saldis are criminals, and our worst enemy. You know that."

"*We're* criminals," Emmanuelle pointed out, glaring at her oldest brother.

"Did you know about this, Francesca?" Stefano demanded.

Francesca didn't reply, and her silence was damning. Dark lines of anger made her husband look very dangerous. "We'll talk about this later." It was a threat. Nothing less. He switched his attention to his sister. "He's manipulating you to get information. We've had this conversation repeatedly. Since you were sixteen, sneaking out of your fucking window and seeing him. He's too old for you, and he's the enemy."

Giovanni didn't want to hear that Valentino was too old for his sister, although he agreed she shouldn't see him. Sasha was only twenty-two. He was older not only in years, but in experience. Of course, so was Valentino.

"You see him again, Emmanuelle, you're going to give me no choice here."

"What does that mean?" she challenged.

"What the fuck do you think it means? Your loyalty has to be to this family. My duty is to protect it and every member in it. The Saldis nearly wiped out every member of our family . . ."

"That is ancient history. Long before any of us were born," she snapped.

"The feud still exists to this day. Go to Sicily, Emmanuelle. You'll learn fast enough. Valentino can't be trusted. If he persists in using you to get to us, he's going to disappear."

Emmanuelle went white. She put down her napkin, her dark eyes never leaving her brother's face. "I would never forgive you. Never, Stefano. I would disappear, and you would never find me. If you think I'm trying to scare you, I'm not. It's the honest truth. I love you. I do. I love all of you. You have no right to harm Valentino when he hasn't done one thing to any of us. He took our side and saved lives when we needed it. He had his men help us," she reminded, almost pleading with her brother.

"I know he did, *bella*," Stefano said. "I'm not saying Valentino isn't a good man. I think he is, but he's loyal to his family. He should be, just as we're loyal to one another. It isn't safe."

"I'm safe with him."

"You aren't, Emmanuelle," Stefano said. "He's a very dangerous man. I'm telling you, I don't want you to see him again. You'll be safe. He'll be safe. We can still be civil to one another. You know I'm right."

She closed her eyes for a long minute. Giovanni wanted to put his arms around her and hold her tight. Something had happened between Valentino and Emmanuelle, something she refused to tell any of them. Most of the time she avoided him, and then there would be short times they would sneak off together. Those times never lasted long. Again, no one knew why.

"You don't have to worry," she said. "I'm not seeing him. I told Bruno, if Valentino called, he wasn't to fill the order, that I'd compensate him for the loss." She lifted her chin. "So, you have nothing to worry about other than my disloyalty to the family."

"I never thought you were disloyal."

"Of course you did. I must be giving away family secrets if I talk to him. I'm a woman, after all, and I can be persuaded by great sex." There was bitterness in her voice, enough that every single member of her family protested at once.

"Emme." Stefano heaved a sigh and pressed his fingers to his forehead as if to relieve a pain. "Honey, I have never treated you as less than you are, a shadow rider of equal value as every man seated at this table. Maybe I'm guilty of loving you too much and being worried every second of my life that something would happen to you. I do the same with Francesca and now, Mariko. I can't help who I am. The obsessive-compulsive streak to surround everyone I love with a huge wall is a battle I fight every day. I don't mean to smother you, Emme. I trust you as a rider. I know you can take care of yourself and that you won't betray family secrets."

"Then stop getting upset if I see Val," she whispered.

Giovanni wanted to protest. He could see on his brothers' faces that they wanted to as well. Valentino Saldi was a good man. They'd all watched him carefully. His family had secrets—but so did theirs. They both were guilty of criminal activities. The difference was, the Ferraro family considered themselves on the side of good. Val couldn't say that. He wouldn't leave Emmanuelle alone. More than once she'd made it clear she wasn't seeing him, and he always seemed to talk her around.

"Honey, you think I don't want to give that to you?" Stefano put his hand over his heart. "On my honor, Emme, with everything in me, I want to give you whatever your heart needs and it seems Val is your choice, but you can't go there. Not with his family and not with yours."

"I know that. I make it clear to him. I just don't like you

threatening him. I have to manage my own life, but"—she held up her hand to stop Stefano from interrupting her—"if I need you, any or all of you, to help me, I promise I'll ask."

Stefano sighed and shook his head but he didn't persist. Giovanni wanted his older brother to lay down the law in no uncertain terms. They all knew Val was dangerous. Emmanuelle, by tacking on the last, made it clear that she thought there might come a time when she would be once again "making it clear" to Valentino Saldi that she wouldn't date him.

"What are you planning to do about your little waitress?" Vittorio asked Giovanni. The peacemaker, changing the subject.

"I have no idea. She already probably thinks I'm the playboy from hell," Giovanni admitted. "And she doesn't like me."

"What else did you do?" Stefano asked, his tone deceptively mild. He hadn't gotten his way with Emmanuelle, so he was quite willing to battle it out with his brother.

Giovanni shrugged. "I did ask her to dance, and when she wouldn't because of club policy, I offered to fire her and then rehire her after."

Ricco groaned. "She had to think you were trying to make her part of that game you invented."

"He *invented* the game?" Francesca echoed. "Giovanni. You didn't."

"I'm sorry." Giovanni wasn't above acting. He hung his head. "Really sorry." He was, now that Sasha had overheard him.

There was no explaining what their lives were like to someone who hadn't been born a Ferraro. Someone whose financials weren't plastered in every tabloid for all to see. Every kidnapper and money-hungry man or woman who thought they would have an easy ride.

"Salvatore thought he'd met a woman who really cared about him for him, not the money. They went on several dates together, and she seemed genuine. We can hear lies as you well know and everything pointed to the fact that their relationship was going in a good way."

"Was she a rider?" Mariko asked, looking around the table. "I thought you could only be with a woman who was a rider."

"Sometimes, we get tired of waiting," Vittorio said. "It isn't easy being alone and feeling as if you're always going to be alone."

"Go on," Francesca encouraged Giovanni.

"She got up before he did and said she would dispose of the condom in the bathroom. She was lying, and he heard the lie. We all have had that trick played on us and nothing makes us angrier. It's a cheap, low blow to have a woman try to get pregnant that way."

There was a small silence. Mariko exchanged a long look with Francesca without comprehension. "I don't understand."

"You wouldn't, *farfallina mia*," Ricco said. "It wouldn't occur to either of you, but some women, when they want to trap a very wealthy man, will try anything including putting holes in condoms, or as in this case, will try to use the sperm in the condom to get pregnant."

"That's disgusting. How could he know she planned to do that?" Francesca asked.

"She had a syringe on her, and when he questioned her, she admitted it, saying she loved him and just wanted his baby. That, by the way, was a lie as well. He heard that, too. She didn't love him, nor did she really want his child. She wanted his money and the prestige of being his wife. It's happened on too many occasions to all of us with a certain type of woman playing one too many tricks on us. So, yes, I invented the game, but it was only played with that type of woman. Certainly, not someone like Sasha," Giovanni said.

"What do you know about her?" Stefano asked.

"She's from Wyoming. A ranch."

"Are you certain about her?" Stefano continued, glancing at Taviano, which meant he wanted the investigators set on her. "Ranch means cattle that are probably artificially inseminated."

Giovanni shook his head. Taviano and Vittorio did the same. Still, it wouldn't matter. Sasha would be investigated. Giovanni needed to know everything he could about her to win her. "I already sent everything that was in her work file to the investigators."

Stefano nodded his approval. Francesca made a face at him.

"If I overheard the rules of the game, Giovanni, I would think you were after me on a dare or a bet," Emmanuelle said. "I can't imagine what you could say that would make me agree to go out with you, let alone be seen in public with you—except that. That's the most disgusting thing I've heard in a long time. Poor Salvatore. He really liked her?"

"He said so. Salvatore wants to settle down. He said he told his parents about her and that he was serious. That's the night he found out she was after him for the money."

"I'd like to pay that woman a visit," Emmanuelle said. "What's wrong with these women? Sometimes I want to lock you all up and protect you myself."

"Speaking of paying someone a visit, Stefano," Giovanni said. "I can't do it myself, or I would." There was a hint of bitterness in his voice. "Darby made a scene deliberately in the club after all the warnings. He had Sasha's camisole torn open and would have exposed her on his fucking reality show. We got the footage."

Stefano's face darkened. "All of it?"

"We think so," Taviano said. "There were a lot of paparazzi there. We needed them to film Salvatore and Geno so they had alibis while Lucca did his job. As usual, Lucca made it out of the plane and back in without ever being seen. As far as the world knows, he was in New York the entire time."

"I'll pay Darby a visit. That little prick needs to be taught some respect," Stefano said.

"I'm with you," Vittorio said. "I wanted to do a little exposure myself."

"That gives me an idea," Stefano said. He glanced at his wife, and forced a small smile to cover the grim darkness in his eyes. "We'll talk about it later."

# CHAPTER FOUR

Sasha smiled as she handed the carefully prepared and wrapped sandwich to Tito Petrov. He was flirting outrageously with her. She'd been getting that a lot since she'd moved into her cozy little apartment above the deli. She *loved* her apartment. She liked the people she worked with at the deli and especially the owner, Pietro Masci. He reminded her of her father.

"Don't just smile," Tito complained. "Say yes. Go out with me."

She shook her head. "I'm sorry, but I'm busy tonight."

The deli suddenly went quiet, the buzz of conversation that was always present hushed.

"Tomorrow night then," Tito insisted, his voice overloud in the unexpected silence.

"I'm working," she said, as gently as possible, lifting her gaze to sweep the room, puzzled at the weird cessation of noise.

Giovanni Ferraro stood in the doorway, his wide shoulders seeming to touch from one side of the doorjamb to the other. He wore a three-piece pin-striped suit and looked so good in it she thought he should be modeling for some high-end fashion company. He wore his hair short as a rule, but lately it wasn't quite as neat as it usually appeared in the magazines, as if maybe he'd neglected a cut or two. He was gorgeous. There was no doubt about it.

His eyes met hers and she couldn't look away. His were

dark and held mystery and had the capability of turning either ice-cold or fiery hot. He had to know he was hotter than hell, and she wasn't in his league. Still, there he was and she wasn't going to delude herself into thinking he wasn't there for her. He was. He was hunting. She knew all about hunting. She'd lived by hunting. Now she was the prey.

Something perverse in her loved that. Her body came to life just looking at him. Staring into his eyes sent heat rushing through her veins. Tito half turned, saw Giovanni and slowly straightened. "Shit," he said, under his breath. "Not again."

Forcing her gaze back to her customer, Sasha pressed the numbers on the pad to ring up his purchase. She turned the entire pad around so he could swipe his card. He did so, muttering to himself. She didn't understand, but she didn't ask what he meant.

"You going out with him?" he asked. "Because I really would like to take you out tonight."

*That*, she heard. Before she could answer, Giovanni loomed over them. He was big. All muscle. Intimidating. He gave off an aura of danger she hadn't realized was so scary.

"She's going out with me tonight," he stated firmly, staring Tito down.

She glared at the two men. "Tito, please sign and take your sandwich. The line is backing up. I'm not going out with anyone, I told you both, I'm very busy tonight." *Men.* She was stumbling over them lately and she wasn't certain why. She had no time for men. She'd heard somewhere that if you weren't open to a relationship, then men knew it and didn't bother to ask you out. Or to dance. Or to have pizza. "I'm not a bone."

Giovanni's gaze drifted over her. Touched her mouth and lingered, dropped lower to drift over her body and then came back to her face. "Definitely not a bone. I appreciate that very much." He glanced at his watch and then looked over her shoulder. "Pietro. Can I steal Sasha for just a minute? I won't keep her long."

She'd felt the heat of that slow, intimate perusal. He'd managed somehow to look possessive, not lecherous. The touch of his gaze sent more heat rushing through her, raising her temperature until she felt hot and edgy. She did her best to glare at him when she really wanted to fan her face, hoping it wasn't red. Her body felt needy, her sex suddenly damp and clenching.

"Mr. Ferraro. Of course. Take your time. You can use my office if you need privacy."

Sasha was horrified. She wasn't about to go into that tiny office with Giovanni Ferraro. Not when she was feeling like she was. She started shaking her head.

"It's Giovanni, Pietro, and thank you, your office is perfect." He stepped right up to the counter, moving around Tito, who was still standing there with his mouth open.

"Smooth, Ferraro," Tito said, snatching his sandwich off the counter and striding toward the door.

"Wait, you didn't sign it," Sasha called after him.

Giovanni leaned over, hit the 30 percent tip, drew an X with his finger and then tapped done. The pad accepted the signature as if Tito had signed it. "There you go. He gave a nice tip as well."

"You can't do that."

Giovanni came right around the counter and took her arm, tugging to get her moving toward the back room. Pietro stepped up to take her place. She turned back to him. "He can't do that. Can he?"

Pietro shrugged. "If it comes back, I know where to find both of them."

Sasha went with Giovanni because she wasn't about to cause a scene, not when the packed deli had every eye on them. The customers weren't even pretending they weren't listening. They stared, and no one said a word in the hopes of hearing more. She was grateful when a corner took them out of sight.

Giovanni took her down the hall to Pietro's office. He stepped back to allow her through the door. Her first thought was that he was very gentlemanly until she realized that put him between her and the door. He even closed it and then leaned against the wood looking at her. His gaze moved over her just as it had done in the store, possessive, hot, making her feel as though it was a physical touch.

She waited him out, mostly because she was shaken by her reaction to him. She noticed each time their shadows touched, she had such an intense jolt of sexual hunger she was a little afraid she might jump him. Thinking that wasn't such a good idea, especially after listening to the finer points of his little game, she backed across the room—which was all of six steps—and perched on the edge of Pietro's desk, hoping she looked casual.

"You didn't tell me you were working here," Giovanni said.

He didn't take his eyes off her, nor did he blink. She felt a little as if she was in the room with a dangerous lion ready to leap on her any minute. One wrong move and she would lose. What, she wasn't certain, but the feeling was so strong, she held her breath and shrugged, afraid of saying the wrong thing and setting him off.

"Why didn't you tell me, Sasha? We talked last night. You know I'm not quite the bastard you thought at first. You could have confided you had a second job."

She took another deep breath, filling her lungs with much needed air. "It didn't seem necessary."

"How so?"

She shrugged. "It didn't fit anywhere in the conversation."

"Of course it did. I wanted to know about you. Everything I could learn, you knew that. I made it clear that I wasn't playing around. You didn't tell me because you knew I wouldn't like the idea of you working sixteen hours a day. You can't keep it up without making yourself sick."

Her chin went up. She narrowed her eyes at him, giving

him her best death stare. "I can take care of myself, thank you very much. I've been doing it for a while now."

"Sasha."

He said her name in a low voice. Almost a caress. Definitely a reprimand. Just her name. Nothing else. She found herself squirming in spite of her resolve to tell him to go to hell. He had no right to tell her what she could or couldn't do. He was rolling in money. Maybe he didn't have to work, but she did. She worked herself up to a self-righteous rant.

"Tell me what you need. We can make it happen."

She closed her mouth before words could tumble out. What did that mean? "Mr. Ferraro . . ."

"We dispensed with that the other night."

"Giovanni then. I don't know what you mean."

"I mean I want to go out with you. Seriously. Not part of some childish, idiotic game, just get to know you. With you working sixteen hours it's going to be difficult. I would very much like to know why you have to work that many hours and how I can help."

There was sincerity in his voice. She usually could hear a lie. It was just some weird little trick she had. A gift, her mother called it. She knew when someone lied to her, but she couldn't believe Giovanni was telling the truth.

"Why would a man like you be interested in a woman like me?" she challenged. She didn't believe in beating around the bush. "It doesn't make sense. Not when so many beautiful women, women in your same circle, throw themselves at you."

"I don't have any desire to be with a woman who wants me because I'm wealthy."

"How do you know I'm not after your money?"

His eyes didn't leave hers and she felt the burn of his gaze all the way to her bones. He was just plain sexy. He didn't have to talk, he could just look at her and she wanted to start peeling off her clothes.

"I know."

"Well, I'm sorry, Giovanni, but I'm not interested."

"You're interested. Don't start lying to me, Sasha." He folded his arms across his chest and kept his gaze on hers. Steady. Unrelenting. "Tell me why you have two jobs."

"It's not your business."

"Everything in our territory is my business. *You're* my business."

"Why?"

"You know why. I'm not playing this game with you. I'm interested. You're interested. I made an ass out of myself, but we got past that."

"You may have, but I haven't," she said. "Just look at yourself in those magazines. You're all over them. You have women hanging all over you. You're practically doing it with them in every other shot. There's a lovely shot of you on a balcony with a woman. She has no clothes on and you don't have your shirt on. There was another with a different woman that same night. *Same* night, same hotel. She was coming out of your room at three o'clock in the morning. Do you really think I would want to be part of that lifestyle? It isn't going to happen no matter how attracted to you I am. You live one way and it's a way I don't understand."

"I told you I was serious about being with you, Sasha. You know damn well I'm not lying to you. You can pretend you think I am, but it isn't the truth, and as far as I can tell, you live by the truth."

She could barely breathe. He sounded serious. And he sounded like he wasn't about to back off or give up. She would give in to him sooner or later if he kept at her. She knew she would. She'd never been so attracted to a man in her life. Her breasts ached. *Ached.* That had never happened to her before. Not one single time.

"Stop shaking your head."

She hadn't known she was shaking her head. Self-preservation was a beautiful thing. "We wouldn't work and you know it." She wished she didn't sound so desperate. It was only because he had caught her off guard. She hadn't expected him to be so direct. She knew his intentions. She wasn't stupid. She'd sat next to him for a couple of hours, his thigh pressed against hers. She was adept at reading men. She'd grown up around them.

She liked direct. She needed direct. She was a plainspoken woman. She said what she felt and expected those around her to do the same. She'd come to the city because she had to, because this was the place that for now, maybe for always, she needed to be. She realized almost immediately that most people here weren't quite as plainspoken as she'd been brought up to be. She liked Giovanni better for it, but it was also harder to resist him.

"We belong."

Her sex clenched. For a moment she thought he was going to take a step toward her, and she flung up her hand to ward him off. He couldn't touch her. That would really get her in trouble. He'd realize she was a little bit in lust with him. Over the top in lust. He just stayed there, draped lazily against the door, looking in complete control while she was a mess.

"Sasha. Did you hear me?"

"I heard you." Her voice came out a whisper. "I am not going there with you. I'm not. I need the work. When things don't work out, and they won't . . ." He'd get bored. Men like him got bored. Sometimes they got bored in the same night, and she had the evidence to prove it lying on her kitchen table, the magazine open to the exact page. "I just can't afford to lose my job."

"Sasha, we're going to see each other. It's going to happen. Just tell me why you need two jobs."

"It isn't your business."

"Men like me investigate women they're interested in. You have to know that."

"Oh. My. God. Are you kidding me?" She was outraged. "Every woman you date is investigated?"

"Thoroughly."

"You have someone looking into me right this minute?"

He nodded. Looked complacent. She wanted to pull out her hair. She might have even yanked at it. At the very least she wanted to throw something at him.

"You don't think that's wrong? Totally messed up?"

"It's something we have no choice in. All of us do it. If you've got skeletons in your closet, you may as well confess now. It won't make any difference. I'm still going to claim you." He regarded her with that steady gaze, his eyes darker, sensual lines cut deep in his face.

"If you're still coming after me, then wasting your money and the time of investigators seems a little foolish."

"Knowledge is always a powerful thing."

"What does that mean?"

"It means stop beating around the bush. Why do you have to have two jobs? The apartment isn't cheap, but you can certainly afford it on what you make at the club."

She had to have the job at the club. If she hadn't needed it, she would have punched John Darby right in the nose. She might have done the same to his obnoxious, very drunk friends *and* the cameraman filming the entire setup. She knew they would have aired it on his reality show, and if she sued, they would have gladly paid her whatever she wanted. The episode would have been worth it to them.

She pulled out Pietro's office chair and sank into it. "I told you I have an older brother, Sandlin, and that he was driving the car the night of the accident." She pushed her fingers through her hair and then scrubbed her hand over her face. "He suffered a traumatic brain injury. Very severe. He . . ." She forced herself to say it aloud. "He doesn't remember me. Not at all. He doesn't remember anything of his old life. I bring photographs to him, but nothing sparks his memory. He can't take care of himself and needs a full-time caretaker as well as rehabilitation. That doesn't come cheap. I researched the country for the best facilities, and there was a really good one here in Chicago."

"You pay for it yourself?"

"There's some insurance. His Social Security. I tried to

hire a lawyer to sue the woman who hit him, but there was so much to do and I haven't had time. That's coming next. You can see I don't have the time or inclination to date anyone, let alone a man who has cameras following him around. My life is real, Giovanni."

"Meaning mine isn't?"

He straightened, and her breath caught in her lungs. He was back to looking like the lion, now stalking her. God, he was scary. He came close, towering over her, making her feel small. Making her feel like a snob. She was ashamed, but before she could take it back, he perched himself on the edge of the desk. He caught the arms of the chair she sat in and leaned toward her. Up close he looked more dangerous than ever. And he smelled delicious.

"I was shot twice a few months ago. The shot to my thigh shattered the bone and I've had to have several surgeries. I'll need another to get rid of the plates and rods. I've been months in physical therapy and haven't been able to do the job I was meant to do for my family. You don't know the first thing about my life, Sasha, but I assure you, it's very real."

She wanted to look away from the intensity of his stare, but she couldn't. She'd said it, and she'd been wrong to make such a statement. "I'm sorry. Of course, your life is real. I can't imagine the things you have to deal with in your life any more than you can imagine what is a hardship in mine. It was really wrong of me to imply that I have things harder than you. I really am sorry."

He caught her chin, his thumb sliding over her skin, sending little electrical pulses zapping through her like little lightning strikes. "You're an incredible woman, do you know that? I don't know many women who would apologize the way you just did. Right away. No beating around the bush."

"It was wrong of me, and I didn't even really mean it." She licked her lips because he kept staring at her mouth and she was suddenly very hungry for his kiss. She craved it when she'd never so much as felt his mouth on hers. She could almost taste him on her tongue. It was ridiculous.

"Sasha, I want to see you. Take a chance on me."

She wanted to. Especially when he was so close. His suit enhanced the muscles. It had to. The coat and vest and shirt just stretched across that wall of a chest and his wide shoulders. He looked amazing. He smelled even better. His mouth was . . . close. On hers.

At the first touch of his lips, she gasped. Firm. Cool. Heating rapidly, or maybe that was her, because the blood in her veins was suddenly scorching and rushing to pool low. His teeth caught her lower lip and tugged gently. His tongue soothed the tiny ache. Her heart thudded. Her stomach did a slow roll. She was aware of him moving, or maybe it was her, but she was in his arms, surrounded by him. Her mouth opened all by itself. She didn't really have a thing to do with it.

He was unexpectedly gentle. That was her undoing. She couldn't resist him. He appeared dangerous and tough as nails, although smoothly sophisticated. He took his time exploring her mouth, and all that fire he ignited in her grew until she felt as if he was pouring flames down her throat so they could spread through her body.

Her arms crept around his neck and she found herself kissing him back, her tongue tangling with his. Her body melted into his. She couldn't think anymore. She wasn't even certain of her own name. All that mattered was his addicting taste and the fire he created with just his mouth alone.

It was Giovanni who broke the kiss with a soft groan. He lifted his head, his breathing a little ragged. She realized she was standing between his legs, pressed tightly against him, her mouth chasing his.

"Baby," he said very softly, "we have to stop. I promised myself I'd do this right with you. I want you more than you could possibly know, and this isn't where we're going to have our first time together."

Sasha inhaled sharply and tried to pull back. What was wrong with her? One moment she was saying no and the next she was participating in the longest make-out session she'd ever been in. The best. No one kissed like he did. She touched her lips to make certain they weren't actually on fire.

"I have to sit down." She did. Her legs weren't going to support her, and if she didn't get away from his body, she was going to be touching parts of him that were definitely off-limits.

He held on to her until she was seated in the chair. She needed time away from his potency. She gave him a rueful smile. "I think that's called being kissed senseless. My brain short-circuited." She held up her hand before he could say anything. "It's coming back. Slow, but it's happening. I love the way you kiss. Obviously. That still isn't saying I'm going to take a chance on you. I don't want a broken heart, and you're that man. You are, Giovanni. Seriously. You have to listen to me. I'm not like those other women you date."

"I don't date them, Sasha. I've never dated anyone. I don't go to their place of work and plead my case. I fuck them. I walk away. They walk away. That isn't how I want to live. I want a woman who actually loves me. I want to love her. I want a family. I don't want to go to nightclubs every night and play stupid games. You're that woman for me."

"How do you know? You met me three days ago."

He waved his hand around the room as if it was the world. "I've traveled everywhere. I've met many women over the years, too many. None of them were the right one. When you've looked as long as I have, believe me, baby, you know when you see her. I knew the moment I saw you."

She had to get away from his charisma. He drew her in like a magnet and she couldn't seem to find the strength to push him away. "I'll think about it, but I have to get back to work. This job is important to me. It doesn't pay anything like the club, but it's forty hours a week solid. Sometimes, if I can do it, he gives me overtime. I like the people, and it allows me to make a few friends."

His face darkened. "Tito Petrov is *not* your friend. If you think I'm a ladies' man, he's worn that title around here since the seventh grade."

She frowned up at him, but there was the tiniest part of her that was a little thrilled. She knew she shouldn't be, but it was there all the same. "You sound jealous."

"I'm jealous as hell. Tito. Aaron. How many others?"

She shrugged. "A few men came in and asked me out. I think I'm new in the neighborhood. And Aaron just feels bad because he and his friend drank too much celebrating his victory and wanted to apologize. Aaron sent me flowers and a really nice note, and his friend, James, sent me a box of chocolates with a beautiful card. I was surprised either of them would do that. Tom came in to apologize in person, as did one of the men who had his camera taken away. I think his name was Sid."

She had been shocked. It was the last thing she ever would have considered—the three men, very drunk, their hands wandering constantly as if they were entitled to anything they wanted, giving her apologies. A man who made his living taking pictures telling her he was sorry he'd gotten angry over losing the film.

Giovanni kept his gaze steady on her face. "Did they include their phone numbers in their nice little notes?"

She nodded. "Yes, but I don't think any of them expected me to actually call them."

He gave a small groan and reached out to tuck a stray strand of hair behind her ear. His fingers moved over her cheek and swept down to her jaw, leaving her shivering at his touch. She found her reaction to him disturbing.

"Aaron is a good man, Sasha, but he's a player. I've known him most of his life. We train together sometimes and he's a very good fighter, one of the best. He's fought his way to the top and he deserves everything he gets. His childhood wasn't the easiest, so I'm always happy when he wins his fights and earns good money. Being a good man doesn't necessarily translate into being a good partner."

"You can't know that."

"I do know that. He's never been faithful to a single woman he's been in a relationship with. I think it's because he's looking for something intangible that he can never find. He needs to know he's worth something, and he's always looking in the wrong places."

Sasha could tell he was very thoughtful about it, not being mean about his friend. She could tell he liked Aaron, but was definitely warning her away from the fighter. "What about you? Have you always been faithful to a woman you've been in a relationship with?"

"I've never had a relationship."

For a moment she almost didn't comprehend what he was telling her. The enormity of that. She heard the ring of honesty in his voice, but to think that he had never been in a relationship . . .

"Not ever? Not even in school?"

"We weren't allowed to go to a school, not like most people. Not even a private school. We had tutors. They were very . . . exacting. We weren't encouraged to have social relationships with our peers. When I said I knew him from school, I meant he was my age during my school years and we struck up a friendship of sorts. Aaron's family life was bad, and I ran across him one evening when I was running in the park. He was skinny, his clothes were torn and he was a mess. It was cold and he didn't have much to keep him warm, so I snuck him into our garage. Our garage is heated and is absolutely clean at all times." There was a trace of humor in his voice when he said the last.

She knew Giovanni felt bad for Aaron and was telling her about his friend, but the story told her so much more about him. He was wealthy beyond most people's imaginations and lived away from others, not encouraged to have friends or relationships, yet he'd taken a boy home and hidden him in his garage to help him out.

"The tabloids always have you with some woman. None of that is true?"

Giovanni shrugged. “I go to charity events all the time. It’s customary to have a woman on your arm. The more famous she is, the more attention you bring to the charity. Being with a woman for a night doesn’t mean I’m in a relationship with her.”

“Why one night?” Sasha was well aware she was asking questions she shouldn’t. She didn’t want to even consider dating him. She didn’t want to be attracted to him, and the more she knew of him, the stronger the attraction seemed to be. She just couldn’t stop herself.

“I don’t lead women on. I don’t pretend that we’re going to be together forever. Even for a few months or years. It’s all or nothing for the men in our family. That’s the way we’re made and we don’t take chances that we’re going to hurt someone innocent. I’m not playing a game with you, Sasha. I’m telling you, you’re the one.”

She shook her head. “I’m not. You don’t know me at all. Not at all.”

“I watched you for most of the night. You’re like a ray of sunshine. The club was dark, and I was feeling angry and maybe a little sorry for myself.” He paused. “*Very* sorry for myself,” he corrected. “I didn’t want to be there, but I had no choice. I was sick of the music and the drinking. I was really sick of the women fawning all over me. My cousin was upset because the woman he thought cared about him did something despicable and he realized she didn’t care at all. It was a shit night, and then I saw you laughing. You were several tables down from mine, serving drinks, and you were like the sun right there, lighting up the dark.”

Her heart reacted, beating faster. Butterfly wings fluttered against her stomach.

“I watched you. I couldn’t take my eyes from you. You chatted with various people and I could see that everywhere you went, those you served drinks to laughed with you. Their faces lit up when you came close. You fascinated me.”

“I think, if that’s true, it doesn’t take all that much.” She had to deflect, make a joke, do something, anything to keep from hearing what he was saying. She liked it too much. She couldn't afford to be drawn into anything with him. She was too busy and she didn't have room in her life for someone else. More, his world was so different from hers. She knew she wouldn't fit in there. How could she? She didn't understand the people in his world, with their false smiles and sense of entitlement.

"I won't lie to you, Sasha. Not now, not ever. I'm about as jaded as a man can get. I've had every trick you can imagine pulled on me. When I saw you, I swear, you were like a breath of fresh air when I was drowning. I watched you all night like some stalker. I lost track of you when you went on your break and that's what got me in trouble."

She didn't have a defense against him, not when he told her things like that. She stared up at his face, all those hard angles and planes. His family scared her just a little bit, looking dangerous and powerful and owning just about everything she could see from her apartment above the deli.

"Tell me about your brother."

The softly spoken command was so unexpected she found herself doing so before she could think it through. She *needed* someone to talk to about him. "Sandlin is my big brother. An absolute sweetheart. We were very close. He taught me to ride and shoot. He practically taught me everything there was to know about ranching. He took jobs away from the ranch and sent the money home when we needed anything extra. He would buy me things my parents couldn't afford to give me. Sometimes he'd sneak me candy he bought, salt water taffy was my favorite, the cinnamon kind, and he'd go to the candy store, pick all the cinnamon ones out and fill up a bag for me. I wasn't supposed to eat it because Mom didn't want me ruining my teeth, but Sandlin would sneak it into my room."

She laughed at the memory and found tears burned too close behind her eyes. "I love him. If I could, I'd take care of him myself, but he needs special care. He has seizures sometimes, and he can't do a lot of things for himself yet. This facility is not only a live-in place, but a rehabilitation center. They've worked miracles on patients. I'm hoping for one for Sandlin. Even if he never remembers me, and the doctors say he won't, I want him to get to a place where he can take care of himself, at least the simplest task. If something happens to me and I can't pay for him to stay there, I want him to be able to do a few things for himself."

"Does he remember you now, as you are, going to see him?"

She nodded. "I'm trying to build our relationship again. I think he looks forward to seeing me." Her voice had a little quiver in it she couldn't quite stop.

He reached down and took her chin with his fingers, lifting her face so she was forced to look at him. She was afraid he was seeing too much so she lowered her lashes, veiling her eyes. She wasn't crying, she hadn't since she lost them all, her parents and Sandlin, but she could feel that burn and was terrified it showed. She didn't want to appear vulnerable to him. She wasn't the kind of girl that needed taking care of and she wasn't about to let him think she was.

"Sweetheart, he sounds like a man I would like to get to know. He might not remember his past, but I'm betting, he's always good to you when he sees you."

She nodded. "He's so sweet." She wrapped her arms around her middle for comfort and forced a smile. The nicer he was to her, the more the tears threatened. "He's never impatient, and that's the way he was before. There are things that make me know he's still there. He's still my brother, he just doesn't know me or remember from before. We had a special relationship and I know I never can have that again, but I'm working on a new one with him." It took effort to keep her voice from cracking.

"How often do you visit him? You can't have much time if you're working sixteen hours a day," he pointed out.

"The club job pays the most, and I start at six. Visiting hours are up until nine o'clock, but I mostly go on my days off the deli. Speaking of which, if I don't get out there, Pietro might fire me and I can't afford that. I'm off tonight at the club, so I'm going to see him tonight. I go as often as I can."

Finding the time to see her brother was difficult though. The facility was across town and she had to take the bus. Sometimes that was uncomfortable at night. More than once, she'd wished she had a weapon to protect herself. Buses were convenient, but sometimes she wished she had a car.

"Let me take you there tonight. My car is comfortable. I'd like to look around the facility and talk to those in charge. If you give me the name and address of it, I can have my people check it out thoroughly."

She didn't want him helping, because that would only encourage him, but she would do anything for Sandlin. "My brother was always there for me when I was growing up. Always. I knew, no matter where I went or what I did, no matter how much trouble I got into, Sandlin would come for me. More than once, when I snuck out to a party, it was my brother I called and he dropped everything, including some pretty hot dates, to get me out of trouble." She knew she was telling him, trying to explain, so he wouldn't think badly of her for taking advantage of his offer. He'd made it, but she felt bad that she needed something from him. She didn't want to be that person.

He flashed a grin at her. "Did you get into a lot of trouble?"

She nodded. "I worked hard in school and on the ranch, doing an adult's work, so I thought I should be able to go wild on the weekends like my friends. Drinking is not my friend. The booze we had was really cheap and hangovers hurt like hell."

She started laughing at a memory, sharing it with him, wanting him to know how wonderful her brother was. "I remember this one time my brother had a date with Ginger Tarter. I called her 'The Tart' to my brother, but she was really good-looking. She had breasts and hips and these lips." She pursed her lips and made fishy noises.

"Sandlin was with her, right at the crucial moment, getting her clothes off her, and I called in a panic. I was pretty drunk and the man I went to the party with was expecting the same thing Sandlin was getting. I locked myself in the bathroom and called him. Of course, he came, and I never heard the end of it, but he never told my parents."

"I'd really like to meet him," Giovanni said. He pulled out his phone. "Name and address?"

She took a breath. Anything for her brother. Anything at all. This wasn't a commitment to Giovanni, simply a friend helping out. She could look at it that way. She hoped she'd chosen the right place for him. She'd researched, and read all kinds of reviews, but she knew any care facility was only as good as the people it hired. She didn't want her brother neglected or mistreated, and she didn't know if he was capable of telling her if someone was hurting him in any way. She told Giovanni and he was instantly texting someone. He was fast at it, too, much faster than she was.

"What time should I pick you up?"

Her heart jumped. "I get off at five today. I usually jump right on the bus."

"Do you want to change first? We could catch dinner after your visit." He held up his hand to stop her protest. "We have to eat sometime. We might as well eat together. I refrained from biting you, remember?"

She narrowed her eyes at him. "Were you thinking of biting me?"

"Absolutely I was. I still am, but I'll make sure you like it."

She shook her head and pushed out of the seat. Instantly the heat of his body told her she was too close, and she stepped away from him. "I'm going back to work. I'll see you later."

He made no move to touch her—or kiss her—a fact that should have made her happy but instead disappointed her.

"Be good. Stay away from those other men. I have that one really unfortunate trait."

"One? You aren't furthering your cause you know," she said, smirking a little over her shoulder. "I believe you have many unfortunate traits." Laughing, she hurried down the hall to the counter, wondering why she suddenly felt so happy.

# CHAPTER FIVE

Sasha went out the back door of the deli, which led into an alley. She glanced at her watch. It was after three. Pietro had let her off early. She'd texted Giovanni and he was probably waiting out front, but just before she left, Pietro had gone to the bank and Aria, the girl who was supposed to relieve her, hadn't shown up right away.

Sasha didn't want to get into his car smelling of deli meat so she ran up the stairs, determined to take a quick shower. At the top of her stairs was a bouquet of roses. They lay there, a little wilted from lack of water, but the splash of color was cheerful against the bleached wood. She bent down to pick them up, thinking for a moment that Giovanni had left them.

She realized immediately that they weren't from a flower shop; someone had hand-picked them, cutting the long stems carefully. Every thorn was gone. She looked around for a card, but there wasn't one. She brought the roses to her face, inhaling the rich fragrance. They were beautiful, and it was sweet that someone would go to the trouble of putting together a bouquet. They were wrapped in red and gold tissue paper.

She straightened slowly and looked around, feeling as if someone was watching her. Fingers of icy fear crept down her spine. She unlocked her door and went inside. The moment she stepped into her apartment, she knew someone else had been there. It felt different. She stood very still, letting her gaze sweep the entire room. It wasn't difficult—her place was small. Easy to manage. Easy to see from the living area to the kitchen because it was really all one room. Everything seemed to be there. As far as she could tell from just glancing around, nothing had been taken, but her things had been touched.

From where she was, she could see someone had put wineglasses, two of them, near her reading chair. Then there was the table: each item on it, mementos of her family, things that meant nothing to anyone else, but everything to her, had been moved. She kept them in a certain order. Her parents' photograph, the one where they were looking at each other with such love. It was inside an antique silver frame. Beside it, she put her mother's favorite pincushion and her father's pipe. She liked to have the two items touching because her parents had always been touching. The pipe was several inches from the pincushion and the pincushion was on the wrong side of the pipe.

Someone had picked up her parents' things. They'd touched the photograph as well. It was turned slightly, so that walking in the door, she couldn't see their faces. Sandlin's picture, the one with the two of them, brother and sister riding side by side on their favorite horses, the sun setting behind them, had been turned toward her parents' photograph, rather than facing out toward the door.

Staying in the doorway, she peered at the table where the little mementos were kept. Her brother's key chain wasn't there. Her heart nearly stopped and then began to pound. She wanted to run over to the table and look all around in case it had dropped to the floor, but the doors to the bathroom and bedroom were closed. She never closed the bedroom door. She wasn't about to set foot in the apartment alone. She backed out and shut the door carefully and extra quietly.

Running down the stairs and across the alley toward the deli, she nearly ran right into Giovanni. He caught her by the shoulders to steady her.

"What's wrong?" The question was clipped, almost growled. He sounded dangerous, and for once she was glad. His gaze swept over her, taking in everything, including the bouquet of flowers she still clutched in her arms. "What is it? You're very pale."

"Someone was in my apartment. They touched my things. I didn't go into the bathroom or bedroom." She didn't realize she was shivering until he wrapped his arms around her and held her close to his body. He felt strong and safe. "The doors were closed and I thought maybe it would be better to get someone to come with me."

"I'm going to call the police and a couple of my brothers," Giovanni said. "My brothers will get here faster than the cops. We'll go in and make certain no one's inside."

She shook her head. "Wait for the police. If someone's in there, they could have a weapon."

He set her aside, texted in that extremely fast way he had and then started up the stairs. She followed. He turned back to her, frowning at her.

"Go into the deli where I know you're safe."

"I can't do that. There isn't any point in arguing with me. I'll just do what I think is right. If you're going in, I'm going with you."

"Where did you get those flowers?"

She glanced down at the bouquet, once again surprised she was holding it. "They were in front of my door."

"Whoever went inside left them for you," he surmised. "At least the probability is high."

She dropped them immediately onto the ground, the same weird tingle of fear slithering down her spine. "That's horrible. Why would someone leave me obviously hand-picked flowers and then sneak into my apartment and touch my things?"

"I don't know, honey, but we'll find out."

Giovanni glanced around the alley, up toward the rooftop of the opposite building and then took her hand and pulled her to him. Taviano and Ricco strode out from around the corner of the alley, both wearing the signature pin-striped suit all the Ferraros seemed to wear.

"Sasha, you met Taviano, and this is my brother Ricco," Giovanni said. "I was just heading upstairs to see what's going on in her apartment. Taviano is going to stay with you. Ricco will go with me. He's tough, he can defend me if someone jumps out at me." He bent his head to hers to brush a kiss along her temple. Deliberately, he took her hand and placed it in Taviano's. "Don't let her out of your sight. I'm putting her in your care."

There was something about the formality of the way Giovanni worded it that had her gaze jumping to his face. He was looking at his brother. Something she missed passed between them, and Taviano nodded.

Giovanni caught her chin in hard fingers. "This time, honey, you stay right here. I can't be dividing my attention, looking out for you *and* sweeping your apartment." There was steel in his voice. Sasha was independent, a woman who went her own way and made her own decisions, but she wasn't about to defy that voice. More, she wasn't going to put him in danger through her own recklessness.

Giovanni took the lead going up the stairs. "Someone's watching from the roof. Text Stefano and let him know. I caught the glint of binoculars. The idiot isn't that good at hiding himself. He's watching us. I'm betting it's the same man who was in her apartment." He kept moving up the stairs. His brother was fast on his phone, even faster than Giovanni, and he could text as he hurried up to the door.

Giovanni bent to examine the lock without touching anything. "There are scratch marks here. He used a pick. I'm going to have to get her a better lock, Ricco, and dead bolts inside, if she's going to stay here."

Pulling on gloves, he opened the door and stepped inside. Her apartment smelled like her—fresh cinnamon candy-covered apples. He loved the way she smelled, and entering her home, knowing it held that same scent he was beginning to be obsessed with, gave him a rush of pleasure in spite of the circumstances. He signaled to his brother to stand to one side of the closed door. He opened it carefully.

Her bathroom was small and very neat. There was no way for anyone to hide in the open space. Her shower curtain was transparent, so even that wouldn't have been a hiding place for an intruder. He looked around, taking in everything she had on the marble sink. Makeup, although she used it sparingly, he knew. A jar of colored bath salts. An electric toothbrush and water flosser. The woman took care of her teeth and it showed. They were straight and white. She had a dazzling smile.

A lipstick lay next to a bottle of perfume. Strange, the perfume was in a beautiful bottle, but it wasn't that cinnamon candy-covered apple he knew was her signature scent; it was a high-end brand he recognized, but the floral scent wouldn't suit Sasha. He couldn't imagine her wearing it.

Her towels were jet-black, which surprised him. He expected her to have chosen more of a pastel color. The two towels were hung with obsessive neatness, which was too bad. He liked neat, but he wasn't always careful about where he flung his clothes, so the fact that her towels were hung exactly symmetrically was probably a bad thing. Again, he was careful not to touch anything. He wanted Sasha to tell him if anything had been moved or taken.

The bedroom was next and he opened that door cautiously, keeping out of the line of fire just in case the intruder was still inside and had a gun. The bed was in his line of sight, the comforter a pale mauve. There were girlie pillows on it, up near the head of the bed. In the exact center was a large heart made of roses, the same type of roses that were now on the ground outside in the alley. Inside the heart, laid out precisely in the center, were a sheer thong panty and bra. They were fire-engine red and nothing more than cord and lace, beautiful, sexy and perfect for his woman. He couldn't imagine that she had placed them there, but he was certain the lingerie already belonged to her.

He looked at his brother. "What the fuck is that?"

One look around the small room told him an intruder wasn't hiding there, not even in the closet. The double doors to the long walk-in were open, revealing a meager amount of clothing. Mostly jeans hung neatly alongside two dresses and several tops.

"There's a note." Ricco removed it from where it lay between the lace bra and panties.

*Wear these for me tomorrow.*

The words were typed out on a single sheet of paper. Giovanni cursed under his breath. "This isn't good. Someone's fixated on her."

"I'm not surprised," Ricco said. "She's beautiful and . . . extraordinary. That smile of hers could stop a war. She has that face, Gee, the kind a man would spend a lifetime wanting to just stare at. I'm not even going to talk about her body because I'm not looking at her that way. I see her and know she belongs to you and the family. Someone to protect, but other men, they're going to see her and want her. She's got something intangible, a magic about her, and you're going to have your hands full keeping the competition away. Think about that, because it's going to be for the rest of your life."

Giovanni knew every word Ricco said about Sasha was the truth. He'd felt the pull of her magic, that mixture of innocence and temptress, her smile, the one that his brother had referred to. He also knew that the assessment coming from Ricco, who loved his wife above all else, was true and stated as a fact rather than interest. Maybe even a warning.

"Let's get her and find out if anything is missing," Giovanni said. He didn't like her out in the alley where she was exposed.

He should have known his brother would take care of things. Taviano had Sasha inside the deli. They stood just inside the back door, Taviano's body blocking the entrance.

He glanced up at the roof. Stefano stood there, lifted a hand and shook his head to indicate there was no one there. Emme and Vittorio paced along the alley, one on the left side and one on the right. They moved slowly, looking for any evidence of a person setting up traps or cameras or just leaving evidence behind.

Giovanni went straight to Sasha and wrapped an arm around her. "He's gone, but he left you a note. I need you to go through the apartment and tell me if anything is missing, or if he's disturbed anything. You'll have to hurry, the police tend to show up fast if we're involved."

"Why?" She looked up at him as they walked toward the stairway. Giovanni wanted to step on the roses and crush them as he passed, but he was careful to step over them just in case the police needed them for evidence.

"They have the misguided belief that we're criminals. Mafia. They've investigated us numerous times, but they always come up empty-handed." He put his hand on her back as they went up the stairs.

Ricco was waiting at the top, and he stepped aside to allow her entry into her apartment. She hesitated, just for a second, just long enough that Giovanni noticed, and then she stepped inside and went straight over to the little table that held the photographs of her family.

"There's something beyond terrifying to know someone's invaded your personal, private space," she said.

Her voice was pitched low, but he caught the slight wobble and wanted to smash something—or someone. She was being brave, but she was shaken. He watched as she looked all around and under the table where the photographs were.

"He took my brother's key chain. He moved the photographs and the things I have here. Why would he take Sandlin's key chain? It isn't worth anything to him, or anyone but me."

"What did it look like?" Giovanni followed her as she circled around the living space and kitchen.

"It was just a key chain with a picture of me in it. He

took it when I was barrel racing and had won a championship."

She suddenly broke off and ran across the room to the armchair. A book lay upside down on the cushion. Next to the chair was a small round side table. Two wineglasses sat out with a bottle of red wine. There was wine residue in each glass. On the side of one of the glasses was a small smear of pink lipstick.

"This isn't mine. I mean, the glasses are, but not the wine and I didn't drink anything with anyone. My book was sitting here on the table when I left. The book on the chair isn't the one I was reading. I don't know where mine is, but that's not it. He staged this. He had to have, and I'm certain that's my lipstick."

Giovanni picked up the book, turning it over to the open pages. Text was highlighted and he skimmed it, his stomach tying in knots as he did. "It's an erotica book. This has a very graphic passage between two lovers highlighted."

Sasha pressed her fingers to her temples as if that might stop a headache. "What's he trying to say?"

"I think he's fantasizing that you're in a relationship with him," Giovanni said.

She turned her head to look at the bathroom door. "He was in there, too, wasn't he?"

"You tell me." Giovanni was certain he had been.

She took a deep breath and started to touch the door handle. He caught her shoulder to pull her back and opened the door with his gloved hand. "Just in case, honey. We don't want to mess up any fingerprints."

She nodded, and stepped inside, her gaze instantly drawn to the towels and then the little cabinet where her things sat. "He was definitely in here. Those towels aren't mine. And I'm not that neat. I couldn't get them on the rack like that." She pushed back the shower curtain, made a face and stumbled back. "He was in here, too. I think he took a shower." There were a few drops on the shower curtain, but the floor of the stall was damp. "He used my soap and shampoo. I'm never touching those things again. What's wrong with him?"

Giovanni stepped up and caught her around the waist, pulling her back to him, wrapping his arms around her. "The cops will get him. What about anything else? Look carefully, Sasha."

She studied the cabinet and then indicated the lipstick. "He used that on the wineglass rim. I keep it in the drawer along with the other makeup. He put that there. The perfume bottle, I've never seen before, nor do I use that particular scent. He had to have brought it." She pressed back into him and turned her head to look up at him. "You don't think he used my toothbrush, do you?"

Giovanni shrugged, trying for casual, but he was buying her a new toothbrush. The idea of her putting her mouth anywhere near where the intruder had put it sickened him.

"Cops are here, Gee," Stefano announced.

Instead of two uniformed officers, two men in suits came through the door. Giovanni introduced Sasha to the two detectives, who he was very familiar with, and then indicated the scratch marks, pointed out the bouquet on the ground and where she'd found it. He circled Sasha's shoulders with his arm and pulled her under his shoulder, keeping it there, letting the detectives know she was not only with him, but under his protection. His hovering family told them the rest.

"Stupid mistake on his part, messing with your family," the one who had been introduced as Detective Jason Bradshaw said. His tone held all kinds of innuendo.

Giovanni didn't rise to the bait. He let them question Sasha, realizing almost immediately they were falling under her spell. Even now, with everything going on, she managed a smile that made them look at her in a way that had him wanting to tear their heads off.

The detectives were thorough, he had to hand them that. Stefano always said the department's detectives weren't always the politest, but they definitely knew their jobs and didn't jump to conclusions; they worked their cases and had a high arrest rate. He respected them, and Giovanni could see why. The two men might not like the Ferraros, or at the very least, suspected them of being a crime family, but they put aside any prejudices and photographed and documented everything. Their questions were polite but probing, leading Sasha to find a few other items that had been touched, moved, or had disappeared.

Her hairbrush was missing. Her mother's silver hand mirror. The book she'd been reading was nowhere in the house. The other two wineglasses that made up her set were gone. She was trembling visibly by the time they entered the bedroom. It was the first time Sasha had been inside it, and she made a small sound that tore at his heart before turning her face against his ribs.

"I take it you didn't leave your bed that way," Bradshaw stated.

"No." She cleared her throat and forced herself to look at them, but she gripped Giovanni's suit vest so hard, her fingers curled into his skin. "But the clothes are mine." She glanced at the dresser just under her window. "That drawer was closed when I left."

The other detective, Art Maverick, walked over and peered inside. He turned his head, his eyes meeting Giovanni's and then his partner's.

"What is it?" Sasha asked.

Giovanni was afraid he already knew. "Baby, go with Ricco. Wait for me outside. I'll just be a few more minutes. You're finished with her, right? She gave her statement."

Maverick nodded. "That's right, ma'am, you can wait outside. I need to talk to Giovanni."

"I should stay," Sasha protested, but they all heard the reluctance in her voice.

Giovanni brushed a kiss on top of her head and gave her a little push toward Ricco. His brother reached out and gently took her by the shoulders. "Emme's waiting to meet you. She didn't want to come in and accidently touch evidence, so she's been not so patiently waiting for the police to be finished with you."

"One more thing, Miss Provis?" Bradshaw said. "Have you ever had a stalker? Do you have any idea who could be doing this?"

She shook her head. "Nothing like this has ever happened to me. *Never*."

Giovanni watched them go. Sasha looked back at him several times, clearly feeling guilty about leaving him to deal with the detectives on her behalf.

"Has she talked to you about anyone she was concerned with?"

"No. She's relatively new to the city. Her brother suffered a traumatic brain injury, and she had him moved here from Wyoming. The Hendrick Center is one of the top in the world for rehabilitation and care of that magnitude." Giovanni volunteered what he knew as he took the necessary steps to cross the room to peer into Sasha's private underwear drawer.

There was a stack of lacy stretch boy shorts as well as lace bras. The intruder had ejaculated all over her panties and bras. Giovanni was aware that he possessed a very volatile temper. It often boiled up out of nowhere, so he was used to the feeling erupting. This was different. This was a rage he wasn't certain he could contain. He turned away from the two detectives, afraid the need to snap the neck of the perpetrator showed on his face.

"He planted cameras," Taviano stated, pulling all interest away from Giovanni. "In the bathroom, bedroom and living area. Stefano found several video cameras on the roof across the street."

"This is one sick bastard," Maverick snapped. "Where do these guys come from?"

"There were a few incidents at the club involving her a couple of nights ago," Giovanni said, staring out the window. The entire apartment was suddenly too small. He could barely breathe with the need to exact justice for

Sasha. "I think she would have admitted if she had a long-time stalker or if she thought she knew who it was. I can have West, our manager, give you the incident reports involving Sasha last night. He can provide the footage from our cameras as well. Darby was there and used her to try to create sensationalism for his show. We stopped him and took the film. Several cameramen weren't happy when we took film from them, but they had signed an agreement with us before they were allowed in."

"Given all the cameras set up in her apartment and outside, I want the names of those photographers," Bradshaw said. "The setup looks professional."

Giovanni nodded. "We'll get you whatever you need."

"She's the kind of a girl who's going to attract attention," Maverick stated. "It could be some asshole she passed on her way to work and she smiled at him. Someone in the deli or club, since she works both places and has to smile to be polite. Now he thinks they're in some kind of sick relationship." He looked around the apartment. "She's in real danger, Ferraro. You don't go to all this trouble without being truly fixated."

Giovanni nodded. "We'll watch out for her," he assured. "You find this bastard."

"You know as well as I do, these creeps are difficult to find. He left DNA, so if he's somewhere in the system, we can get him for breaking and entering, and stalking."

"Why would he exchange towels and get out her wineglasses? Have you seen that before?" Giovanni asked.

Maverick shook his head. "It's all part of his fantasy relationship with her. Having a sexual encounter, sharing wine, showering. The roses he left for her. His towels hung in her bathroom. Some of her things brought back to his place."

Giovanni swore under his breath in Italian as he lifted his gaze to Taviano's. They had to find this man and eliminate him. If Maverick and Bradshaw were concerned, then Sasha was in even more danger than she knew.

"If you're finished with her, I'm going to take her out, get her a few things to wear and a new toothbrush before we go to see her brother."

"Just to warn you, Ferraro, if he's as dangerous as I think he is, he'll be angry with her for having anything to do with you and he'll perceive you as a threat to his relationship. He'll definitely go after you."

Giovanni gave the detective his shark's smile. "I want him to come after me. If he fixates on me as his enemy, he won't have time to harass her. I can take care of myself," he assured. "Just find him."

Maverick nodded. "Then we're finished with her. We'll need to be here a little longer. I want to take these cameras for evidence as well as sweep for more."

Giovanni started out the door.

"Ferraro?"

He turned back.

"Is it possible someone is striking at you through her?"

"She isn't a part of our world." He wanted her to be. He intended to make her a part of it, but she wasn't yet. "She works for us at the club, but no member of my family hired her. We don't do that. She was in trouble the other night because a few customers got out of hand, so I stepped in, but that's something all of us do when there's trouble. My table just happened to be closer than security. I did take her to dinner after and my brothers and cousins joined us."

In his gut, he was certain whoever had fixated on Sasha had done so without counting him in the equation. Maverick nodded as if he had been just as certain but had to ask.

Giovanni joined his family inside the deli. Francesca, Emmanuelle, Mariko and Sasha sat at a table together with his brothers surrounding them. As usual, Francesca had everything under control. Sasha was even laughing. She looked young and happy with the other women, and that made him feel better. He'd had a bad taste in his mouth and just looking at her took it away. He liked seeing her looking as if she didn't have a care in the world.

That was her gift, he decided. She had a crazy stalker and her sanctuary had been violated, her beloved brother didn't remember her, but she could put that aside and still find a way to be happy. She had courage and strength.

She looked up, her gaze meeting his, and smiled directly at him. For him alone. His heart stuttered in his chest. He couldn't help but smile back, the dark, ominous feeling lifting just a little. Already his family was rallying around her, doing exactly what they did—helping out. He could always count on them. He wanted her to understand that she could as well.

Stefano caught his eye, and he drifted across the room to his oldest brother. "I've put guards on her, even when she's with you, Gee, so if you spot them, you know who they are. Demetrio and Drago will be out of sight. Emilio and Enzo are on the two of you."

Giovanni wasn't about to protest as he normally would have if his brother sent the top bodyguards to protect him. He would do anything, even having his brother's guards, in order to keep Sasha safe. "Thanks, Stefano. Are you covered?"

"Of course. Did you think Emilio would let me have five minutes without someone breathing down my neck? I do have that little job to do. I'm not letting Darby get away with his crap. He was warned. Vittorio and I are going to pay him a visit, so that means you, Taviano and Ricco have to be visible. We'll all be at the club celebrating you finding Sasha. I've got all the details worked out. Cousins are coming to help celebrate. We'll have video of Francesca and me there making out like we do. Darby will call the cops and look like a fool. Just make certain you're seen at the club."

"Sasha is working tomorrow night so it will work out nicely. If she's at the club, then I'm at the club. Everyone can show up. I'll alert club security, and we'll need Enrica at the club so if Sasha or any of the women goes into the ladies' room, they'll still be guarded."

"I'll make certain Emilio knows to assign her the days Sasha is working."

Giovanni once more turned to look at Sasha. She appeared as if she belonged with the other women. She had the same sweet innocence about her that all of them did. Emmanuelle glanced up at him and gave him a thumbs-up, her opinion of his choice. He put his hand over his heart and nodded. Sasha caught that gesture. He didn't mind. He was determined to be as honest with her as possible.

"I hate to break up the party, ladies, but Sasha is going to need a few things for tonight and tomorrow."

"Lucia and Amo are waiting in their store. They said to use the back entrance as they're closed. Nicoletta will let you in," Francesca said.

Nicoletta. The problem child. He glanced at Stefano.

Stefano sighed and nodded. "She'll be joining us for self-defense training five days a week. Mariko has struck up a friendship with her and she'll be her first instructor."

"That's a heavy schedule," Giovanni objected. "She works two jobs and has to keep up with her schoolwork."

"I spoke with Agnese Moretti and she's caught up on her work and then some. There will be no problem with graduation," Stefano assured. "Otherwise, I would have been sitting down with her until it was done."

Giovanni nodded his head and held out his hand to Sasha. "Let's get a move on so you can see your brother tonight. I know you don't have much time off."

"I can't do that." There was regret in her voice, but she took his hand. "I can't possibly sleep in that apartment, so I need to find a place to stay and I need clothes and things like a hairbrush, hair products and a toothbrush."

He closed his fingers around hers and tugged until she was under his shoulder. "We're taking care of the clothes now, and I'm certain Emmanuelle won't mind shopping for you so we can see your brother. Lucia and Amo have chosen a few things for you, so if you like them, we can get them immediately without taking much time."

"We'll help," Francesca added. "We can get you the

things you need while you go visit with your brother. No problem."

"I can't ask you to do that," Sasha objected. "Sandlin . . . doesn't remember me at all. I go visit him and he's always sweet, but he has no idea I'm actually related. He doesn't have a clue who I am. If I skip tonight, I don't think he'll care."

"But you'll care," Giovanni said. She was trembling and her voice shook just the merest thread, but he heard it because he was so attuned to her. "Let them help you, honey. They're right here and they can take the things to my house and have them waiting for you." He nodded to the women of his family as he turned a protesting Sasha toward the door. "You can argue with me about staying with me *after* you get clothes from Lucia and when we're in the car. Just hold your arguments. We'll miss visiting hours if we don't get a move on."

He shepherded her right out the back door so they could go down the alley to the back entrance to Lucia's Treasures. The police were still working on Sasha's apartment, and he picked up the pace, not wanting her to think too much about a man invading her space and using her things.

"I'll have a cleaning service take care of your place. They'll sterilize everything. John Balboni owns the local hardware shop and he'll install several dead bolts and better locks on the doors, including your bedroom door."

"Giovanni, you can't do that for me."

"We own the building and it wasn't safe," he argued. "Right here." He indicated the three stairs leading to the back entrance to the little boutique.

Nicoletta waited in the doorway. Her gaze shifted from him to Sasha and she kept her attention centered on her. Her smile was professional. "Hi, Sasha, I'm Nicoletta. I'm so sorry for what happened to you. Francesca called, and Lucia has pulled some clothes and lingerie she thought you'd be interested in. Giovanni told us your size."

Giovanni narrowed his gaze at the teenager. She was eighteen now and looked more of a woman than the scared girl she'd been when she'd been rescued. He was certain she'd tacked the last on just to see him get in trouble, and of course Sasha rose to the bait.

"My size?"

"Your size was on the two garments on the bed," he pointed out, although the truth was, just looking at her, he knew her size.

"That makes sense," she said, mollified. She flashed a smile at Nicoletta. "It's nice to meet you. Francesca was just telling me how proud of you she is."

Nicoletta's smile was instantly genuine. "She could be the nicest person on the planet, unless it's Mariko or Emmanuelle. Well, after Lucia, of course."

"They were telling me about Lucia. I've seen the Faustis in the deli, but haven't really met them. Pietro talks about them all the time. He loves them. When they come in, I'm always busy so I haven't had the chance to get to know them. Emmanuelle, in particular, is fond of Lucia."

"Everyone is," Nicoletta assured as they moved through the back room. "I already love her, and that's saying a lot."

The fragrance in the store was subtle, but with it came a sense of peace. That was also Lucia. Nicoletta stepped back to allow them into the shop. "Sasha, this is Lucia and Amo, my foster parents. This is Sasha. She's with Giovanni."

There was a small silence and then both Lucia and Amo broke into huge smiles. Both went straight to Sasha and kissed her on both cheeks.

"It is wonderful to meet you, Sasha," Lucia said. "Even under these circumstances. We've waited a long time for Giovanni to find the right woman."

Sasha frowned and started to shake her head. Before she could speak, Amo took both her hands and beamed at her. "At last. We've prayed for you to come along. Giovanni needs his woman. We pray and here you are. Please, look at what my Lucia and Nicoletta have chosen for you, but feel free to look around. Anything is yours if you want it."

"Thank you." Clearly, she didn't know what to say or do

because she moved back into Giovanni as if for protection. Going up on her toes she whispered for him alone, "I can't possibly afford anything in here, nor do I want them to give me clothing for free."

"I've already taken care of it," Giovanni assured. "Before you throw something at my head, just accept it and we'll battle it out in the car. We can't stay longer than ten minutes. The Hendrick Center is across town and it takes a little while to get there, even driving fast."

She gave him a dark scowl, which only made his cock ache. God, she was adorable. Everything about her appealed to him, even her fiercely independent nature. He was in for a fight with her, and he was looking forward to it. He grinned at her just to provoke her further.

Sasha turned away to look at the soft jeans Lucia had set aside. There were three pairs and several tees and tanks. Just going by the look on her face, Sasha loved them. She touched the exquisite underwear, a higher end stretch-lace panty and beautiful bras he couldn't wait to take off her. "We'll take them all," he said to forestall any arguments. "She'll need a sweater and something for bed."

"No, Giovanni." Sasha was firm on that. "I can't possibly afford these and you know it." She turned her head to look longingly at the jeans and tees. "Maybe one pair, just because, and the underwear."

"All of it," Giovanni said firmly. "Lucia, why don't you argue with Sasha while Nicoletta wraps everything up for us, and Amo and I will take care of things."

"Absolutely not," Sasha objected, trailing after him.

He didn't even turn around. He heard Nicoletta whispering. "They're all like that. Trust me, if you're considered family, and he wouldn't bring you here or with the others if he didn't, they'll just take over your life."

There was no bitterness in her voice that Giovanni could detect, but there was something he couldn't put his finger on. He turned to look at her. She was looking away from him, down at the clothing she was carefully wrapping in tissue paper. There was a look on her face that made him want to go to her and comfort her. He couldn't stop himself, even though he knew she would probably reject him the way she did all of them.

He strode right past Sasha and tipped Nicoletta's chin. "Are you all right, *sorellina*? Tell me, and I'll take care of it."

For a moment, it looked as if Nicoletta blinked back tears, and his heart sank. She shook her head. "I'm good. Just working a lot lately."

"Will training with us be too hard on you?" He kept his voice low. Gentle. He wasn't certain how to handle her when she'd been stripped of everything. She'd lost her family, was in a nightmare world for far too long before they'd managed to rescue her and was uncomfortable with them because they knew far too much about her. Her body screamed at him not to touch her so he let go of her chin.

"I want to learn to defend myself," she whispered back. "Don't take that away from me."

"We want you to learn. Nicoletta, if you're worried about something, you can talk to me—or to Francesca. You do know that, right?"

She nodded and kept wrapping the clothes. He turned away from her, feeling as if he'd failed her. Surprisingly, Sasha didn't say another word. She retreated to the other side of the boutique with Lucia and left him up front with Amo.

## CHAPTER SIX

"She breaks my heart," Sasha said. When Giovanni looked over at her, she clarified. "Nicoletta. She's so young, but she isn't. She's as grown-up as I am, maybe more, and she shouldn't be."

He was driving the Aston Martin again, her very favorite. Well, at least she thought it would always be her favorite, even though she'd seen a dozen different cars his family drove and some of them looked extremely luxurious. He handled the car the way he did everything. He was absolutely confident and looked casual while he was doing it.

"She's had a difficult time. Like you, she lost her parents too young. She was put in a bad situation, and Stefano was able to get the authorities to allow her to live with Lucia and Amo, but there were a lot of very cruel things that happened prior to her coming here. She's finding her way, and we're all looking out for her."

"The alcohol?"

"Lucia was worried. Like I told you, we were pulling her out of parties all the time. Apparently after the talk Taviano had with her, Lucia says she's been subdued, hasn't gone out with those friends again and has really worked hard on her schoolwork. It's only been a couple of days, so we'll see."

"How can she work two jobs and still go to school?"

"She has tutors. She doesn't go to regular high school."

"Where did she meet these friends of hers?"

"She works at the flower shop with Bruno Vitale. He's

been a thorn in our side for a long while. He just turned twenty-five and those are his friends, none of them from this neighborhood, and she's been hanging out with them quite a bit. It's been worrisome to everyone."

Sasha nodded. "I can see why. She needs friends, though, Giovanni." She knew she was talking about herself as well. Maybe she could befriend the girl, although Nicoletta didn't seem too interested in her.

"We were tutored," he said.

She hadn't meant to put him on the defensive. "You have a very large family. There was no way you were going to get lonely. I understand loneliness a little better than you."

"Don't kid yourself, Sasha. Every one of my brothers, as well as my sister, experiences loneliness. Stefano has Francesca and Ricco has Mariko, so I'm betting they don't, but when you search the world and you believe you're never going to find the right partner, you're lonely. It doesn't matter how big your family is or how much money you have."

She heard the sincerity in his voice and her heart clenched. "I suppose you're right. I'll see if I can befriend her. It would be nice for both of us. What did you mean by training?"

Giovanni shrugged, drawing her attention to how wide his shoulders were. As the car moved through the streets and the lights shone across them, throwing various shades of dark and light, he appeared to disappear as if the very shadows flowed through him.

"We work out together, martial arts, weapons training, that sort of thing, and we want Nicoletta to learn. We thought it would give her more confidence." He flashed her a quick look. "You might be interested in something like that, not that you need more confidence."

"I would be interested if I wasn't already working sixteen hours a day. I visit Sandlin every spare minute I get. Which reminds me, we need to get to the argument where I tell you I'm going to pay you back for everything and I'm not staying at your home."

He was silent for so long she thought he wasn't going to respond. She caught him glancing in the rearview mirror several times, he texted with one hand, and then he turned off the main street she knew led to the Hendrick Center. Before she could ask him what he was doing he sent her a small grin that sent her stomach into a slow roll.

"Start arguing away, but the end result will be that you're coming home with me. My house is so damn big we won't be able to find each other, and in any case, I plan to act the perfect gentleman."

She wanted to laugh at the pious tone. "Really? You're not going to try to kiss me?" She touched her lips because just saying it, just *thinking* about it, put the taste of him in her mouth.

He turned down a narrow street and then again onto another one. He suddenly reversed and backed up right into the open door of a garage and killed the lights. He turned toward her, sliding his arm along the back of her seat. "Gentlemen kiss, Sasha."

"What are we doing here?" Her heart was beating too fast, but she wasn't certain if it was in anticipation or out of fear. Something was wrong and he wasn't telling her.

"Some gentlemen are very good at kissing, but clearly you need to see for yourself."

"We can't just park and have a make-out session in a perfect stranger's garage," she pointed out, trying not to laugh. "Are you crazy?"

His fingers crept from the back of the seat to her shoulder. His palm slid under her curls to the nape of her neck, stroking featherlight caresses against her bare skin. Every nerve ending jumped to life.

Twin headlights lit up the narrow street as a car pulled into the lane, going slow. The lights illuminated the asphalt and brick, but failed to enter the tiny garage. Her heart was already pounding, but now, it accelerated even more.

"Are you trying to distract me? Is someone following us?" She edged closer to him, almost right on the middle console, not realizing until it was too late that she was playing right into his hands. The car went on by and she felt a little foolish.

His hand applied pressure, so that her head continued to bend toward his. Then his mouth was on hers and she forgot all about the fact that they were in a stranger's garage hiding from someone possibly hunting them. Fire swept through her and she found herself wrapping her arms around his neck and giving herself up to the exquisite perfection of his mouth. His kiss.

She'd been kissed before, but this was completely different. This was—extraordinary. Her mind couldn't hold a single thought, but just melted right along with her body. He tasted like male, a spice she quickly found herself addicted to, one she chased, needing more. The kiss went on and on, until she needed air and then he breathed for her, even as those flames he poured into her threatened to burn her alive.

Her body was no longer her own, but belonged to him. Had he tried, he could have taken her right there, on the seat in some stranger's garage. It was Giovanni in control, lifting his head, resting his forehead against hers, breathing a ragged rhythm she tried to follow.

"This is dangerous."

His velvet whisper slid over her skin, stroked and caressed, adding to the terrible need, her body pulsing with demands.

She touched her tongue to her lips, shocked that they weren't on fire. "It is." There was nothing else to do but agree. She couldn't kiss him again. That would lead to . . . She did. She tilted her head just enough to allow her to catch his bottom lip between her teeth and tug. Then she was kissing him, her tongue sweeping into his mouth, sliding along his tongue, taking more of that spice and flame she needed.

His arm nearly crushed her to him, while his other hand slid under her shirt to press against her bare skin. It felt as if his palm burned into her, right through skin and muscle to reach bone, so it was there, his brand proclaiming proprietary rights. She was his exclusively.

His mouth took over, just what she wanted—what she needed. The groan he gave, a mixture of hunger and dominance, sent her temperature soaring. Her panties were damp, her body slick, her nipples tight, breasts aching. She was very aware of his hand, not even his scorching kisses could distract her from wanting him to move it higher.

The long fingers stroked her bare skin, right under her left breast as he kissed her over and over. He pushed his seat back and pulled her body across the console, so that she nearly straddled him. It was a tight fit, but they managed because there was nothing but the two of them, and heat and hunger. It took forever before his fingers moved up over the fine lace of her bra and stroked along the curve.

Her breath caught in her throat and her sex clenched hard. She squirmed, her hips pressing into him, the apex of her legs finding his thigh. The tension in her coiled tighter and tighter. Her breasts felt swollen and needy, nipples pushing blatantly at the thin lace. Then his fingers settled on her nipple and she heard herself cry out, the sound wrenched from her. He tugged, and her hips bucked.

He was more than dangerous to her—that was her one thought of sanity before that slipped away, too, and she dropped her hand, stroking him through his trousers, reveling in the feel of him, so hard and hot, so thick and ready for her. She desperately wanted to open his trousers and explore that heat, but moving required she move her mouth from his and that was impossible. His tongue was velvet. His mouth hotter than anything she'd ever known. Hot. Hard. Commanding. She sank further under his sexual spell, the web closing around her and she let it. She wanted it.

*All clear, Giovanni.* A male's voice came over the radio, shocking her.

She tried to pull back, but Giovanni continued to kiss

her, one hand shaping the nape of her neck, holding her head tilted to his while his other hand explored the full curve of her breasts, the valley between, each nipple, tugging and rolling while she gasped at the streaks of jagged lightning streaking through her bloodstream to pool low in her body. Her sex clenched and throbbed. She curled her palm over his heavy erection, while she rode his thigh, desperate for release.

*Get out of there, man, Harvey is heading your way.*

Giovanni sighed into her mouth. He lifted his head as his fingers stroked her breast slowly, one last time. "Baby, we've got to stop. The owner of the garage is on his way, and we don't want to be caught here."

She tried to move, but her body felt limp, hot and needy. She closed her eyes, desperate to find air, while her sex wept with hunger. Very, very gently, he lifted her off of him and placed her back into her seat. Leaning around her, he caught her seat belt and snapped it back in place. She hadn't known he'd taken it off her in the first place. Or maybe she had. She couldn't think clearly, her mind absolute chaos. All she could think about was reaching into his lap, taking down his zipper and straddling him.

"Baby, help me out."

It was said with a husky groan. Sexy. Almost as desperate for her as she felt for him. Almost. But he'd already adjusted his seat and was pulling the car out of the garage, able to function while she was still having a full body meltdown.

"I'm just sitting here." To emphasize how good she was being, or to keep herself from unzipping his trousers, she threaded her fingers together and locked them that way until her knuckles turned white.

"You're looking at me like you want to devour me."

"I do." She wasn't going to lie. If he wanted a demure, sweet woman, he had the wrong girl. She grew up on a ranch. She knew about sex. Need. Hunger. Right now, he'd taken her higher than she ever dreamed a body could go. She wanted all the way with him.

She looked up at his face, all those sensual lines carved so deeply. He looked like sex and sin incarnate. She touched her tongue to her lower lip. "I want to see what you look like. Feel the weight of you in my palm. I want to taste you. Kissing you, I wondered if your cock would taste as good as your mouth." She watched in fascination as his erection grew even larger, and he had to shift his body just a little as he drove down the little alley to the corner where he waited for a car to flash lights before turning onto the street.

"You're making me crazy on purpose."

"Maybe. You made me that way and then just left me hanging, so turnabout is fair play." She sent him a small smile. He'd certainly made her forget about the fact that her home had been invaded and she didn't want to go there.

"You know I'm going to retaliate."

"You would have anyway and this way I get to have a little fun." Deliberately, she leaned toward his lap as if she might actually carry out her threat. "It's all I can do just to keep from unzipping you and swallowing you down." His cock jerked beneath his trousers, and she couldn't help the satisfied smile. She reached over and stroked her fingers over the hard length. She felt the heat right through the material and her sex clenched again. "Not in the city, though, you couldn't keep us on the road."

"Is that a challenge?"

She loved the intensity of his hunger. His voice had dropped to a growl, the sound sending a little shiver down her spine. She liked being in control. When he was kissing her, she was out of control. Here, she skated that edge. She'd never done anything so daring as she was contemplating. A little, wicked voice kept whispering to her, urging her on.

"Maybe."

"You're playing with fire."

"We're on a very public street. Sooner or later you have

to get back on the main street with all the streetlights. Stop signs. It isn't like you could keep the car under control."

"And if I'm willing to accept the challenge?"

"I'd be in trouble if you lost control."

"We both would be." He turned his head to look at her.

Her entire body went into meltdown again. The tension coiled so tightly in her jerked at her sex, just from the look on his face. She'd never seen anything or anyone look so darkly sensual. So completely wicked. So beautifully masculine. She couldn't help herself. She caught at his zipper and slowly, watching his face the entire time, slid it down.

A muscle ticked in his jaw. His breath caught. Another groan escaped. "Baby, you'd better stop playing around."

She didn't want to play anymore. She wanted her mouth on him. Some part of her knew she was being crazy, she barely knew him, but he made her that way. She'd never met anyone with such animalistic sexuality. Everything about him called to her. She wet her lips again, tugged at her seat belt to give herself room, realized it wasn't going to work and undid it. She was a rule follower and that gave her a thrill. She never did anything like this, and right now, having him in her mouth was all she could think of.

She pushed down his underwear, shorts made of the same material as his suit. His cock sprang free and her breath caught in her throat. He was beautiful. A little intimidating. She wasn't certain how much of him she could take, but she wanted to try. She wanted to claim every delicious inch of him.

She didn't think about anything else but the way her body was on fire and the fact that he wanted her so much. She didn't care where they were, only that she wanted to keep feeling the way she was. It didn't allow for anything else to slip in and freak her out. She couldn't take much more going wrong. For just these next few minutes, her mind and body would be solely occupied with hot, perfect sex.

Sasha licked up his shaft, wanting to feel him, get to

know his cock intimately. She liked how hot he was, how heavy he felt. His heartbeat throbbed through the long vein. His girth was a little intimidating, but it was part of the challenge. She tasted the pearly drops leaking and thought of his taste as an aphrodisiac. A little salty, but mostly the same addicting spice as his skin when she licked at it.

She used one hand to stabilize herself in the moving car, the other fisted him at the base and she licked around him, getting him wet. Very wet. Very slowly she began to take him into her mouth, sucking on the velvet head, her tongue running under the crown, flicking and teasing that sweet little spot that made his body shudder. She smiled, knowing she was getting to him in spite of his steady driving.

Giovanni wanted to pull over and savor the feel of her hot, moist mouth surrounding him like a tight fist. So scorching hot. She sucked at him hard, then released him and changed the tempo. She was humming, a soft little tune that was muffled by the hard cock in her mouth, but that melody vibrated through him, sending shock waves to his groin.

He'd never felt anything like it in his life. He couldn't help but drop one hand to her head, holding her there, not wanting it to stop, even when they came to a red light and anyone might see into the car. He didn't want her aware of where they were in the city. He wanted her mouth on him, sucking hard, running up and down his shaft, taking him deep, so deep he touched her throat, and then she was swirling her tongue around his shaft and teasing the underside of the crown as she came up for air. Every movement sent hot pleasure swamping his body in waves.

She obviously enjoyed what she was doing, moving on him, her fingers dancing over his balls, rolling gently, squeezing, sliding back up to fist his cock, all the while her mouth sliding or sucking or her tongue fluttering and dancing. She never stopped and there was no way to get his balance, or maintain his control, not when he had to keep part of his mind on driving. He was extremely disciplined.

He'd been taught at an early age to be disciplined. She was sucking that out of him every time she took him deep.

It took everything in him not to force her head down on him, so that she swallowed him whole. There was a strange roaring in his head. Thunder crashed in his ears. His body tightened. He hadn't lasted long at all. His balls drew tight, his seed boiling hot, ready to erupt. He knew he had to warn her he wasn't going to be able to stop. He had to make it to the next stoplight before he did. He couldn't let a release burst so ferociously out of him while driving in traffic.

He tried to tap her head, even as he wrapped her hair around his fist and held her down. He thought he heard her laugh, but it came out muffled, and the vibrations sent shock waves through his shaft. The next light was green, and he let her breathe. "Baby, I'm going to blow." He managed to get the words out. Even as he said them, his hand was already applying a little pressure, desperate to feel her mouth again.

She licked at the crown and then swallowed him down. This time the squeezing around his shaft was tremendous. Almost a vise. He felt his cock pulse. Jerk. The light went yellow and he slowed the vehicle, wanting to roar his happiness at something that ordinarily would have annoyed him. The moment the car halted, he closed his eyes because his vision was blurred, colors bursting behind his eyes. He savored the way the pleasure seemed to sweep up his legs, swirl in his balls, rocketing through his shaft until his cock jerked and pulsed, blasting hot seed right down her throat.

It was ecstasy. In a fucking car. Ecstasy. He couldn't breathe it was so good. He didn't realize at first that he had thrown his head back and shouted to the night, roaring right along with his cock. His hand was fisted in her hair, holding her there while she drank him down. It took effort to force his fingers to let go of the handful of hair. When he did, she came up for air and then began to lick at him, cleaning him off to ensure no drop touched his clothes.

When he could think, he glanced around and saw the

truck next to him, the driver staring down at the back of Sasha's head in his lap. He shielded her with one hand, making certain she didn't sit up, so the driver couldn't see her face. In that moment, he knew for certain that Sasha was the one for him. He would never have cared about a man seeing what a woman did or didn't do. That was up to her, not him.

"Baby, don't move until the car is going," he cautioned when he felt her start to sit up.

She used the time to cover his cock with his shorts and then zip up his trousers. The light changed and they sped off. Sasha sat up slowly, reaching for her seat belt.

"*Dio*, Sasha, that was insane. Perfection. I've never felt quite like that."

"Good." She sent him a grin. "I like the way you taste."

"That's a good thing, because instead of an alarm waking me in the mornings, when we're living together, I'll be hoping that's how you'll wake me."

She laughed and pulled down the mirror above the window so she could inspect her lips. The tip of her tongue touched the corner and then her finger did. "You're big. I can't take all of you."

"You didn't have to." He reached over and took her hand. "Are you damp for me? Slick? Hot?"

She nodded. "Very much so."

"I hate that I can't do anything about it right now. But you could. We're about seven minutes out. I could make a circle if you'd need more time." He couldn't keep the excitement out of his voice. "Undo your jeans, baby. Just push them down enough to give yourself room."

She glanced out the window. He had turned off the main road to use one of the less traveled streets. It was a little darker and only two lanes so no one could be next to them. "If I do, it's going to make you hot all over again. We could be at this all night."

"I'm good with that. I want you taken care of. In fact, baby, push your jeans down a little more and turn your body toward me. Put one foot up on the seat, and let your knees fall open." The idea made him hard all over again. He wanted to see her. He liked her like this. A little wanton, unashamed of her sexuality, willing to be adventurous. He wanted to eat her up. He didn't have the luxury of doing that when he was driving, but he could get a little taste.

"You can't possibly . . ."

"I want to devour you, eat you alive, but I'll do the next best thing." He grinned at her, holding up his hand. He had big hands and his fingers were thick. "First you. I want to see you. Show me how you pleasure yourself."

"I have this toy . . ." Her voice was wicked.

He groaned. "We're putting that on the list. From now on, we're carrying a toy in our cars. Maybe several of them. In fact, I think we need to go to an adult store on the way home."

"We have a list?" She slowly slid her zipper down and then began to push her jeans and panties over her skin, leaving her hips bare. Her tight little curls were platinum blond, like her hair. She pushed the jeans down farther, baring her thighs, giving her enough room to draw one knee up so she could plant her foot on the seat.

He found it was much more difficult to drive with her body open to him than it had been when her mouth was around his cock. Well, it was a toss-up. She let her knees fall open as she took her finger and thumb, slowly circling the tiny little hooded bud and then pushing a finger deep. His mouth watered. He swore under his breath, and she smiled. It was pure seduction.

"You're a holy terror, Sasha," he accused. "And we definitely have a list."

She licked at her finger, her eyes on his face. His cock jerked hard in his trousers. He hadn't expected the temptress, but he should have. She had fire in her. Passion. She might hide it, but it still smoldered just beneath the surface. He liked to play, and with her, he found playing not just for the end result, but for the fun-filled journey.

She began to move her fingers in and out, pressing deep and then shallow, curling her middle finger, her thumb strumming her clit.

"Someday, I'm going to put jewelry on you, and you're going to be in my car wearing nothing else and I'm going to do everything I want to your body."

"You'll be driving. I don't have your discipline," she objected, leaning forward, extending her arm to share her glistening fingers with him.

"I'll have a driver, make him drive us all over the city."

She laughed softly, her eyes darkening as he drew her finger into his mouth. "You like cars, don't you?"

"Cars and you. Perfect combination. Push your T-shirt up so I can see your nipples."

"I'm busy. Keep your eyes on the road. You gave me seven minutes. That's not a lot of time to get off. I like to take my time. Prolong the journey."

His cock was raging at him again, which didn't make sense when he'd blown so hot. He wanted to be alone with her back at his house. He'd promised to be a gentleman, but he had given himself the option of trying to seduce her. He'd told her kissing would be involved. He just hadn't said where on her body that kissing was going to take place.

"You've got a wicked look on your face." Her voice was strained. She threw her head back and her hips began to thrust in time with her fingers. Her thumb pressed harder.

He pushed her hand away and took over. He wanted to use his mouth, draw all that sweet honey right out of her body, but he strummed her clit and then pinched roughly, taking his eyes from the road to look at her face just for that moment. She flushed and her mouth opened, eyes darkening even more with lust. He pushed into her with a thick finger, curling deep, finding her sweet spot, hearing her ragged breathing as he began pumping in and out of her slick sheath.

He added a second finger, stretching her, hearing her gasp. He flicked her clit, wishing he was sucking on her and could use his teeth. Her breathing was musical, the sound coming from her throat spurring him to be ruthless with his fingers. He couldn't see her, not when he was driving, so he kept up the work until he saw the parking garage he needed. At once he swept into it, still using his fingers on her.

The moment he parked the car and turned it off, one-handed, he turned, unsnapping his belt, lifting her up by her bottom so he could bring her to his mouth. He felt like a starving man. She screamed when he plunged his tongue deep, when he raked her clit with his teeth, when he used his fingers and mouth in unison, taking her up again and again until that little musical note had a sobbing melody.

Hips bucking, she pressed herself to him, looking for release. He lifted his head away, and she chased after his mouth. He wiped his face on her thighs and rubbed the shadow along his jaw over her lips so the bristles stimulated her more.

"What do you want, baby? Tell me." He'd never teased another woman before. Never played games like he wanted to play. Never let that side of him out. Now he wanted to hear her little cries. Her pleas. He wanted to hear her ask him for her release, to acknowledge it was Giovanni giving it to her. That shit turned him on even more.

"I want you to fuck me, but since we can't do that here, I want your mouth to take me over the edge."

He kissed her. Licked her. Pushed his tongue in her, just to reward her. He took his time sucking her clit and then used his teeth again. "I love how hot you are. Ask me for it."

"*Ask* you?" There was a hint of laughter mixed with the desperation. "I was thinking of ordering you."

"You could try it." He used his fingers ruthlessly and stopped before she could get off. "But I doubt it will work."

"Giovanni, will you please get me off any way that you can? I'm a little desperate right now."

If he hadn't been falling for her, he would have right then. The laughter in her voice was like music, like magic, sliding over and into him. He had been paying attention to every response, what took her high fast, what she liked, didn't like, what had her hips moving out of control. She liked that bite he gave her. The deep thrust with two fingers that stretched and burned. Her response was more scorching-hot, liquid honey. He took her over the edge, watching her face while she shattered. Nothing was more beautiful to him.

He kept his fingers in her, wanting to feel every wave, wishing it was his cock that silken sheath surrounded. He watched the rippling of her stomach muscles, and the way her nipples hardened even more. He was desperate to have her under him, naked, for hours.

She lay back, trying to catch her breath, while he licked her clean before pulling up her panties and jeans. She didn't move, her head resting against the door while she stared at him through half-closed eyes. "You could be a little crazy, Giovanni."

"The good kind of crazy, and you bring it out in me. And I am compelled to point out, you started the whole sex in the car thing, so you're just as crazy."

She threw her head back and laughed. "Where do you want to have sex next? The middle of the street?"

He was grateful she wanted to have more sex with him. He pretended to contemplate the idea. "I don't think the street is good, but I'll definitely make a list."

"Another list?"

He nodded and helped her sit up. "You said you liked lists. I'm all for it, especially if you make a commitment to follow the list and get everything on it accomplished."

"What kinds of things will be on it?"

"I have a favorite restaurant. They have this one table right in the center of the room. It's always gleaming, and every time I go in there, I think, if I had a woman, I'd fuck her right on that table. It's the perfect height. I can take her so many ways and that table is strong. The ceiling is decorated with diamond-shaped mirrors. And each wall has mirrors so the entire room would reflect us."

"A restaurant?" Her laughter rang out. "We'd probably ruin everyone's appetite and they'd call the cops on us."

"We'd rent out the restaurant for the night, silly. I can't have other men looking at my woman's body. I'm a pervert, baby, but not that big of one."

She glanced away from him. She took a deep breath and let it out. "You know, if you told your cousins and brothers about me giving you a blow job and then letting you devour me, you probably could make a lot of money."

His heart jerked hard, laughter fading. "Is that what you think I'd do, Sasha? Is that why you think you're with me?"

"I don't know why I'm with you, but in the interest of reminding you, if you're ever broke, you could make some cash." She reached for the door handle.

He was faster, his hand stopping her. "Look at me."

"I need to go in and see my brother."

"You need to look at me."

He felt her square her shoulders and brace herself. Her chin went up and she turned her head back so she was looking him in the eye. "I'm with you because you're the one. I've looked all over the fucking world for you. I'm not letting you slip through my fingers."

"You don't know me."

"We're sitting in a car outside a very expensive brain trauma rehabilitation, live-in center. You're working two jobs in order to keep your brother in this place. One of those jobs you don't even like that much. I love family, and clearly you do as well. You gave me a mind-blowing blow job. In a car. I'm a very sexual person. I want my woman to be adventuresome and generous, both things you are. When some asshole went into your apartment, invading your space, taking away your security, you didn't flinch or fall apart. You handled it. You're comfortable with my crazy, big family. You're not afraid of me. Baby, the list goes on and on. I'm giving you my word, I'm dead serious about you. I've never taken another woman to my home, to our territory, to the pizzeria, nor have I introduced her to my family. Not ever."

"You scare me," she objected.

He ran his finger over her lips. That mouth he loved. "It's okay to be a little afraid, but you have no problem telling me or my brothers and cousins off. And you would have punched Darby right in the nose. I fucking love that. I forgot to include that on my list."

A small smile curved her mouth. "I wanted to break it. What I really wanted to do was yank down his jeans. I believe in an eye for an eye. Trust me, his cock isn't that big. I felt it when he pulled me down on his lap."

He especially liked that she believed in an eye for an eye. She needed to believe that in order to be with him. There was so much about his life she would have to accept. "You haven't said a word about how you feel about me." Just putting it out there, giving her the opportunity to back out, was scary when he'd always been unafraid.

"Then you weren't listening, Giovanni," she said. "I gave you a blow job in a car while you were driving across town to go to see my brother. Do you think I do that with everyone I meet, because I don't. I don't *want* to be attracted to you, or even like you. Your family is too notorious, and I don't even know if you're good or bad yet."

Relief made him want to kiss her, but instead, he got out, walked around to her door and took her hand as she stepped out. "Why did you give me a blow job? Especially after the stupid things I said to you in the club."

"You're hot as hell, Giovanni, and you take my breath away every time I look at you. I couldn't believe how sweet you were to me. Your entire family came to help. I liked them all. No one was pretentious or condescending, especially not you. I felt safe with you. I still do."

He knew when their shadows touched, the intensity of their mutual physical attraction was amplified, mainly because they each felt the other's emotions. She didn't understand that, nor would she until he told her about shadow riders, what they could do and why it was that she could hear lies.

"Are we done with that silly game, Sasha, because I never want to hear about it again."

She was silent as they walked up to the front doors. He stopped moving, forcing her to stop as well.

"Woman, you didn't answer me."

"I'm considering. It seems a little too early to just put that aside. I think it's letting you off easy. I always make it a point to keep my word, so I'm not just going to give it to you without thinking this over carefully. I might need some leverage, something to even the playing field."

"I'm beginning to see the appeal of whips and handcuffs," he groused, pulling her close to him.

She burst out laughing, the sound carefree and happy. Everything in him should have settled. She wouldn't laugh like that unless she forgave his idiot game. After all that had happened to her, to sound like that . . . He tipped her face up to his and took her mouth. Immediately she wrapped her arms around his neck and pressed her body into his. He loved the way she gave herself to him. Everything. She'd done it earlier as well, holding nothing back. That was on his list of things he loved about her. So many. Especially the way she kissed.

That uneasiness in him didn't subside when he kissed her in spite of the fact that she was clearly over the game he'd invented. Of course, he wasn't about to admit to her that he'd been the one to think it up because he was so damned bored playing the role of playboy that he was sulking all the time. He lifted his head slowly, turning slightly so he could angle his body to keep her between him and the facility's front door and the street. He looked carefully around. His uneasiness grew.

Her fingers tightened on his jacket sleeve. "Giovanni?" Her voice trembled slightly. She kept it low, so it wouldn't travel past him.

"I know, baby. He's out there. He was following us. The

boys set up a trap, but he didn't fall for it. I thought we lost him though. I don't see how he wasn't spotted the way I drove here."

"I wondered why you took such a roundabout route."

"Let's get you inside. I'll tell Emilio and Enzo he's still watching you. We'll visit with your brother and ignore the asshole. Let the boys try to find him. If they can't, when we get back to my home, believe me, there's no way in for him. You'll be safe there tonight. We'll figure out what to do in the morning when we're both fresh."

"But . . ." She trailed off and then nodded.

"Good. Have fun with your brother. Take your time and put everything else out of your head. I want you to introduce me to him. He might not remember this time or next that I visit, but hopefully, he'll come to accept me with you." He was already texting Emilio as they went inside and shut the door.

# CHAPTER SEVEN

Sandlin Provis was a good-looking man in spite of the head-on collision. There were very few scars and none of them were prominent. He had a small one up by his temple and another curving close to his cheekbone, but other than that, he looked as if he was in perfect health and always had been.

Giovanni could see the resemblance to Sasha the moment they entered the common room, where he was sitting quietly in a corner reading a book. His curly hair was the same nearly platinum blond his sister had. His eyes were that exact sapphire blue. The scruff on his jaw was mostly blond.

"Sandlin," Sasha greeted, her voice filled with genuine love. "You look good tonight. I've missed you."

The man looked up, blinking at her, and then a slow, almost childlike smile slipped over his face. "Hello." He marked his place in his book and carefully closed it, his actions unhurried and deliberate. "Are you looking for someone?"

Giovanni was looking at Sasha and he saw the hurt and sadness in her expression, hastily covered by a smile. "You, Sandlin. I was looking for you. I would very much like to visit with you if you have time. My name is Sasha, and I'm your sister. I've brought a friend with me. This is Giovanni Ferraro." She indicated him, but kept her gaze fixed on her brother.

He stood, using the same slow, deliberate movements that he had when closing his book. Giovanni stepped forward and held out his hand. Sandlin took it without hesitation. Surprisingly, his grip was strong.

"I'm the man who is with your sister," Giovanni explained. "I wanted to come and see you so you'll know she's well looked after."

Sandlin regarded him with an open, sweet expression. "That's good." He indicated the chairs closer to the fireplace. "Let's sit over there. I like being close to the fire. It keeps me warm."

They walked toward the fireplace. The flames gave off shadows, some dancing across the wood floor. Giovanni stepped into one and felt the pull against him, the way the shadows tugged at his body. When he stepped out of that one into the next he had a shock. Sandlin's shadow, thrown by the light, had connected with Giovanni's. Like Sasha, he was a potential shadow rider, his shadow throwing out tubes to connect with every shadow around him.

Giovanni watched his face very carefully and saw the exact moment information and emotion hit him. Sandlin turned his head to look at Giovanni, to study his facial features. There was no guile whatsoever in him, but his shocking blue eyes were speculative as he stared at Giovanni.

"Do I know you?"

Giovanni shook his head. "No, I came with your sister to make certain you knew I would take good care of her." He wanted to reiterate that Sasha was his sibling and that Giovanni was good for her.

"You feel . . . scary."

Giovanni nodded. "I can be scary to some people. Not to you. Certainly not to Sasha."

Sandlin frowned and shook his head. "I meant another word. I don't like it when I can't think of what I want to say." His expression cleared, changed at once to glee. "Powerful. You're powerful. Our shadows touch and I know you."

Giovanni nodded. "That's right. When our shadows touch, you can tell whether or not someone is lying to you, right?"

Sandlin sank into one of the armchairs. He gripped the arm with strong fingers. "I don't like lies. They hurt my ears." He rubbed at his temples as if remembering a painful experience.

"That happens to me as well," Giovanni said. He caught Sasha as she started past him, pulling her to him so that her back was pressed tight against his front, his arms around her waist. He moved them both into the next shadow that touched Sandlin's. The jolt hit him hard. All three were connected now, tubes reaching for one another, their shadows intertwining.

Sasha gasped and looked up at him, but he kept his gaze fixed on Sandlin's face. The man felt it, too, that initial hit, a rush of information crowding in, too much to be analyzed all at once. Sandlin and Sasha definitely could have been riders, both of them sensitive to the pull of the shadows as well as to the intelligence pouring in. The ability in them was extremely strong.

Giovanni had known Sasha's character from the moment their shadows had touched. He'd felt her sweet, compassionate nature coupled with her independent, fiery side. Sandlin had a will of steel, but his childlike, open qualities overshadowed that will. He wanted to please those around him, for the most part.

It was important for Giovanni to protect his woman, even from her own brother if it was necessary. Mariko, Ricco's wife, had been targeted by her own brother and the woman who had raised the two of them. Giovanni wasn't about to overlook any threat to Sasha. He was adept at reading shadows and hearing lies. He'd been trained from the time he was a child. He couldn't imagine Sandlin being a threat to anyone, but he wasn't about to make mistakes based on compassion or any other gentler emotion. Sandlin, for all his childlike ways, and the fact that he couldn't hold on to information, at least anything in his memory banks, was a shrewd man.

"I've never felt anyone as powerful or as dangerous as you," Sasha admitted in a low voice. "When all three of our shadows touched like that, your pull was so strong I had to move into you. That was extraordinary and a little scary. I've always been able to hear lies, and so has Sandlin. I can feel other people's emotions, but never that strong. It's nowhere near that strong."

"I've been trained in the use of shadows," he said by way of explanation. He couldn't go into his family's legacy, not there.

Giovanni stepped out of the shadow and led Sasha to the low-slung love seat across from Sandlin. The flames rose up, dancing, as if a breeze had entered the room. Sandlin watched him the entire way. He looked a pale child, helplessly watching a predator draw close.

"What have you been doing today?" Sasha asked as she settled on the small love seat.

Giovanni sat next to her, one arm sliding out along the back of the couch to circle behind her shoulders, trying to offer her reassurance. Her body trembled, small little continual tremors he doubted she was aware of. She kept her smile with a steady, concentrated effort as she regarded her brother.

He ignored her, staring at Giovanni. "You have done *bad* things." It was a child's accusation, sounding a little twisted coming from a grown adult.

Giovanni stayed in complete control, not wincing away from the truth, refusing to give away anything to Sasha through body language. He *had* done bad things, at least those things could be considered bad if the wrong people knew about them. He was a rider, and that meant his job was to bring justice to those who had escaped the law.

He nodded his head. "Yes, Sandlin, that's true. I have done bad things. Not to your sister, but many people might say I'm a bad person, judging me on things they don't understand. But I'm not bad to your sister nor would I ever be. Bad people are afraid of me, not your sister." His voice rang with sincerity and he hoped Sandlin would quit regarding him with suspicion.

Sandlin continued to stare at him with the same frown that Giovanni liked seeing on Sasha's face. She could melt him just with her expressions alone, which didn't bode well for his future. She would be able to play him so easily and, sadly, he could tell he was going to be one of those men who gave her anything and everything she wanted. He bent his head to brush a kiss through her thick hair.

"You don't feel like the other man did," Sandlin said. "He felt funny. I didn't like him."

Sasha frowned at Giovanni. "Who's he talking about?"

"Hell if I know. Buddy, you're going to have to be more precise. Who felt funny to you?"

"He was just here," Sandlin insisted, scowling at them, beginning to look petulant. "Right before you. He interrupted my reading, too. I don't like that. Not when it's at a good part. How am I supposed to figure out who did the killing when I'm interrupted?"

Beside him, Sasha had begun to tense up. He slid his hand under her fall of curls to wrap his fingers around the nape of her neck, massaging gently in hopes of easing the tension out of her.

"He gets agitated sometimes," she whispered. "And he mixes things up. He might have been reading about someone coming into a room and interrupting the hero."

Giovanni didn't think so, and apprehension grew in the pit of his stomach. He leaned toward Sandlin. "Can you describe the man who came to see you tonight?"

Sandlin looked puzzled. "No. He was a man."

Giovanni was silent, trying to think how to get Sandlin's cooperation. "Can you give us clues and we'll try to guess?"

Sandlin's face lit up. Once more he looked like the sweet

child he'd been when they'd first arrived. "Yes. We can solve the mystery. He wore a brown coat. A big one, with a hood."

Sasha frowned, her eyes meeting Giovanni's. "Do you think someone was really here tonight? We don't know anyone here."

"Don't they have to sign in?"

"I thought so. They know me here and I've not signed in for the last month or so. Maybe they've changed their policy."

"We'll ask. I'll want to speak to someone in charge," Giovanni said. He knew once a Ferraro was involved, the Center would do just about anything to keep him happy. He represented the potential of millions of dollars coming their way in donations.

"You didn't figure it out," Sandlin said. "You need to think about it."

"We need another clue."

Sandlin looked deflated. Clearly, he didn't have anything else he remembered. His face suddenly lit up and he fished something out of his pocket. Giovanni heard Sasha gasp. She went pale and leaned toward her brother to better see what he had in his hand.

Sandlin stared down at the object and then held it out. "I think this belongs to her, not me. He said it was mine and he was returning it to me, but it isn't."

"It's the key chain. The one taken from my apartment." She got up and crossed the short distance to take the key chain from her brother. "Thanks, Sandlin, you're right, this is mine. You gave it to me. See?" She showed him the picture. "That's me on the horse the year I won the championship for barrel racing. That same year, you won at bull-riding. You wanted to go on the circuit and you were good enough, too, but then Dad got sick."

There were tears in Sasha's voice, but not in her eyes and that broke Giovanni's heart. She turned back to him. "He was here. How did he know about Sandlin? How could he possibly know about my brother?" Her voice was swinging a little toward hysteria.

"He was in your apartment, going through your things. Your mail. He would have found bills and correspondence from the Center."

She took a breath, desperately trying to be calm. "What if he's in danger? I don't know what to do now."

Giovanni stood up and drew her into his arms. "I'll take care of this, baby. He'll be safe. I'll go now and talk to the front desk."

"They can't do anything," Sasha protested. "It's late and no one is ever here that can answer questions or make decisions." Frustration laced the fear in her voice.

"They'll get their administrator on the phone and he'll come down." Giovanni bent to kiss her. She tasted like cinnamon candy apples. He didn't know why that appealed to him so much, but suddenly that was his favorite flavor. He smiled at Sandlin. "You've stumped us, Sandlin. I don't think we're good at figuring out mysteries."

Sandlin smiled angelically. "I'm not very good, either," he admitted. "I forget the clues."

"Do you want me to read to you?" Sasha asked.

Sandlin nodded eagerly. "Yes. I remember you now. You read to me and you do the voices. I like that."

Giovanni left them to it and strode down the hall to the front desk. Within a half an hour—and he paced the entire time—the head administrator and his assistant were locked in an office with him viewing the security tapes. There was no way to identify the man who had come to see Sandlin. He hadn't signed in. The woman at the front desk had waved the stranger on through, still wearing his hoodie, chatting a couple of minutes and then giving him directions to the lounge.

Giovanni's jaw tightened. He swung his gaze to Sonny Goodman's. The man ran the entire Center, and it was clear he was embarrassed and angry at his employee's behavior.

"I'm sorry, Mr. Ferraro. She was hired a month or so ago and it's clear she isn't doing her job."

"This man is a stalker. He's been stalking my fiancée and now he's here, with access to her brother. He's a dangerous man, and this is a threat. I believe Sandlin is in danger."

"We're so sorry this slipped through," Goodman repeated. "Sandlin will be protected."

"I want to talk to his doctor, and I want a full report of this incident given to the police. Sandlin had better be protected. I will be hiring extra security for him as well. No one should get through to see him other than his sister, me or one of my family."

"I had no idea Ms. Provis was connected to your family," Goodman said.

"Information like that would make her a target of every kidnapper in the country. I would appreciate it if you kept it under wraps." He looked at Goodman's assistant. Harriet Perkins was about thirty, and she kept staring at him and blushing. Goodman wouldn't tell a soul, but Harriet probably wouldn't be able to stop herself. She would want all her closest friends to know she'd met one of the famous Ferraros. "Ms. Perkins?"

"I would never tell anyone," she said. "Not a single word of this."

"I don't mind you telling your friends that you met me, but please don't connect my name with Ms. Provis or her brother." He gave her his most charming smile. He knew from the nearly excited look in her eye that he didn't have a prayer she'd keep her mouth shut. She would want to be in the spotlight.

He cursed under his breath, holding on to his smile grimly, but trying one more time. There would be fallout from this. "You have no idea," he told Goodman, but mostly for Harriet's sake, "the circus that would ensue if reporters found out the connection between Sandlin and my family. They would be bribing your staff, sneaking in and making things up about your facility. This really needs to stay quiet."

"I understand," Goodman said, bobbing his head. He looked at his assistant. "Harriet is very discreet. She's been with me five years."

Giovanni could have told him those five years meant nothing if bribery were involved. Still, he'd done what he could to protect Sandlin from Sasha's stalker. He'd given Goodman the name of a security company his family trusted and assured he'd pay. He wanted Goodman to check them out thoroughly because Giovanni would be sending men over to help keep Sandlin safe. At first Goodman had assured him they could handle it, but Giovanni insisted and Goodman capitulated under the pressure at the thought of the Ferraros being patrons of his Center. Money could be a pain, but in the end, it always talked.

Goodman escorted him back down the hall to the room where he'd left Sasha. Sandlin was stretched out on the couch he'd been originally on when they came to visit. Sasha sat with his head in her lap, her fingers running through her brother's hair while she read to him. Sandlin had his eyes closed, but there was a smile on his face. The long bank of lights overhead shone down brightly, like a spotlight, illuminating the two of them so that with their blond curls, they looked almost angelic.

Twice, while Giovanni watched them, Sandlin caught at Sasha's wrist and said something, his entire body quivering with excitement. She nodded and made some kind of animal sound, a dog barking, a cat meowing, whatever the story called for. Satisfied, Sandlin would subside again.

"How's he doing?" Giovanni asked.

"He's not going to recover," Goodman said, not beating around the bush. "The Center is helping him learn to walk and put on his clothes, but he's never going to be able to live on his own outside a facility. I know that's his sister's ultimate goal. She thinks she'll be able to bring him home with her, but it won't happen. Most of the time Sandlin is sweet and agreeable, but he has periods of agitation and he strikes out at the staff. He has seizures as well. His medication is extremely important and sometimes he refuses to take it."

"When you say agitated, could he hurt Sasha?"

Goodman frowned and stroked his salt-and-pepper beard. "I would hope not, but of course it's possible. He has periods of time where he's in a great deal of pain. The headaches are so severe that we have to sedate him. Unfortunately, they'll grow worse as time goes on."

Giovanni stiffened. "What are you saying? Does Sasha know this?" He didn't care that it sounded as if his "fiancée" hadn't shared all the facts with him.

"The head injury is very severe. His prognosis isn't good. At most, he might live another three years. We're giving him the best possible environment, but there is nothing to be done for him. She's consulted the best surgeons in the country, but the answer is always the same. There was too much damage. She doesn't want to accept that diagnosis, and I can't blame her. She loves him, and he's the last of her family. I can see that they're very close. Sandlin doesn't recognize her face, but somewhere inside him, he remembers her because if she can't visit for longer than three days, he becomes extremely upset."

"Have you told her that?" Giovanni asked.

Goodman shook his head. "What's the use? She works two jobs just to pay to keep him here. Making her feel guilty when she's already trying to do her best for him wouldn't do her any good."

"It's about her understanding that he does remember her. Not the way we would like, but the memory is somewhere inside him. She needs to know that." Giovanni felt his heart clench in his chest when Sandlin suddenly pushed the book to one side and waited for his sister to look down at him. His smile was beautiful, reminding Giovanni of an innocent child's. "He's still very intelligent, isn't he?"

Goodman nodded. "Very much so. It's strange what brain injuries can do. It's wiped his memory so we had to teach him to walk and talk again, yet he can solve incredible math problems. He can read at any level, but he doesn't always remember that he read a book the night before."

"Is he good with the nurses?"

"That's the other remarkable thing. We had to teach him to talk. He doesn't know his sister, but he never fails to remember manners. The brain is still such a mystery."

Giovanni held out his hand. "Thank you, Mr. Goodman. You have my number if you should need it. I'll be checking in regularly, as will my people."

"I'm very sorry that Tammy, at the front desk, allowed a total stranger through." He turned back, looking toward the front of the building, anger building all over again. "She won't be very long in her job." He clearly planned to fire her right away.

Giovanni had to agree with the administrator's decision. All the patients or clients in the facility were vulnerable. It was Tammy's duty to guard them, not just wave people through. "Make certain you get a full description of the intruder from her if at all possible." He suspected that wouldn't happen. Watching the tape several times had him believing Tammy was more interested in doing drugs and talking on the phone to her friends than doing her job. He'd been a rider too long not to recognize all the signs.

He crossed the room to stand behind the couch, one hand sliding into the thick silky curls tumbling down Sasha's back. "It's past visitors' time, honey. They want Sandlin in his room."

She closed the book reluctantly. "I was thinking maybe he should come home with me just for a few days so I know he's safe."

Sandlin sat up, a frown on his face as he took his book from his sister's hands.

Giovanni smiled to reassure him. "It's under control, Sasha. This is home to him and he's comfortable here. He's gotten to know the staff and the routine. Moving him would only make it difficult for him. Easier for you, but much more difficult for him and you don't want that."

Sandlin's fingers bit down on Sasha's arm hard enough to hurt her. He could see the whiteness in the knuckles. "His shadow tells me things."

Giovanni knew that others would think Sandlin was lost in his mind if he spoke of shadows, but nevertheless, it made him uneasy. He couldn't talk to Sasha about his work, not until she had committed. Breaking with a shadow rider had long-reaching consequences once his or her shadow tangled together with a chosen partner's. Already, he could feel Sasha mixed with himself. It was oddly potent, adding to the emotional high he got just from being with her. It also added, evidently, to the intensity of sexual attraction. He'd never been so physically attuned to a woman. It was all he could do to keep his mind from straying to thoughts of her.

"I know, sweetheart," Sasha said gently. "We're good at reading shadows."

"What does it tell you?" Giovanni asked.

Sandlin leapt up, snatched the book from Sasha's hands and hurried out of the room. Sasha stared after him, getting to her feet much more slowly. Tears swam in her eyes, and Giovanni immediately pulled her into his arms. She hadn't cried for herself, but this—this with her brother—was threatening to crush her. He felt the weight of her sorrow. Goodman might not think she knew her brother's prognosis, but she did.

"He'll be safe," he said. "I've already put in a call to a security company we use sometimes. They're all former soldiers, good men, very well trained. Sandlin will have round the clock protection. Goodman has agreed to use them. The woman at the front desk is supposed to have every single visitor logged in, but she hasn't been doing her job. She'll be fired. She's a terrible liability for them. Patients might have wandered off, and if this intruder was looking to harm Sandlin, he could have hurt not only your brother, but any of the other patients as well."

He walked her from the room, down the hall toward the front door, shielding her as best he could with his body when some of the night staff came out of rooms to gawk at them. Really, he knew, at him, but she wouldn't want to be seen crying. She stuck her chin out and kept walking, not looking at anyone as they made their way outside.

Emilio and Enzo were waiting. He lifted his eyebrow, but Emilio shook his head. They hadn't found him. Giovanni was fairly certain they wouldn't. Whoever was stalking Sasha was very clever, a cockroach, Giovanni thought him. One that disappeared into cracks and came out when no one noticed. Emilio walked ahead of him, Enzo just behind. They made a show of it, wanting whoever it was, if he was observing, to know that Sasha wasn't alone anymore.

"Has anyone ever made you uneasy?" Giovanni asked as they walked through the parking garage toward his car. "Anyone at all. In a grocery store. A clerk. Bumping into someone at a bank or perhaps a teller. In the club, someone fixating on you."

She looked up at him and, to his astonishment, those sapphire eyes held amusement and a hint of mischief. "Only you."

He felt the smile start somewhere around the vicinity of his heart. "I guess I had that coming. I did fixate on you, didn't I? Someone *other* than me."

The amusement faded and she shook her head. "No, but then, I've been so busy the last couple of months. I set up my brother in the facility and found my apartment. I was lucky, the former tenant moved right before I applied. Pietro said she wanted to go to Salt Lake to be with her grandson and his wife. I got the job at the club and then the deli. I wouldn't have noticed someone fixating on me if they came up and bit me."

He glanced over his shoulder as if he could still see the Hendrick Center. "What about when you visit your brother? When you first brought him there, you had to be very aware of anyone who came near him." He paused by the car, reaching for the passenger door.

"I wanted to investigate everyone," she agreed, shifting her weight from foot to foot.

It was the only real sign of nerves she'd given. He opened the door, glanced into the car as he stepped back to allow her entry and froze. The bomb was sitting right out in the open, on the driver's seat. There were wires looped all through the steering wheel and going across to the passenger seat.

"Wait." He caught her arm and pulled her back behind him, away from the car. He'd practically thrown her, using more force than he intended.

"Damn it. He got into my car. You can't just break that easily into these types of cars. Emilio. Enzo. Move back. Fast." Even walking, he was already sending a mass text to his family. "We can't stay here," he said, hurrying her back toward the elevator. "If he has a remote detonator, he could kill everyone." The bodyguards closed around them, taking them to the outermost section of the garage.

"This is getting out of hand, Emilio. I want her somewhere safe where this psycho can't get to her."

"Detonator? Is there a bomb??" Her voice was very steady. "Giovanni, I'm not the fainting type. If he's done something else and I see it, there's a possibility that I can identify him through something he's used, or the way he does it. You know that. I don't fall apart easily."

She didn't, but he wanted to protect her from everything. What was the use of his family? Of all his training? He might not be able to ride shadows because of the hardware in his leg, but he still was lethal as all hell. He had money. Power. None of that seemed to matter. All the security at his disposal and Sasha was still being terrorized.

"I'm not calling the police this time, honey. I'm sending you back to the hotel to stay with Francesca."

Sasha remained at his side, not moving around him, not trying to fight him, although her gaze continually strayed toward the car. She waited patiently until he was finished with the text messages and then looked at him expectantly.

Giovanni couldn't have told anyone why, but just the fact that she did that, waited for him to call in reinforcements without harassing him or asking questions when she had every right to, made him want to fall right at her feet. She was amazing to him. He almost couldn't believe she existed—a woman who actually told the truth. She said what she meant. She looked him straight in the eye without guile. She didn't get hysterical or cry to manipulate him—and her tears would work. She had every right to break down, but she didn't.

"He's put a bomb in the car. I only glanced at it, but I didn't see the wires connected to anything. That doesn't mean it's safe. I'm okay with bombs, but Vittorio is an expert. He's going to take a look and tell us if it's legit or not. In the meantime, I'm going to have Demetrio and Drago drive you to the hotel where Stefano lives as soon as they get here; they're on the way. They'll take you up to Francesca."

She was already protesting, shaking her head. "Absolutely not. I'm staying with you. This is my mess, and I'm not taking it to Francesca."

"Francesca is safe at the top of the Ferraro Hotel, Sasha," he said. His brothers were converging from every direction, moving out of the shadows, their pin-striped suits making it nearly impossible to see them until they stepped completely out of the dark. "That's the safest place I know for you, right now," Giovanni said. "If you're there, I won't have my attention divided, trying to keep my eye on you and deal with this mess."

"You can't deal with a bomb. They have professionals for that."

"We were all taught to disarm various types of bombs, honey." He brushed back her hair with gentle fingers. "It wasn't like he had a lot of time to put this thing together. For all I know, it's all show. If he wanted us dead, why didn't he hide the damn thing? Or blow it when we walked up to the car? It's probably not armed, but I'd feel better if you joined Francesca, got a little sleep and then we can figure things out when we're all feeling fresh in the morning."

Sasha looked startled as Stefano and then his other brothers strode up to them. "Where did you all come from? That was fast."

Riding shadows was fast. Sometimes it felt as if his entire body was torn to pieces and parts of him were left behind. The faster the tube, the worse the sensation. Still, it was what he'd been born to do. Sasha and her brother, Sandlin, had also been born with the ability, but it was too late to adequately teach her to do anything but get from one place to another. Giovanni's father had used the ability to carry on affairs. He wouldn't want to think that his wife might do the same.

"Sasha, are you all right?" Stefano asked immediately.

"Yes, I'm fine. I'm actually more shaken up that this man managed to walk right into a closed and guarded facility and see my brother. That made me feel as if Sandlin was extremely vulnerable. He can't take care of himself and I have no idea what this person wants with me, let alone with him."

The little catch in her voice was nearly Giovanni's undoing. He pulled her into his arms and nuzzled the top of her head with his chin. "I'm so sorry, baby. We'll sort this out."

"I hate that you're having to get involved and I may have inadvertently put you in danger." Her head came back against his chest and she briefly closed her eyes. "Tell me why you aren't going to involve the police."

"The fact that he broke into your house made him a stalker, Sasha," Stefano said. "Police can help with that sort of thing, perhaps investigate where we can't as fast. This puts him in an altogether different category. We can work this far faster than they can. You'll have to trust us."

Her gaze was fixed on Stefano's face. "You're saying that you believe he's a real threat to my life, or my brother's life, maybe even Giovanni's. And your family plans to take care of him yourselves."

Giovanni held his breath. His woman was intelligent and reading between the lines.

Stefano nodded. "That's exactly what I'm saying."

"I have a concealed weapons permit," she volunteered. "I don't carry, but I could if you think it's necessary. My guns are locked up in the safe at the deli. Pietro was sweet. I inherited my grandparents', parents' and my brother's. They're all hunting weapons, and the handguns were for shooting ground squirrels and snakes. I'm a good shot. Well, actually a marksman, but that's neither here nor there. Do you think I should be armed?"

"Right now, I think you need to be anywhere but here," Giovanni answered.

"Don't." Her protest came out a whisper. She looked at each of his brothers' faces, then his. "You intend to kill him if you find him, don't you?" She stared Giovanni straight in the eye, just as Emme entered.

He couldn't look away. This was a telling moment. Most people would give them a lecture about taking a life and say that it was up to the criminal justice system. She either accepted that some men were outside that law and got away with crimes all the time, or she wouldn't. He didn't look away. He had to know if she could accept who his family was and what they stood for. He nodded slowly. He'd learned not to speak aloud anything that might incriminate his family. Stefano had all but said the same thing to her.

"I would, too," she said. "I think I'm getting one of the handguns out of the safe."

"Taking a life is never easy, nor should it be done lightly," Stefano warned.

"It's called self-defense," Sasha said. "I have the right to protect myself and my brother. Just because I'm a woman doesn't mean I'm not capable of shooting someone coming at me."

"I'm a woman," Emme reminded gently. She reached for Sasha's hand. "My brothers know a woman can be strong. Right now, Francesca, who we all love dearly, is being guarded by Mariko, a woman. She's trusted to look after Stefano's and our family's most precious treasure. Nothing is going to happen to your brother. We won't let it. You're not alone in this."

Sasha looked around at the tight circle and then the four men standing guard over them. She swallowed hard and nodded. "Thank you. All of you. I don't know why you're helping me like this, but I appreciate it."

"Demetrio and Drago are going to drive you back, Sasha," Giovanni reiterated. "Please go with them and stay in the hotel with Francesca and Mariko. I'll be there as soon as I can. Go to bed and just forget all this."

She glanced at her watch. "I do have to work tomorrow. Both jobs." Before he could protest, she stopped him. "You know why. I can't miss any hours on my paycheck. Sandlin deserves the best of care, and I'm going to give it to him."

"Honey, it's absurd for you to think that I wouldn't help you," Giovanni said.

"I'm accepting the clothes from Lucia's Treasures, which isn't easy for me," Sasha pointed out. "But Sandlin is mine. I don't know how else to put it. I have to be the one to take care of him. He'd do it for me."

Giovanni wasn't going to argue. He'd gotten the concession from her of accepting clothing and he'd had everything sent to his home, including a few extra things she didn't know about. He'd assumed he would have a fight on his hands, she was that independent, but with her allowance, he was getting off the hook.

"We'll talk about it tomorrow. Go to the hotel. Have chocolate, talk to Francesca and Mariko and then go to bed. The place is enormous and you won't be disturbing anyone or putting my brother and sister-in-law out. We crash there all the time."

"We're all here, standing mostly in the dark, with these giant columns around us, why?"

Giovanni didn't know whether to curse because she was so damned smart or shake her. "You notice Emme just joined us later than the others, right? She searched the garage for your stalker just in case he was standing by with a remote to detonate the bomb. Or if he was hiding, hoping the damn thing would go off and he could see us blown to smithereens."

"I see. You kept his attention on you while she searched."

"He was less likely to think a woman would be with us under the circumstances. Emme is very thorough."

Sasha started to step away from him, but Giovanni caught her, turned her around and pulled her body up against his. He tipped her chin up and took possession of her mouth. There was just something about the way she responded every time. Her body melted into his without the least hesitation. Her mouth opened under his and when he swept inside, she gave him everything. Instant everything. She gave herself to him.

He loved the way she did that. The way she tasted. That exotic apple cinnamon that seemed to be always on his tongue where he could just barely taste it, setting up a craving for more. He definitely needed more. He kissed her like she belonged to him and they were completely alone, because when he was kissing her, the world faded away and there was only pure feeling.

Stefano made a sound, clearing his throat, and Giovanni snapped out of it, remembering what he was supposed to be doing. He handed her off to Demetrio and turned back to his brothers, the smile fading to be replaced by the very serious face of the Grim Reaper.

"Let's get this done."

# CHAPTER EIGHT

Pleasure burst through him. Giovanni opened his eyes, acclimating himself immediately in the way he'd been trained. It wasn't easy with hot blood rushing through his veins, spreading flames throughout his body. Silk glided over the bare muscles of his thighs, adding to the roaring in his mind and the thunder in his ears. He dropped his hand onto her head, fingers tunneling into Sasha's mass of curls.

He'd spent the better part of the night with his brothers and cousins, in the parking garage, dismantling the bomb, which hadn't been hooked up. It had merely been sitting on the driver's seat. Still, they took it apart and carefully had each piece sent for analyzing, to find everything they could get from it. He was in Stefano's penthouse where he'd crawled into bed beside a sleeping Sasha.

The drapes were pulled, but he knew it was early, no more than five in the morning. Her mouth was busy, taking him straight to paradise, hot and wet and clamped tightly around him. She swallowed him down and then drew back, all the while her hands stroking and caressing the inside of his thighs, his balls and then the base of his shaft as he emerged slowly from the wet heat.

He recognized the feel of her mouth surrounding him. No one could ever feel so exquisite. A kind of ecstasy, blood pounding through him, his body hot, his heart beating through his cock right into her mouth. He couldn't help himself, he began to thrust lightly with his hips, pushing deeper into paradise, feeling every streak of lightning flash through his body straight to his groin.

He groaned when she tightened her mouth around him, when her tongue danced and flicked, when she teased his crown or took him so deep he pressed into her throat so that she squeezed him like a vise. She had magic in her, a skill that was unbelievable. He caught her hair on either side of her head, bunching it inside his fists, holding her head still so he could control every movement, his body spinning out of control.

She was Sasha, and she gave him that, relaxing for him, letting him take his own pleasure for just a few minutes while his cock swelled, filling her so full she barely could breathe. He was forced to let her head up when he saw her eyes swimming with liquid, but there was laughter there, joy. She loved what she was doing. Her hand slid down between her legs, and that was his undoing.

Giovanni pulled her off him completely, his cock furious, desperate and ferociously hungry. He'd never been like that in his life. "Get on your hands and knees." It was an order, nothing less, and he was already catching her around the waist and lifting her to the position he needed her in. One hand caught the nape of her neck and thrust her head toward the mattress while he knelt behind her, feeling her slickness, ensuring she was ready for him.

He took her hard. The moment he slammed his cock home, pushing ruthlessly through the tightest muscles he'd ever encountered, her sheath bit at him, clamping down like a vise. The friction nearly sent him over the edge. She cried out and pushed back into him. Her bottom was up in the air, that beautiful ass he watched sway every chance he got. He smacked it, watching his handprint appear on her pale skin, feeling the flood of liquid coating his cock.

"You're so fucking beautiful, Sasha." His voice was hoarse. He couldn't stop moving. Surging deep, retreating, thrusting again and again. Between each deep thrust, he added more color to her pale cheeks, reveling in the way she surrounded him with scorching liquid each time.

Her breath came in ragged gasps, little soft cries and whispered pleas for more. He wasn't certain what the more was, so he gave her both, his body a piston now, hammering into hers, while fire streaked up through his body, threatening to engulf him with flames. He didn't care if he burned alive as long as he could feel this ecstasy again and again. He wanted it to go on forever.

One thing he knew, he loved fucking her. He loved her bare ass. The shape of her. The feel of her. The way she moved. The way she responded to his brand of sex. Rough. Hot. Demanding. She made her own demands. She wasn't timid about what she wanted, she used her body to tell him. Slamming back into him, impaling herself while he surged forward. Her breasts swung with every jolt and he wished he could suck on her delicious nipples while he took her. He wanted his cock in her mouth. She was the hottest thing he'd ever known, and he knew no other woman would ever satisfy him after Sasha's brand of lovemaking.

Without warning, her body clamped down hard on his, muscles gripping and milking. He felt his seed boiling. Hot. Rising like a volcano. Vaguely, in the back of his mind, he realized he hadn't worn a condom, but it didn't matter. If he got her pregnant, so be it. He was marrying her. She was going to give him children.

"Giovanni." Her voice was breathless. "I can't hang on. You have to pull out."

"Not pulling out." It was already too late. The orgasm took him like a freight train, roaring through his body until he couldn't think, only feel. Spurt after spurt rocketed through him, blasted into her, his hands gripping her hips, holding her to him while a tsunami seemed to have taken over her. The waves crashed around him, her body squeezing his ruthlessly, over and over, a wild crescendo until she collapsed on the mattress and he went down over top of her.

His heart beat through her body while the aftershocks

shook both of them. They lasted quite a while and he wanted to feel every single one of them with her. His weight had to be crushing her so that she was breathing shallowly, but she didn't complain. He threaded his fingers through hers and held her down, his mouth on her shoulder, then her neck, tasting the cinnamon candy-apple flavor he loved, using his teeth to tease her and his lips to ease the sting.

"You good?" he asked, when he could finally talk.

She nodded. "Giovanni, you should have pulled out. You weren't wearing a condom."

"I'm sorry, baby. I know you wanted me to, but I was so far gone . . ." He should have felt terrible about it. Any decent man would. It was her body. She decided when, not him, but damn it, he wasn't feeling one iota of remorse. He was a fucking dick, but that didn't seem to matter. He wanted her to have to marry him. He wanted his child growing in her.

The revelation was shocking when every member of his family was so careful, had been taught practically since birth never to go ungloved. To be responsible. They were riders and they didn't leave children scattered all over the country.

"I'm not trying to trap you."

Her denial was so unexpected he almost didn't understand what she said. He was expecting righteous condemnation, not her concern that he would think she was deliberately trying to trap him into marriage.

"This isn't your responsibility, Sasha. You told me to pull out." Reluctantly he let his body relax so he could slip away. He hated that loss of connection. He liked sharing her skin. Her body. He rolled over and reached to scoop her close.

Sasha lifted onto her elbows. Her sapphire eyes swept his face. "You don't understand. One of the girls at work, the night Darby ripped my uniform, told me horrible ways to trap a rich man. She said women did it all the time, and the best way was to get pregnant. I know that's what that game was all about. All of you are so tired of having women try to trap you that you really have no respect for them anymore. I don't want you to think I'm like that."

He cupped her face, thumbs sliding over her soft skin. He loved the way she felt. "Baby, you're going to hate me when I tell this to you, but I'm not going to let you feel guilty or allow you to think I believe you're trying to trap me." He took a breath, let it out and stared directly into her eyes so she could see the truth there. "*I'm* trying to trap you. I'm desperate for you to commit to me. I tell you my intentions and you never answer me back. I want you pregnant with my child. I want a ring on your finger. I want the privilege of having you for the rest of my life."

He waited again for condemnation. She stared at him like he'd grown two heads, but she didn't get angry. He didn't see one flare of her temper, and he knew she had one.

"You barely know me. We just met."

"You've said that before. Your shadow touches mine and I know all I need to about you. I know you have that same knowledge when they touch."

She didn't bother to deny it. "You're difficult to read. You're honest with me, yet deceptive with others. Never your family, but practically everyone else. You lead a kind of double life. You're a playboy, but I also feel an overwhelming sense of responsibility. The two things don't add up. I feel a great deal of power and danger mixed together. You love family and you're all about your family. That affection applies to your neighborhood. Or territory. I can't decide if you're a criminal or not. I'm not trying to be negative because I'm not certain how I feel about any of it, just telling you the truth."

"How do you feel about being with me?"

She ran her fingers down his chest to his groin. "Obviously, I like being with you. I think about you when we're not together and I worry. I think you're hot, if that matters. I just don't know if I can really fit into a lifestyle I don't even understand and can't really imagine."

"Kiss me, baby. I need you to kiss me."

She leaned into him, her full breasts brushing the heavy muscles of his chest. An electrical charge flashed through him straight to his cock. He'd just had her, but he wanted her again. And again. Just looking at her did that to him, let alone the memory of how she felt. And then there was that elusive taste.

Her lips pressed against his. Soft. Firm. Cool. Heating fast. He slid his tongue along that delicious seam and his teeth tugged at her lower lip, demanding entrance. If she thought to tease him, it wasn't going to happen. He took over, his tongue sweeping in, claiming that mouth. His hand cupped her breast, fingers tugging her nipple. Rolling. Claiming her breast. His other hand slid from the nape of her neck down her spine and shaped that beautiful bottom, claiming her ass as well.

Once was definitely not enough. He rolled her over, his thigh between her legs, pushing them apart. He kissed his way down her throat to her breasts. They were beautiful. He'd caught a glimpse of them in the club, and just that small, brief sight had taken his breath and fueled his fantasies.

He kneaded the soft flesh, watching the marks come up on her pale skin. His teeth and fingers teased her nipples, his tongue licking and tasting, and then he was sucking her deep into his mouth. He started out gentle and roughened his actions, watching her carefully. Every gasping response to his teeth and fingers told him she'd been born for him and his particular brand of loving his woman.

"I've waited so long for you." He rubbed his bristled jaw in the valley between her full breasts. "I want to have a jeweler make you a special chain that goes from here"—he touched one breast and then the other—"to here. The clamps have to be sapphires to match your eyes." He tugged on her left nipple with his teeth, biting down gently. "Would you wear it for me? Just that and nothing else?"

His gaze caught hers. He was nearly holding his breath.

Even his cock, and it had been jerking and pulsing, went still. Waiting. He didn't honestly care if she would wear it, or if it appealed to her or not. If not, they wouldn't play in that direction. For him, it was more of an acceptance on her part. Did she want him the way he wanted her? Unconditionally? If she said an irrevocable no, then he still couldn't be certain she wanted him the way he was. If she said maybe, he would know she was on board with the way he was made.

Sasha reached for his hand, slid it down her body to press his palm between her legs. "Feel how hot and slick I am just hearing you say that. Of course, I'll wear it for you. I might even dance for you, if you're good and promise me all sorts of things in payment."

"Like what?" He curled his fingers, pushing one into her. At once, her muscles bit down hard. His heart nearly beat out of his chest. She definitely accepted him. She didn't mind teasing or playing. Best of all, Sasha spoke her mind. If she didn't like something, there would be no pretending. She simply would tell him whatever they were doing hadn't worked.

"I think it will be necessary for you to devour me. Eat me. I've been dreaming about that ever since I laid eyes on you at the club. Once was definitely not enough, although it was hot as hell in the car."

"Done." He agreed immediately.

"Your cock whenever I want it."

"I suppose I could arrange that, but only if you promise me I can have you any*where* I want you."

"Like the car and restaurant?"

He nodded, his fingers moving in and out of her. So hot. He wanted her again.

"Where else?"

"I know this little park right in the middle of Ferraro territory. I want to take you there at night when the stars are out, strip you naked and claim every inch of you. The roof of my house. Especially if the moon is full. The plane. That's a must."

"I like the idea. We might try one other place."

"Lots of other places. I'm inventive." He kissed his way down her belly and then knelt between her legs. "Spread wider. What other place?"

"At the club. When the music is playing, each time I'm on my break. I want you to earn several thousand dollars for us."

His eyes met hers. There was honesty in her voice and amusement in her eyes. Also sincerity. "What are you up to?"

"Your cousin was just a little smug with his winnings. Just think, Giovanni, you could get a dance. Feel my breasts, my bottom, get a blow job and go all the way. I'll bet you know every corner where we could get away with it. You'd get your money back and we'd have fun."

"You have a devious mind. Wider, baby."

He loved looking at what was his. She was all his. Every inch of her. He caught her bottom in his hands, pressed the head of his cock into her burning entrance and slammed home. Streaks of lightning ran up his body straight to his brain, and then he was gone again, finding that place she took him to.

"Fuck me, Sasha. Hard. Use your hands on your nipples. Clamp down just like the clamps would bite down on you."

She rode him while he knelt between her legs, her hips moving fast, the smooth roll to her body expert from all the riding she'd done. It was an erotic sight to watch her hands move over her breasts, to pinch and clamp down hard on her nipples, to pull them for him, roll them. To knead her breasts and arch her back while her hips thrust against him. Her mouth opened and her eyes went dazed. She was soaring, her body clamping down on his.

"I love you this way." He reached down and found her clit, pinching her bud hard. "You're so sexy, Sasha."

She cried out and her sheath bathed him in scorching hot liquid, clamping down, biting deep, milking him for every drop of his seed while she soared high. She had taken him over too fast and he hadn't had time to spend in her, but he would. He watched her face as she came back to him, flushed, excited, unashamed of her sexuality. *Dio*, he was way past falling. He'd gone straight to love.

He leaned down and kissed her clit. "I'm getting you a beautiful sapphire clamp for here as well. The chain can extend up to the one across your breasts. Do you think you'd like that?"

"I don't know. It was pretty wild when you pinched me there. I couldn't hold back."

He grinned at her. "Yeah, baby, you're going to love it. You ready for a shower?"

"I'm not sure I can walk yet."

He laughed and picked her up. He hadn't been so happy—ever. Not ever. She turned his life into something fun. He hadn't realized he'd gone to bed exhausted, sliding in next to her, careful not to wake her, looking forward to opening his eyes because she was in his world.

"Are you going to tell me what happened last night?"

"Not much. We found out a few things. It was definitely a bomb, but he hadn't rigged it to go off."

She sat up, her blond curls falling around her face and down her back. One plopped in a long spiral right over her left breast, drawing his attentions to the marks there. He bent his head and kissed the red smudges.

"Wait. He put a bomb in your car but it didn't have a detonator in it? I don't understand."

"Neither did we—at first. The bomb was in the driver's seat. My seat. Had he put it in properly hidden and under the seat, with a pressure switch, the moment I sat down, I would have activated the bomb, not necessarily set it off. That would come when I got out of the car—or tried to."

"Why do you think he didn't do that?"

"Either we interrupted his work, which I doubt, or he doesn't want you killed. You were with me. If I didn't realize I was in trouble and the bomb went off, you'd be killed as well. I think it was a warning to me. He'd take me out if I kept on with my relationship with you."

She stiffened. Her face closed down. He cupped her face firmly between his hands. "Don't even think about breaking up with me. It's not going to happen. The bastard is going to turn on you, Sasha. You're his fantasy. In his mind, you're already in a relationship with him. I'm stepping on his toes. You can't possibly keep up your end when you don't even know him or how he expects you to act."

He stepped back and took her hand. "Come on, baby. Shower."

"I'm tired."

She wasn't. He knew that. He even heard the lie but he didn't call her on it because he knew she wanted time to think. He wasn't about to give it to her. "I'll reward you. I'm not above bribes."

"What's my reward?"

"I'm very, very good with my mouth. You shower with me and I'll eat you like candy. You smell and taste like cinnamon candy apple, and I can't get enough of that."

She was already on her feet, just because he refused to let go of her hand, so he took advantage, pulling her to the bathroom just next to their room. They had this end of the penthouse to themselves, so he had no problems walking naked with her out of the bedroom and into the bathroom.

Giovanni could feel Sasha trying to pull away in her mind so the moment he got the water going, he circled her waist with his arm, pushed her into the shower—a long, tiled affair with multiple showerheads, water coming from every direction—got her against a wall and kissed her. Over and over. He refused to give ground. He claimed her and let her know that was exactly what he was doing. He couldn't be without her, and he wanted her to feel the same way.

He kissed her until her hands were sliding over his narrow hips to find his cock. He knew he'd won when she began fisting him.

"You love my cock," he accused.

"I do," she admitted. "It's clearly going to be your saving grace when you make me crazy—and you will."

He knew that, too. He didn't care. He'd use his mouth or his cock, any damn thing he had to keep her with him—and happy. He wanted her happy. He took some shower gel and began washing her, his hands gentle yet deliberately arousing as he thoroughly soaped every inch of her body. Her breath grew faster and she tipped her head back to let the water soak her hair.

"Tell me, before we start up again, just what you learned about this crazy person."

"He's been in the service at some time. It would help if we knew his age, but we have access to databases and records when we need them. He shot his load all over your panties, and that was a stupid thing to do. We've got his DNA. He used gloves everywhere else so there were no fingerprints. To build a bomb like that, he had to have been in demolition or special forces, one of the branches that would have taught him how to build it."

"Can't you find information like that on the Internet?"

He nodded, rinsing her off, using the wand to spray between her legs, letting the water linger and pulse against her clit. Only when she reached for the shampoo did he stop so he could take it out of her hands. He wanted to wash her hair himself.

"Yes, you definitely can find all kinds of information on how to do anything, but he was fast and efficient. He might have built it elsewhere and carried it with him when he tailed us—and by the way, he was good enough not to be spotted."

"No, he wasn't, you knew he was there."

Giovanni waited a heartbeat before answering her. She was his. Sooner or later she had to know about him. It was dangerous if she knew, dangerous in ways to both of them—him more so than her. He was definitely taking the bigger risk, but she was worth it. He had to make his try with her. There wouldn't be another for him.

"I felt him. Every time we crossed shadows. Didn't you?" He took the shampoo and rubbed it into her hair so he wouldn't have to look into her eyes. He was giving more and more of himself to her, but he wasn't certain she recognized that yet. She was intelligent, and she reasoned things out fast, guessing, of course, but she always hit the mark or close to it.

"We were in a car."

"But the streets were shadowed. The streetlights throw huge shadows. His car kept crossing the shadow of ours." It was one thing to be able to feel their own shadows touching, but very difficult and specific to have car shadows touching and glean information.

"What did he feel like?" She hadn't called him crazy, and her voice held sincerity as if she believed him and wanted to know more.

He rinsed her hair carefully before answering. "Malignant. He's definitely angry. I didn't get much of a sense of him other than that, but it was him. They were only glimpses, but I recognized that same feeling from the alley. When I first got there, I knew he was on the roof."

She pressed one hand to her stomach briefly. "Maybe I did feel him. For me, it was dread. That's what I felt in the alley." She took the gel in both hands and began to soap his body.

It didn't take much for his cock to come to attention. She just had to give him a smoldering look and there it was. "He left behind the bomb, which means we've got men tracking down where everything was purchased and how."

"You still aren't going to the police."

He gave her a look. "It's a family matter." He waited for a protest.

"What time did you come to bed? I thought you'd wake me."

Her voice slipped over him like a caress. Like her fingers. He'd wanted to wake her. He'd even been perverted enough to pull back the covers and look at her. She slept naked. He couldn't blame her, she didn't have much in the way of clothes. She probably didn't want to take the chance that he might rip off something sexy—which he would have done this morning.

He'd wanted her to get some rest. She'd had a rough few days, and he still had to convince her to accept him. He wanted to put a ring on her finger. He'd told them at the Hendrick Center that he was her fiancé because he had to be family in order for them to tell him anything or deal with him in any way. It didn't matter, he *felt* like her fiancé. He knew he was going to marry her.

Her hands were on his cock now, sliding over his shaft, squeezing and pumping until he was full and hard again. She rinsed him off and had him turn around. He put one hand on the wall and let her take care of cleaning him. She soaped him, then rinsed him off. Her lips wandered over his back, exploring like her hands had done.

"I love your mouth," he said. "I dream about your mouth and what you do to me with it. You shouldn't have put that in my head."

"I like doing things to you with my mouth," she admitted and promptly bit him in the butt. "Especially when you're asleep. You wake up so beautifully."

He laughed and swung around, turning off the water so he could step out and hand her a towel. She wrapped her hair in it and took another one from his hands.

Beads of water rolling off both of them, he caught her up, slung her over his shoulder and ran barefoot back to the bedroom. Dumping her on the bed, he yanked her legs apart, pulling her right to the very edge so her bottom was hanging off and held in his hands. He knelt there and put his mouth to her. He felt like he'd been waiting forever to have her like this. At his mercy, unable to move unless he allowed it. He didn't plan to allow it for a very long time.

The moment his mouth touched her body, she cried out, squirming, pushing into him, not away. He smiled because he couldn't help it. There was so much joy in her. So much life. It didn't seem to matter what waited for her when she was alone, she lived every single second. She was in the precise moment.

He took his time, refusing to allow her to hurry him. He used his tongue first, licking and then sucking, savoring her flavor. He'd known she'd be perfection. "I could exist on this alone. Feed on you three times a day and be satisfied."

She bucked against his mouth, and he swatted her bottom. "This is for me. You had your fun this morning and I owe you payment."

"If you owe me payment, you dolt, you're supposed to pay me the way I want it paid."

"You didn't negotiate that," he pointed out and went back to his slow enjoyment. He wanted to build the burn slowly. He wanted her heat smoldering. He was ruthless with her, licking, stabbing with his tongue, circling her clit, flicking it hard and then ignoring that taut little bud altogether. He fucked her with his tongue and then his fingers, never letting her get off. He brought her to the brink repeatedly only to back her off, his teeth nipping the insides of her thighs.

She was sobbing his name, her fists clenched in his hair when he lifted his head. "What is it, baby? Can't you see I'm busy?"

"Take me over," Sasha said.

"Mmm. That's not what I want to hear." He went back to that hot little meal that was all his. He devoured her, made growling noises, driving her even higher, getting her right to the edge and then he pulled back.

"What do you want to hear, you maniac? Giovanni. You're torturing me."

"Pleasure, baby, it's called pleasure. I'm loving this. You taste so good." He wiped his face on her thighs. "You want a taste?" Deliberately, he half rose to lean over her, licking his way up her belly to the underside of her breasts. All the while he pressed his body tightly against hers so she rubbed her clit on him, desperate to get off. He kept moving up her body, allowed himself to be distracted by her breasts and spent some time there, enjoying the way she squirmed and mewled.

Giovanni pushed her a little more, making certain she enjoyed the things he was doing to her body. His teeth teased her nipple, biting down, while one hand squeezed her breast, clamping tighter, tugging, pulling, while she arched and cried out. Her hips bucked against him, and he kissed her throat and then took her mouth, giving her a taste of cinnamon candy apple.

His hand went to her sex, pressing on her clit, pinching until she nearly came, but he pulled away. "Do you like the way you taste?"

She nodded and slid a hand down her body toward the junction of her legs. He pulled back, flipped her onto her stomach, dragged her once more until she was bending over the bed and spanked her—three smacks on each cheek. He kicked her legs apart. "You want something, baby? It's mine to give, not yours to take."

She cried out, her body bucking, hot liquid spilling out of her.

"What the fuck, woman? Don't you have any control? I thought I just said this is my orgasm, not yours."

"That's not my fault. You're deliberately making it impossible to stop." There was excitement in her breathless voice.

"I guess I could spank you until you have an orgasm, but it isn't what I have in mind."

"*Do* something. Anything. Eat me. Spank me. Fuck me. Anything at all. Just do *something*." There was desperation in her voice.

"It's in your hands, baby. You know what you have to do."

"Just remember this when I've got your cock in my

mouth," she warned, her voice muffled by the sheets. "Giovanni, you bastard, will you please fuck me hard until I come? I need it very, very badly. Please?"

"Aren't you going to ask my permission to come?" He used his finger, pushing into her, retreating, pushed in two. He flicked her clit hard and felt her body tighten around his fingers. He couldn't help smiling when he swore she ground her teeth. Playing. Teasing. He'd never had those experiences and he loved that she was willing to play with him. "I'm not asking you to call me master, that might come later."

She growled, but turned her head toward him. "Giovanni. Dear. Honeypot." She batted her eyelashes at him. "Please allow me to come? If not, I might have to hurt you."

He caught her hips, jerked them back to him and slammed into her. She shrieked and instantly her body clamped down on his like a vise. The walls of her sheath contracted, strangling his cock. He plunged into her over and over, right through her orgasm, letting the friction and heat drive them both straight into another realm. He held on to his control through two more wildly long quakes that rippled through her entire body, and then when he built the last one higher than the previous ones, he let her take him with her.

Her sheath was so tight he could barely breathe. It was either hell or paradise. He only knew he never wanted to leave. His release, as he emptied himself into her, flung him back to that place where her mouth had taken him, somewhere he'd never been. He floated while his body went up in flames, and he felt reborn.

She lay limp on the bed, facedown, her narrow channel still gripping his with aftershocks while he kissed the nape of her neck and rubbed her body gently. Soothingly. She turned her head to one side to look at him. "We might not make it out of this relationship alive."

He grinned at her, flopped on the bed and pulled her up and over him like a blanket. "I'll go out happy." His stomach tightened. "What about you? If we killed each other with sex, would you go out happy, too?"

She lifted her head to rest her chin on his chest. "How could I not? I didn't know sex could be like this. It's so good sometimes I never want you to stop."

He could breathe again. He pushed at the wet hair tumbling around her face. They'd lost the towel somewhere. It didn't matter. His heart hurt just from looking at her. *Ached.* She did that to him. "*Dio*, baby, I'm falling in love with you. Really falling."

Her lashes fluttered. They were long, a dark gold, and very thick. He held his breath, knowing his declaration was probably too soon for her. She was embattled on too many fronts and having him just come out and tell her he loved her . . .

"Strange, Giovanni, and I can't believe I'm saying this because we haven't spent that much time together, but I'm feeling exactly the same way."

He heard the honesty in her voice. That ring of truth. Part of him rejoiced. The other part knew he wasn't out of the woods yet. She didn't know his life, and he had to tell her soon. The more ties they had between them, the more their shadows tangled together. Theirs had knitted together very quickly. Once the shadows were woven together, there was only one way to get them apart. She wouldn't remember him, and he would no longer be able to ride the shadows. That was the very worst thing that could happen to a rider. It was who they were more than what they were.

"I never expected to really find you." He hadn't. Somewhere in the back of his mind, even when he was actively looking, he hadn't believed he would find her. "Going around the world and looking for you, and here you walk right into my club. Shocked the holy hell out of me." He lifted his head to brush a kiss in the fall of wet curls. "And you had to see me at my worst."

She laughed and rolled over, sitting up on the edge of the

bed. "I doubt that's you at your worst. Your worst is going to be when you try taking over my life."

He sat up as well. "Why would you think I would take over your life?"

She looked around the room for her clothes. "I said 'try,' and where are my clothes? I folded them neatly and left them on top of the dresser."

"They're in the laundry."

"I'm not going naked to breakfast. You can give me your clothes."

"In the drawers. I put a change of clothes there for you last night when I came in. The others are already at the house."

Sasha gave him a look that told him they'd be having a discussion about her going to his house. That look made him want to smile. He loved that she thought he wasn't going to get his way in everything.

She went to the bureau and took out underwear. He couldn't help watching her dress. He knew that was always going to be one of his favorite things. He'd never get tired of it. Instead of dressing as well, he remained quiet, never taking his eyes from her.

Sasha started laughing again. "Quit staring."

"You might disappear on me if I let you out of my sight or just blink." He knew she would laugh again and that sound did something to his heart. Made it lighter somehow. All the bitterness over the wasted months of pulling playboy duty after getting shot disappeared, suddenly worth every moment because he had her.

"I'm going to find Francesca and breakfast," she announced.

"Not without kissing me first."

"Kissing you is dangerous. It leads to other things and we're never going to get out of this room if we keep it up."

"Kiss me, baby." She was right, his cock stirred at the thought of her touching him. That mouth. Her body.

She shook her head, blew him a kiss and ran out of the room laughing.

Giovanni listened until the sound faded away. He pressed a hand over his heart where his chest ached. Very slowly he dressed and wandered down the hall and through his brother's penthouse. Francesca had made the very cold apartment a warm, welcoming home. Sasha would do that to his home. He could tell already, just being in her little residence.

Stefano sat at the table alone. A cup of coffee was near one hand, a tabloid, of all things, was in the other, and he was frowning. He glanced up at Giovanni and then back toward the kitchen where their two women were talking together.

Immediately Giovanni knew something was wrong and it involved either Sasha—or him. He held out his hand. "What is it?"

Stefano sighed. "You aren't going to like it." He glanced toward the kitchen again where his wife was laughing with Sasha over something she'd said and then he put the paper in his brother's outstretched hand. "Someone got a picture of Sasha that night at the club. They took a couple of them and obviously sold them to a tabloid. I called, of course, but they're already running them in the magazines as well. It's all over the news. A woman employed at the Hendrick Clinic gave an interview to the newspapers and let it slip that you're engaged to Sasha. With that news out, of course whoever took the pictures was going to sell them to the tabloids. He must have made a mint."

Giovanni looked down and his heart dropped. Sasha was on Darby's lap, both breasts exposed. Not only exposed, but the camisole, lace gaping open, pushed her breasts up and out, emphasizing them. In the photograph, it was impossible to see that the laces were torn. From the angle the photo had been taken, it appeared as if Giovanni was reaching for her breasts.

He swore. "Whoever took this was on the same tier we

were, Stefano," he said. "They were too close and had too good of a view. Someone at Aaron's table took this."

"We don't know that."

"Look at it. Damn it, I haven't locked her down yet. You know why? Our lifestyle. Too much money, too much jet-setting. This is going to shake her up. This is exactly the kind of thing that she can't stand. We're in the tabloids nearly every week. Sometimes more. Every story we've inserted, every picture we've orchestrated, is coming back to bite me in the ass."

He threw himself into a seat across from his brother and pressed the tatty little gossip rag that just might very well lose him Sasha to his forehead. "I hate this."

"I know you do. We're going to have to do damage control, and you're going to have to show this to her. You don't want her getting broadsided."

The elevator buzzed just before the doors opened, and the brothers exchanged a long look. Both looked up as Eloisa burst into the room, her expression furious, her gaze snaking around the room, seeking a target.

Francesca and Sasha turned toward her, and Eloisa gasped and, ignoring her sons, stomped toward the women, purpose and fury in every step.

# CHAPTER NINE

Giovanni nearly knocked over the table in his haste to stand up. "Eloisa." *Dio*, *Dio*, he didn't need this now. Nothing good ever came of Eloisa's confrontations, and it was clear she was determined to have it out with someone.

Eloisa held up her hand to stop him, not that it was going to do any good. He was already in position, standing between his mother and Sasha. Stefano had risen much more elegantly, but also glided between Eloisa and the women.

"I had no idea you planned to visit this morning, Eloisa," Stefano greeted. "Come sit down." He indicated the table. "Would you care for coffee?"

"No, I wouldn't care for coffee. What I care for is an explanation of how my son ended up engaged to a complete bimbo." Both hands went to her hips and she glared at Giovanni.

Stefano glanced at Francesca. One look, that was all, and she immediately caught Sasha's hand and whispered to her, hoping to get her out of the room. They'd taken two steps when Eloisa cut them off.

"Don't you dare leave this room. Do you think I haven't seen all the pictures? Exposing your breasts in public? Declaring to the world that you're engaged? You are not trapping my son into marriage."

"That's enough," Giovanni snapped. He knew his face darkened with temper—he had one, and it was rising fast.

"You don't know the first thing about what you're talking about."

"Wait." Sasha's soft voice had him spinning around. She looked puzzled. "Is she accusing *me*? What does she mean, pictures? Exposing my breasts in public? I thought you got all those pictures. You told me you did." She put her hands behind her, feeling for the counter.

Giovanni nearly groaned aloud. The action only served to emphasize her generous breasts, and he knew that would drive his mother into further tantrum. Sasha hadn't denied her breasts had been exposed; in fact, from her statement, the circumstances would only sound worse to Eloisa. She would be certain Sasha had been partying.

"You little whore." Eloisa actually curled her fingers into two tight fists and stepped toward Sasha aggressively.

Giovanni stepped with her, keeping his body between Eloisa and Sasha. "Eloisa, as usual, you have no idea what's going on. Just stop."

"Eloisa." Stefano's tone held a wealth of warning.

Giovanni knew all along Sasha wasn't the kind of woman to hide behind her man; still, he wasn't prepared for her to step around him to face his mother. Eloisa tore other women to shreds, especially if she thought she was protecting the family name. The minute Sasha was nearly toe to toe with Eloisa, his mother attacked.

"I know all about you and that brother of yours, kept locked up because he's totally gone, out of his mind. If you think I want someone like you—"

"Don't you *dare* talk about my brother," Sasha hissed, her step toward Eloisa every bit as aggressive as his mother's had been. "You don't know the first thing about him. If you had one shred of decency, one tiny bit of patience, you'd know he was in an accident and suffered a brain injury. If you *did* know that, it just goes to show you don't have one ounce of compassion in you and you aren't worth very much. If you all will excuse me, I have to get to work. This horrible *bitch* has ruined my appetite."

For once, Eloisa looked stunned. She stood there, her mouth open and her eyes wide with shock that another woman had stood up to her. Sasha went on around her and stalked toward the elevator doors. Giovanni wanted to shove his mother out a window. Instead, he followed his woman. Her shoulders were set and her head high. Color flagged her cheeks. *Dio*, even that made him hard—and so fucking proud he wanted to kiss her—the way she stood up to Eloisa.

"Do you deny trying to trap my son into marriage?" Eloisa demanded.

"Absolutely I deny it." Sasha kept walking.

"If anyone is trying to trap anyone, Eloisa, I'm doing my best to make certain she marries me," Giovanni snapped as he put his arm around Sasha.

"That was so unkind," Francesca reprimanded, sending her mother-in-law a frown of condemnation.

"You can leave now," Stefano said, indicating the elevator.

"Wait." Eloisa sounded conciliatory, not commanding.

Sasha stopped and slowly turned around. Giovanni turned with her, but he dropped his arm and stepped back. She wanted to deal with his mother on her own, and she deserved to do so. As long as she was holding her own, he wasn't about to interfere.

"I'm sorry about your brother. You're right. I should have learned more before I came here. The investigators showed me the pictures and told me you had a brother in a hospital and I didn't look any further."

She glanced at Francesca. "You'd do to learn a little from this one. She stands up for herself and her family. Still, I can't have a woman who exposes her body to the world as one of our family. Giovanni, you know the rules. Your duty is to follow them."

"Well, fuck duty," Giovanni snarled.

"You can get angry all you want, but I'm not having this exhibitionist in our family. It's bad enough that your brother chose . . ."

Stefano let his breath out in a long, slow hiss. "Did you come here just to piss me off? Because you don't want to do that, not now. I'm already there. State why you're here without shrieking at everyone and hope I don't throw you out."

"I'm your mother whether you like it or not, Stefano, and you can show a little respect."

Stefano's eyebrow shot up. "The problem you're running into, Eloisa, is that in order for me to respect you, I have to have a reason, and coming into my home, harassing my wife and screaming at Giovanni's woman before you even know the facts is not the way to get it."

Eloisa slapped her hand over the tabloid. "I think I know the facts, Stefano, they're here in black and white for the world to see. Giovanni's engagement to this woman is a complete farce."

"What engagement?" Sasha asked. "What pictures? Show me."

Giovanni glared at his mother as she held out the tabloid.

"Don't try to pretend that isn't you because it clearly is," Eloisa snapped. "You're on rather prominent display." There was sarcasm in her voice.

Stefano handed his paper to Francesca, who stood with him. There was a long silence as the two women stared at the damning photographs, tension stretching out until Giovanni wanted to break it. He didn't, he just kept his gaze fixed on Sasha's face. No one else's reaction mattered. No one else mattered.

"Well." Eloisa broke the silence. "What do you have to say for yourself?"

Sasha glanced up. "I don't owe you an explanation. Not one word." Her gaze switched to Giovanni. "I'm sorry, honey, I know this is going to be terrible for you." Her finger moved over the lurid headline declaring playboy jetsetter Giovanni Ferraro was engaged to a party girl waitress. "You wouldn't be in this position if you hadn't tried to help me." She tossed the tabloid away from her as if it were a snake. "I really do have to get to work. If you all will excuse me . . ."

"Baby, you know you can't go to work. You have a very dangerous stalker after you. He put a bomb in our car last night, or don't you remember?"

"*What* is going on?" Eloisa demanded. "A bomb? *Dio*, Giovanni, you've gotten yourself into more trouble than your brothers ever thought of and they were bad enough."

Everyone ignored her.

"Someone at Aaron's table snapped that picture," Giovanni stated.

"A series of pictures. Of course, the article left off the part where you were attacked and your clothing ripped," Stefano said. "I reviewed the security tapes."

"Do you think Aaron did it? Or his friend James? Tom Mariland was there as well," Sasha said. "Aaron sent me flowers, and James had a box of chocolates delivered. Tom came to the deli and apologized in person. But . . ." She trailed off, frowning.

"We'll find out," Stefano said. "We've got ears and eyes on the tabloids. They sold the pictures anonymously, but there's always a money trail."

Sasha shook her head. "I never thought about what you all go through on a daily basis. My life is much simpler." She made a small move as if she might separate herself from Giovanni.

He didn't like that she had referred to her life as being simpler. She was in his life now, which meant their life was hers. He slipped one hand around her upper arm very lightly. He didn't want her to notice, but he wasn't letting her leave the building. She couldn't possibly conceive of the firestorm waiting for her outside the hotel. Their engagement had been announced, and the paparazzi would be out in droves. No one and no amount of money was going to stop them from trying to get her picture. She might think it was fake, but he was going to do his best to make their engagement real.

"We need to double the guard at the Center to keep her brother safe. In fact," Giovanni said, "we'll have to make certain only those we trust are looking after him."

Sasha stiffened. "What do you mean by that?"

"The tabloids will want his photograph and any information they can get on him. They'll bribe the staff to cooperate. The woman who gave the interview was named Harriet. She's Goodman's trusted secretary. She was the one who announced our engagement. In order to speak for you and Sandlin's care, I had to be a family member."

Sasha put the heel of her hand to her forehead. "Giovanni, I'm really, really sorry. I seem to always be apologizing to you. You're so deep in my mess, I'm not certain how to get you out of it."

"Giovanni will have to go to Europe. We'll send you to Sicily . . ." Eloisa began.

"Baby." Giovanni ignored his mother. "I told you I was in love with you. As far as I'm concerned, the engagement stands. I hope we're past that."

He waited a heartbeat. Two. She didn't pull away, nor did she respond, but he took her silence as a response. He wasn't going to allow her to pull away from him, not with his heart pounding, roaring in his ears, and desperate chaos threatening his mind.

He took a chance that she wouldn't argue in front of his mother. "I'm grateful we are. It gives us the opportunity to focus on what's important here, which is the safety of your brother as well as your own."

"I can take care of myself. You don't have to worry about me," Sasha assured.

"I know you can. You're strong, Sasha, but the paparazzi are relentless. Let me protect you just a little. Give this to me. I need you to trust me. Trust my family. We've been doing this a very long time."

Sasha's sapphire eyes searched his face for what seemed an eternity to him. He felt the tension fade from her body before she nodded. "That makes sense. Thanks, Giovanni.

I'm not exactly certain how to handle a picture like that on every counter of every grocery store in America. It's the first time I'm grateful my parents aren't around to see it. Or maybe not. I'd rather have them and be embarrassed than not have them."

She moved into Giovanni and he put his arm around her. "I know you have to be hungry. Come have some breakfast."

"I really do need to make certain Pietro can find a substitute today."

Giovanni shared a look with Stefano. Stefano had already made the call, waking Pietro as soon as the tabloid was delivered to the penthouse by one of the bodyguards. No way could Sasha go to work at the deli. The family had already been through that nightmare with Francesca and they didn't want Sasha to have to go through it as well.

"And I *have* to go to work tonight at the club."

"She still works at the club?" Eloisa's voice nearly squeaked with outrage. "Seriously, Giovanni? A waitress? Can you set your standards any lower? At the very least, she should have been fired."

He all but pushed Sasha into Stefano as he whipped around to face his mother. "That's it. I've had it with you. You barged in here and as usual are spewing crap you don't know a damn thing about just to stir up trouble. You aren't breaking us up. I'm in love with her. I'll always be in love with her. She isn't beneath us, if anything she's way too good for me."

"Really? You don't think she's after your money?" Eloisa turned to Sasha. "I'll give you five million dollars right now, under the table, tax free, to walk out of our lives."

Francesca gasped. "Eloisa, stop. I mean it. You've done nothing but insult Sasha since you walked into my home. It's one thing for you to insult me, but not a guest in my home. I understand you love your children and are trying in your own very abrasive and rude way to protect them, but you're going too far and I'd like you to leave my home."

Eloisa glared at her. "The little mouse thinks she can throw me out of my *son's* home. This hotel, this penthouse, it belongs to Stefano and my sons and Emme, not you. Never you." Her furious gaze slashed at Sasha. "Well? I mean what I say. My word is good. Will you accept the money?"

Stefano put his hand on his mother's arm while Sasha simply stared at her. Eloisa shook him off. "Ten million then. Ten million right now to leave my son alone."

Sasha sighed. "You won't be able to understand this because clearly you were raised to believe money is some kind of measure of worth. I wasn't. I might need it in order to give my brother the best care possible, but I'm willing to work for it."

"Would you stoop so low as to prostitute yourself for money?" Eloisa sneered.

"For my family? My brother? In order for him to have the chance to live better, regain his abilities? Give him the best care?" Sasha leaned forward and stared Eloisa straight in the eye. "Damn straight I would. Fortunately, I have a job that allows me to make a good deal and I don't need to prostitute myself or take money from someone like you. I have no problems with working for what Sandlin and I need."

"Stefano, I would like you to remove your mother from our home," Francesca said.

"You're done," Stefano said immediately, when his mother opened her mouth. "You've insulted Giovanni's fiancée and my wife for the last time in our home. This is Francesca's home. If you're too blind to see that, it's on you, not us." As he spoke, he walked his mother toward the elevators. "Francesca was nothing but nice to you, Eloisa. She tried hard to get us to accept you into our lives, but this is the last straw. You should have known better than to insult her in front of me. She might keep your poisonous barbs to herself, but I protect what's mine, and Francesca is definitely mine."

"Ours," Giovanni corrected. He strode across the room to pace along with Stefano. "Francesca is the center of our family. She holds that place you should have had but were too busy to bother to take, Eloisa. Sasha is my choice. She's forever my choice. You didn't bother to get to know her before you accused her of being a gold digger."

Eloisa shrugged off Stefano's hand and stomped to the elevator. "The two of you are absolutely ridiculous. At least Francesca has the right blood, and if she'd just get pregnant and do her duty, I'd be happier. That one"—she waved her hand toward Sasha—"she waits tables. Why would we want children from her? She isn't even of our blood." Clearly, she hadn't noticed Sasha's shadow, although the lights were dim in the early morning hours.

Giovanni would have hit her if she'd been a man. The contempt in her voice lashed out at his woman. He had never understood his mother. She appeared cold and unfeeling most of the time. Certainly, when he was young, he couldn't remember a time when she held him. There were no sentimental pictures of her holding any of her children. It was Stefano, a young boy, who had taken the role of caretaker of his brothers and sister, never Eloisa. Francesca had made every effort to integrate her back into the family circle, but rather than embrace Francesca, the longer it took for Francesca to get pregnant, the worse Eloisa acted.

The elevator doors slid open and Eloisa stepped inside. She turned to face her sons. "Giovanni, you have a duty to our family. You *must* produce the right children. You can't marry a woman who does not have what that takes. You've known this since you were a toddler."

The doors shut before Giovanni could respond. Sasha could produce riders, but Eloisa didn't know that because she hadn't seen shadows cast by her in the dimly lit rooms. It didn't matter to him whether she knew or not, she had no right to make matters for Sasha worse than they already were by jumping to conclusions and raining a nasty, barbed diatribe on her.

Stefano whipped out his phone and called down to the manager. “Did I not say I wanted the code changed on my private elevator?” There was silence. “If it was changed, then how did my mother get up here?” Again, there was silence. “I didn’t put her on the list of people who could have the code.” He listened, his face darkening. “No, it wasn’t an oversight and if you want to keep your job, you’ll have the code changed again. Not a single person who is *not* on that list is to be given the code. If this happens again, you will not be working here. Do you understand?” He slammed the phone down.

Giovanni and his brother exchanged a long, frustrated look before turning back toward the kitchen. “Are you certain that woman is our mother?”

Stefano shot him a look that slowly turned into a grin. “I don’t know. If there are aliens, it’s possible they stole our real mother after I was born and left behind a robot. That would mean the robot is your parent, and I got the real, sweet mother.”

Giovanni couldn’t picture his mother being sweet. He’d never witnessed her sweet, not even when Emmanuelle was born. Stefano had held the new baby, looking down at her with love on his face, but not Eloisa. She’d immediately gone to the training room and had begun to work to get her figure back. None of them believed for one moment that anything said or done would change Eloisa. None of them tried anymore. Only Francesca seemed to see Eloisa’s goodness beneath her abrasive, nasty barbs. Francesca insisted Eloisa’s concern for her children was there, and that she tried in her own way to protect them. Maybe after this she’d give up trying, but he doubted it.

Sasha and Francesca, both seated at the table, were calmly drinking coffee. He could have kissed Francesca. He could always count on her, the way they counted on Stefano. She’d kept on as if Eloisa hadn’t just insulted the hell out of her and she’d made certain Sasha was put at ease in doing so.

Sasha looked up when they entered the room, her gaze moving over him and settling on his face. She sent him a small smile. "Are you all right?"

That was supposed to be his question. Giovanni felt warmth infuse his body and the tension coiled tightly in his belly ease. He hadn't even known it was there, but Eloisa could do that to all of them—make them tense and edgy just by walking into a room.

He stalked across the room and bent to brush a kiss across her mouth. "I did neglect to mention my mother. I was hoping I'd actually have the wedding ring on your finger before you met her—or even knew about her."

"She who must never be mentioned," Stefano intoned in a ghostly voice.

Francesca burst out laughing. Stefano had followed Giovanni into the room, eyes only for his wife. He relaxed the moment she laughed. He took the chair across from her. "I'm just grateful I already ate before she arrived."

"Sometimes I wonder what she thinks is going to happen when I have a baby," Francesca said. "Does she believe that she'd suddenly turn into a doting grandmother?"

"Not a chance," Stefano said. "That woman won't touch one of the babies. Not ever."

"You can't possibly know that," Sasha said. "Babies transform people. You put a baby in their arms and they turn to mush. It just happens."

"Not with Eloisa," Stefano said, helping himself to the fresh coffee Francesca had put on the table. "She gave birth, sent the baby to the nursery, summoned one of her sisters to the hospital and they carried the child out. I fed them. I was just a little boy and remember getting up because the baby was crying. She never got up. Not one time that I can recall."

"Really?" The shock showed on Sasha's face. Like everyone else, she had tremendous difficulty believing the reality of their lives.

Giovanni nodded. "It was always Stefano who took care

of us. Eloisa rarely even showed her face, and there was hell if a baby cried for more than a few minutes. She would fly into a rage."

"She hit Giovanni more than once because he would always guard the door to slow her down so I could get the baby outside where she couldn't hear it cry anymore," Stefano said.

"You couldn't have been very old," Sasha said to Giovanni.

He shrugged. "Ricco took more of a beating than I did. If she was really angry because the baby had the croup or something and cried at night, he was the one who had to face her."

"She wasn't turned into Child Protective Services? No one knew?" Sasha asked. She put down her coffee cup and looked around the table at their faces. "This is for real? And you still have dealings with her?"

It was obvious to Giovanni that she would have tried to kick his mother's ass had she been in the room. He loved that Sasha was outraged. She was all about family, and he could see she'd take care of their children, not palm them off on someone else. In a weird way, Eloisa felt the same. Family came first with her, and he knew, once she calmed down, his mother would respect Sasha for standing up to her and for the way she felt about supporting her brother.

"She's our mother," Stefano said. "The weird thing was, even as children, we knew no one else could ever touch us or she'd eat them alive. She was fierce in her protection of us. Even from our father. Only she could 'discipline' us. She doesn't come around that often, just enough to stir up trouble and then disappear again."

"She doesn't like me," Francesca said.

Giovanni was happy there wasn't hurt in her voice. He took the chair beside Sasha, moving it just a few inches as he did, so they were close. He wasn't certain why he liked being near her all the time, but he did.

"She doesn't like anyone," Stefano said. "I know you try

to see the good in her, but, baby, it isn't there often enough to make the effort."

"That's not true," Francesca protested. "You know, with her, she's all about family. She was harsh, but you said she didn't allow anyone else to punish you. It's clear she doesn't realize Sasha has shadow blood in her."

Sasha held up her hand and both men stiffened, going alert immediately. Francesca looked horrified and put her hand over her mouth, shifting her weight toward her husband, her gaze meeting his.

"I don't know what 'shadow blood' means. I do know that both my brother and I have this weird thing where we can feel other people when our shadows touch theirs. We talked about it all the time. We could hear lies, and sometimes, I could persuade people to tell me things I wanted to know. Sandlin could do it all the time. His ability seems to have amplified since the accident and the brain injury, almost as if it magnified the capacity." She looked at Giovanni. "Is that why you're interested in me? Because of my strange abilities with shadows?"

He shook his head, reached for her hand and pressed her palm over his heart. "I saw you in the club, in the dark. Then, the colored lights were flashing and we were moving through crowds. No shadows, remember? I couldn't take my eyes off you and was mortified when you overheard our conversation."

"Why is having 'shadow blood' so important to your mother?"

Giovanni took a breath and let it out. This was one of those moments he hadn't wanted to get to until he knew Sasha was as much in love with him as he was with her. His eyes met Stefano's. He detested that he would either have to put her off or risk losing her.

"Baby, I'm going to ask you to wait for me to answer that. I swear to you I will, but I fell in love with you because of *who* you are, not what. I'm hoping you did the same with me. Can you wait on that answer? Trust me that much?"

She was silent, studying his face. Her gaze went to Francesca and then Stefano. The clock seemed overly loud. Time stretched. Giovanni didn't realize he was holding his breath until his lungs began to burn.

Sasha nodded slowly. "I won't stop thinking about it, and just to let you know, I'm very good at solving puzzles. For instance, I know whoever broke into my apartment is someone who was in the club that night. I know it. Nothing else makes sense."

"Babe, someone can be across the street and see you and begin to fantasize," Giovanni said gently. "It could be anyone."

She nodded. "You're right of course, it could be, but it isn't. It's someone in Aaron Anderson's or John Darby's party. Or one of those cameramen who were close to them."

"Tell me why you're so certain."

"Because when someone's shadow meets mine, I feel them. Sandlin felt you immediately and he could tell certain things about you. He practiced more than I did and he's very good at reading people. I just get feelings, like dread." She pulled her hand away and pressed it to her stomach. "I feel slightly sick if the person's intentions aren't very nice. I felt that in the club. The camera light and cell phones threw shadows all over that upper tier, and in particular, those two tables. That feeling was there and it was the same when I was in my home and also in the parking garage."

Giovanni couldn't deny that she was right. He'd felt dread as well. Even inside the Hendrick Center, he'd had the feeling that something wasn't right, that they were in danger. Or he was. Or Sandlin was.

"That's pretty damning evidence," Stefano said. "If you felt that and recognized it, Sasha, why didn't you say something to Giovanni?"

"Umm, maybe because we barely knew each other and I would have sounded like a loon?" The smile faded and Sasha shrugged and speared eggs Benedict onto her plate from the warmer. "I don't ever talk about how my shadow connects with someone's shadow and I can tell if they're lying. Or that I can feel what they feel. It doesn't matter that Sandlin talks about it all the time, no one believes what he's saying because he has a brain injury. If I said it, they'd lock me up."

Stefano nodded. "There are a few people in the world who can do that—feel emotions and intent when shadows touch. It's exhilarating to say the least and nice when others have that ability so you don't feel like you're slightly crazy."

"I definitely would have felt that way without Sandlin. When he first talked to me about it, I was really young. I'd been to the doctor's office and they said I probably wouldn't have to get a shot, but they all knew I would. I was upset that they'd lied to me and it didn't make sense when I knew they'd been lying. Of course, I went to my big brother for answers because that's what I always did. He told me that sometimes when my shadow touched another's I would feel things about that other person. He said when I did, I needed to believe it. That I had it right. Then he explained that he had noticed it when he was very young as well."

"Did you look at your shadow?" Giovanni asked. Francesca buttered toast fresh from the toaster and handed it to him. He took a bite and chewed, waiting for her answer.

"Of course. My shadow is different from others. It isn't as solid. Well, that's not the right way to put it. It's got little shadows reaching out like arms or something, so my shadow can touch multiple shadows at once." She reached for the pot of coffee.

Stefano got there first and poured the hot liquid into her mug. Francesca nudged the cream and sugar closer. "Did your mother or father have that same kind of shadow?"

Sasha's gaze jumped to his face. His voice had been casual, but it was clear they were all waiting for her answer. "Both, as a matter of fact. They were extremely close and doted on Sandlin and me."

"From what country did your family originate?" Again, Stefano sounded extremely casual. Too much so for someone like Sasha not to understand what he was asking was important.

Sasha sighed. "You know, if you just tell me what *shadow blood* means, I would understand what you were looking for and just give you the information. I don't have anything to hide."

"*Shadow blood* is a term we made up," Giovanni said. "We didn't have anything else to call those who have shadows like ours, so when we were children, we referred to anyone with shadows that had those feeler tubes as someone with shadow blood."

She nodded. "My grandparents on my father's side immigrated from Russia to the United States, but his great-grandparents had gone from Sicily to Russia. Of course, our name changed from Spataro to Petrov and then to Provis when my father's family came here. My mother's family also came from Sicily, and her great-grandparents changed their name as well. My father said his great-great-grandfather had to change the name because it was too dangerous at that time to keep their original name, Spataro."

Stefano and Giovanni both sat back in their chairs and regarded her with more care. Clearly, her father had been from a shadow riding family. Of course, the riders had escaped when the Saldis had attempted to wipe out every member, no matter how little blood in their veins; they wanted anyone related to the Ferraros stamped out. Only the riders escaped because they were able to slip into the shadows unseen. Most were gone when the massacre took place, and they took care to save the remaining family members before trying to avenge the deaths of their loved ones.

The mafia had risen to power, nearly taking the place of the government. Any other family who opposed them eventually came under attack. Most relocated. The Spataro family had been riders—at least her great-grandfather had been one. Giovanni leaned toward her. "Did your mother's family settle in the same region of Russia as your father's family?"

She shook her head. "No, according to the family history, the family immigrating from Sicily to Russia split up and hid in various regions. Whoever was hunting them would be looking for a concentrated amount of families from Sicily living close to one another. By splitting up, they were able to be safe."

"How did your parents meet?" Giovanni knew, for his family, for all riders, and especially his mother, Sasha would be considered gold. A treasure, just like Mariko. When they had babies, those children would be strong in the gifts and abilities of a shadow rider. There were so few that all riders were expected to have children in order to always have protection for their families.

"Both were born here in the United States. My father's family settled in Wyoming. His father liked the open spaces and the life of a cattle rancher. My mother was actually on vacation, and she happened to go into a bar where there was dancing. My father was there and they just hit it off. From what she said, they were inseparable from the moment they met."

"Did they talk to you about their shadows?"

She shook her head. "Cattle ranching is an all-consuming business. We worked hard, from daylight or before until well after sundown. We grew our own food so there was gardening to do. We hunted for meat and fished for the same reason. My parents were loving and sweet, but they worked harder than any two people I've ever seen. At night, my dad would fall asleep in his recliner with Mom sitting on his lap. She'd sometimes talk to us in a hushed voice, but mostly she fell asleep on top of him."

"Did you meet your cousins? Any aunts or uncles?"

She shook her head. "There weren't any. As far as I know, my father was an only child, as was his father before him. Same with my mother."

"Don't worry too much about that picture of you in the tabloids," Stefano said. "We'll get to the bottom of it and find out who sold it."

"I don't really think it matters, do you?" she asked. "It's out there. There's no getting it back. Everyone's got a good look at what's under my blouse."

"You're beautiful," Giovanni said. "So, fuck them."

She flashed him an appreciative smile. It was brief and faded fast. "I guess Darby got his way in the long run." She shrugged. "When I go to work tonight, is West going to be upset with me and relegate me to the bottom tier? He told me the other night if I took the top and did well, he'd keep me there. Nancy wants to drop to part-time. If I can get the top tier, I can make enough money to pay for Sandlin's therapy in that place without working at the deli. I love the job there, because I'm beginning to know the neighborhood people, but I don't get to see Sandlin as often as he needs me to."

Giovanni exchanged another long look with his brother. Neither thought it was safe for Sasha to work at either job. The news of their engagement was out and that set her up as a target for any kidnapper bent on making money, not to mention the paparazzi. There was no way to tell someone until they experienced the crazy way they had to live in order to guard their privacy.

"Sasha"—Giovanni kept his voice as gentle as possible—"right now, it will be very difficult for you to work without constant harassment."

"I can live with harassment, but Sandlin can't live outside that facility." She didn't look at him but continued to eat.

"It isn't safe," Stefano said. When she continued to chew in silence, he sighed. "Look at me, Sasha." It didn't matter that his tone was pitched low, it was a clear order and no one disobeyed Stefano. When her eyes met his, he continued, "We'll cover the cost of your brother's facility because this wasn't your fault. Our security didn't get to you in time to stop what Darby did. We're responsible for not collecting all the cameras. Aaron Anderson is a friend of ours. We made the mistake of not looking at those at his table when we should have. Stop shaking your head and listen to me."

"I'm not allowing someone else to pay for my brother's care."

Giovanni could hear the stubbornness in her voice. Her sapphire eyes practically flashed with fire. He leaned into her, unable to keep the grin off his face. "Obstinate little woman. Are you insane? Stop thinking with your heart, baby. Of course, you want to take care of him yourself. I completely understand that, but—"

"You can argue all you want to, Giovanni," Sasha said, "but it won't do you any good. If I don't show up for work, people will think that stupid picture sent me running and hiding. Most everyone else will think I'm with you because of your money. I happen to know, because I was told, that some of the waitresses are out to snag one of you. Can you imagine what they're going to think—"

"Do you think I give a damn what they think?" Giovanni snapped. "The point is to make certain you're safe. People are going to run their mouths no matter what."

She smirked and picked up her coffee cup. "Exactly."

"I can see I might want to strangle you a few dozen times a day."

"Probably. I know I'm going to feel that way about you." She sounded complacent. "What exactly are we going to do about this engagement? I know you had to tell them you were family at the Center in order to get Sandlin some help, but now it's plastered all over the world in every news outlet."

"We'll have to put the engagement ring on your finger," Giovanni said. He hadn't won the battle about her job, and he clearly wasn't going to, but he gave her his don't-mess-with-me-on-this-one voice. She took the hint, glanced around the table, shrugged and subsided.

He didn't know if she figured she would argue with him later when they were alone, or if she could tell by his face it wasn't up for discussion—and it wasn't. He wanted to make that very clear. He believed in marriage. Having babies. Sandlin was his family as well as hers. That meant he was just as responsible. They'd have that discussion again. So yeah, he'd concede on the work argument and put about a hundred bodyguards on her—he'd be there as well. That way, she could win that battle and give him the important one, because, first things first. Get the ring on her finger and her promise. They'd work out the rest of it later.

"You're on the schedule tonight?" Francesca asked.

Sasha nodded. "Luckily my other uniform is in my locker at work. I know I have to go back to my apartment, sooner or later, but not yet." She gave a little shudder. "Knowing that man was in there, touching my things, using my toothbrush and shower, the things he did in my bedroom, I don't particularly want to be there anymore."

"Fortunately, we've already worked that out," Giovanni stated.

She looked at him with her eyebrow raised, but she didn't protest.

# CHAPTER TEN

Stefano walked into the club, Francesca on his arm. Taviano and Vittorio followed close behind, Emme in between her two brothers. Ricco and Mariko followed them with Emilio and Enzo bringing up the rear. Their New York cousins were in town and were already at the club, waiting with Giovanni at their reserved table. A celebration was in order, although Giovanni's fiancée had insisted she was working. Even so, the family came out to celebrate, the way they did most things—together.

Flashes went off all around them. Of course, the paparazzi were there—with the exception of Sid Larsen and Chesney Reynolds. They had been relegated to staying outside the club and hoping for a good shot of the newly engaged couple. The family made it very clear that photographers who cooperated with Ferraro policy were welcome. In fact, Giovanni had promised them a shot of the ring, a photograph that would be worth a tremendous amount.

The family made their way up to their table where Giovanni waited with all three cousins. Salvatore, Lucca and Geno laughed with Giovanni, clearly giving him a very bad time. Giovanni glanced up as they approached the table and he stood, as did his cousins. Francesca smiled at him as he leaned over to kiss her cheek and then Mariko's. Mariko was new to the family and she wasn't used to their affectionate way with one another, but she smiled and returned the kiss to his cheek.

He caught Emme around the waist and hugged her. "I got the ring on her finger, Emme, but it wasn't easy."

"How'd you manage? Stefano said she was giving you trouble."

He grinned, elated now that he knew his ring was on Sasha's finger. He wished it was a size too small so she couldn't get it off even if she wanted to—which he was sure she did. "I wrestled her to the floor, sat on her and put it on her finger. It was the only way."

He knew they thought he was joking, but he'd done exactly that. He'd taken her to his home, seduced her, managing to get her naked in under seven minutes, and then, when she was too sated and drowsy after their lovemaking, he slid the ring on her finger. It was a special ring, made by his famous cousin, Damian Ferraro. Out of New York, Damian made custom jewelry for those who could afford his special talents. For the shadow riders, he used a special alloy that could move through the shadows with them.

Each rider went to him in person, was interviewed and then the ring made up. The interview consisted mainly of conversation and their cousin just asking a few questions. It was almost impersonal, but all of them knew he had a gift. He knew things. He read people. He was a seer in the sense that he "saw" inside each person who came to him.

Damian didn't take suggestions. The ring was made in advance of the rider ever finding his woman. Somehow, he always chose the exact ring—the one that was perfect. Giovanni had been shocked when he'd gotten the ring from Damian. The engagement ring had no gemstones, which meant it was possible he would find a rider. The alloy could withstand the pull of the shadows, but the gemstones could not. If his partner wasn't a rider, then she was a woman capable of going into the shadows. That, at least, meant he could keep her safe.

The ring was a work of art, just as everything Damian made was. On Sasha's finger, it looked beautiful, as if made just for her—which, technically, it had been. He should have cautioned his cousin to smear superglue on the inside of it.

"She really is working?" Emme asked.

He pulled out a chair for her. "Stubborn as all get-out," he responded and seated himself beside her so they could talk above the pounding music. "Even Stefano talked to her and got nowhere. He'd pull out his hair if Sasha was his woman."

"She'll need to be stubborn if she's going to really marry you," Emme stated. She grinned at him, obviously happy for him. "Stefano and Francesca really like her. That's saying a lot." She glanced over to the table of men a few feet from the stairs. "I see you have bodyguards everywhere."

"Let's hope she isn't as adept at spotting them as you are. I've got two tables on this tier and one on the one below us. Four roving patrols and more scattered throughout the club. We did go over the rules, and she knows how to signal for security. She did ask that they wait for the signal."

Emme rolled her eyes. "Does she know you yet?"

"She does. She laid down the law to me. When I smiled at her she shook her head and stomped away."

That made Emmanuelle laugh. "Do you really think this stalker is going to come tonight?"

"Don't you?" Giovanni took a long, slow look around the club. "He's here. Where else would he be? He can't get to her anywhere else. He wants contact with her and he'll make it, too. I'm betting on it."

"Look who else showed up tonight," Emmanuelle said and gestured to the large party moving up the stairs to the VIP section.

Giovanni clenched his teeth to keep from swearing aloud. Aaron Anderson. The man was a walking menace. Women fell all over him, he was that good-looking. He was charming as well. He always had an entourage with him and this time was no different. He recognized several of the men moving up the stairs. As usual, they were all mixed martial arts fighters, and good ones. Aaron was friends with most of the fighters.

"You wouldn't consider sacrificing yourself and flirting your little ass off, would you?" he asked his sister. "He's always had a thing for you."

"He has not."

"Emmanuelle, every man has a thing for you. You just don't see it. Or you choose not to. At least with everyone but Val Saldi." He glanced at Stefano and lowered his voice even more, turning his head so there was no chance that his brother could pick up what they were saying. "If you care to share what happened between you two, I'm a good listener. I know he matters to you. If he matters to you, he matters to me. He did come through for our family."

Emmanuelle's mask slipped, just for a minute, and he glimpsed pain there. "It's always been him. You know that. Since I was sixteen years old. I thought I'd outgrow it, but apparently, that's not going to happen." She sighed. "He isn't exactly pining away for me the way I am for him. In any case, we both know it would never work between our two families so there's no point in talking about it."

"Of course there is. If you're hurting . . ." He wanted to wrap his sister up and hold her close to him. He detested that she was in pain. He knew it wasn't Val's fault, but he still would like to punch him.

"I'm good. I'm just working through accepting it. As long as I don't have to see him with other women or read about it somewhere, I'll be good."

He touched her face gently. "You know I'm really sorry, *bella*. If I could fix it for you, I would." He'd do anything for her. Any of her brothers would—including Stefano. Especially Stefano.

She turned to watch Aaron seat himself two tables away, in Sasha's section. "He is good-looking. Maybe I'll ask him to dance."

Now that she said it, perversely, Giovanni wasn't too certain he wanted his sister to have anything to do with the man. He liked Aaron and didn't want Emme breaking his heart—which she would. She was beautiful, intelligent and sweet. It would be impossible not to fall in love with her, but Emmanuelle, like the rest of them, had a duty to their family. She had to marry a rider—or a man capable of producing children who could be riders.

"Eloisa is pushing me to meet some of the riders from other countries." Emmanuelle made a face. "I think she wants to hold a ball. Like I'm some kind of prize." A little shiver of revulsion crept through her body. "I suppose it doesn't really matter, does it? It's not as if Prince Charming is going to show up and rescue me from the evil dragon."

"It happened for me. Not Prince Charming, but definitely the Princess." Giovanni's gaze sought out his woman. She was smiling and nodding as she served drinks to the table farthest away from the Ferraro table. Her smile faded when she put down drinks at the next one. She shook her head twice and stepped back as she collected her tip.

Drago and Demetrio made as if to stand and then settled back in their seats as Sasha moved away from the table and went to the bodyguards' table. She took their orders with that same smile plastered on her face—the one he knew didn't mean a thing. She was going to Aaron's table next, and he found his belly tightening.

"She can't run away. Half the room is guarding her."

His sister's soft laughter made him aware he was also clenching his fists. He didn't like that he could be jealous and possessive. Sasha was a woman of her word. There was no mistaking that. Those traits he had, and they were far stronger than he'd like, were not attractive ones in his opinion. He was even slightly ashamed of them. Aaron was his friend and would respect the engagement ring on her finger. There was a code of honor between men. That ring was the line one didn't cross. He wasn't going to embarrass Sasha or himself by being jealous.

He made himself join in his sister's laughter. Sasha looked up, and his heart nearly stopped and then accelerated when her eyes met his. Her face went soft when she looked at him. He didn't deserve that look on her face, like he was something special, her white knight. Still, he wanted her to look at him like that for the rest of their lives. He was glad he'd overcome such a petty reaction as jealousy. He put his hand over his heart and to his shock, she reciprocated.

Two hours went by, Stefano occasionally dancing with Francesca. Ricco spent a great deal of time dancing with Mariko. Emmanuelle mostly danced with her cousins, and refused invitations politely when other males asked her to dance. Giovanni decided he needed to keep a better eye on his sister. She seemed sad, too sad for a woman of her age. They had duties and it weighed heavily on them, but he didn't think forcing Emmanuelle to carry them out if she wasn't happy was right.

Sasha worked the top tier where the family could better protect her. Like the VIPs she served drinks to, she was protected from the others in the club. Giovanni wanted her sitting at the table with the family, but his woman was stubborn and very determined to work in order to pay for the care of her brother on her own. He could see he was going to have to choose his battles with her carefully.

He enjoyed watching her. It no longer mattered if everyone saw him. Their engagement had been announced and his ring was on her finger. She had the protection of the Ferraro family, and that made him happy. Still, he couldn't help but be on edge. The feeling of dread persisted in the pit of his stomach and kept him on alert.

Sasha came to their table often and each time she came up to his side, her body subtly brushed up against his. He was careful, knowing others watched, to not touch her where anyone could see, but it was easy enough to drop one hand below the table and stroke her leg, up her thigh, taking in all that smooth skin.

Sasha did small things to make him aware of her. She dropped a napkin in his lap, and when she retrieved it with a small, shocked apology, her fingers slid over his cock. She didn't need to touch him for his body to react to her presence, but when she did, it wasn't just about the sexual response, it was the fact that she was playing. Teasing him. Making him the center of her attention without seeming to do so. He had never had that before, the way she made him feel as if he really were the center of her universe, and he looked forward to each time she came to their table.

The club was in full swing, packed with people dancing and drinking. Midnight had come and gone. Giovanni wanted the night over so he could spend time with his woman.

"If you'll excuse me," Francesca said. "I need to use the ladies' room and then I would very much like my husband to dance with me again."

Stefano kissed her hand and rose with her. At once, all the men stood. Two tables away and below them, Emilio and Enzo came to their feet. Francesca looked at Emmanuelle and rolled her eyes and laughed.

Salvatore held out his hand to Emmanuelle. "Dance with me, cousin. I'm not in the mood to hold women at bay."

Emmanuelle stood and gave him a little curtsy. Giovanni glanced at his watch. His woman would be on her break in another five. He rose to his feet and stretched, wishing the metal was out of his leg and he could accompany Stefano. His family would be exacting payment for what John Darby had done to Sasha. He wanted to be there. He needed to be there, but those pins, bolts and plates that had saved his leg also prevented him from doing his job.

Emilio stepped in front of Stefano and Francesca as they started down the stairs. Ricco and Mariko followed. Emmanuelle and Salvatore were right behind. Giovanni's other brothers, Vittorio and Taviano, all but prowled down the stairs. Geno and Lucca followed them. Enzo closed in behind them. Giovanni turned toward the bar that was set up in between the two tiers. There were two of them, one serving the upper level and the other the bottom row.

He watched as the Ferraro family captured the spotlight as they moved together, the men as well as Mariko and Emmanuelle wearing their signature pin-striped suits.

Francesca wore a little black dress that hugged her breasts and flared at her hips, the hem short. She wore heels and sheer stockings, her thick hair falling free to her waist. She was beautiful, and flashes went off, capturing every movement. Stefano walked with her, his arms around her, his mouth on her neck, then her shoulder, one hand sliding over her hip. Stefano was rarely with Francesca without touching her. Giovanni knew what that felt like. The moment he was with Sasha, he wanted his hands on her.

Stefano nuzzled Francesca's neck as they threaded their way through the crowd. "You look beautiful tonight."

She put her head back and smiled at him, her eyes warm and loving. "You picked out my dress."

"It isn't the dress." He ran his hand over her hip. "I like touching you."

"I like you touching me." They were nearly to the ladies' room, and he spun her around and took possession of her mouth. Francesca did what she always did, no matter where they were, no matter who was around, she gave herself to him, kissing him without reservation, trusting him to control the situation if they were in public.

Stefano loved that she gave him that control and trust. He spent a few long moments indulging himself. He loved her beyond everything and everyone in his life. She was his entire world and if anything happened to her—if anyone threatened her the way Giovanni's woman was being threatened—he'd lock her up so fast her head would spin. Then he would go hunting until he found the culprit. He knew how frustrated his brother was, frustrated and angry. He couldn't imagine being sidelined while his woman was in danger.

He watched Francesca disappear behind the door and, as always, when she wasn't directly in his care, hard knots of tension developed in his gut. Mariko sent him a small smile and followed his woman in. Emmanuelle was added protection and then finally Enrica, Emilio's sister. Emilio had trained her and she was a damn good bodyguard. That meant with Mariko, Emmanuelle and Enrica with Francesca, he could breathe easier.

He stepped into the men's room, his cousins and brothers moving in a tight group after him. The lights threw shadows in all directions. He stepped into one and was instantly pulled into the tube, his body feeling as if it were flying apart. Somewhere behind him, he knew Vittorio had also chosen a shadow. They moved from shadow to shadow, unerringly seeking one house.

John Darby resided in an upscale community. Everyone knew where he lived because the parties were endless and his neighbors reported him often to the police in hopes of some relief from the continual noise and drunks vandalizing their neighborhood. Security gates were closed tight, presumably to keep out anyone who would protest the wild party going on.

Stefano blew past the gates and went straight to the two-story house. Wide, open balconies provided space for the men and women spilling out of the house. Glass broke as drunks smashed bottles and glasses against the walls or tossed them over the railing. Music blasted from somewhere inside, the sound reverberating through the entire valley. It was no wonder the neighbors complained. At one o'clock in the morning, they would want sleep, not to listen to John Darby's particular brand of shrieking guitars.

Stefano moved unseen through the house, seeing the smashed furniture, the drugs and the half-dressed women and men as they wound themselves around one another. Cameras were mounted everywhere, so many in each room that every angle of the interior was being recorded. On the outside, each balcony had been given the same treatment.

Not seeing Darby anywhere throughout the house, Stefano caught another shadow and rode it to the master bedroom. The room was dark and Darby was alone in his bed. Porn was on the huge screen taking up one wall of his room. He was lying naked on the sheets, alternating looking between the screen and the mirror above his head while he frantically worked his very soft and uncooperative cock.

Vittorio emerged in the mouth of the shadow tube beside Stefano and pointed to the cameras that were set up to catch bedroom activities should a woman be so foolish as to join Darby in his room. The reports Stefano had read on Darby's reality show proved more than one woman had made that mistake. The cameras were off, all four of them.

Vittorio was very, very good at disrupting energy as well as causing power surges. One quick surge and the cameras began recording. Darby was too busy trying to get himself off and having no luck to notice the tiny red lights shining, signaling the cameras were on. Because he found the entire thing distasteful, Stefano signaled his brother and they moved back into the main part of the house, staying to the shadows so the cameras couldn't catch a glimpse of them.

They had to keep their eye on the time. By now, Francesca had left the ladies' room and his cousin, Lucca, playing the part of Stefano, had caught her to him right in the center of his family and had taken her to the darkest corner, a lover's tryst, while his family blocked all access to them. He could be seen from the back, nuzzling his wife while his brothers, the women and his cousins visited. It was necessary in order to keep the illusion of his presence that he return quickly with Vittorio.

They reentered Darby's room after shutting off the cameras in all other parts of the house. He was sitting up, looking down at his flaccid penis in disgust. Vittorio took care of the cameras, making certain they were no longer recording.

"Having problems?" Stefano asked.

Darby yelped and fell from the edge of the bed to the floor. Stefano glided closer. "You really shouldn't have messed with one of my employees. I had a talk with you and you promised you would behave yourself."

Darby started to move, but Stefano stepped on his hand

hard. Darby screamed, but Stefano didn't move. He just stood over him, smiling down at him. "Did you think it would up your ratings to show her naked body on your television show?"

Darby tried to crawl away, but Stefano didn't move. He ground down harder. "When I speak to you, I expect an answer. And Johnny boy, I can hurt you in ways you never imagined."

"No, no." Darby held up his other hand to ward him off. "You don't understand, bitches like it. They want to be seen on my show."

"No, they don't. They don't sue you because you blackmail them with the crap you're recording. You give them date rape drugs in their drinks and then you record your friends with them and tell them you're going to release those videos. You make a little side money that way, Johnny boy? You blackmail them on top of raping and humiliating them?"

Darby kept shaking his head, still trying to scoot away.

"You do though. I had you investigated. I do believe that the day of reckoning has arrived. That little porn film you're watching, the rape of that girl by a couple of frat boys? Is that the only way you can get off now, hurting women? I think the world wants to see that, don't you? The ratings of your show will go right through the roof."

He waved his hand toward the screen. Vittorio, from the shadows, produced the necessary surge of electricity and the recording of Darby on the bed, mixed with the film and the mirror moving back and forth, showed the reality star's underwhelming cock and the frantic pace he'd set with his fist that had clearly done no good. Audio had picked up his continual hoarse shouting at the two frat boys on the bed with the restrained girl, urging them on, telling them to hurt her and shouting graphic instructions to them.

Darby looked horrified. "You can't . . ."

"It's playing all over town right now. Live feeds, you know. It wasn't hard to arrange." Stefano leaned down.

"You ever touch a member of my family or a person under our protection again, I'll come after you and you will wish you were dead before you die. Do we have an understanding?"

Darby frantically nodded. The music had stopped and the house was eerily silent. Stefano stepped back into the shadows. Vittorio's foot snapped out of the shadows, delivering a kick between Darby's open legs. He howled and doubled over. The Ferraros were gone, riding the shadows into the next room where the screens were all playing and replaying the same video of John Darby.

Sasha was a little tired of the men smirking at her and staring pointedly at her breasts, held in by the lace of her camisole. If she hadn't needed the money so badly, she would gladly have taken a few days off in the hopes that another scandal would have taken the attention of the bored celebrities and their entourages she served drinks to. Most groups were polite, but there were a few that annoyed her.

She had to laugh at herself about that, because she'd been fantasizing pretty heavily about playing Giovanni's game. She would ask him to dance first. She'd already scoped out the darkest corners in the club. She knew when they took the dance floor the paparazzi would go crazy, and that was okay. Hopefully they'd get bored. She hoped to enlist Mariko, Francesca and Emmanuelle in her little dance of seduction. They just had to get the attention of the paparazzi and give her some time alone with her man.

If she managed to do half the things she wanted to do to Giovanni, she would definitely deserve the smirks and knowing looks she was getting. Then, after being completely sated and feeling smug, she wouldn't mind those looks. The thought made her smile. She glanced up at his table. His family had headed down to the dance floor. They all seemed to like to dance and they were very good at it.

She had to admit, the Ferraro family was very good-looking and drew the eye. She had been known to stare a bit at them when she first was hired, earlier in the month. Of course, she worked the floor far down below their elevated status. She'd found herself staring at Giovanni every time he went onto the floor until she realized he was such a player. Now, she wasn't so sure. He didn't seem like one when he was with her. He kept his gaze fixed on her. Not once, even now, when his brothers were on the dance floor and he would have had an excuse, did he look down at the other women.

Sasha looked. She made a slow perusal of the club and the women while she waited for the tray of drinks to take up to two of the tables. Most were beautiful. Really, beautiful. Their clothes were quality, clearly designer. Their hair was styled perfectly and most dripped gold and diamonds. How had Giovanni overlooked them to find her?

It wasn't that she thought the others were better than her in any way—she didn't. Sasha had confidence in herself as a woman. She could take care of herself and her brother. On the other hand, she knew her heart was very vulnerable, and she'd always protected it. When she loved, she loved with everything in her. She was intensely loyal and expected the same. She wanted a home and family. She also believed in a strong partnership. She didn't want Giovanni to make the mistake of thinking he was going to take care of her.

Her gaze was pulled inevitably back to him. He was so handsome he took her breath away. He really did. She could barely breathe sometimes when she got close to him and inhaled his scent. He had the kind of body artists sculpted or painted. He was sweet to her and caring. She hadn't planned to fall for him. She'd started out thinking he was the worst kind of human being and somewhere along the line she'd fallen under his spell.

"You look like you got it bad, Sasha," Alan, the bartender, said.

She laughed and turned back to him. "I do. He's very sweet to me."

"So, it's really true? You're engaged to him?"

She held up her left hand and showed him the unusual band. "I am." It was important to play along with the engagement so the Center continued to believe she was with Giovanni and the Ferraro family. She wasn't the best security possible for her brother. And the truth was, she liked the thought of being engaged to him, but that she kept to herself.

Fingers brushed her wrist as if the person wanted to see her ring. She turned toward the man standing that little bit too close to her. James Corlege and Tom Mariland, the MMA fighters who always came in with Aaron, stood close, crowding her against the bar. She dropped her hand to the tray, but James and Tom could clearly see the ring.

"Looks like your little ploy worked," James snickered. "I told Aaron you were interested in the Ferraros. All the servers here are. Pay someone to rip your blouse, and he's all about saving you." His voice was nasty. Sneering.

She stepped back away from him. When she stepped back, she did so right into his friend, Tom. He didn't move. He felt like an oak tree, his body hard from all the workout and training for fights he'd done. She was used to men with hard bodies—she was from an area of cattle ranchers, men who rode and worked for a living—so Tom didn't intimidate her.

Sasha glanced at him over her shoulder. Tom wore the same mask of contempt as James did. She stepped to the opposite side, moving closer to the bar and away from both men. She knew she could signal the security guards. Right now, they probably thought the men were being friendly. The fact that she could summon help made her feel confident.

"What did you do to get his attention?" Tom sneered. "Give him a blow job? I hear that's one way girls like you snare wealthy men."

James nudged her with his foot, keeping the action small so Alan, behind the bar, couldn't see him. "You like giving blow jobs, Sasha?"

She sent him a small frown, feigning confusion and a wealth of being sorry for him. "Doesn't your girlfriend like to give you blow jobs? Because if she doesn't, maybe you need to figure out why. Cleanliness is at the top of the list, and then there's what you eat. You want to take care of yourself or she's just not going to go there." She switched her attention to the bartender. "Do you have those drinks up yet, Alan?"

He grinned at her. "Right here, Sasha." He pushed the tray toward her and then switched his attention to the two men. "What can I get for you? Usually your server will take your orders."

"Our server is too busy flirting her ass off with the Ferraros to bother with us," Tom said.

Alan glanced at his watch. "I don't know when she would have had time to do that, sir. We keep strict watch on all servers and she's more than meeting the requirements to keep drinks on the table, but if you want to file a complaint . . ."

James cursed and shook his head, turning away to start up the stairs after Sasha. She was very conscious of the two men coming up fast right behind her. She could actually feel hot breath on her neck as she neared the top. They were deliberately harassing her and she wasn't certain why. As she gained the top tier she spun around and faced them.

"Did I do something to offend you?" she asked James deliberately, looking him straight in the eye. Let him defend himself for a change. "As I recall, you were the one who was all over me the other night, and in fact, you sent me chocolates to make amends. What changed between then and now?"

"You didn't even bother to look around you at any other men," James accused. "You set your sights on Ferraro, yet you flirted your ass off with Aaron, making him think he had a chance. You also made certain I was looking and so was Tom."

Her breath caught in her throat. "I didn't. I didn't flirt

with anyone that night. You were all drunk, and I thought all of you were a bunch of wealthy players with far too much money and no manners. None of you impressed me."

Tom narrowed his eyes at her. "Yet you're wearing Giovanni Ferraro's ring."

She supposed that was a bit of damning evidence against her. She shrugged. "I did nothing to either of you, or Aaron. If he wanted to see me outside of the club, he gave no indication. I appreciate that you're both his good friends, but I'm a little tired of you acting as if it's your right to persecute me."

She swung away from them and went to the table where the four men waited for their drinks. One smiled at her. "Are they giving you a hard time?"

The question sounded casual enough, but something in the man's voice caught her attention, as if he was really asking, not just being nice. She had the feeling that if she answered in the negative, he—and possibly the others—would jump up, pummel the two men and throw them out. She hadn't noticed just how fit these men were beneath their flawless suits. More, they weren't dancing. In fact, they weren't even looking at the women on the club floor. She had put the table down to out-of-towners, businessmen looking for relaxation. Now, she wasn't so certain.

"Seriously, honey," another said. "If they're giving you a hard time, say the word and we'll take care of it."

She flashed a quick smile and pocketed their generous tip. "Thanks, really, but I can handle them." She turned away, hesitated and then turned back. They had to know, just to keep them safe. She didn't want them taking matters into their own hands. "They're mixed martial arts fighters. All of them at that table, and I believe most have won championships in their divisions. I really appreciate the offer, but security is excellent here. You just enjoy yourselves and the evening." She gave them her high-wattage smile and moved to the next table.

Two gentlemen gave her smiles. They'd gone down to the dance floor twice the entire evening, but not at the same time. Both had been respectful as well as being generous tippers. She put their drinks in front of them and turned to go back down the stairs. Her stomach sank. Aaron stood waiting for her a few feet away.

"Ma'am"—one of the men stopped her, his voice pitched low—"if you need help, just shout out."

Did she look that fragile, or worried? She didn't like to think so. She wasn't a woman who depended on others to defend herself. She flashed a smile and shook her head. "No problem, really. I'll be fine." She hoped she wasn't lying to them—or to herself.

"Mr. Anderson? Is there something I can do for you?" She went straight up to him, deciding to get it over with.

"Aaron. Call me Aaron."

She nodded. "Aaron then. What can I do for you?" She walked past him to his table, ignoring James and Tom.

Aaron leaned close to her. "I need to talk to you. Somewhere private." He kept his voice to a near whisper, as if just standing there with her wasn't going to cause undue attention.

"I'm working." Sasha pointed out the obvious, setting his drink in front of his seat. She turned to go.

Anderson caught her wrist, a wad of bills in his other hand. "I'm serious. It's for your own good. I'm not trying to be a dick, but someone needs to warn you." He pushed the cash into her hand. "Please, just give me two minutes. And take your tip."

Sasha hesitated and then nodded. "I'm heading to the bar to grab more drinks. You can either walk with me and talk, or be down there and talk while I get the drinks." She was firm about that. She wasn't going anywhere alone with him. She just didn't trust anyone.

Giovanni was close, but that didn't mean he could get to her if some crazy man with too many fantasies tried to hurt her. Sandlin needed her alive. It was possible—even probable—she'd been too stubborn about working this soon.

Aaron followed her as she made her way around the tables toward the stairs. There was just enough room for the two of them to walk side by side as they descended. She didn't so much as glance at Giovanni. She had the feeling he wouldn't like Aaron walking so close to her. She didn't like it, especially every time his body brushed against hers. She was fairly sure Aaron was sliding up against her deliberately every chance he got.

"He's a player," Aaron announced.

Sasha glanced up at him. It wasn't what she expected. Not at all. She'd braced herself for something different, something to do with the picture of her breasts exposed. She'd been getting a few propositions, and after what James and Tom had said to her and the way they'd treated her, she was expecting the same from Aaron.

"Excuse me?"

"Giovanni. He's my friend. I've known him a long time, if anyone knows a Ferraro, but he's a player. Straight up. A good man, but a player. He's never going to go through with the wedding."

She continued down the stairs, keeping her eyes on where she was going. He put his hand under her elbow and gripped, as if helping her down. She didn't like to be touched when she hadn't invited it, and after that ghastly, very public picture in the tabloids for the world to see, she *really* didn't like it. Too many men, as she served them their drinks, had brushed against her body as if they had the right. It wasn't anything she could call security over, but it made her skin crawl. His friends had been the most disrespectful, and that seemed to be on his behalf.

When she didn't reply, Aaron continued. "Look, I know you're going to think I have an agenda, and maybe I do. I noticed you right away and tried to get your attention. I was drunk and went about it wrong, but it was genuine interest.

Giovanni knows that. He's competitive. Do you think this is the first time we've competed for a woman?"

She hadn't paid attention to anything he said until the last. It made sense given what she knew about Giovanni. He was competitive, and he detested the way women threw themselves at his brothers, cousins and especially him. She couldn't help the sideways glance she gave Aaron. She knew immediately he would take that as a go-ahead to continue.

"End it. Give him the ring back. Tell him you don't want anything to do with him."

She didn't know what to say or how to react. She wasn't someone who doubted herself. She knew she was good-looking. Okay. More than good-looking. She also knew quite a few men thought she was sexy. She had curves and confidence. She wasn't a shrinking violet. She liked sex and what's more, she enjoyed giving her partner pleasure, in particular Giovanni.

"Give me a chance."

"This competition you and Giovanni are supposed to have. Does it involve money?"

He shot her a quick glance and then shifted his gaze away, nodding. She couldn't judge his voice by his nod. She had to hear the lie, she couldn't see it.

"So, you bet whether or not you could lure me away from him?"

"No, God, no. Of course not. I wouldn't do that."

"Yet you have money on the table between you. How exactly did the bet go?" She stopped and turned so she was right in front of him, challenging him. She wanted to hear his voice. "And look me right in the eye. If you're betting on my downfall, the least you can do is look me in the eye when you tell me about it."

He sighed. "He bet me a thousand he could wrap you up before I did."

Her churning stomach settled. He was lying. She saw it in his eyes and heard it in his voice. Why he was lying, she didn't know, but he was definitely trying to break up her and Giovanni.

"We're done. Please don't talk to me again," she said. "And I hope Giovanni realizes you aren't his friend at all." Deliberately she turned her back on him and went to the bar to get the drinks for her other tables.

# CHAPTER ELEVEN

A half hour later, Sasha finally got a well-deserved break. Nancy was supposed to cover her tables much earlier, but she continued to have headaches and had lain down in the lounge to try to combat the one she had, so Sasha had taken both tiers. The Ferraro family sat in full force at their table, which made it just a little intimidating to approach. Still, the ring on her finger gave her an added boost of confidence.

She went right up to the table, stood across from Giovanni deliberately between Geno and Salvatore, his two cousins who had played their game. She smirked at both of them and then locked eyes with Giovanni. "Would you care to dance with me, Giovanni?" She sent him a sultry smile, her voice pure seduction.

Geno groaned. "I don't think this is going to be a fair competition."

"No one had better be competing at all," Francesca decreed.

Giovanni's lashes lifted and his dark eyes met Sasha's. She felt the impact right down to her toes. He couldn't possibly fake that kind of desire. The sensual lines carved in his face deepened. Lust rose, sharp and terrible to settle wickedly in her deepest core. He could do that to her with one look. He rose immediately without a word.

Sasha dropped a hand on either cousin's shoulder. "Perhaps there is a lady or two ready and willing to ask you to dance." Smiling, she took Giovanni's hand, threading her fingers through his as they walked away together.

"Was that a challenge?"

She laughed. "Of course it was. I know you lost a good deal of money to that awful Geno. He was bragging. We'll have to see just how many points you earn tonight."

"It's late, baby. We'd have to hurry if we were going to win back all our losings."

They moved down the stairs together. Around them flashes went off as the paparazzi went crazy trying to get photographs of the two of them together. A couple had managed to sneak up to the top tier—although to do that she was fairly certain security had to have cooperated. They managed to take pictures quickly before they were escorted back down the stairs. She'd noted no cameras were taken away from the photographers. In fact, everyone had been polite.

Once on the dance floor, Sasha let him guide her through the mass of writhing bodies to the darker edges where she let the music take her. She'd always loved music and dancing. She found the rhythm in the pounding beat immediately and began to move her body to it. Giovanni came up behind her, his body against hers, following the same beat so that they moved almost as if they were already joined, skin to skin.

His hands came up to her hips, guiding her more intimately into him so that she felt his erection pressed tightly against her buttocks. Every time she moved, she rubbed her body over his. She reached down and brought his hands up to her breasts. The moment his warm palms covered her, her nipples pushed against him, begging for attention.

Her breasts felt swollen and achy, hungry for his touch. Her panties were damp, her body going hot and slick. There was something about the pounding beat of music, the dark, his body, so hard and masculine up against hers, just a thin layer of clothing between them. Heat blossomed in the pit of her stomach and spread like wildfire through her veins.

His thumbs strummed her nipples, rubbed through the thin top until she wanted to scream in an agony of need. Her eyes were closed and she found herself sinking deeper into a haze of desire. She took his hand and slid it along the seam of her blouse. It wouldn't be easy to slide his hands under the camisole, but she should have known he would be able to figure it out. The zipper whispered and the camisole loosened, allowing his palms to slide up her rib cage to the sides of her breasts.

She sighed and pressed back into him again and again, rocking her hips. He kept one hand around her waist, locking her to him while his other cupped the weight of her right breast, his fingers and thumb busy, stroking and caressing, kneading and tugging. Rolling and pulling. Lightning streaked from her breasts to her clit. Her body pulsed with need. For him. She was wrapped in a web of sheer physical hunger.

His breath was warm against her ear as his teeth tugged at her earlobe. More lightning. More fire. Her sheath spasmed. Clenched. Went hotter and slicker. "Baby, you have to ask me to put my hands on you."

She wanted that more than anything. Skin to skin contact. Her entire body felt as though she was going up in flames. But . . . a tiny little part of her hesitated. She could have this moment—this intimacy, locked with him surrounded by a sea of people, but it was only the two of them. If he really was playing her, was this moment going to be enough for her? Would she look back on it with regrets?

"Sasha?" His hands went from moving over her body to swinging her around to face him. His palms framed her face. "Look at me."

Butterflies fluttered in her stomach when she raised her gaze to his. It was impossible not to see the worry in his eyes. The emotion. Stark. Intense.

"We were playing a game here, but for me it's real. Touching you. Kissing you. The moment my body is next to yours I heat up. Catch fire. I thought this was fun for you, too, but you're not into it." He zipped up her top and enfolded her immediately into his arms, his body tight against hers.

She was into the game. She had been. She'd initiated it. She had thought to put the game to rest. The worry she had that he was playing her long term. She didn't believe Aaron. In fact, she knew he lied, but still, that little nagging worry told her this was all happening too quickly. How could Giovanni fall in love with her so fast?

For her, it wasn't about his looks. It wasn't about the money. She'd fallen because when her shadow had touched his, she'd known him. She'd "seen" him. That first night when he'd taken her to the pizzeria, then walked her home, she'd felt him. His sincerity. His need to protect and care for others. Giovanni was many things, but beneath that mask he wore in public, the playboy, he was something very different. He said things, things she normally wouldn't believe, because everything between them had happened so fast, but she knew he was sincere. She knew he was telling the truth because her innate ability to hear lies told her she could trust what he said and did.

Still, she doubted herself at times. She didn't understand how it happened so fast for him. For her, it made sense. She was alone. Everything around her was crumbling. Her brother—that beautiful man she loved so much, her last relative—had little time to live and barely knew who she was from one day to the next. Need was a strong motivator even for love.

That pulled her up short. Was she with him only because she needed someone to help her get through the terrible fears she had over Sandlin? She pressed her face deeper into Giovanni's immaculate jacket. Was she that shallow of a person that she would cling to a man she barely knew, convince herself that she was falling in love?

"Baby, stop."

She knew he was moving them through the couples, but she didn't look. She just went with him. She heard herself sobbing, but she was disconnected, and there was no stopping anyway.

Giovanni took her to the edge of the dance floor and was immediately surrounded by his family. He didn't know how Stefano was always aware of each and every one of them as well as their state of mind, but he was. He had the bodyguards there as well, so they moved easily through the crowd toward the back hallway where the offices were located. No one was the wiser that anything was wrong. Even the paparazzi was used to the family walking from place to place together.

The moment they got to the hallway door, Giovanni yanked it open, took Sasha on through and, still holding her to him, brought her into the family's office. It was large. They each required space. Maybe it had to do with spending so much time in the shadows, but they all preferred wide-open spaces if they could get them.

He sank down onto the plush couch, taking Sasha with him, cradling her close to him. Maybe if she hadn't spent hours serving drinks and being brave, or if she hadn't set out to seduce him using his own game, her tears wouldn't have gutted him the way they did, but the longer she sobbed as if her heart was breaking, the more he wanted to fight someone, slay dragons, do whatever the hell he needed to do to get her to stop.

He massaged her scalp and rocked her, holding her to him, the entire time murmuring soothing reassurances in Italian. He let her cry, wracking his brain, trying to think of what could have happened. He'd been careful to keep them in the shadows, so much so that at times, the pull on his body had been tremendous and his leg had ached until he thought it might shatter. Still, every second of her seduction had been worth the pain to him.

He loved her all the more for her courage and sense of fun, for her willingness to forgive his stupidity and turn his game into something beautiful and intimate between them. He rubbed his jaw and then his cheek along the top of her silky head. Strands of hair caught in the five-o'clock shadow that had seemed to be a part of him since his late teens.

She hiccupped. Coughed. Clearly made an effort to stop. He kept her head pressed against his shoulder, knowing she wanted to hide from him. He was content to let her, as long as she was in his arms.

"Can you tell me, Sasha? What's wrong?"

"I just need . . ." She trailed off.

His heart clenched and sudden fear swept through him. He knew what she was going to say. He was that tuned to her. She wanted to put space between them. She wanted to rethink her decision to be with him. Go backward.

"Don't, baby. I'm asking you not to say it. Not that." He struggled to keep his voice from breaking. Her wild emotion seemed to be contagious. "Just talk to me and tell me what you're feeling. I know you're overwhelmed. We can be an overwhelming family. I know it has to feel as if everything is happening too fast, but we can deal with those things together. Just talk to me. Trust me enough to talk to me."

She squirmed, her hands coming up to his chest, but she didn't push him away. She just kept her hands there while she pressed her forehead against him, still struggling to gain control. "I'm sorry, Giovanni. I don't know what happened."

He wanted to let her get away with it, but he couldn't. They had to always be on the same page. That was part of being a shadow rider. "You need to tell me what happened."

She sighed and lifted her face so her eyes could meet his. His heart stuttered, and he brought his hand up to cup her face even as his other arm continued to lock her to him.

"I think I panicked. I'm getting in too deep here, Giovanni. I don't know how to play games, and if that's what's going on here . . ."

That was a knife, striking deep, straight through his heart. He couldn't even be upset with her for thinking it, although he thought they'd put that to rest. He cursed himself and the stupid, *idiotic* idea of the game he had played with his brothers and cousins. He thought Ricco was going to have problems with the ridiculous things he'd done before he found Mariko, but this was just as bad if not worse.

"Does it really feel as if I'm playing games with you, Sasha?" He leaned into her, brushed her trembling lips with his. That shock of electricity he'd come to expect when he touched her raced through his body. He brushed those velvet soft lips a second time, his heart accelerating.

No one had ever told him that he could fall so far so fast. There was something about her, that combination of vulnerability and independence, strength and yet compassion. He liked her honesty, even when, like now, she didn't want to admit what she was feeling.

"No." Her voice was a whisper. A thread of sound. "No, but . . ."

She tried to turn away, the tears tracking down her face obviously embarrassing her. He could tell she didn't believe in letting anyone see that evidence of vulnerability. "I'm not just anyone," he reminded. "That ring on your finger means something to me. I've never told a woman she matters. Or that I'm falling in love with her. I've never wanted a woman to wear my ring. The sad truth is, Sasha, I knew when I told Goodman, the administrator, that we were engaged, that the news would be leaked all over the next day—I wanted it to be."

"To protect my brother," she agreed.

"To wrap us tighter together. I didn't want you running from me. I know you're the one. The moment I saw you working, I couldn't take my eyes off you . . ."

"That's physical attraction, Giovanni," she pointed out a little desperately.

He nodded, sweeping one hand down the back of her head. He leaned forward to sip at her tears. He wanted them gone any way he could get rid of them. "I know that's physical attraction, Sasha. Believe me, I know what my body feels." Before she could say anything more, he had to tell her the rest. "I watched you all evening. I saw you give that bottle of very expensive champagne to the couple who couldn't afford it. I saw you pay the bartender out of your tips."

She ducked her head. "They were celebrating their tenth anniversary. He'd gotten the special tickets for that private table and it was all they—"

"I know that. I made it my business to find out. The money for their tickets was refunded to them and they were comped a dinner at Salvo's. Thank you for bringing them to our attention. You also helped a young woman whose blind date was a nightmare."

She frowned at him. "I couldn't just leave her sitting there crying when he told her to get herself home and she could pay the tab."

"You didn't have money to pay his tab."

She shook her head slowly. "No, but I asked Alan if I could make payments. He consulted you, and you said you'd take care of it."

He had taken care of it. The man who had run up a very big bill and was down on the floor dancing with his real girlfriend, leaving his "blind" Internet date with his mess, had been escorted by security into one of the offices. He'd paid the bill and was then escorted to the door, thrown out and told never to return. The woman sitting alone on the second tier was given a free cab ride home.

"I could go on to tell you several other things I discovered about you by just observing you, but you get the point. I got there just after we opened. You were an interesting pastime, and the various tables that were filled. People come and go throughout the night, but I was more interested in you than watching any of them. I learned more than the fact that I was seriously attracted to you. And at that point, I didn't even know about your brother."

She pressed fingers to her mouth to try to suppress the last of her hiccupping tears. "Why do you say it as though knowing about my brother is a good thing?"

"You love family and are loyal to them no matter the circumstances. I'm the same way. I want that trait in my wife. I want it instilled in my children. Your brother is a highly intelligent man and he's also strong in what Francesca refers to as 'shadow blood.' That means, when his shadow touches mine, I can read him just as he can read me."

"What does your shadow tell you about him?"

He heard the curiosity in her voice. She was becoming distracted, calming down from the storm of tears. He could breathe easier. If she cried like that again, he knew he'd be on his knees, promising her anything, and as a rule he was as tough as nails.

"He's a good man. Doesn't have a mean bone in his body, but he's strong. He'll stand when it's for something he believes in."

She pressed her forehead against his chest. "He *was* like that, Giovanni. What's he like now?"

"Baby." He tipped her chin up. "You're adept at reading shadows. Why are you asking me? You know the answer."

She shook her head. "I don't." Her eyes met his and there was pleading there. That look shook him just the way her tears did. "What you told me and what I read are the ways he was *before* the accident. He can't remember anything. How could he remember what he believes in? The answer is he can't."

"I don't know what he remembers and what he's forgotten. He accepts you coming to visit him," Giovanni pointed out. "He likes you reading to him. It makes him feel peaceful when so many things upset him. He doesn't like that he can't remember and becomes agitated in his mind. You have to have felt that."

She nodded. "That's why I read to him. It calms him down."

"*You* calm him down, Sasha. Not the reading. You. When you sat on that couch with his head in your lap while you read to him, I stepped into your shadows. He was feeling you. The way you love him. He might not know your name, but he knows who you are to him. You represent love. His world. His family. He doesn't believe in a what. He believes in a who. That who is you, honey. He becomes agitated if more than a couple of days go by without seeing you, according to Goodman. No, he doesn't know what being your brother or sibling means. He doesn't know your name from one day to the next, but he recognizes you. Never think he doesn't."

He spoke the raw truth to her, looking into her eyes, willing her to see the honesty. He wasn't lying to soften a blow, he knew the truth of every word. He'd read Sandlin's shadow. His shadow had deliberately connected to her brother's in an effort to assure himself that there was no threat to Sasha.

"He doesn't understand that we're siblings," she insisted.

He shook his head. "That doesn't really matter. His life is all about you, waiting for you, seeing you, listening to you. He likes that you tell him stories of his past. He might not remember them, but he hears the love in your voice when you talk to him about the ranch, the cattle, the horses and your parents. He listens for the sound of your footsteps. That's love, Sasha. It might not be what you had before, but you still have your brother."

"How did you get that from just his shadow?"

How did he tell her he'd been reading shadows from the time he was a child? He cleared his throat, hoping she wouldn't think he was a stalker. She already had one of those and didn't need two. "I went down the hall several times to check on you while I waited for Goodman to arrive. I listened to you talking to your brother, telling him funny and loving childhood stories, and I watched Sandlin's face. I deliberately connected our shadows so I could feel his emotions. Sandlin was acutely aware of me because

I was so locked on to you, yet during the telling of those stories, his attention didn't wander once. He barely knew I was there, he was so interested in what you were telling him."

Sasha framed his face with her hands and looked into his eyes. Twin sapphires, so brilliant, a deep blue, stared straight into him, looking past the façade he wore for everyone else. Seeing him—seeing the man he was inside.

"Thank you." She whispered it. "I am falling very hard for you. Very fast. I let myself doubt you and I'm sorry for that, but seriously, Giovanni, I can't afford to get my heart broken, not with everything I've been through these last months. You're that heartbreak. I can't seem to resist you no matter how hard I try."

"Please don't. I'm right there with you, Sasha, just as vulnerable." How could he make her believe him after the stupidity of his game? The sad truth was, it had been his invention.

He'd been sidelined far too long from his real purpose in life. He was a shadow rider. He meted out justice. He didn't know who he was without being a rider. Just sitting around acting like a bored playboy, flying into various locations and having women climb all over him while his picture was taken for months and months while his leg healed, was enough to tip him right over the edge. Maybe it had. He'd come up with the game thinking it would relieve his boredom—and truthfully—maybe to get back at the women hunting his brothers, cousins and him for their money. He'd been an idiot and now he was paying the price.

"How can I possibly know I'm not just one of those women you compete with Aaron or some other men for?"

He stiffened, adrenaline rushing through his body. He'd seen her with Aaron. He'd forced himself to sit at the table while his friend talked and laughed with her. While the MMA fighter had walked her down the stairs, engaging in what appeared to be a very serious conversation with her.

"What are you talking about, Sasha? Competing with Aaron? I've never done that. Not with him, not with any other man other than what you overheard. I would never take something so far that I'd ask a woman to marry me—"

"You didn't ask me, Giovanni," she interrupted.

Everything in him stilled. "I didn't?" Surely, he hadn't been that big of an idiot. No, he'd been that arrogant. He'd declared it to the world, put the ring on her finger, but he hadn't asked her because . . . "You might have said no to me. We talked about this."

"How it came about. Wearing your ring. That we might actually make it work, but you didn't really ask, Giovanni."

"If I ask officially, are you going to say yes?"

She burst out laughing. "You can't cheat. Either you do the right thing and ask me or you'll never know."

"Are you serious?"

She nodded her head, but there was a teasing glint in all that sapphire staring into his eyes. She took his breath. His heart. She liked to play. To laugh. She gave that to him in some of their worst moments, and he knew she always would.

"Giovanni, if and when you really ask me, you have to be serious."

"Baby, you're still doubting me. Go over there, where your shadow can touch my shadow." He practically tossed her off his lap. She wanted a proposal, she was going to get one and she was going to be standing where their shadows touched so she could feel exactly what he was feeling. He didn't want her to doubt him again.

"What did my good friend Aaron say to you?" He should have obeyed his first instincts and broken that up immediately, but he wanted to show her he could overcome jealousy.

"Just nonsense apparently. I knew he was lying and I still was worried. Maybe it's me I doubt, not you. I don't seem to know what I'm doing anymore."

"You work too much and you're tired, Sasha."

She shook her head. "I'm used to working long hours. On a ranch, the work is never done. It isn't that, it's Sandlin."

Her voice broke, and he wished he still had her in his lap.

"I lost my parents, the ranch, my entire world. And they keep telling me I'm going to lose Sandlin. I'm fighting for him the only way I know how, but sometimes, I can't sleep worrying that when I'm not with him, something terrible is going to happen and then I'll lose him, too. I just can't, Giovanni. I just can't lose him."

He would give his fortune to keep that from happening. He had to consult with the acknowledged best doctors in brain trauma that he could find. He had to make it a priority immediately. That didn't mean he was going to be distracted. He knew Aaron had said things their friendship should have prohibited and he needed to know what those things were in order to do damage control. He was *not* going to lose the best thing that had ever happened to him.

He slipped off the chair and waved her toward the light where her shadow would be cast straight across his. When she backed into that position, he moved as close as possible and knelt down. Her eyes widened and she shook her head. He could see that she hadn't really expected him to ask her. Not formally. Not on his knee.

"Sasha Provis, would you do me the honor of becoming my wife and living the rest of your life with me?" His heart pounded and thunder roared in his ears. He hadn't expected to be so fearful. "I need you. Your laughter. The way you know how to love. I want you for a million other reasons. I know you're the one, the only for me. I don't cheat, in spite of whatever you may have heard to the contrary. I believe in loyalty and family. I swear on my family's code that I will do everything I can to make you happy."

He knew she would have to feel his sincerity. This wasn't about that anymore. This was about whether or not she felt capable of loving him. He didn't take his eyes from her, taking in every detail. The slightest nuance, her every expression.

She touched her tongue to her lip. "Are you hiding something from me? Something about your family business that might change how I answer?"

She might as well have shot him—put a fucking bullet right through his heart. She was smart, and there was no hiding the fact that his family was powerful and dangerous. They wanted people to know they were a force to be reckoned with. That was how they protected themselves and their territory.

He took a deep breath. "Yes." It was the only answer he could give. The only answer he would give. He had to be honest with her, and in any case, their shadows were connected. She came from a family straight from Sicily. She might not have been trained to be a rider but she certainly could have been one. Her brother as well.

Sasha stepped close to him. "Will you tell me what it is?"

"I'm not at liberty to tell you until we're together." That was the truth, too.

She studied his face for what seemed an eternity. Very slowly she nodded her head. "Then yes, Giovanni, I'll marry you."

For the first time in his life, he actually felt so weak he thought he might hit the floor. "After what I just told you?"

She was there, sinking to the floor beside him. Her hands framed his face, her thumb sliding over the bristles on his jaw. "I know your family has to have secrets. You didn't lie to me, Giovanni, and you promised you would explain when we were committed. I'm committing to you. Tying my life to yours. You come with secrets, and your mother. I come with stalkers and Sandlin. We'll find a way to work it all out."

"Eloisa." He sighed.

"Stalkers." She matched his sigh.

The two of them burst into laughter, and he gathered her

into his arms, pulling her onto his lap again. He liked her there. He liked the way her arm naturally curved around his neck and she leaned into him. Almost melted into him. "Have that ridiculous game and your worries been put to rest?"

She nodded. "I really wanted to play the game and get your money back from Geno. He was very smug about his winnings."

"I lost a ton of money that night, but it was well worth it. I found you. I wasn't about to leave that table and have you thinking I was playing that game."

She laughed again. *Dio*, but he loved her laugh. Her fingers curled around the nape of his neck, and just that touch, the way she brushed his skin, made his heart pound and his cock stir. There wasn't anything at all sexual about the way she was acting with him, but the intimacy of her touch and the way she was so naturally sensual were arousing. She didn't have to try very hard with him.

"I noticed, too. I was watching."

"Tell me what Aaron said."

"He lied about you. He said the two of you competed for the same woman and he implied you would go so far as to get engaged and then dump the woman just to win."

He didn't have many men he counted as friends and that hurt. Deeply. He liked Aaron. He'd helped him often with his training.

"That was never true. I've never come close to an engagement. You can go back through every tabloid and every speculation. I was never photographed with the same woman twice. I was careful never to escort a woman more than once to a charity event or any public event, for that matter. I never in my life have led a woman on. I have never been with one that didn't know the score."

She closed her eyes and let her head fall on his shoulder. "You don't like your life, do you, Giovanni?"

"Do I sound bitter? I don't mean to. I don't like every aspect of my life, but sometimes, it is necessary to do things for the family. I can't perform my regular job, so I play the part of the playboy. That's a job and I've learned, over the last few months, to be very good at it, but no, honey, I don't like it."

She pulled back to study his face, her eyes thoroughly examining every line carved deep. "You really don't. Are you going to tell me why you have to be a playboy? Why all the men in your family act that part? I presume they're all acting."

He nodded. "Yes, it's part of our jobs. Stefano and Ricco no longer have to play that role, so that narrows it down to the rest of my brothers and me. As a rule, we try to take turns, but I have this metal in my leg and it's going to be there for a while. My fear is, I'll have to fly out of town and be seen in a club somewhere and you'll get the wrong idea."

"You fly somewhere and have to appear in a club, I'll be right there with you." A mischievous smile lit her face. "I could be that sexy stranger asking you to dance. If Geno's anywhere around, he'd be begging you to let him give you back your money." She rubbed her hand down his jaw, feeling the five-o'clock shadow with her fingertips. "Honey, now's the time to fill me in on your family's business. I said yes to you, which means I've made that commitment. We're sorting things out. Tell me."

He shook his head. "Give me a little more time, Sasha. I'm not stalling. I'll tell you, but the timing is critical. It matters. Trust me a little bit longer."

She studied his face for a long time before she nodded slowly. "Not too long, Giovanni." She slid off his lap, stood up and held out her hand. "I'm way out of time. Lucky I'm with my boss because otherwise I'd be fired. As it is, West is probably going to give me a whale of a lecture. He's so good at them."

He laughed and took her offered hand, getting up to stand beside her. He wrapped his arm around her waist. "That better not happen. The only one who gets to lecture you is me. Or maybe Stefano, too. He's bound to do it sooner or later."

They started to the door. Giovanni stopped, pulling her to him. He cupped her chin in his hand. "Do you have to work, Sasha? We're getting married. Soon. Do you really have to put yourself in danger when we don't need the money?"

"I need to work. Sandlin is mine. My responsibility. If I can keep this job, working on the top tier, I'll have enough to pay his medical bills and my apartment. Then, as soon as Pietro finds someone to replace me at the deli, I can drop that job. It will give me more time with my brother, but I need to work this job. I absolutely am going to be the one paying Sandlin's medical bills. I've worked all my life and I can't imagine just sitting at home twiddling my thumbs."

"You wouldn't be doing that. Francesca could use some help with all the things she does. You're used to working on a ranch with a tremendous amount of responsibilities. That's what she's doing, trying to hold together the neighborhood and take that off of Stefano's shoulders. You have no idea what a relief it would be to have someone helping her. Organizing for her. She's been thinking about advertising for a personal assistant. It's better pay than being a server in the club. You don't even like it," he pointed out.

"I'll think about it. I don't see how the pay could be better considering the tips I make on that top tier."

"It will even out. At least talk to Francesca before you say no." He was going to be talking to Francesca first. She did need the help, but she would be too sweet and say she was doing fine even if she was drowning. He needed her cooperation to get Sasha out of the club and where he could better watch over her. And he was going to have a few things to say to Aaron.

"Emme and Eloisa will make our wedding a huge event. I'm just warning you ahead of time, Sasha." He opened the door for her and waved her through.

"Is my makeup running? I forgot to check. And we just

got engaged. I think two to five years of getting to know someone is good before marriage. Especially when contemplating marriage into a family like yours with all those secrets."

The woman didn't pull her punches. He sent her a small knowing grin. "It isn't the secrets you're dragging your feet over, it's Eloisa. And no, your makeup is fine."

She shrugged. "That could be the truth. When are you going to tell me whatever it is you can't tell me now?"

"When we're in bed and my cock is buried so deep in your body I'll know you can't escape and you have to hear me out before you make your decision." He opened the door and the music hit him. Loud. Obnoxious now. He didn't want to dance or watch her serve drinks. He wanted to go home and be in bed with her with his cock buried in her.

He tried to make it a joke, but the consequences, once he told her the family secrets, were too costly. He risked who he was. If their shadows were woven too tightly together, and he knew that had already happened, then when they were torn apart, when she rejected him and their way of life, he would no longer be able to ride the shadows. She would forget she was ever with him, but the cost to him was his ability to ride. That was essentially who he was. He would always be a shadow of a man if she left him.

She stopped right before they got to his family. They were all there, patiently waiting. He felt them before they reached them. Their love. Their loyalty. Their support. They wanted him to succeed, and if they could have made Sasha fall in love with him, they would have collectively willed her to do so.

"It's bad, isn't it?" Sasha asked.

"No, at least I don't think so, but if you can't accept my family, the cost to me is more than losing you. I'm not influencing you by telling you more than that. If you accept me and can love me in spite of the public and private life we lead, then my world is right. If you can't, Sasha,

I'd rather know before we're together and have several children."

"Several?" Her eyebrows shot up. "What exactly is several? Can two be considered several? Or is it more like . . ." She frowned at him and then looked toward the group of people waiting.

He followed her gaze and found himself laughing all over again. There was a considerable amount of Ferraros standing there. He took her hand and pulled her in close, her front pressed tightly to his side. He walked her toward his family and then, just before he reached them, pulled her toward the wall, needing to kiss her. His palm wrapped around her jaw and he turned her face up to his.

Movement was all around, except directly in front of them where his family cut off all sight from the dance floor and any paparazzi waiting to see what Giovanni had been doing with his employee in the back offices. He knew they were there, crouched like vultures, waiting to get a photograph of Sasha.

As he bent his head to hers, a man stepped into the darkness, quite close. Giovanni instinctively shifted his body just enough to shield her if he had a camera. The man walked past them, swinging his arm out. Giovanni didn't have the help of shadows, there was little light spilling near them. Pure instinct had him shoving Sasha away from him and blocking the arm coming toward them. The slice of a blade burned as he slammed a block hard enough to break bone. The man tried to run, even as he cried out in pain.

Giovanni was on him, taking him to the floor hard. His assailant's face smashed into the floor with the force of Giovanni's weight behind it. He rolled the man over and punched him hard several times in the face, breaking the nose and several teeth. It was Stefano's hand on his shoulder that stopped the killing punch to the throat.

Giovanni rolled off him and allowed Taviano to help him to his feet. "You're bleeding. He get you with that knife?" Taviano toed it without touching it.

Giovanni glanced down at his arm. "Shallow. I'll clean it. No worries." He glanced around him. "No one saw this little mess." It was a statement.

"No, he's a drunk. We'll fix him right up." Stefano turned to Emilio and his bodyguard nodded as he reached down and secured the knife. Instantly they were helping the injured man to his feet and hustling him back through the door to the office. He was gone in seconds and several men were already mopping up the blood.

# CHAPTER TWELVE

"What was that?" Sasha asked as she looked around Giovanni's house curiously. She was very nervous. Much more so than she thought she would be. "That man who attacked you and cut you with a knife."

Giovanni wasn't going to get away with pretending nothing had happened. She'd been sent back to work by Stefano. Sweetly, but still he'd given the order. By the time she had looked up from the wall where she'd been tossed, the assailant was gone and several men were wiping the floor clean.

Giovanni had come back to his table with the others several minutes later as if nothing had transpired. They were so casual and laughed so often she would have thought she'd hallucinated the entire incident, but his hands were swollen, his knuckles torn and there was a streak up his arm where the knife had sliced right through his jacket.

"That's the kind of thing that happens when you're a celebrity. People with mental illnesses fixate on you and you're not even aware of it. He had too much to drink and got a little crazy. We've been talking about putting metal detectors at the doors for some time."

His tone was casual and he waved his hand as if the entire thing was just an everyday occurrence, but she wasn't buying it. "Where is he now? I didn't see the cops arrive." There was no way to keep the suspicion from her voice and she didn't try.

"I'm not certain, Sasha," Giovanni said. "Are you hungry? I don't think you've been eating much since your stalker made his appearance. I watched you at Stefano's and I'm fairly certain you ate three bites."

"I wolfed my food down. I'm not one of those women who never eat," she declared. "I'm always willing to eat, but I would like a shower."

She desperately needed to breathe deep. She was in Giovanni Ferraro's home. It was beautiful. Not at all pretentious. It was impressive, but beautiful. She loved the way the house was shaped in a long U. One side of the U was the master bedroom, bathroom, what appeared to be a training hall or very well-equipped gym, a theatre room and a large library that she could get lost in, as well as what she was certain was a nursery. Just looking into that room made her heart start to pound, as if she was looking at her future. She'd always loved the thought of children because she knew her brother would make the best uncle in the world and her parents, wonderful grandparents. In a way, that nursery was comforting.

The kitchen, dining room and great room formed the curve of the U with two bathrooms and a large pantry. She hadn't visited the second side of the U, but she was certain it was equally as impressive. In the courtyard between the two long sides of the house was a swimming pool, an outside kitchen with a fireplace and a garden that easily could have been in a magazine. She was very glad, in spite of the money he had, Giovanni didn't have a home with thousands and thousands of square feet. She would have been lost. His home felt like it still was cozy and comfortable to her although it had every modern convenience and in terms of square footage was large.

Sasha let the water pour over her body. She was exhausted, and yet just being in Giovanni's house with him, knowing she'd be in his bed, was exhilarating. She should have waited to agree to marry him until she knew the secrets of his family, but something had tied them together.

Something unbreakable. She had no idea what it was, but those ties were strong. She wanted to be with him. She wanted to make him happy. She knew he could make her happy.

If what she felt for him had only been sexual, she could have resisted. She was strong, and she weighed things carefully as a rule. This whirlwind romance with Giovanni Ferraro was almost unbelievable to her if she examined it too closely. She wished she could talk to Sandlin. He'd always advised her when she was growing up, and his advice had always been spot-on. Still, there was a part of her that knew it wouldn't matter what he said. She was too far gone. Whatever it was that bound them together tied her so tightly to him she couldn't think straight. So yes, she was taking that chance.

When she had dried off, feeling refreshed, she wrapped a towel around herself and wandered back into the master bedroom. Her heart thudded when she saw him sitting there on the bed, a tray beside him. Suddenly she was starving. She looked around a little helplessly, not wanting to sit on the bed in a towel.

"Clothes in the drawers."

She loved the sound of his voice and the fact that he always seemed to know when she needed something. The closet held a series of drawers, and she cautiously opened the top two. Panties, bras and lingerie were stacked neatly. The top item was an apricot gown in a fabric that stretched, but wasn't more than delicate lace. She picked up the thong panties. They were made out of the same fabric, but twisted cord.

Just looking at the lingerie made her sex clench. She loved beautiful, sexy undergarments. It was the one thing she spent money on. She wore them beneath her jeans when she rode horses on the ranch. She wore them beneath her uniform when she went to work. Now, she would wear them for the man she was falling off a cliff for and who turned her on.

"So, that man, the one you took down to the floor in zero

point one seconds and who your entire family surrounded just as fast and then he was gone . . ." She glanced over her shoulder to look at his face. His expression hadn't changed at all. She stepped into the gossamer panties. They might as well have been nonexistent, but she settled the thin, rolled cord between her cheeks and reached for the short gown. "How did you manage to disarm him, take him down, beat the crap out of him and get him out of there right under the noses of the paparazzi and me?"

Sasha didn't turn around that time. She knew she wouldn't be able to read him. He would either tell the truth or he wouldn't. He'd been so fast she questioned what she saw, but the more she replayed the incident in her mind, the surer she was that something significant had happened. Giovanni Ferraro looked like a hot businessman, a playboy jet-setter, but he was far more than that. He moved too fast, was too good at fighting. He'd put that man down so fast she honestly hadn't even seen it.

"Practice."

Her heart thudded. She pulled the matching gown over her head. The stretch lace was apricot, the color barely there. It was short, falling to just below her bottom so that every step would have her bare cheeks peeking out. The material settled over her body like a glove, a sheath emphasizing rather than hiding her curves. She stared down at herself. "Um, Giovanni? There seems to be a little flaw in this gown." The material wrapped around her breasts, framing them beautifully, but there wasn't so much as a stitch over them.

"Turn around. Let me see. I approved that one myself."

"I'll just bet you did." She took a breath and turned. His eyes went dark with pure lust. The sensual lines in his face were carved deep, making him look like the epitome of sin and sex. There was no way the transparent panties were going to do much good when she went damp, slick with desire for him. It was impossible to feel anything but sexy in a gown so exquisite, one that left her breasts on display for him. Already, her nipples were tight little buds and her breasts ached.

"You look beautiful. Come eat something."

She went to him, her breasts swaying with every step, making her acutely aware of them. The moment she got close, Giovanni pulled her between his thighs and cupped her breasts, his mouth settling immediately over her left nipple, drawing it into the heat of his mouth. Fire streaked straight to her clit. More liquid heat rushed to dampen her panties. She was afraid she was going to be more than damp by the time he was finished, but she couldn't bring herself to push him away. Instead, she cradled his head to her, arching a little to give him better access.

Pleasure shot through her as his teeth raked her nipple and then he was sucking hard, his tongue and lips sliding over the other breast. She gasped when his mouth worked on her swollen, needy flesh. She wanted his fingers between her legs, but he didn't comply, even when she bucked her hips in invitation.

When he lifted his head, she wanted to yank it back to her. Nothing felt so good. Nothing. "Have you considered whether or not you want to try jewelry on your nipples for me? We talked about it, but I want you to be sure." He licked around her areola and then caught her nipple between his teeth and pulled gently.

She shook her head. "I've always wondered what it would be like."

"Sapphires, to match your eyes. Sparkling gems." His hands kneaded her breasts. "You're so responsive." He reached over and pulled a small box to him. "Would you wear this for me?" He opened the box and pulled out a chain. There was no doubt the sapphires were real. They were gorgeous gems. They dripped down from small to larger, a long, beaded row of fiery blue. Between them was a chain of platinum. The links weren't delicate, but rather a winding of strands of platinum so the chain appeared to be a vine running from one blue gem to the other.

Sasha couldn't help the little gasp of pleasure looking at it. She didn't want to think about the cost. Giovanni had bought it for her, and she loved it. She cupped her right breast. Already her heart pulsed through that soft flesh, desperate for his touch. He leaned into her again and suckled, bringing her nipple to a hard peak. He fastened the clip, watching her face.

She gasped again at the shock of the bite. He instantly had his mouth on her left breast, repeating the same ritual. Once he clamped her nipple, he went back to the first one and tightened it, again watching her face. She kept her hands under her breasts, offering him her body, trusting him to know when it was enough. The bite sent streaks of fire to her clit, as if there was a live wire running straight to her core. He tightened the second clamp and indicated for her to step back so he could look at her.

"Put your hands down, baby. Let me see."

She dropped her hands and the loss of support set her breasts swinging. The chain followed suit, as did the heavier sapphires. More fire. More liquid. This time she felt the inside of her thighs dampen. It was hot. It was sexy.

"You're so gorgeous. Look in the mirror." Giovanni indicated the wall across from the bed, the one that was mirrored from the floor to the ceiling.

Sasha turned and walked over to it. Every step she took set her breasts swaying. She'd never felt anything like it in her life. Her breasts were on fire, so was her sex. She looked . . . enticing. Sexy. Her body was flushed beneath the gossamer gown. Her hair was still piled on top of her head, leaving her shoulders bare. Nothing was really left to the imagination, yet the stretch fabric seemed to enhance her natural beauty. If nothing else, it gave her courage.

Her gaze was drawn immediately to her breasts. Giovanni's marks were all over the soft mounds. The blue of the gemstones caught the light and sparkled. The chain was loose and swung with every movement. If there had been music, she would have been tempted to dance.

"Come here and eat something, baby."

His voice. She loved the way he sounded. She tried to think about the conversation she'd planned on having with him, but the fire shooting from her nipples to her clit short-circuited her brain. It was easier to follow his instructions. She went back to the bed slowly, loving the way his gaze was glued to her body.

He patted the middle of the bed, and she crawled up. Even that was sensual, her breasts swinging as she went to all fours. The weight of the sapphires sent fire licking over her nipples and breasts. She was deliberately slow, wanting him to be as aroused as she was. The tray held strawberries and whipped cream along with cheeses and honey.

"Scoot all the way to the headboard, Sasha. It will be more comfortable." He put the tray beside her and then stood up to unbutton his shirt and remove the rest of his clothes.

She took cheese and smeared the slice with honey before eating it, all the while watching him. He was definitely every bit as aroused as she was. He moved back up the bed and nudged her legs apart. She accommodated him but it wasn't enough. He pushed her thighs much wider, caught the little panties and yanked. They hadn't been doing that much good anyway.

She took another bite of cheese. It was delicious. Really delicious. A glass of ice was on the tray and a bottle of water with the cap on it. He'd thought of everything. His hand moved up her inner thigh to settle over her entrance.

"I love that you're so ready for me."

She was. Just his touch brought more heat. He dipped a strawberry in the whipped cream, put it in his mouth and leaned over to kiss her. His chest brushed her breasts, and she gasped as fire burst through her like a roaring conflagration. Instantly the strawberry was in her mouth, and he was rubbing ice all over her breasts and around her nipples. The contrast of fire and ice bordered somewhere between pain and pleasure. Maybe both. It didn't matter. She wanted more.

Her clit pulsed and throbbed. Her sex wept and clenched.

He caught her hand and brought it down to her dripping, slick sex. "Put your fingers in. You feel that scorching heat? That's all mine." He brought her hand to his mouth and licked her fingers.

She had no idea why she found everything he did so sexy, but his every action just made her want him more. He let go of her hand and took a finger full of whipped cream and painted her with it, then pushed more inside her. He chased it with his tongue, and she couldn't help the cry of need that escaped.

He took his time, devouring her, making it impossible to do anything but push into him, desperate for more. Giovanni kept all control, refusing to do one single thing other than torment her with his fingers, his tongue and his teeth. He used the ice on her clit and then flicked her, nearly bringing her off the bed. The fire was in reverse now, rushing from her sex to her breasts. That didn't seem good enough for him. He suddenly reached up, caught the chain and pulled it to him.

Her nipples had been settling but that movement caused explosions to go off, both through her breasts and deep inside her core. Her sheath spasmed. "Giovanni!" She cried out his name, uncertain whether she wanted him to stop or go on forever.

He smiled and tugged a second time. His smile was pure sin. Pure wickedness. Her breath rushed from her lungs and her body nearly went over the edge. She was close. Tension coiled tight. She needed . . . "More."

He moved the tray, setting it on the floor, and then his fingers pushed an ice cube deep into her. She cried out, her bottom lifting off the bed, when his teeth raked her clit. He caught her waist, dragged her down the bed and flipped her over. The moment her clamped nipples hit the mattress, the weight of her body on them, a burst of fire radiated outward. He caught her hips and dragged her to her knees. Now her breasts swung free, the sapphire gems pulling, stretching. Fire poured over her skin, until every nerve ending in her body was alive.

His mouth was everywhere, his teeth, his fingers. He took full advantage of her position, claiming every inch of her as his own. She tried to impale herself on his hard cock. It was so close, at times pressed against her buttocks as he kissed his way down her spine. His hand smacked hard on her firm cheeks. Her sex spasmed. Her breasts rocked. The sapphires swung. The smacks grew harder as she bucked her hips, seeking more.

"So close. I'm so close." She sobbed it. Chanted it. "More." She just needed.

Her brain was gone and some part of her knew it, but it didn't matter. Her body was going up in flames. Then he was inside her, a brutal, shocking invasion, one she welcomed. The cry turned to another sobbing demand. "More." He had to move. He had to be as out of control as she was.

His fingers tightened on her hips and then he was driving into her, over and over. His ferocious thrusts jolted her breasts, sending them swaying and bouncing. The sapphires danced with the heavier chain, tugging and pulling, pinching the way his fingers tugged and pulled. The nerve endings on her reddened bottom sent heat flaring through her. There wasn't a place on her body that wasn't his.

"More." He was taking her to a place she hadn't known existed and she wanted to go there with him. She needed to.

One hand slid up her back, caught her around the throat and tilted her head back. That arched her back even more, increasing the fire streaking through her nipples to her core. Her body tightened around his cock.

"No. Breathe through it. It will be worth it, I promise," he said. "Don't let go yet."

She tried to breathe. His palm, curled around her throat, restricted her air somewhat. She didn't care, she loved that her head was pulled back and her breasts were on fire. It was a good fire. It was pleasure beyond her imaginings. She fought off her orgasm, concentrating on making it every bit as pleasurable for him. Thinking only of him. What he wanted. What he needed.

"So fucking hot," he whispered. "That's my girl. So beautiful."

She felt like molten lava. She hoped it felt that way to him. She tightened her inner muscles, tried to strangle him with her sheath. She could count his wild heartbeats right through his cock. He was stretching her, growing wider and longer as he pistoned into her. So deep. So much a part of her. Swelling. Pushing at her inner walls. His cock was hot steel, scorching her, branding her.

"Giovanni!" She wasn't going to be able to hold back.

"Now, baby." He smacked her buttocks again as he slammed his cock deep. Hard. Jolting her body. Her breasts jolted, too, gems tugging while the clamps pinched tighter. Heat radiated outward, seemed to encompass her entire body. She couldn't catch her breath, feeling dizzy and on fire. Then she was exploding, fragmenting, rocketing out to space. It went on and on, long vicious but luscious waves that kept her gasping and shuddering—that kept her body clamped down on his, milking every drop of his seed from him.

She eventually collapsed, and the burst of fire as her nipples dragged over the mattress triggered another massive tsunami. His cock was still hard and very sensitive. The scorching wave of liquid honey bathing him made him shudder right along with her. He collapsed over top of her, adding his weight, crushing her, but she didn't care. Her body still pulsed and throbbed, as the aftershocks shook her. She floated somewhere, maybe with the stars, they seemed to be all around her. Giovanni threaded his fingers through hers and they lay like that for a long while.

He moved first, rolling off her and gently turning her over. "Stay still, baby," he said, his fingers at the clamp on her left nipple. He took it off and pain rushed through her, a thousand needles, each one hotter than a flame. She cried out and he latched on, his mouth engulfing her, sucking gently, his tongue lashing occasionally so that deep in her core her muscles spasmed in delicious reaction. He kissed her breast, and then his fingers were on the other clamp.

Sasha held her breath. He leaned down and bit the side of her neck. "Breathe, baby."

She forced air through her lungs, and he removed the clamp. The blood surged in and a thousand matches flared against her tender nipple. His mouth took that sting, too. He spent time on her breasts, each strong pull of his mouth or flick of his tongue on her nipples sending another spasm through her sex.

"Can you sit up?"

She did so reluctantly. She was tired and sated, although his cock was still semihard. She couldn't believe he could still need more. She pushed into a sitting position.

Giovanni took ice into the palm of his hands and held it over her nipples. "Did you like the clamps?"

She had. She was fairly certain she could have come just from the clamps alone. She nodded. "They're beautiful and they make me feel sexy. I like the pinch. It feels like your fingers on me. I think I could get addicted to them."

"I like the way you respond in them, but I don't want you too sore."

"Sore can be good. It reminds me of being with you whenever I move. I like that."

His smile told her he liked that as well. "You wanted answers regarding my family, Sasha. I want to give them to you, but you're going to need an open mind. I want you to think about what I tell you before you react."

She couldn't think. She was still a little dizzy and she wanted a clear head when he talked to her about his family. The way his hands were moving on her breasts, swirling the ice around, making little patterns, and as it melted following the drips with the pads of his fingers, was distracting. Still, she didn't want him to stop. She liked looking at his erection. He was impressive, and thick. Even resting he was thick. Unbidden, she thought about taking him in her mouth. How would she make all of him fit? She wanted to be able to take all of him.

"Baby, are you going to pay attention?"

She nodded her head and pulled her gaze back up to his. He was looking at her breasts, stroking his fingers over her nipples gently, as if to take away any lingering ache. Instead, he was producing an ache. It was deep inside her core, small, but persistent. Pulsing there.

"Sometimes, there are people—criminals—who get away with their crimes. For some reason, they're able to fall through the cracks, or a jury finds them not guilty when in fact they are. Oftentimes they are powerful individuals, men or women who buy or threaten their way out of trouble. The crimes can be petty or they can be serious, anything from rape to murder. When our justice system has failed, that's where our family comes in."

His hand moved down her rib cage to drop to her thigh. She was acutely aware of the heat. His palm seemed to burn right through her skin. She needed to focus on his words, not his hands. Again, she couldn't summon up the strength to tell him not to touch her. She wanted his touch. She loved the way he stroked and caressed her skin as if she meant something to him. As if he couldn't stop any more than she could stop him.

"How would someone know to contact you, and how do you keep the police from coming after your family, if you're the ones to carry out justice when no one else will? That has to be done by illegal means." She knew it would have to be. More than just intellectually knowing, it was the blatant aura of danger and mystery surrounding his family that gave them away.

"Anyone can make an appeal for a meeting, and all meetings are conducted in person."

"That's risky, Giovanni. You could have a cop or FBI agent investigating your family."

"Ssh, baby." His hand slipped around to her inner thigh. "Let me tell you how it works and then you can give me any objections."

She nodded, since the hand caressing the inside of her thigh distracted her from being able to breathe, let alone speak.

"Eloisa takes those meetings. She, like all of those with what Francesca calls 'shadow blood,' is able to hear lies. Most of us have other gifts as well, but that one in particular is extremely important. That allows her to weed out any potential threat to us. She chats casually with a potential client. That establishes a pattern in breathing. Heartbeat. Inflections in their voice."

Her gaze jumped to his face when his finger began to make circles on her inner thigh. The circle took him very close to her now throbbing mound. Her heart seemed to beat right through her clit. He wasn't looking at her face, but at her breasts. The moment she realized where he was looking, her nipples tightened. Just that little movement sent a fresh flood of liquid to coat the walls of her sheath in anticipation.

His finger swiped across her entrance, collecting the liquid. He brought his finger to her left nipple, smeared it with her cream and leaned in to suck it off. She closed her eyes. He was so naturally sensual. Everything he did made her feel as if she was the sexiest woman in the world. He couldn't keep his hands or his gaze off her.

"I love the way you respond to me." He kissed his way up her throat to her mouth. He spent a good deal of time kissing her over and over. When he finally lifted his head, he gave her a mock glare. "You have to quit distracting me. I need to tell this to you."

"I'm not taking responsibility," she denied, but she shifted her legs, drawing them up tailor-fashion, which opened her thighs for him just in case he wanted to keep making those little circles that were driving her out of her mind.

He cleared his throat. "Eloisa is considered a 'greeter' now. Greeters can be anyone in the family born with the gift to hear lies. There are normally two greeters so that the petitioner can be heard by both. The greeters need to be in agreement about whether or not an investigation is warranted. Phillip, my father, is gone now, so she does it alone."

"That's so sad for her."

He didn't comment on that. "The greeter listens to the potential client. Once they get casual conversation out of the way, the greeter will ask the client why he or she came. After that, they remain silent. They don't encourage or discourage any part of the client's story. They don't comment one way or the other. That way, if they do miss someone from law enforcement, no one can say they did or said anything that could be construed as illegal. Once the client has finished, the greeter simply thanks them for coming and escorts them to the door."

"So even the client doesn't have a clue if your family will help." She wanted to take his hand and put it back on her thigh. Instead, she reached for the water bottle. The action had her breasts swaying. Once again, she was totally aware of every nerve ending in her body.

Her gaze dropped to his groin. He was beautiful. There was no question about it. If she could have drawn, she would have drawn him. Or sculpted him. He was that beautiful.

"That's right, they don't," he continued. "The greeter makes up the report, and if he or she thinks it's warranted, they pass the information on to the investigators. Each family has two teams of investigators. My aunt and uncle form one team, and two male cousins form the other. I have two female cousins who are hell on wheels with computers. They do all the necessary research into the crime and pass it on to the investigators."

"Why are there two teams?"

"One team works the crime, and the other learns everything they can about the client. The investigators hear lies, but they also can compel others to talk, to open up and tell them anything they want to know. They investigate quietly and with great patience. It's important we don't make mistakes. We have to know everything there is to know about both the client and the criminal. We need to know routines, where they live and work, who lives with them, who works with them. Every detail of their lives. Both teams of investigators have to agree that the criminal did in fact commit the crime and the client wasn't just trying to get back at someone they didn't like."

Sasha was fascinated with Giovanni's cock. She was listening, taking in what he said, and that was fascinating, too, but just the way he was formed made her mouth water. She really thought that she could listen while she tasted him. She was that talented. She let her hand slide up his thigh while he dipped a strawberry in whipped cream and fed it to her. Her tongue slid around his finger the way it wanted to do around his cock. His cock jerked. So receptive.

"This is where we come in. My family. We're riders. That's what you and your brother would have been had you been born in our family. Your training would have started at two. One has to start early or the tearing at the body can be deadly."

Okay, that distracted her. Her palm rested on his inner thigh, nestled close to his velvetlike balls. She could feel the heat on the back of her hand. "What would tear my body apart?"

"People like us are capable of riding the shadows. Essentially, we can move from one shadow to the other unseen. The shadows form tubes. You can see how your shadow throws out tubes, or connecters. It's very different from other people's shadows. Our shadows connect and take us inside those tubes. We can go anywhere in a city. A door can't keep us out if the shadow moves under the door. It feels almost as if . . ."

"Your body is flying apart. The pull is very strong." She said it absently, as if it came from some memory long ago. She raised her eyes to his. "When I was little, I used to feel that sensation sometimes. Sandlin told me it was the pull of the shadows. It never took me anywhere, but both of us could step into the shadows and kind of disappear. Not really, but it was very hard to see us."

Now that he had reminded her, she remembered the sensations very vividly. "It's hard to believe a person could really move from one shadow to the other and get across town, but . . ." She remembered hiding from her father once when she was little when she'd refused to eat something her mother had cooked. She knew she was in trouble, and she also knew they'd never find her if she remained very still right there in the living room with the shadow across her. When she'd first stepped into it, her body felt as if it was being pulled deep into a tunnel. If she hadn't been afraid of getting in trouble, she would have leapt away from it, but she had held still.

"We have to slide through portals, the shadow tubes, and we need to have a photographic memory. Or a damned good one, like yours. We also should have enough energy to disrupt electrical devices if need be, or cause a power surge, to turn things on or off."

She glanced at him again. "That's why you don't always worry about cameras."

He shrugged. That little movement pressed the velvet skin against the back of her hand and she turned it over so her palm cupped him. He felt amazing. She made the mistake of looking down at him. He was fully erect again, his cock pressed tightly against his stomach. She couldn't help stroking a caress over his sac. When she did, his cock reacted, jerking hard. Deep inside, she felt an answering pulsing.

He didn't protest, but he did move the tray again, shoving it up near the wall. "We wear special clothing. The cloth is made up of material that will go through the rigors of the shadow tube. When we're sent out, the investigators continue to gather evidence right up until the last minute so there is no chance of a mistake. If we're charging money, it is at that time that the client must pay us. Usually that client is very wealthy and we take a ton of money. That money is laundered through our legitimate businesses. It also pays for those who can't afford our services but need them."

She frowned, looking up, remembering how fast he'd been in taking down the man who had come at them with what she suspected was a knife. Practice, he'd said. He had a huge training room with all kinds of equipment. He knew Aaron Anderson and had trained with him. His body didn't carry an ounce of fat. When he held her close, she could feel that every muscle in his body was developed. "Giovanni, if this is all true, how exactly do you bring people to justice?"

He didn't change expression. "That depends on the crime. Sometimes it is just a matter of retrieving stolen property. Seeing that any money taken is given back. Some things that appear trivial to us are huge to someone else. Once we retrieved an item that had been in someone's family for many years. Other times, if the crime is truly great, such as murder or rape or torture, justice is served by removing the threat to others."

She pressed her hand to her stomach. She expected his answer. It even made sense on some level. She had been raised to believe in an eye for an eye, but that usually involved a brawl that ended with the two combatants sharing a drink together. She sank back against the headboard and held out her hand for the bottle of water. He seemed to know what she wanted and handed it to her.

His gaze never left her face. "Can you accept our way of life?"

"I don't know. I have to think about this." She should have expected something of the sort. His family was shrouded in mystery. She knew many people thought they were a mafia family, and it made sense. The aura of danger surrounding them was there for a reason.

"I suppose you are well versed in the art of combat."

"We're required to be proficient with any weapon as well as hand-to-hand combat in most styles. Not just proficient, we need to be excellent. We train daily. Our training starts when we're toddlers. We're also required to learn multiple languages. Riding the shadows is dangerous and it takes a toll on the body. We have to stay in shape at all times."

"You appear to drink copious amounts of liquor, but you don't really, do you?"

He shook his head. His eyes never left her face. He didn't seem to blink. He held himself so still he might have been made of stone.

She wanted to tell him she understood and of course she could accept his way of life, but what he was telling her was huge. She needed to absorb it. Really study it from every angle. If she agreed, she would be in their family, shrouded in those same secrets, apart from everyone else. Her teeth tugged at her bottom lip while she thought about what he was really telling her, all the implications.

"You kill people."

He nodded. "Yes."

"Have you killed people?"

"Yes."

She took a deep breath and another long drink of water. She needed the time to think. Of course, he'd killed people—so had his brothers and probably Emmanuelle, too. It was in the very way they held themselves. She realized there was no real surprise or outrage. It was one thing to talk abstractly about having her man kill someone, and another living with it. She had to be sure.

"What kinds of crimes would bring that sentence down on someone's head? Give me an example."

"A serial rapist. More than once we've been called in for that. A murderer. We're careful. The investigators never make a hasty decision. When the report is turned over to the rider with the approval to act, the rider still has to agree. If, after reading the report, he is uncertain, it is turned back to the investigators to be given to the other team. They start all over. If the conclusion is the same, then the rider still has to agree or the job isn't taken."

"Aside from the fact that you can move so fast from one area to the other, how do you keep from getting caught?"

"It is rare for a job to be taken in one's own city. We rarely work in Chicago. Our team investigates, and riders are called in from New York or San Francisco. We go to either city. That's where the playboy image comes in. We fly in, party like crazy, get photographs taken and splashed over the tabloids and then go home. We're the alibi. The cousins from that city party with us. No one can accuse them of being involved."

"So, if you went as the playboy to New York to party with your cousins, Stefano or one of the others would be along but unseen. He would be the one to carry out the sentence."

Giovanni nodded again. "That's correct."

"Your cousins were here to do a job."

"Exactly."

"That's pretty clever." She liked that he was so patient, allowing her to process the information he gave her. She moistened her lips and took another drink of water. Stalling. She knew she was stalling. "What did you mean by consequences if I didn't agree to being with you after you explained everything? Would you harm me?"

"Of course not. How could you think that? I'm in love with you, Sasha. I would never hurt you, nor would I ever let anyone else. Our shadows have woven together. The longer we spend with each other and the closer we get, the tighter that weave. That's what happens with shadow riders when they come together with the right person." He touched his chest. Rubbed it over his heart. "It's as if, when I saw you and heard your voice, you unlocked something in me that was locked up tight. I think that starts the process. No one really knows how it works."

She liked that concept. "That still doesn't explain what happens."

He shrugged. "If your shadow and mine are torn apart, in other words, if we were to break up, you wouldn't remember me at all. You would have no knowledge of ever being with me. I wouldn't be able to ride the shadows."

She gasped. He said it so quietly she almost didn't catch the magnitude of what he was revealing to her. He had risked everything. Who and what he was. For her. He didn't have to tell her about his family and what they did. He could have married her and let her find out gradually, but he'd promised to answer her questions and he had.

"What about all the pictures of us in the tabloids?"

"They will be there, but you won't remember. You won't care. I'll just disappear from your mind altogether."

Her heart clenched hard in her chest. Hard enough to hurt. She never wanted to forget him. Never.

Very slowly she leaned over to put the water bottle on the floor. When she did, her breasts dragged across his thighs and she hissed as the fire streaked through her.

He caught her in strong hands around her waist and pulled her over him so she was straddling his thighs. "Ride me, baby. Get yourself off."

He didn't move and she didn't care. She knew how to ride. She was very, very good at it. She caught the base of his cock and slowly engulfed him, feeling the spectacular burn of his shaft stretching her tight muscles. She began to move, taking him deep, rising and falling, slowly at first, getting a rhythm. Feeling that wonderful stretch. The heat. The fire.

At once his mouth was on her breasts, first one, then the other. Those streaks of fire raced straight to her core and she moved faster and harder. The more he worked her breasts, the more she rode his cock until she couldn't hold off. Until there was no air in her lungs and her body was screaming at her that she was going to fly apart.

He threw his head back as his cock painted her sheath with his seed, with so much fire she knew she could burn there for eternity.

"*Dio*, I didn't know a man could love a woman the way I love you." He whispered the words to her as she collapsed against him, her body still trying to milk his. Her face buried between his shoulder and neck.

"Every time you touch me, it's amazing. Really amazing, Giovanni."

"Baby, you haven't given me your answer."

She laid her head on his shoulder. "I think I just gave it to you, honey. Yes. The answer is yes. I don't go back on my word, and I said I'd marry you. I think I'll fit very nicely into your intriguing and infamous family."

# CHAPTER THIRTEEN

Giovanni lay with his body curled around Sasha, listening to her breathing. She was very quiet, almost as if she wasn't in the bed at all. He liked the feel of her against him, her silky soft, bare skin moving against his. He cupped one breast in his hand, while he stroked caresses along her hip and let his mind drift a little as he waited for the all-clear, his signal to go.

It was almost impossible to believe that she had committed to him. That she'd said yes. He'd never really believed he would find his woman—that any of them would. He nuzzled her hair, the braid she wore when she wore nothing else. She'd been—magnificent. She was wild in bed. A demanding little tigress and yet willing to do anything he asked. He knew he would be willing to try anything she wanted as well. It went both ways, but he loved the fact that his woman was adventurous in bed.

He stroked a possessive finger down the curve of her hip and let his fingers close around her breast so that her nipple pushed into his palm. There were things that he needed to consider. Aaron Anderson, for one. The man had been a friend—or at least he thought so. He didn't have many outside his family because he couldn't let people get too close. Aaron had been different, and he liked the man. He didn't like to admit his betrayal had struck deep, but it had. Usually when something hurt, he reacted with anger. He couldn't even summon up that negative emotion this time.

He closed his eyes and inhaled Sasha's scent. She had a fragrance that teased his senses and stayed with him even when she wasn't near. He knew she needed to sleep, but he wished he could talk about Aaron with her. She was thoughtful. She weighed her answers. He sighed again. Her breast moved. The smallest push against his palm. He tipped his chin so he could find the nape of her neck with his teeth. He couldn't help biting her gently.

"What's wrong?"

Her voice was drowsy. Sexy. It got to him. He had already nestled his cock between her cheeks and he felt the hot jolt right through it at the sound of her voice.

"Nothing. Go back to sleep." He wanted her awake, but he needed her asleep. Stefano would be calling him any minute.

"Don't say 'nothing.' I hate that, and you can't lie worth crap to me." She pushed her face deeper into the pillow and her bottom tighter against him. "Tell me."

He sighed. He would expect her to answer. He couldn't do less. "The things Aaron said to you really bother me, Sasha. I thought he was my friend."

"I'm sorry, honey. I think, for him, it *was* a competition. He saw me that night in the club and made his play in front of his friends. I said no. It didn't matter that all those other women were throwing themselves at him, he probably bragged, and then I was with you. That hurt his ego. His friends definitely had a lot to say on the matter."

He stiffened. "What the fuck, Sasha? His *friends* talked to you about this and you didn't think it was important enough to tell me?" He bit her shoulder. Not hard, but not gentle, either. Enough to make her yelp.

She didn't turn over, but she did lift her head to glare at him. "I don't respond well to your word choice, Giovanni."

She sounded so snippy in spite of how grave the situation might be, he felt laughter bubbling up. He tugged hard on her braid. "I don't like the fact that you have the stalker from hell and some asshole sold your picture to the tabloids. That asshole has to be Aaron, or one of his friends. It's possible, although I don't want to think it, that Aaron or one of his friends could be your stalker. So, yeah, I'm a little pissed that my woman held something back from me. Whether you were in danger or not, some asshole says crap to you, I want to know about it."

"Are you going to beat them up?" There was a little snicker in her voice.

She was laughing. He felt her body shake, causing her breast to press more tightly in his hand. Her warm bare cheeks tightened around his cock, massaging it. The action took his breath away. He was sated after so much sex. He'd been brutal the first time. She'd blown him, her mouth the best he'd ever known, and then later, he'd taken her slowly and gently before she'd drifted off to sleep. He couldn't imagine that his cock would grow hungry so soon. He was just plain addicted to her.

"Because, seriously, Giovanni, if that's okay, I'll just punch them myself when they're being an asshole. And they were. It was the one called Tom and the other one, James."

"That would be Tom Mariland and James Corlege. They run with Aaron a lot. Both are up-and-coming fighters in Aaron's weight division. They're good, but nowhere near as good as Aaron because they lack his discipline. And, just so you know, sweetheart, the only one punching and drawing blood in our family is going to be me. You can serve drinks in the club if you insist, but you can't beat up the customers. You point them out to me."

"You go ahead and think that. I'm going to punch them if they ever talk to me like that again. James first accused me of paying someone to rip my blouse so you would be gullible and play the white knight. Tom asked me if I gave you a blow job. He said girls like me snag men like you all the time with that ploy."

Giovanni was silent. He wanted to rip Tom and James in half. Instead he forced a small laugh. "If you had given me that blow job before my marriage proposal, believe me, baby, I'd have asked immediately. I'm all for being on the receiving end for the rest of my life." He nuzzled her neck to keep from swearing. "What else was said?"

"James asked me if I liked giving blow jobs, and I told him yes, with you, but didn't his woman like to give him one? Perhaps it was his hygiene." She sighed. "The thing was, he got a little too excited over the blow job issue. Both of them did. Just saying the word got the two of them aroused. It wasn't that difficult to see. It was kind of sick."

"Where were the security guards?"

"There wasn't anything really to be construed as an attack so I didn't signal for them. It just looked like that's what he was doing, being friendly and looking. I don't think Alan liked them so close, but again, they weren't doing anything, just seemingly talking to me and no one else could hear, not with the music blaring so loud. I can take their crap. It's meaningless."

"It's harassment and you shouldn't have to take it." He wanted to punch the two men and shake her. He was going to have a word with security. More, he was assigning a bodyguard to her while she worked whether she liked it or not. "You should have told me immediately."

"I'm sorry about Aaron, Giovanni. I know he meant something to you. He's jealous of you. He doesn't want to be, but he is. Truthfully, he has reason to be. You're so good-looking it hurts, and then there's all the rest of it. You have everything he wants. Money. Family. A life. I step in and out of shadows all night. You aren't reading him because you don't want to."

That was probably true. Once they'd established a friendship, Giovanni didn't want to pry. He felt it was wrong to read emotions. If Aaron wanted him to know something, he'd tell him.

His phone, sitting on the nightstand, vibrated. A color strobed for a moment, a soft green lighting the ceiling and then it was gone. He pressed a kiss to the nape of her neck again. "I've got something I have to do, Sasha. You go back to sleep."

She rolled over and looked at him from under her lashes. She looked sleepy. Sexy. All his. He forced himself to let her go and sat up on the edge of the bed. She watched him dress without saying a word. He had set out his clothes. Not his suit this time. Old jeans. An old T-shirt. A sweatshirt to pull over the tee. Disposable clothes. Gloves. He had another set of clothes and shoes packed to go with him.

She looked him over carefully, her eyes seeing too much. He wanted to kiss her for that. He loved that she was so intelligent and quick, even when she was sleepy.

"What are you up to, Giovanni? It's five o'clock in the morning."

"Got a call from Stefano. He needs my help with something." That was strictly the truth. Or maybe Giovanni needed Stefano's help. Either way, they had a lot to discuss. "Go back to sleep, baby. I'll be back soon and take you out to breakfast. Biagi's Café has the best breakfast around." He bent his head, brushed a kiss over her temple and backed away from the bed, watching her. It was difficult to leave her. He hadn't expected that. Her eyes followed him right to the door. "You'll be safe. The alarms are set and no one can get into the house. Sleep, Sasha. You're working again tonight and you need it."

She didn't answer him, but those sapphire eyes of hers kept watching. He paused in the doorway, drinking her in, his heart doing the weird stuttering he was becoming familiar with. "I never expected to find you, Sasha. Never. You're like some gift that dropped out of the sky right into my lap. I can barely comprehend that you're here, in my bed, in my world. I know you're taking a huge chance on me. I know you're scared, but you have no reason to be. I'd very much like to see your brother this afternoon. I want to talk to him about letting me marry his sister."

She half sat, forgetting to take the sheet with her. She was beautiful, with her curls escaping, wilder than ever, her full breasts and that expression on her face. Almost stunned. So pleased. He'd said the right thing.

"Go to sleep, baby," he added softly. "I'll be back soon and we'll go to breakfast with the family." He looked at her one last time. His woman. That gift that was for him alone. Then he forced himself to turn and walk out of the room, closing the door firmly behind him.

The moment Giovanni was walking down the hall and was certain Sasha couldn't overhear him, he contacted the security guards in the control room. "I'm leaving for a few. I want Sasha guarded at all times. Wake Drago if she gets up. She doesn't leave the safety of this house. Do you understand that command? She doesn't leave."

There was a small silence and then a crackle before the young man on the other end spoke. "I understand, sir."

"Stay alert, Leone. The threat to her is very real." He wanted to emphasize that so the kid would do his job. Giovanni knew he was a second cousin, a young man sent to be trained by Emilio as a bodyguard. Emilio always had the younger ones work in the control rooms while they were training as bodyguards.

"Will do, Mr. Ferraro."

Giovanni hurried down the hall to the door leading to the back of his house. His youngest brother, Taviano, waited in the car under the covered drive. He slipped in and settled against the leather. His brother immediately set the car in motion.

"She asleep?" Taviano's voice was clipped.

Giovanni glanced at him. "Not quite, but she'll settle quickly. She's too damned intelligent to get much over on. She knew I was going somewhere she might not like."

"Just how much did you decide to tell her? How much do you think Stefano tells Francesca?"

Giovanni shrugged. "I can't imagine Stefano tells Francesca much about any violence. He treats her with kid gloves and wants the world to do the same."

Taviano laughed. "He *demands* the world to do the

same. He adores that woman." He was silent a moment. "Of course, so do I. I know she's upset that she hasn't gotten pregnant. Eloisa didn't make the situation any easier."

"Stefano had a private chat with her," Giovanni volunteered. The car raced through the streets, heading toward their family home. The men usually visited their mother, not the other way around. It was only Stefano's home Eloisa ever went to, and that was just fine with the others.

Taviano looked at him, a slow smile spreading over his face. "I wish I'd been there. Stefano doesn't pull his punches when he's laying down the law in anything regarding Francesca. I'll bet Eloisa wishes she never confronted Francesca about why she couldn't get pregnant."

"Something is going on with the entire pregnancy thing. Stefano and Francesca have both been sad and upset for months." Giovanni sighed. "Eloisa is a serious drawback to our chances with the right woman, Taviano. A *serious* one. We might have all the money in the world, but none of us want to be wanted for that reason, so what the hell else do we have to offer? Our reputations are shit. We have a legacy we can't get out of. We don't want to get out of," he corrected, needing to be strictly truthful. "So, she has to live with it, no matter what. And then there's our mother."

Taviano pulled into the long drive leading to their family home. "You don't have to tell me. She's seriously screwed me, not that I already didn't do that for myself."

Giovanni regarded his brother carefully. No one had said a word to Taviano, but all of them suspected. "Nicoletta is the one, isn't she?"

Taviano parked the car and turned toward him. His face was partially in shadow, but Giovanni could make out the lines in his face, the stubble on his jaw that would make Eloisa want to scream. They all did it, just to be bastards, but right now, Taviano was hurting and Giovanni didn't much care whether or not they needled their mother.

"You can talk about it, Taviano," he encouraged. "We're all behind you."

He shook his head. "She wants no part of me. Of any of us. I fucked up bad this last time with her. I was drunk and I knew better than to be alone with her. I was so mad, seeing her with those friends of Bruno. She had no business being with them. She'd been drinking and she was . . ." He shook his head. "It was bad, and I totally fucked up. She won't look at me. She won't talk to me. There's no way to make it right, and worse, she's a fucking baby. She's barely eighteen years old. She's not even out of school yet."

Taviano rarely swore. He'd said the f-word three times. Whatever had happened between Nicoletta and him had to have been extremely bad. "Are you certain she's the one for you? Your shadows? The chest thing." Giovanni touched his own chest, right where Sasha had unlocked something deep inside him, allowing his emotions out, unchecked, the ones that told him Sasha was all his.

"I'm absolutely positive. I like sex, Gee. Correction. I *love* sex. Sometimes, sex is the only thing that gets me through a day. I'm never attached. I don't want to be attached. I like sex a certain way. My way. I'm in control and I make certain my partner knows it. I've never wanted any kind of restrictions on me. I'm rough and I like it that way. My partners always know the score and they like it that way."

Giovanni saw the problem and stayed silent. He had no advice for his brother, as much as he wanted to give it.

"Suddenly, I'm there with Stefano, facing three brutal men who raped a girl and are about to give her to the worst man they know, and it happens. In the midst of breaking necks and killing, I feel something give way in my chest. It opens, as if some lock preventing me from giving a damn about a woman is gone, and I just know that girl belongs to me. She's mine. She was born to belong to me. She's been beaten down for a good part of her life. What the fuck am I going to do with that? How do I even know how to be her man?" Taviano pressed the heel of his hand to his forehead. "This is the biggest mess."

Giovanni shook his head, knowing exactly what Taviano was talking about when he described the lock. He'd felt that same sensation and knew only the woman truly meant to be his partner could do that for him. "All I can tell you, Taviano, is that every one of us will do whatever it is we need to do in order to help you."

"Help me what? Change my personality? My needs? The way I was born?"

"It's possible dominance comes with being a rider." Giovanni had speculated on that for some time. "In different degrees, but . . ." He shrugged.

"Emmanuelle doesn't seem to need to always be the one in control." Taviano sounded as if he wished he were like his sister.

"I'm not certain exactly what's going on with Emme, but she isn't very happy."

Taviano nodded. "I agree. I tried to get her to talk to me, but she just shook her head and looked as if she might burst into tears. Fucking Eloisa probably told her she better have fifty kids like tomorrow."

It was back to Eloisa and the f-word. Taviano was really angry at their mother. "Eloisa hasn't actually talked to Nicoletta personally, has she?" Giovanni asked.

"Of course she has. She's been very vocal that she shouldn't be living with Amo and Lucia."

Giovanni wanted to swear himself. That was Eloisa, always interfering. "Maybe you need to tell her that Nicoletta is her future daughter-in-law."

Taviano shook his head. "Nicoletta isn't going to agree to that."

Giovanni stared him down. "She's yours, Tav. That means you step up and take control. You lose her to somebody that she shouldn't be with and neither of you is ever going to be happy."

"She isn't going to be happy with me if I take away her choices since she hasn't had many to make in her life. And she sure as hell won't be happy with my brand of sex."

Giovanni didn't say anything, but he knew Taviano well enough to know that if someone made a move on Nicoletta and his brother considered her his, the wrath of the demons from hell would fall on everything and everyone. Maybe it already had. Maybe that night when he'd been drinking and he'd seen Nicoletta with Bruno's friends, he'd already said or done something terrible. Taviano was certainly capable of it.

"We've got to get inside," Taviano announced. "Talking about Nicoletta or Eloisa makes me want to beat the shit out of something—or someone. I'll do the 'talking' when it's needed."

Giovanni ordinarily would do his own "talking" when someone tried to kill him, but if that's what his brother needed, well, it was the least he could do. "I hear you."

They avoided the front door, winding around toward the back end of the massive garage. Once inside, they hurried across the end concealing the small door leading to the basement. In the basement, there was a hidden door, nearly impossible to find, in the wall. They stepped inside the tiny, claustrophobic closet and punched a code into the keypad. That opened another door to another stairwell. Both men hurried down to the last measure of protection. The staircase ended in a small room. That room had one other door. Giovanni bent down, allowing the scan to move over his eye, recognize it and unlock the door.

Stefano, Vittorio, Ricco and Emme were already there with Emilio and Enzo, their cousins and head bodyguards. The man who had attacked Giovanni was seated in a chair. He had a black eye and swollen jaw. His nose was broken, but the dripping blood had ceased. His mouth was swollen and his front teeth were jagged. He looked up as Giovanni and Taviano entered. Recognizing Giovanni, he half rose, revealing that no one had bothered to tie him.

Giovanni went right over to him. Stefano handed the report to him. His cousins had done a good job of finding out about the man in the short time they had.

"Giles Newborn. Forty-eight. You're a freelance hit man."

Newborn shook his head, groaned and looked at Giovanni through his one good eye. "Part-time. Nothing permanent."

"Yeah, I can see you're not one hundred percent committed to your career. If you were, I'd most likely be dead. You're shit at your job."

Newborn glared at him, looking a little like a cyclops. Now that he was closer and the lightbulb overhead spotlighted their prisoner, Giovanni could see the massive bumps that had formed all over his face from the beating he'd taken.

"I nearly got you and the bitch."

Giovanni went very still. Newborn hadn't gotten near Sasha, but if Giovanni hadn't seen him coming, hadn't noticed the arm swinging toward him with something held tightly in the fist, and the knife had come across his body, it very well would have gone across Sasha as well. He leaned close. "The hit was on both of us? Her, too?"

Newborn shook his head. "You. I was supposed to scare her. Extra in it for me if I fucked her up a little."

The tension eased in Giovanni's gut and air slipped back into his lungs. He stepped back, handed the report to Taviano and went back to his questions. He kept his voice mild. Casual even. Not in any way threatening. "Who paid you?"

Newborn shrugged. "Don't know. I was contacted via email. Don't know how he got a hold of that."

"Must be your extraordinary reputation," Giovanni said.

The man scowled. "You're being sarcastic, but you know you almost bought it."

Giovanni shrugged. "*Almost* doesn't count in your business, Newborn. Hasn't anyone ever told you that?"

Newborn spat at Giovanni's feet.

Taviano hit him. Hard. He used blurring speed, snapping the would-be assassin's head back and planting his fist in the mess that had been his nose. Newborn's chair went over backward and the back of his head bounced on the concrete. He screamed. Wailed. Drummed the heels of his boots on the floor.

Giovanni waited, drifting over to Stefano. "Eloisa is becoming a real problem with Nicoletta. She got better for a few weeks after Phillip's death." He referred to his father. "Now she's back to interfering in everyone's lives. What's wrong with her?"

The rest of the family looked at Stefano expectantly. He shrugged. "Whoever knows what's wrong with Eloisa? If she's having a bad day, she tends to take it out on everyone around her, especially Francesca. Mariko doesn't react, so she doesn't bother, but Francesca wants to repair the damage between us all. She sees good in Eloisa and keeps trying to bring it out."

Giovanni frowned, shaking his head. "She's too kind-hearted."

"I had a talk with Eloisa. I think I scared her enough that she'll leave Francesca alone. If she doesn't, as head of the family, I'm going to take drastic action, and I told her so." Stefano clapped his hand on Giovanni's shoulder. "I like your woman. She isn't going to take shit off anyone, not even our mother." He grinned. "Of course, that means she won't off you, either."

Giovanni flipped his brother off, even as his answering grin began to form as he drifted back to the man on the floor. He loved Francesca. *Loved* her as a sister. He would give his life for her. She would never suit him. He loved Mariko the same way, but she was perfect for Ricco, not him and not Stefano. Sasha, his sassy, sweet, independent woman, would never suit either of his brothers or Taviano, but she was exactly what Giovanni needed.

He reached down and straightened the chair. He caught Newborn under his arms and lifted him easily, planting his butt in the chair. Deliberately, he paid the man no attention, wanting it to sink in that he was strong and he didn't really give a damn one way or the other about Newborn or his comfort.

"Regarding what we were talking about earlier," he said, facing Taviano and turning his back to the prisoner. "It has come to my attention that once that lock is opened"—he held his hand over his chest so his brother would know what he was referring to—"it is only opened by the perfect partner, the one holding the key. She has to be perfect in every way, or it's impossible to be the right one."

He turned back to face Newborn. "How were you paid?"

Newborn's eyes darted from man to man, as if for the first time realizing these men might not let him go. He glanced toward the door then back up at Giovanni. "He left money in a Dumpster behind a store just a few blocks from the club. If I got you, there would be more."

"When did he contact you?"

"Yesterday morning."

"What's his name?" Giovanni's shadow was connected with Newborn's, the light overhead providing really strong shadows of both men. He needed to hear the truth.

Newborn shook his head repeatedly. "I don't know. He never told me. I didn't want to know."

"How were you going to fuck up the woman?"

"I wasn't going to," Newborn said hastily.

Giovanni didn't need shadows to hear the lie. Evidently, neither did Taviano. He hit the man square in the face. Once again, the punch was so hard it sent Newborn flying backward out of the chair. The chair flew several feet away and landed upside down.

Giovanni walked around the writhing, screaming man, back to his brothers and Emme. Taviano came with him. "You want to tell Stefano what's going on?" Giovanni asked his youngest brother.

Taviano shrugged. "Pretty certain all of you know Nicoletta was supposed to be my woman."

No one looked surprised. They nodded, but Stefano just stared at his youngest brother. Nothing ever got past him. "*Was* supposed to be your woman? What the fuck does that mean? She *is* your woman. You don't have many chances as a rider to find a woman who is your partner. She was made for you. She's everything you need, Taviano. I explained how this works. You can find a woman compatible that you will feel affection over time for. That's what Salvatore was hoping would happen, but you're not capable of loving her. Not really loving her. Nicoletta is that woman you will love with everything in you, deep down in your soul. She'll own you. She'll be everything to you."

"She would have been that woman," Taviano corrected. "I would have been the man for her, but I'm not. Not with the things that happened to her. Life shaped her in ways I can't undo. I can't be any different, and neither can she." He sounded matter-of-fact, but his shadow was connected with every one of his brothers as well as Emme's. He was hurting. He was raging. His every instinct was to go get his woman.

Stefano stepped close to Taviano. "She belongs to you. You were put on this earth to see to her every need. You do your job. Whatever it is you need from her, those instincts, those desires and needs are in her. You might have to go slow and find your way, but it's your duty to her. In any case, you're going to go out of your mind the first time some man puts his hands on her. I don't want to be cleaning up dead bodies after you. Figure it out."

"Yeah, well, I pretty much blew that entire go slow and find my way thing," Taviano admitted. He glanced across the room, saw Newborn crawling toward the door. Unhurriedly, he crossed the room. "I wasn't exactly gentle with her when I took her home the other night."

He kicked Newborn in the ribs, a vicious front kick snapped out with tremendous force. Newborn howled and rolled over, holding the ribs that had been broken like twigs.

Taviano walked back to his family without missing a beat. "She doesn't want anything to do with me."

"What exactly did you do?"

Taviano shook his head. "Suffice it to say, I was drunk, furious and out of control. Not a good combination, especially when she needed sober, calm and complete control. I'm surprised she didn't try to run."

"She quit the job at the flower shop," Emmanuelle volunteered. "She got a job at Salvo's restaurant. If you take another woman out, you'd better avoid that place."

"We don't take women to our territory ever unless they're our proven partner," Stefano reminded. He glanced at Vittorio. "You're quiet."

"I guess it skipped me."

Stefano frowned. "What do you mean? Skipped you?"

"You found Francesca, Ricco found Mariko, and now Giovanni found Sasha. I should have been next, but Taviano has Nicoletta. Emmanuelle comes after him."

Emmanuelle shook her head and stepped back to distance herself from her brothers. Stefano frowned. "Taviano found Nicoletta before Ricco and Giovanni found their partners. She'll come along. Have faith."

Vittorio looked a little shocked. "I didn't think of that. I suspected Nicoletta was Taviano's, but until he confirmed it, I guess I didn't count that time."

"What did you find out about traumatic brain injuries?" Giovanni asked as he slowly made his way across the room to stand beside the moaning, rocking body. Newborn had pulled his legs up and was writhing in the fetal position.

"Sandlin has one of the best doctors in the country," Stefano said. "Sasha did her research. I contacted him and told him the family would pay for any additional therapy or resources he felt would help her brother. I also asked about other doctors and therapies here in the States as well as other countries. I'm sorry, Giovanni, he said they were doing everything that could be done. He was willing to try a couple of other noninvasive techniques, but as to his memories, they aren't coming back. As for the prognosis, the longevity of his life, that doesn't look that good, either. They want him comfortable and happy."

Giovanni had been fairly certain that was what Stefano was going to tell him. He'd done a little research and the doctor's name came up often along with headlines using the terms *leading edge*, *cutting edge*, *the best the United*

*States has to offer the world.* He sighed and planted his feet on either side of Newborn's head.

"I was afraid of that," he admitted. He looked over at his brothers and sister. Each of them nodded. He reached down and grasped the hit man's head between his hands and yanked hard, breaking the neck in the grip he'd been taught and had to perfect since he was young. All the while he looked at Stefano. "Did the doctor specify how long he thinks Sandlin has?" He dropped Newborn on the floor and stepped back, dusting off his hands.

"He didn't think long. Maybe three years, but that's best-case scenario. He has chronic subdural hematomas. They operated once already, drilling holes to relieve the pressure, hoping to curb the seizures. The leaks continued. They're slow, but even trying twice, they've been unable to repair them. He's getting worse. Eventually, it's going to kill him."

Giovanni went to the corner and began to peel off his clothes. He threw his gloves and shoes into the bag. Taviano did the same. The others weren't close enough to Newborn to get even a drop of blood on them. The two changed into the clothes they'd brought with them.

Emilio glanced at his watch. "Sal will be arriving any minute. You can get home, he'll take care of this."

They nodded and started back up the stairs. "Let's meet at Biagi's in a couple of hours. That should give us time to get ready," Stefano said.

Giovanni thought two hours would be perfect. He couldn't wait to get back to Sasha. He was silent, as was Taviano, on the way home. He didn't have the right words to say to his brother. He could feel Taviano's temper smoldering beneath the surface. He understood, because if he knew who his woman was, after waiting so long, he'd want to go after her as well. Nicoletta was eighteen and traumatized. Being with an older and very controlling man wasn't going to be easy for her—or for Taviano. His brother was right, she needed careful, gentle handling, and that wasn't in his personality.

He lifted a hand and sent Taviano a small, regretful smile as the car pulled away. When he turned around, his entire body came to life. She was there. In his home. In his bed. Waiting. Heat sang in his veins and rushed to his groin. His heart beat hard, and it felt like a rhythm of joy.

Giovanni entered the bedroom already stripping his shirt from his chest. He kicked off his shoes, his gaze on Sasha's body. She lay on her back, her full breasts on display. The sheets were tangled, and one arm was flung out toward his side of the bed. Her curls had come out of the loose braid and her hair was a mass of golden and platinum waves spread over the pillow. Her legs were sprawled out, not too wide, but wide enough to see her golden curls and a flash of pink beneath. Her face was beautiful. Her long lashes lay like two thick crescents on her cheeks. Her mouth was a bow, lips full. Her skin looked and felt like silk.

He crawled up between her legs, on his stomach, hands to her thighs, spreading her legs farther apart. He didn't wait for her to wake slowly, he put his mouth exactly where he wanted and kissed her intimately. His tongue swiped her lips and then made its way deep. Liquid honey greeted him. Sighing, he caught her hips and began to devour her.

She said his name on a gasping breath, both hands going to his head, fingers curling in his hair. He didn't stop. Didn't hesitate. He fed. He ate. He devoured. He loved her taste. He loved her response even more. Her clit was sensitive to every rake of his teeth, every hard flick of his fingers, to the laving of his tongue and the sucking of his mouth. He used his tongue and fingers ruthlessly in her, driving her up again and again so that her hips bucked helplessly and her demands grew passionate.

Her orgasm was fierce, the waves rushing over her, taking her hard so that her stomach muscles rippled and her thighs danced. He wiped his face on the inside of her thighs and moved over her, surging deep right into her orgasm so those muscles clamped tight around his cock. It felt like a silken fist, scorching hot and tight as hell, grasped him, clamped down and pumped. So slick. So perfect.

He moved in her, watching her face. Loving the look he put there. Loving the way she embraced sex with him. He bent his head to her tempting breast, sucking deep, but mindful that her nipples might be a little sore. His hands stroked over satin skin, taking her in, claiming her, while her hands moved over his body. She lifted her legs around his waist, locking her ankles and riding him hard.

He loved the way they came together. Looking down, he could see his cock sliding out of her body, slick with her honey, and then disappearing deep, her muscles grasping him so tightly he thought his brain might explode.

"Look at us, baby," he whispered. "It's a beautiful sight."

She lifted her head to look and he saw the flush of beauty on her face, the way her eyes widened and breath caught in her throat. "We are, aren't we?" Her eyes met his. "Kiss me."

"I'll taste like you." He wanted her to kiss him. He wanted to share her taste. To him, it was sexy as hell.

She lifted her face and one arm curled around his neck even as her body kept riding, kept tightening. He found her mouth. So hot. So tempting. Everything he could want. The walls of the bedroom disappeared. Sounds became ragged breathing. Hearts beating. Their bodies coming together with a hard slap of flesh on flesh. Her moans. His name on her lips. His love swelling until he knew he was going to burst with it, but he couldn't stop. He never wanted to stop. He kept alternating between kissing her, sucking her breast and rocking her with hard, deep thrusts.

"I can't stop it," she gasped against his lips.

"Then don't," he whispered into her open mouth.

Her body clamped down so hard for a moment it felt as if his cock had been seized by a vicious, scorching-hot vise and then the scalding seed in his balls blasted into her, splashing the walls of her sheath, triggering one wild orgasm after another. He closed his eyes and let her take him straight to paradise.

He collapsed over her, trying desperately to regain air in his lungs, unable to move. He had no idea how much time went by while her body clenched and spasmed around his. Each movement sent waves of euphoria rushing through him. Her hands moved over his back and down to his buttocks. He felt possession in her touch and he smiled, turning his head to claim the side of her neck. He bit down, and felt her body tighten again around his.

"That's a good way to wake up," she admitted. "I could get used to it."

"Good. I'm very addicted to your taste." He took her mouth again. "Good morning, Sasha. This is the best morning I've ever had."

"We're just getting started," she pointed out, with her slow, sexy smile.

# CHAPTER FOURTEEN

Giovanni and Sasha joined his family for breakfast at Biagi's Café, in Ferraro territory. Giovanni had never felt as much happiness as he did waking up to Sasha. She'd taken such amazing care of him, her mouth working his cock the night before, taking him to paradise. He'd wanted to return the favor in the morning, to wake her, his mouth between her legs, devouring her. Next time, he decided, he would take his time, making sure she felt love in every stroke of his tongue, his hands and his cock. He wanted every morning to be perfection. He wanted her to feel loved every minute of the day.

She kept her hand in his, even though the people around them stared as they entered the café. Imeldia, Bernardo and Leah Biagi's oldest daughter, greeted them. She showed them to the massive Ferraro table where his brothers, their wives and Emmanuelle sat waiting for them. Imeldia wove around the other tables like a pro. She'd been a waitress since her early teens and now was the hostess. She was one of the people in their territory Giovanni particularly liked.

"Melda, I'd like you to meet my fiancée, Sasha Provis," he said, as they reached the table. He brought Sasha closer to him, not because she needed the added confidence, but because he liked her close. He liked holding her hand. Or having his arm around her shoulders. He liked bringing her in close, under his shoulder, her arms tight around his waist. He just plain liked touching her, and she never seemed to mind.

Imeldia's smile brightened. She had that high-wattage smile that could charm a snake. He knew quite a few of the work crews ate breakfast in Biagi's just to see Imeldia smile at them.

"How lovely to meet you," Melda said instantly. "I've known Giovanni for years and he's always up to no good, so watch him closely," she cautioned with a wink.

Sasha smiled back. "I'll do that."

Giovanni pulled out her chair for her and waved at John and Suzette Balboni, owners of Balboni Hardware. John had taken a bullet the same time Giovanni had, when the Ferraro family had been attacked. John looked good. Fit. Giovanni knew Stefano and the others had visited him twice in the hospital and a couple of times at his home. Francesca and Emmanuelle had kept close tabs on his progress and the needs of the family while he was laid up.

"It's good to see John out," he told his brothers as he seated Sasha and dropped into the chair beside her. Close. He reached out and put one hand on her thigh. As always, she didn't flinch away from him. She rested her palm over the back of his hand.

His brothers and their women greeted Sasha. Emmanuelle just smiled. She looked tired and unhappy. So did Taviano. Giovanni squeezed Sasha's hand. He understood his brother and sister, how their lives could be lonely right in the midst of their large, loving family. "How's John doing?" he asked Emmanuelle. He knew Francesca would probably have all the information, but he wanted to engage his younger sister.

She nodded. "He's so much better. I actually think physical therapy helped him more than just recover from his injury. He and Suzette joined the gym, and they work out together. You see them together much more often. They laugh all the time. I think they both realized John could have been killed and they pay attention to their marriage more."

"It's all about sex," Vittorio announced gravely, using a wise voice. "Good sex with the perfect partner. She nearly lost him and she's all over him. He's happy again."

"Is that what it takes to make a man happy?" Emmanuelle asked.

"Yes," her brothers chorused, Giovanni included.

Emmanuelle rolled her eyes.

"Fast cars," Ricco added. "And ropes."

"Food"—Vittorio indicated the menu with the bread he was holding—"really good food."

"Good sex and good food," Emmanuelle echoed. She shook her head, but there was a ghost of a smile curving her bottom lip. "You boys."

Giovanni leaned into Sasha and put his mouth against her ear. "Nipple clamps," he whispered.

Her skin flushed a delicate rose. She tried hard to give him a quelling look, but her laughter was too close to the surface.

"*Dio*, I'm in love with you," he added, his lips brushing her earlobe deliberately. He couldn't resist temptation. He caught her lobe in his teeth and bit down just hard enough for her eyes to widen in shock and her mouth to open slightly. Her breath slipped out in a heady rush. She dug her fingers into his thigh.

Very gently, he put his hand over hers and pressed her palm into the muscle of his thigh. "Breathe," he whispered and brushed a kiss over the little sting.

A young waitress approached their table. She smiled at Ricco, looking at him as if he might be her hero. Ricco inclined his head. "Rita. I heard your studies went very well this last semester. How are you doing?"

"Great. I really appreciate the scholarship, Mr. Ferraro," she said. She glanced over her shoulder, smiling at the boy bussing the table just over from theirs. "Maso is doing awesome as well. He really likes working here, and he's gotten fast." She made a little face. "There was some breakage at first. A lot of it," she corrected with a grin, "but he's over that phase."

"Good. I hear very good things about both of you," Ricco said.

"What can I get you this morning?" she asked.

As they were giving their orders, the door opened, allowing in a swirl of cool air and two obvious detectives dressed in long, brown, almost identical trench coats. Giovanni tightened his hold on Sasha's hand. He made a small sound, one that alerted his family to the presence of the two policemen.

They fell silent as the cops approached. Both showed their IDs, although it was silly to do so as Giovanni recognized both from when they had come to Sasha's apartment. "Detectives Maverick and Bradshaw." He nodded to them. "What can we do for you? Or have you come in for breakfast? The food is the best."

Art Maverick looked from Sasha's face to Giovanni's. "How are you, Ms. Provis?"

"I'm good, thank you for asking," Sasha said. "I haven't been back to my apartment."

"I've arranged for a cleaning company to come in," Giovanni said. "I'd prefer she doesn't go back until we're certain we removed every single camera and there is no evidence whatsoever of her stalker anywhere in her home."

"You might think about changing the locks on the doors and windows as well," Jason Bradshaw advised. "Have you had any more trouble with him?"

Giovanni pressed her palm harder into his thigh. He didn't dare look at her. His family sat very silently, waiting to see how Sasha would handle her first test—lying to the police. She shook her head.

"That's odd. He was so aggressive in your apartment. The wine, the lingerie, the entire scene, using everything in your bathroom and leaving his own towels. I would have thought he would have come at you more aggressively,"

Maverick said, the frown on his face revealing he was attempting to figure out her stalker's next move.

"What can we do for you?" Stefano asked.

Both detectives immediately turned their attention to the head of the Ferraro family. "John Darby has made allegations against you. He claims you came to his home and beat him up, staged him looking at porn and released the video to every outlet imaginable."

Stefano frowned and looked first at Francesca, and then at his brothers. "John Darby?"

"He's a reality television star," Giovanni supplied. "He came to the club several nights ago and caused problems. Security threw him out."

"I wasn't even there, was I?" Stefano asked. "I don't remember dealing with him."

"He claimed you came to his house," Maverick supplied.

"While I might not be opposed to beating someone up if they deserved it, I'm not in the habit of making porn films, or whatever he is alleging I did." He sighed. "I suppose we're going to have to call Vinci. Our lawyer can deal with this. I keep hoping people will leave us alone, but they always seem to find new ways to try to get money."

"When was this supposed to have taken place?" Francesca asked, glaring at the two detectives.

Maverick gave the date, and Francesca looked outraged. "We were at the club. Celebrating. All of us. Stefano included. We danced most of the night. Drank a little too much and closed the place down. In case you're wondering, I was the one dancing with Stefano."

Mariko nodded. "We were all there."

Bradshaw glanced at Sasha. She nodded her head. "It was crazy busy that night. All the Ferraros were there. Even a couple of cousins from New York. They stayed all night. Stefano and Francesca danced nearly every dance, and when they weren't, they were at the table."

"There're cameras everywhere," Stefano said, sounding bored. "This man picked the wrong night to accuse me.

Most likely he was angry at getting thrown out of the club. I don't know what he's talking about with his little porn accusation, but I can call West, our club manager, and ask him to have all the security tapes pulled for that night. You're welcome to go through them."

Bradshaw nodded. "Thank you, Mr. Ferraro, we'd appreciate that."

"You might remind whoever this man is that falsely accusing someone is a crime as well. I have half a mind to sue the bastard."

Both detectives nodded, turned and walked away. Francesca looked at her husband. "Porn?"

Stefano shrugged. "I didn't quite understand that allegation."

"There's money to be made in making porn films," Vittorio announced.

There was silence around the table. Emmanuelle wadded up her napkin and threw it with deadly accuracy at her brother. She hit him right in the face.

"Hey. I was just stating a fact."

"A random fact. Why do we need to know that?" Emmanuelle demanded.

"It's good to be up on all the latest information," he argued. "You might find yourself down-and-out and in need of funds."

"Are you suggesting my baby sister become a porn star?" Stefano asked, a hint of true menace in his voice.

"No, I was suggesting she *produce*, fund, get behind the moviemaking industry if she's out of money."

"Do you remember what that detective accused me of doing?" Stefano asked.

"Making a porno?"

"No, beating the asshole up."

Vittorio grinned at his brother. "Francesca, he's threatening me."

"I'm going to threaten you if the subject of pornography continues at our breakfast table."

Sasha started laughing. "I think you all are a little crazy. Stefano sounds like my father, and Vittorio sounds a little like Sandlin."

"And Francesca?"

"She sounds like me." She made a face. "The difference is, she wouldn't beat Vittorio up, and I would."

Francesca burst out laughing. "There you go, Vittorio, the women are banding together to take you out."

He put both hands into the air in surrender. "I'm the good brother, remember? Why are the tables suddenly turning?"

Rita arrived with the food, expertly putting plates in front of each person, not mixing them up. Ricco looked up and smiled at her. She beamed, as if he'd given her all kinds of praise. Her smile was a little shyer as she placed a plate and a pot of tea in front of Mariko.

Mariko inclined her head. "Thanks, Rita. It looks lovely."

Giovanni smiled at the waitress. He'd heard about her from his brother. Rita and Maso's parents had been killed in a car accident. Mariko identified with Rita because she'd been an orphan with a younger brother and she'd tried to support and take care of him. He knew Sasha would identify the moment he told her Rita and Maso had lost their parents. The Biagis had taken both children in. Rita and Maso preferred to work in the café to help pay expenses. Ricco was paying for Rita's college. She was a good student and could have gone anywhere, but she preferred to stay close to her brother, who was still in high school.

When the waitress walked away, Stefano pulled out a packet of papers and handed them to Taviano, who was sitting beside him. He indicated with his chin to give them to Giovanni. "The report on many of the components from the bomb. Where each item was purchased."

Giovanni didn't like the heaviness in his brother's voice. He took the papers from Taviano and flipped them open, scanning the report. His cousins, Rigina and Rosina Greco, were amazing and invaluable on a computer. They did most of the work for the investigators that wasn't legwork or actually talking with real people. Once on a task, neither stopped until it was done. He knew they had to have worked with very little sleep.

"Who?" Sasha asked, looking up at the lines set deep in his face.

"Some of the items were purchased with a credit card that Aaron later reported stolen."

"How much later?" Vittorio asked.

His voice was strictly neutral, but it pissed Giovanni off anyway. Aaron had been his friend. "He might betray me for a chance at a woman, but he wouldn't try to kill me."

"The bomb wasn't actually set," Ricco reminded. "It was just put on your seat as a warning. Aaron served in the Army, didn't he?"

Giovanni cursed under his breath. "He wouldn't be so stupid as to use his own damn credit card. I know a lot of people think fighters don't have brains, but they're wrong. Aaron's intelligent."

"Which means he might know how to put a bomb together and take one apart," Stefano said. "You know we're going to have to pay him a visit."

When one got a "visit" from any Ferraro, it didn't end well. He glanced at his brother and handed the report back to Taviano. "I'll talk to him."

"Giovanni"—Stefano's voice was the one that no one argued with—"I know he's your friend, but it isn't wise to go visit someone who may be trying to kill you. I'll handle it."

Giovanni shook his head but refrained from arguing. What would be the point? He couldn't tell Stefano not to kill his friend, not with Sasha sitting there and others in the restaurant perhaps overhearing. He would have to plead his case later. Aaron might have betrayed him, but Giovanni didn't believe for one moment that the fighter would want him dead.

"There's more," Stefano said. "I'm sorry, Sasha, but both of you need to know. The picture sold to the tabloids came from Aaron's phone. It was sent directly from his phone. The money, however, was not put in his account."

Giovanni's gut tightened. "No way would Aaron be that stupid." But he'd taken the picture. He had to have been the one to snap the picture of Sasha in such a compromising situation. Damn the man to hell. Maybe he deserved to have Stefano unleashed on him.

Sasha's face burned but she kept her head up. Giovanni leaned down to brush a kiss over her temple. "We live in a fishbowl, baby, and what they can't get, they manufacture. All of us have had really terrible press."

"It's true," Emmanuelle said.

Of course, they'd been born to it and had learned to use the paparazzi. They'd also learned to live with the publicity their name and lifestyle generated. Sasha had no idea of the firestorms that could happen.

"I've got to go with Giovanni on this one," Vittorio said. "Aaron couldn't be that dumb. And he'd know our family would go looking for evidence. He's been around Giovanni. He knows we don't stop."

"Are Rigina and Rosina tracing the money?" Giovanni asked.

"They're trying. They'll do it. You know the two of them," Stefano assured. "It seems to be a very convoluted trail."

"No one is going to pass on that kind of money. Whoever is doing this is going to find a way for the money to ultimately get back to him," Ricco said. "The girls will find it."

Giovanni nodded. "I think Aaron needs to know all this. It isn't that hard to determine whether he's lying or not."

"That's right," Stefano said. "Ricco and I will be talking to him, not you."

"I want to be there," Giovanni insisted.

Stefano shook his head but then seemed to change his mind. "I'll give it some thought."

Giovanni knew that was the best he was going to get. If Aaron was Sasha's stalker, and he'd tried to have Giovanni killed, there was no saving him from Stefano's wrath. It was personal, and technically, Salvatore, Lucca and Geno should be handling it, and maybe that was what would happen in the end, but Giovanni doubted it.

"What have you decided to do about Eloisa?" Emmanuelle asked Stefano.

Giovanni shot her a quick smile of thanks. Sasha started to say something, but he stopped her by biting the end of her finger and shaking his head when she looked at him. She took the cue and remained silent, but he knew he would have to have that discussion with her.

Francesca's head snapped up. "What do you mean, do about her? What's Eloisa done now?" There was a distinct sigh in her voice.

"She's wreaking Eloisa-havoc on everyone," Stefano said. "Nothing to worry about, baby. We're used to it."

"It's fine if she comes down on us," Taviano corrected, "but Nicoletta's off-limits. She's a kid, and she's been through enough. I'm not going to put up with it."

"I'll talk to Nicoletta about her," Francesca offered.

"That's not the point. She talks to Lucia and Amo, trying to get them to kick Nicoletta out. That's bullshit. What if they listen to her?"

"Lucia is incapable of kicking anyone out, let alone a young girl. She'll gently tell Eloisa to mind her own business," Stefano reminded.

"That's true, but Eloisa doesn't hear or understand gentle reminders. She's going to continue, and sooner or later, Nicoletta will leave just so Lucia and Amo will have peace."

"She's going to want to leave soon anyway. She missed all that schooling, so she's being tutored, but Agnese Moretti said she's nearly finished high school and can graduate. The moment she does, she's going to want to get out of here," Giovanni pointed out. He hated upsetting Taviano further, but it had to be said. They needed to plan for it.

"That's not going to happen," Taviano said, his voice tight.

Sasha's fingers dug into Giovanni's thigh. She didn't like the idea of the powerful Ferraro family pitting themselves against a young girl and her desire to leave their territory.

"It's too dangerous for her to leave," he said. "Benito Valdez is still searching for her. He's called in favors and offered them to other gangs, to try to find her whereabouts." Giovanni wanted Sasha to know they were protecting Nicoletta, not making her a prisoner. "Valdez is president of the Demons gang out of New York. He ran the gang from a prison cell for a few years and is known for his brutality. He wants Nicoletta. He saw her and claimed her for his own. He knows she's alive and he wants her back. She's safe as long as she's here. There's no connection to us so no reason for him to look here, but if she goes outside our territory and someone sees and identifies her, he'll go after her."

"That's awful," Sasha said. "Clearly I've led a very sheltered life."

Giovanni was happy she'd led a sheltered life. On the other hand, she knew what heartache was. Sasha had confidence in herself that Nicoletta was never going to have, thanks to the brutality her step-uncles had put the young girl through.

"What are we going to do?" Mariko asked. She had a special bond with Nicoletta. "I've heard her talk about making a new start, but I didn't think she meant away from all of us."

"Don't worry." Ricco immediately ran his hand down the back of her head, his touch clearly reassuring. "She's not going to leave us."

Giovanni knew Ricco was right, but he wasn't going to do any explaining, not to Sasha. He noticed none of his brothers volunteered any information, either. It was one thing to ask the women to live with them, another for them to realize just how ruthless they could be if it was needed.

"Have you set a date yet?" Emmanuelle asked.

All eyes turned to Sasha. She squirmed under the spotlight. Giovanni brought her hand up to his mouth and bit down on her fingertips. She took a deep breath and shook her head.

"A fall wedding would be really nice," Emmanuelle ventured. "What do you think, Sasha?"

Giovanni shook his head, worried about Sandlin. Sasha would want her brother there, and after the report Stefano had shared, he was concerned her brother could go at any time. His seizures had gotten worse, and the surgeon had admitted that even if they went in to relieve the pressure on his brain, that could kill him, and the fix wasn't working.

"I was thinking earlier. In a few weeks." Before Sasha could protest, he brought her hand to his heart and pressed it there. "I planned to go by the Center today and ask Sandlin officially for Sasha's hand and maybe talk to him about the when. We'll consult with the doctors about the where because we want Sandlin with us."

He willed Sasha to understand that he wasn't pushing her. As much as he wanted to marry her, he was worried about her brother.

She smiled up at him. "Thanks for including him. I definitely want him with us."

Giovanni took a drink of his coffee and sat back, waiting for her to finish. He liked watching her eat. She didn't pick at her food or shove it around her plate. She enjoyed food the way she did everything else in her life. When she was finished he stood up and held out his hand.

Stefano glanced toward the smaller table where several bodyguards were eating. "Take Emilio and Enzo, Giovanni."

"They guard you," Giovanni protested. "I can take—"

"Emilio and Enzo," Stefano repeated, icicles dripping off his voice.

Giovanni wasn't going to argue about it; after all, the two very experienced bodyguards would be looking out for Sasha as well. She took his hand and rose. She looked up at him. "So that man, last night, was after you, not me. Was he after you because of me? Or do you have multiple enemies?"

He gave her a quelling look. She just laughed at him, and somehow that lightened his heart. He tucked her hand in the crook of his arm, and they left Biagi's with Emilio and Enzo, one in front leading the way, and one behind them. Giovanni was so used to bodyguards he didn't think anything of it. He'd grown up having them around him. He might be well-versed in the art of protecting himself, but riders were too valuable to the family and they were guarded at all times. Riders were nearly revered. The bodyguards took their jobs very seriously.

Sasha clearly was uncomfortable, but she didn't say anything. Giovanni matched his steps to Emilio's as he bent his head toward Sasha. "I probably have multiple enemies, especially now that our engagement has been announced, but yes, last night, that man attacked me. He was a hit man, hired anonymously. He didn't have much information. He was called, the arrangements made, the money provided in a Dumpster. He came to the club to kill me and, I quote, 'Fuck the woman up.' What that means, I have no idea."

"Has the world gone insane? This kind of thing didn't happen in Wyoming. The horses or cattle never got jealous or murderous." She slid into the backseat of the car, and he followed. "Well, occasionally, one did, but it was easy enough to stop them. We ate the steer that gave us trouble and worked with the horse until it behaved."

Giovanni laughed. "Well, I don't think Aaron or the hit man would like it if we ate them."

"I guess not." She sounded glum. She leaned her head against his shoulder. "I'm beginning to be afraid for you. I'd feel better if you really could disappear into the shadows." She glanced at Enzo, who was driving, and put her hand over her mouth. "Sorry."

"Emilio and Enzo are very aware of what we do as riders. They've been guarding us nearly their entire lives. Nothing is going to hurt me."

"I wish I was as certain of that as you are."

"Sandlin is extremely vulnerable," Giovanni ventured. "Right now, your stalker is angry at me because I'm fucking with his fantasy, but if he turns that anger toward you, he'll start ramping up his threats. You have one brother, one person he can get at you through."

"Sandlin is very childlike," she said, rubbing at the frown lines between her eyes. "He would take someone at face value. If they came to him and pretended to be his friend, just like before, he wouldn't question it."

Giovanni wasn't so certain. "He can still read lies when his shadow connects with someone else's. I don't think he's vulnerable that way. I don't like the fact that the Center has so many staff and volunteers. Even the security force we're using could be penetrated." He was thinking out loud, trying to figure out a way to better protect Sandlin. Even if he assigned one guard to be with him at all times, how would the guard discern between someone who wasn't supposed to be there and one of the staff?

"Other patients, too. They all share the common rooms and are encouraged to interact with one another," Sasha said. "If Sandlin was kept away from the others, he would be so sad. I don't want him to have to live like that because of me."

"It isn't because of you," Giovanni denied. "The stalker is doing this, not you and not anything you've done."

"Do you have an idea who it is?"

He sighed. "I've thought a lot about it and I just can't conceive that it would be Aaron. I think he's being set up to take the fall. Most likely the stalker thought we'd go to the cops and they'd be doing all the investigating. Aaron would be taken in for questioning, and as the evidence piled up against him, the only question would be, where's the money? He wouldn't have an answer, and they'd think he was being cagey."

"But you don't go to the cops. You handle it as a family."

He nodded. "Technically, this entire mess should be

handed over to my cousins in New York. We're too close and we don't normally take chances that anything can ever be traced back to us. If Aaron disappeared or ended up dead somehow, there's a link to us."

"Why hasn't it been handed over to your New York cousins?"

Emilio glanced back at them. Enzo looked at her in the mirror. Giovanni looked down into her too-innocent eyes. She really didn't know. "My cousins might not be as close to this as we are, but it would be personal to them as well. You're one of us. You're considered family. Sandlin is family. No one hurts our family, Sasha." He picked up her hand and kissed the ring. "They know I'm in love with you. I don't try to hide it from them. They see the way I look at you, the way you make me happy. My brothers, sisters and cousins are not going to allow anyone to take you away from me."

She sat back, her eyes on his. All that beautiful blue shining up at him. His heart did a weird stuttering thing he was beginning to recognize whenever he looked too closely at her. He definitely was attracted to her looks, but more than that, he found himself wanting to be in her company because she made him smile. She didn't have to do anything to make him happy. He just was happy because she was in his world.

Sasha glanced at the two men in the front seat. Both were facing forward again. A mischievous look slid over her face. Sexy. His cock jerked hard. "What are you up to, baby?"

She didn't answer, but undid her seat belt, letting the shoulder harness drop back out of the way. She shifted on the seat, facing him, swinging one leg over his thighs so she could straddle him. She put both arms around his neck and leaned in close to nip at his ear. "Guess what I'm wearing under my clothes?"

Her voice was a thread of sound. Barely there. Her lips brushed his earlobe, just as he'd done to her earlier. She could have called down lightning. It was the same effect. A white streak of fire raced from his ear to his cock. One hand slid up her belly to her breasts. He pressed his palm tight into her. "Not the jewelry I bought you." There was some disappointment in that. He would have done anything to pull that chain into his mouth and tug.

"No, but something else you'll like."

He tried to think what he'd purchased for her. So many sexy things. Lucia's Treasures had a spectacular collection of delicate and very sexy lingerie. Just with her straddling him, pressing tightly against his cock, he was already hard as a rock. He caught her by the nape of her neck and kissed her. Long. Slow. Commanding. She tasted like the paradise he remembered from waking her up. The more he kissed her, the more he wanted to kiss her. He wished they were alone in the car, or that there was a privacy screen.

"Tell me," he whispered.

"You have to guess."

"You're deliberately getting me worked up before we go see your brother."

She gave him her impish grin—the one that told him he had it right. "Too bad these bodyguards are here. I can think of all kinds of things we could be doing."

"You aren't safe."

"I'm safe enough." She kissed her way up his neck to his throat and then flicked her tongue in his ear.

"I'm going to retaliate. Tonight. After work. I've got a few more surprises for you. In fact, woman, I'm going to torment you until you scream for mercy," he threatened. Already his mind was spinning with ideas.

"Bring it on, baby," she whispered. "I'm more than up for the challenge." She dropped her hand between their bodies and stroked.

White lightning streaked up his spine. That fast she'd changed the entire course of the day. He'd been so upset over the thought that Aaron could be in any way responsible for Sasha's picture ending up in the tabloids, or for trying to kill him, that he'd felt almost sick. Sasha had changed everything, laughing with him, teasing him, arousing him, giving him something else to think about when he couldn't do anything about Aaron.

"I'm accepting your challenge," he said. "I'm looking forward to tonight."

"So am I." The car slowed and pulled into the circular driveway in front of the Center. Enzo parked the car, and Emilio got out and opened the door for them.

"Seat belts are worn for a reason," the bodyguard said as Sasha slid out.

Her laughter teased every one of Giovanni's senses. "I was making certain Giovanni's was on properly."

"I'll just bet you were," Emilio said.

Sasha gave him her best innocent smile, but Giovanni was sure Emilio wasn't buying it. He took her hand and walked inside, the two bodyguards following behind. Sandlin was in the common room, the one he preferred with all the books and lots of couches and chairs. There were a few other patients in the room with him.

The moment they walked in, Sandlin noticed them. His gaze jumped to his sister's face.

"Good afternoon, Sandlin. I'm Giovanni Ferraro. Do you remember me? I came the other day with your sister, Sasha." Deliberately, he stepped into the light spilling down from the overhead bulb so that his shadow was thrown across the room. Sandlin's shadow didn't reach his, but both shadows threw out tubes, so it was only a matter of time before they connected.

Sandlin regarded him with a sweet smile. "Nice to meet you." His gaze moved past Giovanni to rest on Sasha, then dropped on their linked hands. His smile faltered. "Wait. You came before."

Giovanni knew he wasn't talking about Sasha. He might not remember she was his sibling, but she came often. She spent hours with him. She read to him. He had protective instincts for her, and those hadn't been wiped out by the accident.

"That's right," Giovanni acknowledged. "I came with your sister." He stepped closer so that the two shadows merged. "I'm very much in love with her and I want to marry her. I can take care of her and protect her, but we need you to say it's all right with you. You can feel me. Feel that the things I'm saying to you are true."

Sandlin looked from Giovanni's face to Sasha's. "I want her to come and read to me." He sounded innocent. Like a child.

"Of course, I'll come and read to you. I'll always read to you," Sasha said.

A woman wearing a volunteer's jacket came in carrying a tray with cookies and hot chocolate. She offered Sandlin's bodyguard the refreshments first. He smiled at her and shook his head. Giovanni liked him. He took his job very seriously. The entire time she walked around the room, handing out the cookies and chocolate, the bodyguard watched her. It was somewhat of a relief to know Sandlin was being looked after.

Sandlin stepped closer to Giovanni. "Is she going to live with you?"

Giovanni nodded. "As my beloved wife. I'll cherish her, Sandlin."

Sasha's brother scrunched up his face as if thinking about it. "You feel scary."

He was scary. Giovanni knew he was. He was a trained assassin. A bearer of justice to those able to wiggle their way out from under the system. "Never to Sasha, or you, Sandlin. *For* you, but never *to* either of you. I'll protect you both. Sasha has an enemy. He was here the other night. He brought you your key chain with the picture of Sasha on it."

"I lost it again." Sandlin looked around the room as if he might spot it. "My friend brought it to me."

"No, no, Sandlin." Sasha was alarmed. She let go of Giovanni's hand and stepped close to her brother. "He isn't a friend. The man who was here, who gave you the key chain, he's trying to hurt us. You can't ever be alone with him again."

"I lost my key chain, Sasha," Sandlin said.

"You gave it back to Sasha," Giovanni reminded.

Sasha moved around Giovanni and took the book that was pressed tightly to Sandlin's chest. "Don't worry, Sandlin. I have your key chain. I'm keeping it safe. I'm going to read to you."

"Right now?" His face lit up.

Sasha nodded and gestured toward his favorite couch. He liked it because it was positioned directly below the row of lights and it illuminated his book no matter if all other overhead lighting was off. Sometimes, if he stayed up late reading, the staff turned off the other lights.

Sasha sat at the end of the couch as she often did and Sandlin immediately lay down, his head in her lap. He handed her the book he was reading. Giovanni glanced at the cover. It was *The Complete Works of Sherlock Holmes*. The volume was old and worn, but Sandlin held it like it was a golden treasure.

While Sasha read to him, Giovanni drifted over to the bodyguard. "I'm Giovanni Ferraro." He held out his hand.

The bodyguard's grip was firm but brief. "Nolan Rockman. How's it going?"

"My question to you?"

"It's been fairly quiet. Visitors were all confirmed. Some workmen were working on a couple of windows that were broken. They checked out, but to be sure, I kept Sandlin on the far side of the building until they were gone. He's a sweet man, Mr. Ferraro." He looked over Giovanni's shoulder at the siblings on the couch. "I can't imagine anyone trying to harm him."

Giovanni half turned to look at them, too. His heart melted every time he saw her. Enzo had stayed with the car to make certain there weren't any presents in it when they came out, but Emilio was draped against the wall, just to the right of Giovanni, trying to look less lethal and failing miserably.

It was Sandlin's expression that caught his eye as he looked at the two of them on the couch. He looked as if he was sitting in heaven surrounded by angels. His face held a light as he looked at Sasha as she read to him. Her face held a similar expression. Filled with love. Sweet, unconditional love. His woman had plenty of it to give and she did so without thinking once of the cost to herself.

The light dimmed for a brief second and seemed to sway. Sasha coughed and rubbed her eyes, but continued to read. When she did it a second time, Giovanni saw tiny bits of dust floating in the rays from the bank of overhead lights. It looked for a second as if white powder spun in the flickers. The lights shimmered, as if they'd moved, and he caught a glimpse of a thin transparent line running from the seats in the couch to the light above it.

He was moving before it really registered what was happening. Why the lights kept dimming and appeared to sway. The trip wire one identified with the military. He threw his body over Sandlin and Sasha, covering her head with his shoulders and arms, his body completely blanketing Sandlin so that his chest smashed Sasha's brother's face.

## CHAPTER FIFTEEN

The crash, as the bank of lights fell onto Giovanni's back, reverberated through the room and shook the building. He was hit so hard, for a moment he thought his back was broken. Glass shattered and fell around them, covering the couch. Shards were hot as they pierced through his clothing. The metal rod holding the bank of lights hit across his back and bounced off, rolling onto the floor. Broken plaster rained down, a cloud of it so that for a moment the room seemed white. The ceiling cracked all the way across the room and down one wall. He tried to move his bad leg, but something bit at his calf and hurt like hell.

Emilio was there immediately, pushing the metal rod aside and gently brushing glass and plaster off Giovanni's back. "Wait, don't get up," he cautioned. "You're covered in blood."

Giovanni took a moment to assess his physical condition. His back hurt, but it wasn't as if anything was broken. His calf hurt the worst. He lifted up just a bit, to ease his weight off the two under him. Immediately there was a flare of pain as if needles were poking into his back, but he knew the wounds were more superficial than anything else.

"Sandlin?" Sasha's voice trembled. "Sandlin, say something. Giovanni? What happened?"

He realized she couldn't know what had happened. He had her pinned down under him, his arms surrounding her head, his chest over her face. Poor Sandlin was in a very uncomfortable position, but he was alive. Giovanni could feel movement under his body as Sasha's brother squirmed.

"I've got to get off them before I crush them," Giovanni warned Emilio. In three minutes his entire family was going to show up, and Stefano was going to lose his mind. Emilio would get chewed out and so would Sandlin's bodyguard. He forced his body to roll off the couch but he landed on his belly. A groan was torn from his throat as pain shot up his injured leg and flashed through his back. He knew he'd been hit with the heavy metal rod. That was the pain in his back. The leg pain worried him. He'd been off work too long waiting for the damn thing to heal to have something go wrong with it.

"Giovanni." Sasha's voice soothed him. He could hear the alarm and a part of him was happy she cared enough to be worried.

Emilio's hand on his shoulder prevented him from pushing up off the floor. He couldn't see Sasha or Sandlin, but he was aware the staff was already checking on the few patients who had been in the room and hustling them out.

"You've got a large piece of glass from one of the lights in your calf," Emilio explained. "And several pieces in your back. That was an explosion," he added.

"I got that," Giovanni said, trying not to laugh at his cousin. Emilio sounded so affronted. "Just get that shit out of me, but check Sandlin first. I think I crushed him."

"You smashed my face." Sandlin crouched beside his head, leaning down to peer into his eyes. There was a trace of amusement, as if the man found the entire thing funny. "You have blood all over your back."

Sasha sat on the floor beside him, stroking caresses in his hair. There were tears running down her face. "You could have been killed. What happened?"

There was no way they could keep this to themselves. The police would already have been called by the staff. He knew the detectives assigned to Sasha's case would be coming, but Giovanni wasn't going to tell them anything he had learned—his brothers would get that information. "Baby, don't cry. I'm all right. The light structure above the couch the two of you were on fell."

"What the fuck happened, Giovanni?"

That heralded the arrival of his oldest brother. He found himself grinning. He reached for Sasha's hand, the movement sending another flash of pain through his back. "In case you were wondering, Stefano, I'm all right."

"You don't look it. Emilio, where the fuck were you?"

"That's not a very nice word," Sandlin said. "Why are you so angry? Giovanni is going to marry Sasha." He patted Giovanni's arm. "I have to go now."

Giovanni could see the man assigned to Sandlin hovering, worry etched into his face. He kept glancing at the ceiling, as if afraid the rest of it would come crashing down. That was entirely possible. "Get Sasha out of here. I don't want anything falling on her head."

"I'm not leaving you. The ceiling is fine. It has a few cracks, but it's intact," Sasha assured. "Even if the entire thing was falling, I'd be staying, so don't waste your breath."

Emilio continued to pull the shards of glass from his back. Giovanni could see that Vittorio had shown up. Taviano came striding into his line of vision. He crouched beside Stefano.

"What happened?" Stefano asked, his voice a thread of sound.

"Bastard definitely has skills when it comes to setting charges. He rigged a line between the couch and the lights and just got lucky that we were all here in one place. Sandlin's bodyguard mentioned a glass company was working on repairing windows. He kept Sandlin on the other side of the Center. The bastard has military experience, Stefano, which means, since we have his DNA, we should be able to identify him. He's an expert. That trip wire was nearly invisible. I just got one glimpse of it because the light shone just right on it," Giovanni told him.

He wanted to curse at Emilio as the man patiently removed the shards from his back. "Get the one out of my leg. It hurts like a mother."

"Stop complaining," Stefano ordered. His hand on Giovanni's shoulder and the worry in his voice belied his words. "He's waiting for the doc."

"I don't need a doctor. It's a piece of glass." Giovanni wanted to sit up. He felt vulnerable lying on the floor facedown. It helped that his brothers had arrived. He could hear Ricco talking to some of the staff, gathering information. "Did the bodyguard go with Sandlin?"

"He's safe, in his room. The guard is in with him," Stefano assured.

"Check out Sasha. Make sure she wasn't hit by any of the glass," Giovanni ordered.

"I'm fine. You had me completely covered," Sasha assured.

"Cops are here. Bradshaw and Maverick," Taviano whispered. "Emmanuelle is giving them quite a performance, wringing her hands and looking as if she's going to burst into tears any moment. They're both occupied with reassuring her the world isn't coming to an end."

"Anything else you can tell us?" Stefano asked Giovanni.

"He's clever, methodical and an expert in explosives. He has military training. He isn't afraid to take chances and he knows how to blend in. He set those charges to blow exactly the direction he wanted them to. He scouted this room and knew this couch was always in poor lighting and the overheads had to be on and it has a lamp if the overheads are off."

"As long as I've been coming here," Sasha added, her voice pitched low to match Giovanni's, "no other patient used this couch because of the way it's always darker in this corner. Sandlin likes it because he thinks of it as his."

"So, he somehow got that information out of someone on staff or a volunteer. He knows how to manipulate people," Stefano murmured. "We're dealing with a professional, not some shmuck off the streets."

"Mr. Ferraro." Detective Maverick announced his arrival. "Is your brother all right?"

"I'm alive," Giovanni said. "But a little worse for wear."

"Ms. Provis? You and your brother okay?"

Sasha's fingers tightened in Giovanni's. She inched a little closer to him as if she could protect him. He liked that. The detective represented conventional authority, and ordinarily, his family would have welcomed the investigation and helped it along as best they could. Sasha's attacker had attacked someone they considered a family member, and that meant it was family business. She was already thinking along those lines.

"We're fine thanks to Giovanni. He shielded both of us."

"That's what the witnesses said. We'd like you and your brother to give us your accounts."

There was something in the detective's voice that bothered Giovanni. He detested not being able to turn over and see the man's face. He was at a distinct disadvantage, but he was surrounded by family.

"My brother is back in his room and has a bodyguard. He has a brain injury that prevents him from being able to answer your questions, Detective," Sasha said. "His doctor will confirm that. I'm very concerned that my stalker is out to kill my brother, and I don't understand why you haven't gotten any closer to finding him."

Giovanni could have kissed her. He squeezed her hand in an effort to try to tell her he was proud of her.

"Giovanni, we're going to remove the shard in your calf," Emilio said. "The doc is here. We can try to numb it."

"Just take the fucking thing out," Giovanni snapped. He was done with lying on his belly while dust settled around them and the cops questioned everyone.

"What happened?" Maverick asked.

"You can't wait until the doctor finishes with him?" Sasha sounded outraged. "Seriously, Detective. Someone rigged the light fixture to blow while I was reading to my brother. I don't know if his intention was to kill us or injure us or just plain scare us. My brother is fragile as are the other patients here." Her voice wobbled.

Giovanni realized she was close to breaking down. "Baby, I'm right here. Sandlin's okay and so am I." He didn't want her to cry, not without him able to hold her and shield her from the two detectives. They were good men. He knew they were and they were just doing their jobs, but they didn't like the Ferraros. They believed the family was involved in criminal activities rivaling their enemy, the Saldi family. Neither detective wanted a war between the two powerful families in their city.

"I'm sorry, Ms. Provis," Maverick said immediately. "If the doctor says your brother can't talk to us, of course we'll leave him alone. We do need Mr. Ferraro's account."

"My account. *Fuck*, what the hell are you doing, Doc?" He was much more dramatic than needed.

Sasha fell for it, her little gasp and the way she hitched closer to him, her hands in his hair, was gratifying. "Be careful," she hissed to the doctor.

Giovanni wanted to pull her into his arms. She was protective of him, but he knew she was sliding close to the edge of a cliff. So much fear and trauma could send one cascading over. She had lost her parents and the brother she knew forever. She was clinging hard to Sandlin, even though the doctors had cautioned her that his life expectancy wasn't long. To have him menaced in any way, to have a persistent stalker threatening her brother's life, was too much. Anyone was bound to crumble, even for a few moments.

"Hurry up, Doc, just get it out," Giovanni said. He gripped Sasha's hand. "I'm good, baby. Really." He glanced up at the detective. "I can't tell you very much. Sasha was reading to Sandlin. I was talking to Nolan Rockman, Sandlin's bodyguard. He told me about the broken windows and that the repairmen had checked out, but he still kept Sandlin on the other side of the Center until they were gone. I think he was saying something about how childlike or innocent Sandlin was, and I turned to look at him with Sasha. I noticed the plaster swirling around in the rays of light shining down. At first it didn't register and then I just dove to cover them."

He stayed as close to the truth and what he knew Rockman would tell the detective. He could give a word-for-word account of what was said, but witnesses usually couldn't do that. He also had incredible speed, which Rockman would probably mention, but he was deliberately vague in his own account, not mentioning distance or how he'd gotten there in time.

"You really could use a couple of stitches," the doctor announced.

"Just use glue or whatever you do now," Giovanni said. He was done being at a disadvantage and growing impatient with all the questions.

"We need everyone out of this room." Goodman was there, worried the rest of the roof would cave in and his Center would be liable. "Please go into the other room."

"Doc." Stefano ignored everyone. He was a law unto himself and it showed in everything about him. "Put in the stitches right here. It's the only chance you're going to get. You don't do it, it won't get done."

"Infection could set in," the doctor warned. "I have everything I need with me." He was already setting up a small tray to get it done. "But I'm warning you, with all the dust in here, this could get septic."

"You say that every time you have to sew one of us," Giovanni griped.

"That's because I find you in the worst circumstances."

It took forever to get out of there. Giovanni had to answer more unnecessary questions, as did Rockman and Sasha. Several staff members and the volunteer who had served chocolate and cookies were detained for more questions. Giovanni repeatedly told the detectives no one saw or heard anything because the others hadn't. Rockman was upset with himself, but really, he couldn't have done much, either. Their enemy was a man who was cunning and bold. He was also very well trained.

Sasha insisted on going to work. Goodman had made noises about removing Sandlin from his Center, and she panicked. Giovanni made the mistake of telling her it was a ploy often used to get more money. She was associated with the Ferraro family. No one minded price gouging them, so of course Goodman would expect them to pay to keep Sandlin there. It wouldn't occur to him that Sasha was paying the bill herself after their engagement.

In the end, even Stefano stopped arguing with her when Giovanni gave a slight shake of his head. She was becoming more and more agitated. There was no way to resolve the situation. The Ferraros would negotiate terms with Goodman without Sasha and then they'd continue to look for better places and other doctors. They had the means and they'd use whatever it took to give Sandlin the best care possible.

Giovanni knew Sasha loved her brother and she would put aside pride in order to make certain he got the best care. Right now, she was feeling raw and possessive and definitely protective. He knew she needed space and he was going to give her whatever was necessary to make her feel in control. If that meant she needed to go to work, to be in her normal routine, then it wasn't a big deal to sit at a table all night and watch her. Of course, he was doubling the guards, and she would have one of the experienced ones moving around with her, that was nonnegotiable.

Giovanni hadn't counted on how tired he was, or how much a petty thing like a few stitches in his calf was going to hurt. He felt like a whiny baby, although he hadn't complained, nor had he taken pain pills. He did, however, have a shot of whiskey halfway through the night. He told himself it had everything to do with pain and not with the fact that Aaron Anderson had come in with an even larger number of his friends than before.

Mixed martial arts fighters trained all the time. They didn't frequent nightclubs, and they didn't pay for the top tier of a club like the Ferraros'. That table cost Aaron thousands of dollars. He was normally a man very careful with his money, but all of sudden, he was spending cash as if he had it to throw away, and judging from the cash tips at the table and the amount he would add in to his tab at the end of the night, he was doing it to show off for Sasha.

He didn't want his woman anywhere near Aaron, just in case, and he'd tried to get Sasha to change tiers with Nancy, but she was so damned stubborn he wanted to shake her. He found himself glaring at her as she served drinks to Aaron's table. He wanted Aaron banned from the club, but he had no real reason; the investigators hadn't handed in their final reports. Yes, he had military training. Yes, he was capable of setting charges, but then so were a number of the men at his table and the two cameramen who were giving the Ferraros trouble.

Giovanni realized why the rules were in place regarding bringing in other riders to serve justice close to home, especially if it was personal. He wanted to break a few necks, do whatever it took to keep his woman safe. He thought cavemen had it right, throw his woman over his shoulder and carry her off where no danger could get to her, but he lived in modern times and his woman believed in carrying her own weight.

The thing was, and he couldn't find the right words to tell her, she was a miracle to him. Everything to him. His world, the way Francesca was Stefano's world and Mariko was Ricco's. They'd been raised to believe having children was their duty and they had to find the right women to give them shadow riders for babies, but in the end, when they found the right women, it wasn't about that at all.

He knew Stefano wanted children with Francesca, but not because they would be shadow riders. He also knew, if Francesca couldn't have children, Stefano would never give her up and never go to another woman to provide those children. Ricco felt exactly the same about Mariko. Giovanni knew, because more than once Ricco had told him if Mariko chose not to have children, he wouldn't push her, no matter what Eloisa or the council said. Fortunately, Mariko wanted children. Giovanni knew he should have that conversation with Sasha, but it didn't matter to him anymore. He wanted children with her, but not if she was unhappy.

He watched Sasha go up to Aaron's table. Instantly all attention was on her. Aaron spoke at great length to her. Tom Mariland was there, along with James Corlege. Both men looked as if they were apologizing to her. She gave them a small nod and brief smile. Giovanni knew her now, and that smile was in no way genuine.

He willed her to look up at him, but she didn't. She was withdrawing, pulling in to protect herself. He couldn't blame her. She had to be scared. She didn't understand what was happening or why. Her stalker hadn't made demands. The threats to Sandlin were very real, and her brother's health was fragile. If the heavy rod had come down on his head, it could have easily killed him.

Taviano and Vittorio had come with him in an effort to help protect Sasha. He was grateful to them. Taviano was distracted and danced more than usual. Vittorio seemed more introspective, as if he had something on his mind but wasn't sharing. Each time Giovanni thought he would try to pry it out of his brother, either Taviano returned to the table or Sasha was serving a table full of rowdy celebrities.

The paparazzi was present in full force. To his dismay, the two cameramen he'd hoped wouldn't be allowed back were there as well. Apparently, the deal made with them when their film was taken was that they could return in a couple of days. Chesney Reynolds was a man who was extremely aggressive at getting his shots. In spite of the fact that the Ferraros were considered cooperative and usually worked well with the photographers, he still tried to jump out at them and followed them relentlessly. Instead of being of use to them, the man was a constant threat to them.

He was more surprised at Sid Larsen. He was, as a rule, extremely cooperative. At the time the shots had been taken, Sasha was a cocktail waitress at the Ferraro Club; otherwise, she wasn't affiliated with them in any way. Larsen had had no way of knowing that Giovanni would ask her to marry him. Why had he been so adamant about keeping his photographs of a waitress when giving them up meant a shitload of money and a favor owed by the Ferraro family? He'd added both photographers to the list of suspects, and their investigators were working to uncover everything they could about both men.

Giovanni couldn't stop himself from looking toward Aaron's table again. There was a part of him that wanted to walk up to the man he'd called his friend and smash him right in the face. He didn't like the fact that Aaron had lied to Sasha. He'd sparred with Aaron to help him out. He'd never competed with him for a woman. He didn't do that kind of thing. He was already ashamed of the stupid game he'd thought up to play with his family to get back at the women so blatantly trying to use them, but that wasn't competing for the same woman. That wasn't making a woman feel special or trying to take her away from a friend or brother and then dropping her. The idea turned his stomach.

Gritting his teeth, he turned his head toward the sudden, overpowering scent of roses. Meredith Benson, a powerful actress who had won her share of awards, stood far too close. She'd made a million overtures toward him. He'd made one very bad mistake a few months earlier. He'd been in Los Angeles and had been angry with Stefano for insisting he play the role of playboy yet again. The doctors had made it clear he was sidelined for at least six more months. He'd drank too much. He'd known Meredith was a predator, just like he was, and he'd spent the night with her.

He forced a smile. "Meredith. Good to see you." He was already feeling as guilty as hell, he didn't need Meredith making him feel worse. She was a shark, a woman who enjoyed men and got off on dumping them as publicly as possible. She liked her reputation as a femme fatale, and she wanted as much publicity as possible.

Meredith was the kind of woman who constantly schemed to use the paparazzi, just as his family did. He could respect her for that. He respected her business sense, but she didn't have one-night stands, she developed relationships with men. Those relationships sometimes lasted as long as six months. That, Giovanni didn't like or agree with. Inevitably, she dumped a man who cared about her and it often shattered her partner. Once, a few years back, one man had committed suicide. She'd gotten a lot of publicity out of that, playing the part of the regretful, mourning young woman. Even then, Giovanni had known her emotions weren't real.

She put her hand very possessively on the nape of his neck, her fingers dancing a seductive massage. "I was told you'd be here tonight. I'm so glad my sources were right. Come dance with me, Giovanni. I want to hear all about your engagement."

"Take a seat. I can tell you right here." He patted the chair next to him, the one Taviano had vacated to take the dance floor.

Meredith smirked a little, using the expression she was so famous for. Half seduction and all secrecy, she wiggled until her tight dress slid up her thighs as she sank into the seat. "I couldn't believe it when I heard. I kept expecting you to call me right up until I realized our little tryst meant nothing to you."

"It didn't mean a damn thing to you, either, Meredith, so don't pretend it did."

Her smile stayed intact, but her face got hard. "There's a right way and a wrong way to end things, Giovanni. You're a big boy, you know that, and you knew it going into it."

"I drank too much and we hooked up. It wasn't a long-term affair and you knew that going into it. That's why you took advantage."

She tilted her chin and then put her elbow on the table and her chin into the heel of her palm so she could smirk at him. "How so?"

"I didn't like the publicity you got out of it."

Her eyes widened and one hand went defensively to her throat. "Did you think I arranged for those photographers to be at my gate at that hour? They're always there."

He rolled his eyes. "You aren't playing with someone who's wet behind the ears, Meredith. I was born in the game. It wasn't that hard to bribe one of them to tell me how they all came to be there. You had them called. It was a great shot, the two of us kissing, you in a short robe, nothing else and me still buttoning my shirt."

"Compromising," she said.

She almost purred the word, and just the way she said it bothered him. He knew she was someone who knew the score. She went through men the way others went through candy, of course she was always the one caught cheating, not her partner. He didn't think she felt very much in the way of emotions. In fact, he didn't think Meredith was capable of true feeling.

No one had ever thrown her over. She had tried calling him dozens of times. She'd issued even more invitations. He'd stuck to the ways of his family, seeing a woman just once. That way there could be no emotional ties. Her ego hadn't allowed her to drop it.

"I had no idea they were going to be there or I'd have been more discreet," he said.

"Dance with me and make up for it. I'm sure your little waitress won't mind."

"Don't call her that." He sounded harsher than he intended and glanced toward Sasha. She was back at the bar talking to Alan the bartender and not looking his way. He would have felt better if he could have caught her eye, maybe introduced Meredith to her. "Her name is Sasha."

"I'm sorry, Giovanni. I don't want us to be awkward when we meet. I value your friendship, and I'm trying to do damage control, but I seem to be failing miserably. Is she the jealous type? Should I just go? Aren't you allowed women friends?"

*Dio*, he detested this bullshit. He glanced up at Vittorio. So far, his brother had been silent. Vittorio had never cared for Meredith. Vittorio shrugged. He didn't know what to do, either.

Giovanni rose, trying not to feel the way his stomach lurched. His calf hurt like a son of a bitch in spite of the whiskey, but he could take it for one lousy dance. A part of him was certain Meredith was playing him again. She couldn't possibly have been hurt that he hadn't called her, but there was that tiny little bit of doubt. "Of course, I'll dance with you, Meredith." He held out his hand. "Sasha definitely isn't the jealous type." He hoped Vittorio got the message and would apprise Sasha of what was happening.

Meredith beamed at him. She took his hand and, as they moved around the tables to the top of the stairs, she slid right under his shoulder, her arm curving around his waist. She was tall with long legs that went on forever—she looked good and knew it. She leaned into him, pressing her lips against his ear so she could be heard above the loud music. He inclined his head just enough to let her so he could catch what she was saying.

"I'd really like to meet her. Your Sasha must be very special."

He smiled, because hell yes, Sasha was special. He had to turn his head to press his lips against her ear so she could hear as they continued down the stairs. "I'd like for you to meet her. She'll be on a break in a few minutes. You'll have to come back to the table with me and meet her." He didn't want to give up one minute of his time alone with Sasha, especially now, when he knew she was upset over her brother, but keeping Meredith from trying to sink her teeth into his woman was wise. Giving up a few more minutes wouldn't kill him.

The music was slow, so he swung her into his arms. Every Ferraro knew how to dance. That was one of the thousands of requirements put on them from the time they were very young. He was good at it, although Vittorio was the best. Still, Giovanni could make his partner float across the floor in perfect sync with him.

He realized, as he pulled her in close, that he didn't like her body sliding over his. That was for Sasha. Only his woman. He kept his frame perfect, but Meredith's body melded to his and she kept looking up at him, smiling into his face with a look of near adoration. That made him uncomfortable.

"I'm very much in love with Sasha," he felt compelled to say.

"What?" She went up on tiptoe, in spite of her height and heels. Her arms slid around his neck and she leaned her body right into his. "I couldn't hear you." Her lips were against his neck, close to his ear.

He turned his head toward hers. "I'm very much in love with Sasha." He proclaimed it a second time, wanting her to understand.

His mouth was a breath away from hers and she pressed her red lips to his, holding his neck like a boa constrictor, giving the performance of her life as she kissed him. Flashes went off from every direction. He caught both arms and dragged her away from him as he jerked his head back, his heart sinking. He'd underestimated Meredith once again.

She smirked at him. "Now, we're even. You're going to

be all over the tabloids as a two-timing asshole, Giovanni, and you deserve it."

Everything in him stilled. "Did you once think how Sasha might feel?"

"Who gives a damn? She's going to have to get used to seeing you in the tabloids accused of screwing everything in skirts that comes near you. Fuck her. You didn't think how I might feel when the tabloids speculated that you dumped me."

He regarded her for a long time, and something in his expression wiped the smirk from her face. "The problem you have right now, Meredith, is that I won't forgive a hurt to my woman. Me? Yeah. That's part of the game, but you knew before you did this that you were going to hurt her and you didn't give a damn. Money talks. It always has. It doesn't matter how big a star you are, your career can be ended in a heartbeat." He snapped his fingers. "Consider that the heartbeat."

He turned to walk away, wiping his lips with the back of his hand, despising her. Despising all the women like her. They were ruthless and greedy and willing to hurt innocents to get what they wanted. Sasha had enough to contend with without having to deal with what was going to be in the papers the next morning. There was no way to stop it. Even Meredith couldn't stop it now. She'd set the paparazzi on him and even made certain to bring in Reynolds and Larsen. Both would be more than happy to take on the Ferraros.

Cursing, he took the stairs two at a time, ignoring Meredith's frantic call after him. Already, he had his phone out and was texting their Hollywood contacts. All of them. Every producer the family knew and all those they didn't have relationships with. Money talked. He had tons of it, and Meredith was going to be hit where it hurt. No producer was going to get behind her films. He would make certain if she was being considered for a part, he would take it away from her. Had she kept her revenge to him, he wouldn't have done a thing, but she knew better than to fuck with his woman. The Ferraros had a certain reputation. She thought herself out of reach.

Sasha stood at the top of the stairs, waiting. She'd seen the kiss. The flashes. Meredith's arms entwined around his neck. He could tell by the look on her face. Flashes continued to go off. Several photographers tried to follow him. He didn't know why since they all had zoom lenses, and they had to know security was going to stop them. He ignored that little byplay, too, his eyes on Sasha's, willing her to keep looking at him and nowhere else.

He held out his hand. She stared at it a beat too long, and his heart clenched so hard in his chest he feared he might be having a heart attack. He kept his hand out, waiting. With great reluctance, she put her smaller one in his. He closed his fingers around hers and pulled her to him as they moved together back to his table.

He pulled out a chair for her and then sank down into the one closest, dragging her chair right up to his, arms caging her in just in case she tried to escape him. "That woman . . ."

"A former lover?"

The words bit deep. Fuck. Fuck. What the hell could he say but the truth? "It was a fuckin' one-night stand. Stupid of me hooking up with a shark, but I was having a pity party because the doc told me at least six more months on playboy duty and I hated it."

"So, fucking Meredith Benson, the hottest actress in Hollywood right now, was part of your little pity party."

He raked his fingers through his hair. The hurt in her voice nearly destroyed him. He didn't want to see himself through her eyes. He looked bad. Maybe he was. Hell, he didn't even know anymore. It all came back to that game that never seemed to go away. "Baby, I know that hurt, to see that on the dance floor—"

"*That?* You mean you kissing another woman? Not just kissing her, but your tongue down her throat?"

He shook his head. “My tongue was nowhere near her throat. She kissed me, Sasha. For revenge. Because Meredith likes to dump her lovers publicly for the publicity. She craves the camera and the drama. She thrives on it. This was all about revenge. She set me up with the paparazzi, and like an idiot, I fell for it. I’m sorry. I know this is going to be a firestorm and every time you go into a grocery store or see a magazine, or watch television, it’s going to be in your face, but you have to know, I wasn’t a party to that.”

“Giovanni.” She sounded tired, and his gut tightened in alarm. “Your world is so far removed from mine. These games you all play so casually are beyond me. I don’t understand them, and quite frankly I don’t want to. Maybe you weren’t kissing her back. Maybe that dance with your bodies all over each other didn’t mean anything to you, but it did to me. I suppose if I was a woman in your world, I’d just grab Aaron and dance with him like that. Kiss him like that and smile for the cameras. It isn’t my world no matter how much I want to fit in for you.”

“Don’t. Baby, don’t do this. You’re tired and scared and I understand that. I do. But you know damn well I didn’t betray you. I’ve had a lot of one-night stands. I can’t pretend I didn’t. Hell, I think they’re all pretty much documented. You hear lies. Am I lying when I tell you I love you and I’m not capable of being unfaithful? I’m not. I told you about my life. I need you, Sasha. You think your brother needs you, and he does, but not like I do. Not in the same way. I’ve never had one fucking thing for myself. I’ve done my duty and played my part for the family. You’re everything to me. Don’t let a vindictive, petty woman rip us apart.”

He hated the tears turning that beautiful sapphire to liquid. He caught her chin and leaned in to brush her mouth with his.

She jerked back. “You still have her lipstick on your mouth, Giovanni.”

The accusation was harsh, but he wasn’t about to let that

stop him. "Wipe it the fuck off, Sasha. Right now. Use the water in the glass if you have to, but get her off me."

Sasha responded to the command in his voice. She dipped a napkin into the water and rubbed off Meredith's lipstick. He despised the woman all the more. Leaving the evidence behind had obviously been part of her plan. He'd tried to wipe it off, but apparently, she'd made certain it was smeared everywhere.

"Thank you. I want you to take a deep breath and really look at me, Sasha. I could never give you up. I don't care what the circumstances were, I couldn't. If you were dancing with Aaron and he kissed you, I might go to jail for beating the holy hell out of him, but you, you I love, I wouldn't touch you, nor would I break up with you. I'd try to figure out what I wasn't giving you that you needed. Meredith Benson was looking to fuck me up with you. Don't let her succeed."

Sasha hung her head, shaking it. "I have to step back, catch my breath and figure out what I'm doing. I need Sandlin safe, but I also need to think about us realistically. I can't do that when I'm with you. I can't do that with people around us every second. I want to go back to my apartment by myself and really have time to think."

He shook his head. "It isn't safe and you know it."

"Then make it safe. Surround the place with a million guards. You have to give this to me, Giovanni. I need to figure out what I'm doing. If you can't give this to me, I'm going to say we're done, because right now, I can't get rid of the image of you and that woman kissing on the dance floor with all those cameras going off. It's burned into my mind for all time." She held up her hand when he would have protested. "It doesn't matter that it was all about revenge. It's your world. It's how you live. She represents a good many of the people populating your world. I need space, and I'm asking for it."

He knew he had no choice. The only play he had left was to comply. That gave him a night to fuck up Meredith's life even more than she could ever conceive of him doing. What was the use of having billions of dollars at one's disposal if they couldn't ruin an enemy? He hated that Meredith had hurt Sasha, especially on the heels of someone trying to kill her brother. He brought her hand to his mouth, kissed her knuckles and conceded with a nod.

## CHAPTER SIXTEEN

The problem with pity parties and crying one's eyes out, Sasha decided, wasn't the red, puffy face or the swollen eyes. It was the headache. She didn't get headaches as a rule and tended to be a baby when she got one. She took a couple of over-the-counter pills that did nothing for it and lay down with every curtain pulled. She'd pulled them to keep out anyone like a nasty stalker who probably was lying in wait with binoculars. She wasn't giving him or anyone else a show.

The paparazzi could be out there, too, hoping to catch her reaction to Meredith Benson kissing her man so they could put it in front of the world. She didn't like crying in front of anyone and she wasn't going to do it where her picture could be taken for display on a rack in a grocery store.

Still, she was too restless to lie down. She was up and pacing through the small apartment, making a slow circuit, trying not to think about anything because her head was so crowded with everything that had been happening she couldn't think straight. After an hour of a wild storm of weeping, fifteen minutes of trying to sleep and another fifteen of pacing, she threw herself into a chair and tried to sort through things the way she always did—she made a list.

Compiling problems was ridiculous, but the way her mind worked, she needed to see them, figure out the most pressing and how best to handle it. Number one always, *always*, was her brother. His care and safety. The Hendrick Center was the best that she could find, and the surgeon was renowned. She wanted Sandlin to stay there. The moment Goodman had made noises about removing him for the safety of the other patients, she'd panicked and couldn't hear much after that.

Granted, she'd wanted to break down and cry right then. It had been such a relief to have Giovanni and Stefano talk to Goodman in their calm, quiet voices. She could listen to those voices all day. They sounded reassuring and safe. As long as Giovanni was around, she felt Sandlin was safe. He had provided the extra security and the bodyguard. Her stalker had still gotten in—and she was certain he had been the one to rig the explosives, although Giovanni had pointed out to Goodman that they didn't know that for certain yet.

She had checked out of the conversation for a few minutes, but now, thinking it over, she knew they had quietly offered him more money for Sandlin's care. For the extra trouble of security and bodyguards. For more background checks. In return for allowing her brother to stay there, they had been willing to add another desperately needed wing onto the Center and to fund the equipment for that wing as well.

Her breath caught in her throat. She hadn't been paying attention. She'd stood by the window in that stuffy little office, shaking, terrified she'd have to remove her brother, and all the while, Giovanni had been negotiating on her behalf. He'd taken care of it without hesitating. He hadn't asked permission from his family, nor had Stefano balked, treating her as if she'd been born into the Ferraro family solely because she was engaged to Giovanni.

A small groan escaped. She'd been so prideful, insisting she take care of Sandlin herself. She couldn't afford extra security for him. It wasn't Giovanni's fault that someone was stalking her, and he certainly didn't have to continually provide her with protection or pay for her brother's protection—yet he did. She wasn't even certain if she'd thanked him. She'd been so busy resenting him for even offering because Sandlin was her brother and she wanted to be the one to take care of him.

What in the hell was wrong with her? Loving Sandlin meant utilizing whatever she had access to in order to give him the best possible care available. Was it her ego that dictated to her that she not use Giovanni's money? She rubbed her temples, put her head back and stared at the ceiling. It was the fact that she didn't want Giovanni or anyone else to think she was with him for his money. Everyone used him. They used his family. They wanted something from them.

She'd seen the women in the club throw themselves at every family member in the hopes of hooking one, not because they liked them, but for their money. What would that be like? She didn't want Giovanni to think she wanted his money, not for her and not for Sandlin. She wanted Giovanni. He made her laugh. He made her feel safe in an unfamiliar world. He seemed to value her opinions. He listened carefully to every word she said, as if it was terribly important to him.

She let out another groan and wrote down "stalker." How had she managed to catch the eye of some insane person? The detectives had told her it could be someone who passed her on the street and she'd absently smiled at them. She worked at the deli in the daytime. She smiled at a lot of customers. She worked at the club at night. She'd worked the floor at first, and who knew how many customers she'd served?

Giovanni thought the problem had started when she took over for Nancy that first night of serving on the top tier. She was afraid he was right. It felt right, but how did one explain that to a cop? The Ferraro family was doing their own investigations and she'd gone along with them, not telling the police everything. She knew why. She couldn't deny that she knew if Giovanni and his family figured out who was threatening her and those around her, they would send for their cousins and the man would disappear or be found dead. What did she think about that?

She began to pace again, thinking about the way the light structure and a portion of the ceiling had fallen on the couch where her brother always sat to read. Everyone knew he sat there. That light fixture had been deliberately rigged to fall on him. She knew the stalker was escalating his behavior. He'd threatened Giovanni. He'd targeted her brother. What was next? Who was next?

Was any of that Giovanni's fault? Of course not. She would have the stalker and the threat he presented hanging over her head without being engaged to Giovanni. If anything, Giovanni had tried to make both her and her brother safe.

She had been targeted by John Darby and his college frat boys for an ugly prank so he could boost his reality show ratings. Was that Giovanni's fault? Nope. She had taken that job because it paid so much money. West had told her about the dangers of drunken celebrities and how they often felt very entitled. He'd even told her about the specialized training servers got before they worked the top tier and told her he was worried because she hadn't had it yet.

She'd insisted she could do the job. She wasn't involved with Giovanni at the time. The incident would have happened no matter what. Even her picture in the tabloids might have happened without her name being attached to his because Darby would have tried to get mileage out of his prank.

She picked up her cell phone, needing to call Giovanni. She just wanted to hear his voice, but she knew if she did, he'd want to come to her—or have her go to him. That told her something right there. She had confidence that it was her he wanted, not someone like Meredith. She believed him when he told her he would be faithful to her. She believed he had a code and he would always live by that code.

She pressed the cell phone to her forehead and continued to pace. Why was she so angry at him? His world? He was born into it. He'd had no more choice in who gave birth to him than she'd had—she'd just gotten luckier. Was she really going to throw him over because he had far too much money? Because he lived life in a completely different lane than the one she was used to?

She was a fighter. She'd always been a fighter. Her mother told her she came out of the womb kicking and screaming. As a toddler, she never let anything defeat her when she wanted to learn something. She could be defiant, go her own way, be stubborn until she got what she wanted. Was she going to let Giovanni's lifestyle defeat her? Why? Pride? Ego? Worry about what the rest of the world would think of her because she was becoming part of a very wealthy family? Fear that she'd have to constantly battle the paparazzi and what was written about her?

She'd never cared before. Never. Why had it suddenly become important now? There was a sound outside her door. It sounded like something had hit her balcony rail. Everything in her froze, driving out her inner dialogue. She went to the front door, but she wasn't about to open it. Nobody knocked. She took a breath and slowly pushed aside her curtain.

She'd left the light on so that it shone on the small porch just outside her door. It wasn't much more than a landing, really, but she called it a front porch. Had she sat out there, she'd be staring into the alley, and at the surrounding buildings, but still . . . Right now, she was looking at the wooden railing, obviously broken. Something had hit it and it was pushed outward. *Outward.* Someone had stood just outside her door and shoved that railing, or hit it with something. She knew a bodyguard had been sitting out there. Where was he now?

She pressed Giovanni's number and prayed he'd answer immediately. A crack sounded so loud she jumped. Simultaneously, the glass around her porch light shattered and the light went off. Her heart thudded and she stepped back from the window. It was a good thing she did, because the glass in the large pane splintered apart in hundreds of small pieces, flying into her house. With it, liquid sprayed in every direction, as the thrown bottle spun through the air, releasing the fluid inside.

"Sasha?"

Giovanni's voice was so calm, she sagged with relief. She equated him with safety. "He's here," she said. "I think he hurt the bodyguard. He broke out one of my windows."

Even as she said it, the second window exploded, glass hurtling through her residence. Again, whatever had been thrown spilled a liquid all over. She could smell accelerant and knew the next thing coming through the window would be fire.

"He's burning the place. Call the fire department. Hurry, Giovanni."

He was swearing now. Not so calm, but she could tell he was on the move. "Get out of there, baby. You can't stay in there. Where the fuck are your bodyguards?"

"I think he did something terrible to them."

"That's impossible. Too many. Get out of there. I'll find out where they are."

She had no choice. Already the next cylinder came hurtling through the window, and she saw this bottle was stuffed with a fiery rag. Instantly, it was as if her apartment exploded with flames. She didn't have time for anything but grabbing her pictures of her parents and Sandlin as she raced to the front door. When she tried to open it, it wouldn't budge.

Her heart nearly stopped. There was a back way out, but it was a small balcony off her bedroom—nothing more than a fire escape. It was even smaller than the front landing and the stairs were really a fire ladder. If she didn't go now, she wasn't going to make it. Flames were licking up the walls to the ceiling, climbing the drapes, racing across the floor toward her bedroom.

She ran. The heat was intense. Fear was worse. Her heart beat out of control as she slammed the bedroom door closed and tried to open the one to the fire escape. Her fingers were shaking so badly, it took a few moments to unlock the door. As she did, a Molotov cocktail was thrown through her bedroom window and landed on the floor on the opposite side of the bed.

Sasha shoved the door open and jumped out, grabbing for the railing. The window was on the opposite side of the apartment so she figured there was a good chance her attacker couldn't make it around to this side of the building before she could make it to the ground. She nearly fell down the metal ladder and hit the pavement. She screamed when arms came around her.

"You're safe." It was Stefano's voice. "We're here now. Giovanni's on the way. The bodyguards were pulled off duty. I'm *killing* Cosimo for falling for an order like that. They left behind a new guy, and he was beaten senseless." There was distaste in his voice, although he still sounded matter-of-fact.

All the while he talked, Stefano had swirled a long trench coat around her, covering her. She was wearing pajamas and little else. Her pajamas tended to be very skimpy because she liked feeling feminine after a long day in jeans and a tee when she'd been riding horses and working cattle. Also, she was the type who was always too hot. Going naked in bed or wearing a minimal amount of clothing was always what she preferred.

He kept walking with her. She couldn't stop shaking. "Is the bodyguard dead? What's his name? I didn't have a chance to meet him." Even her teeth were chattering.

"Raimondo Abatangelo. He's actually Cosimo's youngest brother. Cosimo and Tomas, the oldest of the Abatangelo brothers, were both shot during the attack on our family last year. This was the first assignment given to them since it happened. We thought it was going to be an easy one. Raimondo has a military background and trained for becoming a bodyguard, but you were also his first assignment."

"You didn't say if he is alive." She was terrified he was going to answer in the negative and she knew she'd never forgive herself.

"He's alive, but just barely."

"I should never have insisted on going home. If I hadn't, my stalker couldn't possibly have hurt him." Where was Giovanni? Stefano was holding her close, keeping her shaking, rubbery legs from letting her fall.

She didn't know how many people were putting out the fire, keeping it from spreading to the buildings on either side, but they seemed to have come from everywhere. She closed her eyes. "The deli is going to be ruined. There were flames on the floor of my apartment. It had to have burned through. And the smoke and water will ruin all of the food if the fire doesn't burn it to the ground. What am I going to tell Pietro?"

"We can rebuild," Stefano assured. He had walked her down the alley. Lucia, Amo and Nicoletta waited. All three immediately put their arms around her and all but dragged her toward the open back door of Lucia's Treasures.

Stefano shook his head. "I'd prefer all three of you to evacuate. Amo, my men are going to take you to the pizzeria. I've already asked Benito to open it. Taviano and Vittorio will go with you, and Giovanni's meeting you there."

"I don't understand why he wants me dead," Sasha said. It was true. What had she done that was so terrible to this unknown man? "What could I have done to set him off like this?"

"You haven't done anything, honey," Stefano assured. He glanced at his brother over her head, and Vittorio immediately put his arm around her. "Men like this, they're sick. They have paranoid fantasies. When you don't react the way their fantasies dictate, then they lose it."

"I don't want everyone around me," she said. "Not Lucia, Amo and Nicoletta. He could burn down Lucia's Treasures or harm them just because they're associating with me."

Sasha looked around her, suddenly afraid for everyone. "What if he has a gun? He could be about to shoot someone right now. He's got military training. All of you have said that." Even to herself, her voice edged toward hysteria. She didn't want to sound out of control because she wanted them taking her seriously. Everything she said was the truth and the threat was very real. Especially for Giovanni. "He can't come near me," she whispered. "I mean it, Stefano. You have to tell Giovanni to stay away from me. He's going to go after him next."

"There is nothing you or I can say to keep Giovanni away from you, Sasha," Stefano said. "If you know him at all, you'll know that."

She shook her head. What was there to say? Stefano was right about Giovanni. He wouldn't stay away, but she suddenly had a very bad feeling that everything her stalker had done was to bring Giovanni out in the open. The Ferraros protected their homes. Security was tight, and it wasn't as if someone could easily get close to the actual house where Giovanni resided. It was much easier to draw him out. What better way than to attack Sasha?

"He's going to go after him," she said. "Stefano, you have to listen to me on this. I think Giovanni is the real target."

"Maybe, but if you get to the pizzeria, honey, you'll find Giovanni isn't so easy to get to. Hurry up. Go with Vittorio and Taviano."

Vittorio tightened his arm around her. Taviano shepherded Lucia, Amo and Nicoletta. Around them, a tight shield of guards formed as they made their way quickly up the block to the pizzeria. Benito had the back door open, and they were swept inside.

"Helicopter will land on the roof," Benito said to Vittorio. "Use the attic stairs. There's a trapdoor. Wait inside the attic with her, Vittorio. The guards are going up to the roof now. It's flat and has plenty of room. They'll clear the surrounding rooftops. If he's up there on any of the buildings waiting with a rifle, he'll make a run for it. Giovanni's going to hunt him with the chopper first and then he'll bring it in to retrieve his woman."

Her heart jumped. Giovanni was going to hunt him with a helicopter? "Can't he bring down the helicopter?"

"It isn't as easy to do that as it looks in the movies," Vittorio explained, turning her away from the others so she could climb the narrow stairs leading to the attic. "He'd have to take out the pilot to bring it down, or make the shot of his life. Giovanni isn't going to make it easy to shoot him. There's going to be a hell of a bright spotlight sweeping the rooftops. If that gets in his eyes, he's not going to be able to see to shoot at the pilot."

"Wait, *Giovanni* is piloting the helicopter?"

Vittorio shrugged. "We were all trained to fly helicopters, planes, and drive fast cars. We have very specialized training. Flying a helicopter is very different than flying planes, I might add. We are required to maintain licenses for all three, and that includes very large trucks and motorcycles. In case you're worried about your man, we're also required to be more than proficient in hand-to-hand combat."

"The stalker beat up that guard and he was trained."

"We began training at the age of two, Sasha; granted, it was in the form of playing at first, but we still had to learn the moves. We've trained just about every day of our lives since. You know that friend of Giovanni's? The mixed martial arts fighter? He sparred with Giovanni, but Gee took it easy on him. Really easy. Giovanni's reflexes are like lightning. He's as strong as an ox, and when he hits you with power behind his punch or kick, you're going down, and most likely, he's broken something, your face or your arm, leg, ribs. If he hasn't broken something, it's because he was careful."

Sasha closed her eyes and wished she could just disappear. Giovanni was in the air searching for her stalker. "He figured out that he's the real target, didn't he?"

"Yes."

Her stomach lurched. "You're telling me how safe he is up there in that helicopter, but he's really setting himself up to draw him out, isn't he?" She waited, her heart pounding. Her mouth was dry. She knew. She wanted to punch Vittorio.

She pushed him hard, out of the way. It was the last thing he expected and he rocked back, giving her just enough room to squeak past him. He caught at the trench coat Stefano had put around her, and she let the coat fall from her shoulders. If she ran out onto the roof and waved her arms, the stalker would try to shoot her, and Giovanni might have his target without exposing himself to certain danger.

Vittorio caught her just before she managed to unlock the trapdoor leading to the roof. "What are you doing, crazy woman?"

"Let go." She tried to kick him off her, but he had her in some kind of a hold that wrapped her up so tightly she was like a mummy.

"Does Giovanni realize what a little hellion he has?" Vittorio asked. "Sheesh, woman. Stop struggling. It isn't like you're going to get away and this is a rather . . . intimate hold for being with my future sister-in-law."

That brought her up short. She was locked against him, and it wasn't like she was wearing much in the way of clothes. She relaxed instantly, embarrassed that she'd put them both in such a weird position.

He pointed to the attic. Reluctantly, she went down the steps. He sat on the top one. "What exactly did you think you were going to do? Run out there and make yourself a target?"

She picked up the trench coat and wrapped it around her body. "Yes. Better me than Giovanni."

"If you were my woman, I'd turn you over my knee and

spank you until your ass was raw." His voice was utterly calm, but it still sent a shiver down her spine because she had the feeling that calm, soothing Vittorio was capable of such a thing. "Are you insane? Do you think Giovanni would just let you get shot? He'd leap out of a helicopter to save your life. He'd do anything to save you. Men like Giovanni protect their women. He's fine with you being whatever you want to be, and do whatever you want to do, but that ends when the cost could be your life."

"Has it occurred to you that I feel the same way about him?" she hissed.

"No. Frankly, I don't believe that."

Again, he spoke so calmly that at first she didn't understand what he said. And he meant it. He didn't believe she felt the same way about Giovanni as he did her.

"Why do you say that, Vittorio?"

"You're a highly intelligent woman, Sasha. You aren't blind or deaf. You're a planner. You take great care of your brother and it's clear you put him first. That adds up to a certain personality. If you loved my brother with the same intensity as he loves you, you would never have put him in the position he's in. You would have recognized the danger and avoided it. You wouldn't have gone to your house licking your wounds because some woman put her tongue in your man's mouth. You wanted out. You knew he was uncomfortable and wanted no part of Meredith Benson. You weren't jealous of her. I saw your face. You didn't get Giovanni out of the situation. You used it to remove yourself."

She had done all that. She had. She didn't like his world and she'd thought to remove herself. It was only when she was alone without him that she realized she loved Giovanni enough to face that world with him.

"You put yourself in danger. He loves you enough to let you because you're the type of woman to get angry and say it's your right to do that. And yeah"—he shrugged—"it is. Absolutely. But having a man like Giovanni means if you love him, you'll do the right thing and take the protection offered."

She almost protested. She had taken his protection. She'd been surrounded by guards. But she knew that wasn't what Vittorio was telling her. She knew there were all kinds of men in the world. Some of them wouldn't have cared what she did. If she wanted to go, she could go. There wouldn't have even been a discussion. With a man like Giovanni, her safety and the safety of her brother were real issues. When she took him on as a partner, she took that part of him on as well.

"I hear you, Vittorio," she said. "I won't be making that mistake again. I would like to see what's going on though. Is there a way to do that without putting us in danger?"

He nodded. "But you do what I tell you. I'm not like Giovanni." It was a warning. Gentle. Delivered in a mild voice, but again, a little shiver of awareness crept down her spine.

She was fairly certain he wasn't that gentle man they all thought he was. No one else seemed aware of this side of him. He was just so calm, but he was being calm now, just scary calm. Giovanni referred to him as the peacemaker. She suspected he was the peacemaker for a reason other than what the others thought.

"Have you heard anything about the fire?" She had been afraid to ask, afraid it would have jumped from her apartment to the buildings on either side of hers as well as Masci's.

"It's out already. It was out almost before the fire department got there. Why didn't the sprinklers go off? They were installed last year."

She hadn't thought of that. "The only thing I can think of is that when he got into the apartment the first time, he disrupted the line to them? I don't know how they work. I never thought about it, but he had to have done something. If he did it when he first got into my apartment, doesn't that mean that he planned on killing me all along?"

Vittorio nodded slowly. “So, if he really had planned to kill you, why didn’t he just do it immediately? Why take all these chances?” He frowned as she started up the stairs. He began texting. “Sending a mass text to the family. They’re pretty good at figuring things out.”

“How much damage did the fire do?”

“Your apartment is a mess and so is the deli, but nothing else was touched. We’ll get a work crew in the moment the investigation is complete and tear the building down and rebuild. The nice part is, Pietro has wanted to remodel for a couple of years now. His place has gotten popular for lunch, and he would like to expand the inside to include an area for more tables. Or have an outside court. Clearly that would have to be built in the back, but he’s got all kinds of plans. Stefano will look them over and either approve or not.”

“I don’t know how you can make a fire sound like a good thing,” she said. “As if Pietro is going to be happy.”

“He will be. In the end. Besides, we can send him on a vacation to the home country. He’s been wanting to go but claimed he couldn’t because of his business. Right now, he’s upset, but once he sees what Stefano is willing to do with that place, he’ll be happy.”

“Like what?” she asked suspiciously.

“That little apartment could be used for his offices. You’ll be living with Giovanni.” He grinned at her and reached up to cautiously lift the trapdoor. “Straight ahead is a thick railing. It’s low, no more than three feet, so you’re going to have to stay low. I mean it, Sasha. If you start to rise, expect to find me on top of you.”

“Has anyone ever told you that you’re annoying and bossy?”

She edged out of the attic, staying low, going to her hands and knees and even lower. She didn’t want Vittorio flattening her.

“No. Everyone thinks I’m sweet. In fact, I think my reputation is sterling among my family members.”

She would have rolled her eyes, but he couldn't see her. Light was already streaking through the dark as the sun began to rise. Working all night and then having a madman burn down her apartment and try to kill her made the hours pass fast. She made it to the railing and stayed low, waiting for instructions.

Vittorio annoyed her by putting a hand on the nape of her neck, so that even if she thought about lifting her head above the railing, it was impossible. She clenched her teeth. She was a woman of action, not someone to be pushed into a little room and guarded. Giovanni understood her. Vittorio did as well, but he didn't care. He would have locked her in that little room and let her be angry with him. Giovanni took the consequences of her actions.

She heard the helicopter. It sounded close. Every instinct was to rise up and look for herself. She wasn't certain what Vittorio was doing. He certainly was looking over the railing.

"Raimondo is a good fighter," he said suddenly. "Giovanni pointed that out in his texts. He isn't trained the way we are, but he's training with Emilio and Emilio is a hell of a fighter. He wouldn't have allowed Raimondo to go out on an assignment if he didn't think he was ready. He was beaten nearly to death."

Her stomach twisted into knots. "That's on me."

"He would have been guarding Giovanni's residence," Vittorio said. "I'm not certain you can claim that one. Giovanni thinks he was beaten deliberately."

"Aren't all beatings deliberate?"

Vittorio lifted his hand, and she turned, staying low, scooting even farther down in order to rest her back and head against the wall.

"Giovanni says only a seasoned fighter, someone with a great deal of experience in combat and martial arts, could have possibly beaten the kid to that extent. Raimondo got in a few good ones, his hands were damaged, but this man nearly beat him to death."

Her breath caught in her throat. "You think it was Aaron."

Vittorio shook his head. "I don't know what to think. Aaron's smart. If he wanted to do this, if he has some problem with Giovanni, and this looks as if it's aimed at Giovanni, he could easily make it look as if he's being set up. He took that picture of you and it was on his phone. No one else had it. It ended up being in the tabloids. Some of the material the bomb was made from was charged to a credit card he later reported stolen. He served in the military and has training in explosives."

"Don't you think that's all a little too neat?" Sasha thought it was. Aaron was smart, at least Giovanni always said he was. "He wouldn't stack the evidence against himself, would he?"

"It is all a little too neat, as if we're being handed Aaron with a bow tied neatly around the package. Don't you think a very intelligent person could pull that off? Make it look as if he's being framed?"

"What would be his purpose?" She didn't want to hear that little voice inside that repeated Aaron's lie about Giovanni and him in competition over women, but it was there. He'd lied when there was no reason to.

Vittorio shrugged. "We've got a lot of money, Sasha. People think we live magical lives. They see us as wasted human beings with far too much money."

"You all play the part of playboys deliberately. You want people to think all you do is race cars and chase women."

He gave her a small smile. "Someone who lived a good deal of his life on the streets, struggling for every penny, can build up a great deal of resentment. Aaron may think everything has been handed to Giovanni. If he had his eye on you and Gee managed to grab you out from under him, he might tip over the edge."

"But Aaron never so much as asked me out."

"He sent you flowers, honey. On his phone, it turns out there are a number of photographs of you. Quite a few."

That brought her up short. She turned her head to look directly at him. Straight into his eyes because she had to know the truth. "What are you talking about? How could you possibly know something like that?"

Vittorio shrugged, looking casual. Calm. As if nothing ever ruffled him. "I know Giovanni told you about riding shadows. It isn't that difficult to get into someone's house and look through their things. If Aaron is a threat to my brother, then I'm going to remove that threat. If not me, one of my cousins or another brother. It's that simple."

Another shiver went down her spine. If Vittorio had been showing an intense emotion such as anger, she wouldn't have been so affected by the way he stated so calmly that Aaron was probably living on borrowed time. Clearly, if the Ferraros found out that he was behind all the threats, he didn't have long to live. She realized they carried out their work without passion. It was their job, and they didn't allow emotions to get in their way.

Vittorio was a mystery to her. He didn't appear to give off the aura of danger the others did, but somehow, spending a little time in his company, she was beginning to think he might be the most dangerous of all of the Ferraros. He reached out unexpectedly and put his hand on her shoulder. His touch was gentle, but she felt his strength.

"I didn't mean to scare you, Sasha. You have enough to worry about. Giovanni is going to be fine, and we'll figure out who is doing this and why."

His cool assurance made her feel more confident. She nodded her head just as a shot rang out. Instantly a volley of shots answered, the sound coming from all directions. Instinctively she ducked. Vittorio moved away from her, coming up in a crouch, peering over the wide concrete barrier.

A bright light lit the sky. The helicopter that had been flying back and forth in a grid pattern suddenly dipped low and raced toward a rooftop across from the pizzeria and down three buildings. The light beamed along the roof of that building, illuminating a man with a rifle running across the roof toward a door. He dropped the rifle and disappeared inside just as more shots rang out.

"Taviano and Stefano are not with Nicoletta, are they?" she asked.

"That was three rifles. Emme's a crack shot as well. No one was able to get a good angle on him. Giovanni hung out there, but he didn't take the bait."

"Do you think he was waiting to get a bead on me?" Again, she looked straight at him, needing an answer.

Vittorio wasn't looking back at her. His attention was centered on the drama playing out as his brothers and sister tried to race the assailant down to the street. Giovanni kept the helicopter in play, using the powerful light to illuminate the streets and alleyways below to see where he would come out so the others could trap him. The problem was, there were so many routes he could take. He could move from building to building without being seen.

"I don't know, Sasha. It's impossible to know what this man is looking to do."

For the first time, she wasn't certain whether someone was telling the truth or not. Usually there was a note of discord, but Vittorio was too smooth to give her one. Still, there was something . . . "You think he was looking to shoot me, don't you?" A much better question.

"Yes. That's exactly what I think. Giovanni thinks so as well. That's why he went up in the helicopter. He wanted to distract him. The shooter wouldn't think in terms of us using a helicopter. He was up on that roof waiting for Giovanni to join the fray so he could shoot you in front of him."

Her heart clenched hard. "That's why he didn't shoot me when I came out of my house. He wanted to do it in front of Giovanni."

"I believe that."

"So, my stalker isn't stalking me because I'm important to him. I'm so confused. I don't understand any of this."

She turned around and rose up onto her knees so she could look down at the streets. “Just so you know, it’s far easier living and working on a cattle ranch in Wyoming than living in Chicago. If anyone tries to tell you differently, point them my way and I’ll straighten them out.”

“Come on, let’s get out of here. The cops are going to want to talk to you. It’s going to be a while before we can get you home and in bed.”

She looked toward the deli where her little apartment had been. Now, there were only smoking ruins. “I don’t have a thing. No clothes. No anything.”

“You’re going to be fine, honey. We’ll take care of you. You’re doing great. I know it’s been a crappy day, but hang in there. Giovanni will be here soon, and we’ll have our lawyer present as well when they ask you questions.”

“I don’t know what I can and can’t say.”

“Just tell them about being in your apartment and all hell breaking loose.”

“If they ask me why I was there instead of with Giovanni?” Because it seemed ridiculous to her that she hadn’t been with Giovanni. She should have been. Her apartment would still be intact, and Pietro wouldn’t have lost his deli.

“Don’t.” Vittorio’s voice was low. He took her arm and indicated she make her way back to the trapdoor. “There’s no point in wondering what would have happened had you been with Giovanni.”

“How could you know I was thinking that?”

“Your face is an open book. I can read every expression.”

Strange, when her brother had always told her she was difficult to read and would make a good poker player. Vittorio was definitely an enigma.

# CHAPTER SEVENTEEN

A bath had never felt so wonderful. Sasha had spent a long time in the shower, hoping to get rid of the smoke smell. The water pouring over her had felt like heaven on her tired, sore muscles, but nothing felt like luxuriating in the bath. The water came up high and was just the perfect temperature. Steam rose and with it the perfumed scent of candy apple with a dash of cinnamon. How Giovanni knew that was her favorite scent, she didn't know—or care—she just breathed it in and let it transport her far away from the reality of the night.

Her head rested on a very comfortable pillow and her hair was wound up in a tight spa wrap. She opened her mouth and Giovanni obligingly put a forkful of beef Stroganoff in. The sauce seemed to explode in a myriad of flavors on her taste buds. How he'd managed to get such a five-star meal delivered to his home at such a crazy hour, she had no idea, but she was okay with indulging.

He put another bite to her lips, and she sighed with happiness. She didn't know how she could go from being terrified for her brother, losing everything she owned, finding out her stalker really wanted her dead, to complete bliss.

"I think I could live here," she stated.

Giovanni grinned at her. "That's the idea, baby. If I knew it would take beef Stroganoff to convince you, I would have had the chef fix it for you the day I met you."

"I'm talking about the bathtub. Living in the bathtub."

His eyebrow shot up and he removed the fork just before her lips could close and ate it himself.

"Wait. The Stroganoff is going a long way to showing me the error of my ways," she hastily amended. "I should have moved in, no questions asked, and accepted every little thing you offered me."

He smirked. "It is that good, isn't it?" He fed her another bite. "Stefano found the chef in New York and had to offer him a fortune to relocate. The man makes more money than our bank does, but he's worth every penny."

"I'm sorry," Sasha said, because she had to apologize. It had been weighing on her since they'd entered his home and he'd been waiting on her hand and foot as if she was the most precious thing in his world. "I should have come here with you. I don't know what got into me. It was never you, Giovanni. I was scared for you, for Sandlin and for myself. I was also very angry and wanted to strike out at someone. Not just anyone, whoever is doing this—manipulating all of us. But I made you my convenient target and I'm really sorry."

He leaned down and brushed a kiss over her forehead. "Sasha, I'm angry. Who wouldn't be? Of course, you needed time to sort things out. You haven't been with me that long. Seeing me with Meredith . . ."

"Please don't," she said softly, ashamed. "I knew Meredith was the one doing all the kissing, and I don't much care what the tabloids say. I never believed them anyway. Long before I ever met you, I didn't read them because I knew mostly they were filled with bullshit. I took everything out on you, and that was wrong of me. I put you in danger. I put myself in danger. It was silly and I'm not a silly woman. I'm intelligent and I usually think things through. I was being emotional instead of logical."

He fed her another bite of Stroganoff. "Are you back to being logical?"

Her eyebrows shot up. "Sitting in a perfumed bath, being fed the most wonderful meal I've ever eaten by a very handsome man? No, babe, I'm pretty sure this falls under the category of fantasy, but I'll take it."

"Do you plan to sleep in there?"

His laughter teased every one of her senses, bringing her own joy to life. She loved his smile, the way it lit up his eyes. "Is there a way to keep the water hot all day?"

"Not happening. You're sleeping with me," he decreed and fed himself two bites of the Stroganoff in a row.

She narrowed her eyes. "Stop eating all the food. Share." Which wasn't quite fair since he'd given her the lion's portion already. "And if I'm in the bed with you, I doubt there will be much sleeping, and I'm exhausted."

"If you're exhausted, baby, I'll do all the work. I don't mind." He fed her another bite.

The food was so delicious she closed her eyes to savor it. "If you're 'working' on me, I won't be able to just lie there quietly."

"I can tie you up. Make sure you don't move an inch. I know you worked on a cattle ranch so you'll recognize my skills when you see them. My brother Ricco is a rigger. A good one. He's been teaching me, and I have to admit, I'm pretty damn good with knots. I won't mind showing off my skills."

She looked at him from under her lashes, giving him her best scowl. "Um. I'm not familiar with that term. *Rigger.* What the heck is a rigger?"

"In some circles, Ricco might be known as a rope master. He has certain skills with knots. He creates art with rope on the human body. His particular skills can be transferred to tying prisoners in remarkable and sometimes painful ways or to the other end of the spectrum, which would be erotic bondage."

She sat up straighter, one hand going to her throat. "Are you telling me, Ricco practices bondage with Mariko?"

"She's his rope model for Shibari so I would assume they would also practice erotic bondage together, but I've never been in their bedroom and don't plan to be."

"Mariko looks so sweet and demure."

"She's a tigress. You should see her in action when she's working. No nonsense with that woman. She gets the job done fast and efficiently. She was trained as a rider as well, but in Japan. Her life wasn't easy. Ricco adores her. They're pretty much inseparable."

She took her time with the next bite, chewing it thoroughly. He tipped his head to one side. "What are you doing?"

"Contemplating the merits of being tied up so I can't move while you indulge your every whim. And you would. I know you. You'd have a field day with my body."

He skimmed his finger down her throat and traced over the swell of both breasts before trailing down to her nipple. "If I had you tied up where you couldn't move, I'd make you admit that your body belongs to me whenever we go to bed."

She rolled her eyes. "There it is right there. The reason I'm reluctant to let you have your way. You think I'm your plaything."

He frowned. "Aren't you? You have that hot little body, and no one else gets to touch it but me. I'm pretty sure we've established you were made for me. Put on this earth just for my sole pleasure."

She laughed. "You are so crazy. That's not true at all. It's the other way around."

He managed to look genuinely puzzled. "It is? How so?" He put the plate to one side and circled the impressive girth of his cock. "This belongs to you?"

She nodded. "I'm afraid so, Giovanni. All mine. In fact, now that I've had my meal, I may just demand dessert."

"I don't know. I think you're a little mixed up."

She couldn't take her eyes off the sight of him, sitting on the wide edge of the bathtub, his hand sliding over his shaft with a lazy fist. She loved the way he looked. She loved the fact that he was so easy about sex. She'd been raised to believe sex was natural, a part of life that was fun with your partner and there were no limits as long as both consented.

She liked that Giovanni enjoyed it and was willing to have fun and be adventurous.

"Come here," she enticed.

"Get out of there and lie on the bed." He turned the knob to allow the water to drain out of the tub.

The sinful gleam in his eyes excited her. Her sex clenched and her breasts suddenly ached. She was so tired, and yet just that look, just the sight of him sitting there naked, his cock gloriously erect, could wipe out the exhaustion. "I don't know how I could have been so silly," she murmured aloud. Thinking she could leave him. Thinking she wanted to leave him.

She stood up slowly, letting the water run off her. She'd shaved in the shower, feeling deliciously wicked, baring her mound so she could feel every stroke of his tongue. She felt sexy and wanton as she stepped out of the tub to be enveloped by the thick, soft towel he put around her shoulders.

"Braid your hair."

"It will be wet when I wake up."

"That's all right. Braid it."

She dropped the towel on the floor and undid the spa towel. She liked that he watched her every movement. That made her aware of her body. The lift of her breasts as she raised her arms to separate her hair into three sections. She had thick, curly hair and it wasn't easy, especially when he crouched down next to her thighs and licked at the perfumed drops running down her legs. Fingers of desire danced up and down her thighs. Her sex reacted, clenching hotly. Still, she managed to braid her hair quickly and secure it with the tie he handed her.

She tried not to hurry into the bedroom, but she wanted him suddenly with such a deep need she could barely keep from flinging herself at him. She saw the heavy drapes were pulled over the privacy screens. One small light, a dim spray of gold, came from the ceiling light directly over the middle of the bed. She stretched out under it, watching his face the entire time.

There was no way to put into words the way she felt lying there under that golden spotlight, the rays beaming out over her body, displaying every naked curve to him. His expression showed his appreciation, the way his gaze moved hotly over her, the way the sensual lines of lust carved deeper into his face so that he looked as if he was the very definition of sin.

Her heart accelerated and she suddenly couldn't lie still, her hips rocking gently in anticipation. She wanted to look at his body. It was so beautiful. So masculine. But all she could do was watch his face as his gaze traveled over her. In that moment, she felt truly his, as if she really had been born for him. As if he was so hungry for her, no one else could possibly do for him. Only her. Only Sasha Provis. He looked at her as if he was the Big Bad Wolf about to devour her ravenously.

He reached out one hand, his eyes never leaving the rise and fall of her breasts as he stroked caresses over the curves. Every brush of his fingers sent heat curling through her body. She found she liked the fact that she was tired and felt lazy and yet sensuous as she lay there in the soft glow of the light. "I want to be yours, Giovanni," she admitted.

His mouth curved. Just a little, as if her admission meant something to him.

"I like that you want to be mine, Sasha. You're so damn beautiful, sometimes I can't believe you're real. The fact that you're in my bedroom, in my bed, is still shocking to me."

She liked that, too. Giovanni had every reason to be arrogant, and to others, she knew he seemed that way, but with her, he was different and that meant something to her. Lying on the bed with a few drops of water still clinging to her skin, his gaze hot as hell as it moved over her, brought her nipples to a peak and sent hot liquid gathering at the vee of her legs.

She swiped a finger through the liquid and lifted it up toward his mouth. At once he bent his head and drew her finger into his mouth. He was sexy, the way he looked at her, carnal sin his very expression. She dug her heels into the bed and shifted her body around so she could hang her head slightly off the bed.

"Come here, honey. I need to feel you in my mouth."

Giovanni stared down at the perfection of the woman enticing him—*seducing* him. He didn't understand how it all had come about, how he'd managed to find her—his woman. Perfect for him. She never shied away from anything in the bedroom. She made her demands and expected him to do so as well. She reveled in his demands of her. He moved around the bed and brought both hands to frame her face.

"I love watching my cock disappear down your throat. It's the sexiest thing imaginable."

She gave an adorable pout. "Why are you just standing there out of my reach?"

Her gaze moved over his hand, the one he circled his cock with. He did it deliberately, staying just out of her reach. He waited, knowing her, knowing what she would try next. She reached for him and he caught her hand, whipped the soft cotton rope out from under the bed and lashed it around her wrist, flipped her over, caught her other hand and tugged it behind her back so he could knot the two together. Putting one knee gently in the middle of her back, he caught her ankle and drew it up so he could tie one leg to her hands. He flipped her back over and reached for the other leg. That one he stretched out from her body and tethered it to the bedpost.

"What are you doing? I'm not a calf." But she was laughing.

"No, you're not," he agreed. He pulled her to the edge of the bed again so her head could tilt over the side. "Now, you're my woman, ready and willing to do anything I want."

"I'm always ready and willing to do anything you want."

"I've got interesting ideas, some might shock you." He

leaned over her, his chest sliding over her breasts, his cock filling her mouth as he reached with both hands to hold her little flower open for the exploration of his tongue.

Her cry was muffled around his cock. He hadn't given her much time to catch a breath before he'd stuffed her mouth. He was big and her lips had to stretch to accommodate him. Still, he pushed deep to feel the amazing suction of her mouth and the lash of her tongue. He held himself there, letting her suck hard, feeling the heat of her mouth wrapped around him like a silken fist. He pulled back, not all the way out, and then pushed deep again. When he pushed into her, he stabbed deep with his tongue, his finger flicking her clit.

She cried out around his cock, her hips bucking, but she couldn't go anywhere, not tied, and not with the weight of his body holding hers down. He lifted his head as he eased back to give her a chance to breathe. As he waited for her to draw in air, he pinched her clit gently. Most of the nerve endings were there on the sides and the breath exploded out of her.

"I want to buy you jewelry for here, too," he whispered and kissed her clit. "You're so sensitive and you'll like the stimulation." He pushed his cock back into her mouth before she could answer him. "Suck hard, baby." He proceeded to do the same.

He began to move his hips, a slow indulgence, pushing deeper, drawing back and pushing deeper again. She caught his rhythm and worked with him, until he thought the top of his head might come off. He worked her hot little channel, drawing honey and spice, playing with her clit, getting all sorts of ideas on how he could enhance her pleasure as he did so. Knowing he wouldn't last if he kept it up, he reluctantly withdrew from her mouth and stood up.

"Wait." Sasha glared at him. "That was mine. I wanted it all."

"Such a greedy girl. You're supposed to be lying back, exhausted, remember? I was nice and gave you a taste of dessert like you asked, but you told me I had to do all the work." He pulled her around to the center of the bed again. This time he untied the leg that was stretched out and once more flipped her onto her stomach. "I like being able to just put you in any position I like."

He dragged pillows over and shoved them under her hips to raise her ass. He rubbed it. "Have I told you how much I love your ass? Because I do. I dream about it sometimes, and all the things I can do to it."

"Hmm, I'm not certain that bodes well for me." There was laughter in her voice. "You be very careful of what you choose to do. You're going to have to go to sleep sometime, and what goes around comes around."

His hand smacked her left cheek. "Are you threatening me?" He caught her free ankle and added it to the tie at the small of her back. Both legs were drawn up at the knee so she essentially was on her knees, laid out over the high stack of pillows.

"Well, yes, but it was more like a promise. And I'm not so certain about jewelry on my clit, crazy man. Can I just say 'ouch'?"

His fingers slid into her. "If you said ouch, it isn't on right. It isn't for pain, it's for pleasure. You're going to have to learn to trust me. I'm not into the lifestyle, but with you, I want to play. Let me have my playtime, woman."

She laughed again and then gasped as his mouth was back between her legs. Her entire body jerked as he took his time claiming every inch of her. He used his fingers, his tongue, his teeth, his lips. He kissed, sucked, licked and probed, drawing sweet cries out of her and wringing three separate orgasms.

"Hands okay, baby?"

"Yes," she gasped.

He knelt up behind her and very slowly began to push into her. Her muscles were tight. Her silken sheath hot as Hades. She tried to push back to force him inside, but he gave her several hard smacks, which only caused moaning.

She couldn't move much, and he loved inching in slowly. That burn engulfed him, inch by slow inch. So good. He could barely breathe and it didn't matter. He wanted to live right there.

"Sure you're okay, Sasha?" She *had* to be. He would stop if he had to, but it was so damn good, a paradise of heat and fire.

"Move. Just move."

"Demanding little wench." He didn't move, not like she wanted. He liked the hitch in her voice that told him she was burning up the same way he was. He kept pushing into her slowly, exquisitely slow. Murderously slow. Sweat broke out on his forehead, beading there—that kind of slow.

Finally, *finally*, he was seated all the way, his cock pushing against her cervix, the ring of flames holding his shaft like a vise of pure fire. He threw his head back, one hand kneading the cheeks of her ass, feeling the amazing reaction. Every time he massaged deep, or smacked her, a wave rippled through her sheath so that without him moving, she clamped down, a thousand tiny tongues stroking, a thousand muscles milking his cock. The sensation was incredible.

He was very cognizant of her hands and legs being bound. He couldn't get her comfort out of his head and decided that maybe tying his woman wasn't for him. Still, he liked that she couldn't move and he had complete control. With Sasha, that wasn't bound to happen too often.

He loved her beyond anything he ever thought he was capable of. Maybe it was because he was aware he could have lost her at any moment, or maybe it was because she made him feel alive when he hadn't for a very long time.

"Get moving," she demanded, sounding like she was gritting her teeth.

He threw his head back and laughed, sheer joy bursting through him. "You're such a bossy little thing," he said, holding her still, keeping the same slow, burning movements. He leaned forward and kissed the nape of her neck.

His fingers dug into her hips and he surged into her, burying himself deep, feeling the fire race up his spine. "That hard enough for you, baby?"

"No. And faster."

He obliged because the need in her voice overcame the need in him to tease her. He took some things seriously, and pleasing his woman was at the top of his list. He forgot about everything when he was inside her. That hot paradise. He loved when they were sharing the same skin. When they were so connected there was no one else in their world.

"I'm so close, Giovanni," she whispered, her voice ragged. Panting. "Hurry, baby."

He loved that, too. His woman waiting for him. She didn't have to. He felt the tension in her coiling tighter and tighter. The way her body gripped his. He was beginning to know her body so well now, every nuance. She was close, her breath hitching. The moans that grew into a musical of hunger and need. Her voice, so soft and plaintive, so demanding and bossy, played over him, adding to his building pleasure.

Then there was no holding back. No possible way. "Come with me, baby," he whispered. "Be with me." He felt it moving through him, rising like a volcano, while her body clamped down, those tight muscles milking him. Hot seed splashed over her walls, claiming her, branding her. Causing ripples and quakes that sent more fire crashing through him like a perfect storm of intense beauty.

He fought to catch his breath, his fingers working at the knots and ropes to get them off her. Still buried deep, he rubbed at her ankles and wrists, making certain there was plenty of blood flow. It disturbed him to think that might have made her uncomfortable. "You okay, Sasha?"

"More than okay, but I can't move. If you expect me to do anything but fall asleep, you're going to be disappointed."

She hadn't moved from the position he'd put her in. She

was still over the pillow, her legs drawn up. Only her arms had moved. Now she was hugging the pillows. Her braid hung in a thick rope, the sheets wet under all that hair.

"Baby, just roll over." She was in the middle of the bed. He was still kneeling behind her, his body buried deep.

"Go away. I'm not moving. I think you killed me."

"You couldn't talk if I did you in," he reasoned. His arms slid around her and he leaned his body over hers, blanketing her. "I suppose I could go to sleep right like this."

"Yes. That's perfect. I like you in me."

He felt her love surround him. Hold him. He'd always known the love of his family, of Stefano, but this was different and it moved him. The contentment in her voice made him feel as if he was everything to her. He wanted to be everything to her. He ran his hand down her body and over her bottom possessively.

"I love being in you and once here, I never want to leave," he admitted. "I don't know how I survived without you. That's the fucking truth, baby. I don't know how I got up in the morning, got through the day and went to bed at night. I know I've never laughed so much. I never felt so much joy. You make me feel alive."

"I love you, Giovanni."

"Me? Or my cock?"

Her laughter was muffled by the pillows. "That's a difficult choice. I'm very much in love with you, the man, but you are arrogant and bossy. Your cock is pretty spectacular. Although, now that I think about it, it can be arrogant and bossy as well."

He smacked her ass for that. She yelped and then spoiled the glare she shot him by giggling.

"My cock is perfection."

"Oh. My. God. You're *such* a man."

"Thank you."

"That wasn't a compliment. I want to go to sleep now. I can't take much more of your macho bullshit. Speaking of which, your brother Vittorio scares the crap out of me. Talk about macho."

"Vittorio? He's my nicest brother. He shouldn't scare you. Seriously, babe, he's a good man and one you can always count on." Very slowly and reluctantly he pulled out of her.

Her body shuddered as the action of dragging his heavy cock over her muscles caused more friction and sent another ripple of pleasure moving through her. He hated missing that. He detested not being inside of her. He caught her folded-up body in his arms and rolled, nearly taking them both off the side of the bed.

She burst out laughing as he threw himself back toward the middle of the bed, taking her with him. They landed back on the stack of pillows.

"Cool move, Mr. Sauvé."

He caught up one of the pillows and hit her with it very gently. She wasn't nearly as gentle in retaliation. The next thing he knew, they were in a full-blown pillow fight. He was definitely the loser because he spent more time looking at her naked body and making certain he was careful not to hurt her than he did protecting himself.

She wasn't nearly as careful about being gentle with him. They both collapsed on the bed, and she flung her arms out wide and stared up at the ceiling. "Babe?"

"Right here, Sasha." He stretched out beside her.

"You have stars on your ceiling."

"Really?" He'd had the house built. He'd needed escape routes, hidden hallways and rooms. "I never noticed that."

She turned her head, and he felt the impact of her eyes. He loved those sapphire eyes. So startling blue. Now they regarded him with so much love in them he felt his heart stutter in answer. He rubbed his palm over his chest.

"I'm really in love with you, Giovanni." Her voice was a soft whisper. He heard the love. "I never want you to think this is about your money or your power. This is about you.

The man. You make me laugh. You make me feel beautiful. I love the way you are with Sandlin and the care you take of him even though you barely know him. I can't ever explain to you what that means to me. I just want you to feel loved and I swear, I'll spend a lifetime making you feel that way."

He found her hand and brought it to his heart. "I feel the same way about you, Sasha. I love you very much."

"I'm sorry I didn't listen to you earlier. The way I acted toward you in the club after I saw you with that actress, that was so wrong. I felt raw and afraid and angry, but it wasn't at you. You didn't deserve the way I treated you, and in the end, through my stupidity, I put all of us in danger."

"That's not true," he denied.

"No, it is. I should have listened to you."

"Sasha, the fact that this bastard tried to bring down the ceiling on the patients at the Center tells me he doesn't care who he hurts. I was feeling angry and pretty raw myself. Don't beat yourself up because you're human."

"Do you believe it's Aaron?"

He stared up at the ceiling. At the stars swirling around above them. Did he? Did he think Aaron was capable of such hatred and jealousy that he'd hurt everyone around Giovanni? "I don't like to think so," he mused. "Aaron had a rough childhood, but he pulled himself up out of that by his fists. By his feet. He literally fought his way up. He's good, too. There was no fixing fights or anything underhanded. Aaron is where he is because of his determination and skill. That skill was hard-won. Practicing every day. Working at his craft. Honing it. Finding people who could help him make it better. He worked hard and had the discipline to get up every day whether he was hungry or not. Just get up and work."

"You admire him."

"Damn right I do. I know what it takes to work like that. I had Stefano driving me. My duty to my family. Aaron had to find that drive in himself. He had to be the one who forced himself up on those days he wasn't feeling like it. Motivation only goes so far when you're doing it yourself, but he managed."

"Would Aaron be so jealous of you that he would be willing to kill me? Kill my brother? Hurt people?"

Giovanni thought that over. It was a good question. Aaron might have reason to be jealous. It looked as if Giovanni had everything, but Aaron had never struck him as that kind of man. He was too busy working his way to the top to feel jealousy. He had goals and kept his eye fixed on them until he accomplished them. When he did, he set new goals.

"I don't know, baby," he said softly, but he was shaking his head. "I just can't see Aaron doing all this. Of course, I would never have believed he would lie to you and say we competed for women. Why would he do that unless he was motivated by jealousy?" That was the one note that struck the biggest chord of argument. It made no sense that Aaron had lied to Sasha unless he was jealous.

He sighed. "I hate like hell to think this has been Aaron all along. And what set him off, if it is? You? He was there that night, but he had at least three women fawning all over him. He was drunk, and that's unusual. Believe me, it isn't his normal unless he's been drinking. Aaron stays away from booze and women because he trains daily. A night out like that is rare and having the women and the alcohol fogging up his brain . . ." He closed his eyes. *"Dio."* It exploded out of him. "I don't want this to be Aaron. I really don't. I hate that he's in any way attached to it."

He knew the hurt in his voice showed, and that embarrassed him. He was a man and in his world, a Ferraro didn't show weakness. Allowing an outsider to hurt him showed he still had vulnerabilities, and those weren't tolerated. That was a direct edict from his mother. She made certain they never showed real emotion in public. Their circle only included family. While other members of the family were allowed outside friendships, riders were not. He rubbed his eyebrow, keeping his eyes closed, afraid of giving too much away to her, afraid she would think less of him.

He felt her move, roll, so she was pressed to his side, and then she draped her body over his, almost as if she were protecting him. He opened his eyes and looked up to the mirrored tiles cut in the shape of stars, surrounding the golden light still shining down on them. On her. Sasha. He could see the line of her back, all that smooth, silky skin. The curve of her spine as it met her buttocks, those dimples and the swell of her cheeks. One still carried a flush of rose where his hand had been. Without thinking, he covered the spot and began to rub.

Her face was buried in his throat and her arms were flung out to wrap around him. He felt the press of her soft breasts pushing into the heavy muscles of his chest. Her legs wrapped around his. She looked beautiful. Enticing. More, she looked as if she would fight off an army for him. His love felt so large, so encompassing, it actually hurt. Physically hurt. His heart felt as if it could shatter.

Giovanni didn't say anything to her, he just stroked her hair and her butt. He loved the feel of both. All soft silk and satin. After a few minutes her breathing evened out, her breath warming his skin.

"You asleep, baby?"

"Just drifting."

"Marry me. Right away. Let's get married. We can marry at the Center. Sandlin can give you away. He'd love that. I know he could do it and he'd be happy to."

"Honey." She moved her head. Rubbed her chin along his chest and then looked at him. Her eyes met his. "I'm not going anywhere."

He concentrated on rubbing her bottom. "I love your ass." He did. He was an ass man; well, he was also a breast man. Right now, he could see that bitable, spankable bottom, so he was all about her ass, but if she rolled over, his fickle cock would be all about her breasts.

"Good, because I'm madly in love with your cock. I love

how it feels right now, pressed against me. I'm thinking about going to sleep with it in my mouth. I used to suck my thumb when I was little. It drove my mother crazy. I might have to have a substitute to get to sleep."

"You're supposed to be so exhausted you can't move."

"Well, I can't. I'm contemplating whether or not I have the energy to put my plan into action, or whether I'll have to wait until tomorrow night."

"While you're contemplating, consider marrying me immediately. We'll get a license and get Goodman to agree. He will. He wants a new wing and more equipment. He also wants a Ferraro on their board. It always helps with fund-raisers."

"He's gouging you for money because my brother's there. That's not right."

"That's the way the game is played. We could do some good though, baby. I've been thinking about it. I hate that you've had to work so much just so your brother could have decent care. There are so many families that can't afford the Center, families with loved ones that really could benefit from the therapy. We could establish a scholarship in your brother's name and pay for the care and therapy of recipients."

He felt her swift intake of breath. Her eyes met his again. Liquid turned the sapphires to sparkling gems. "You would do that?"

"*We* would do that, Sasha. What's mine is yours. Remember? There isn't a divorce in the conventional sense of the word. If our shadows are pulled apart, you would never remember being married to me. All the pictures in the world won't allow you to remember. The money belongs to my family. We might be wealthy and have the ability to use the money any way we want, but in a divorce, the family trust can't be broken. What that means is, there isn't a prenup. Once we're married, all you have to do is say, I would like to build another wing onto the Center, and we get the people in place to make it happen."

"I don't know if I'm ready for that." Reluctance was clear in her voice.

"Then put the money aside. Are you ready for being with me? Living here with me? Being part of my crazy family?"

"I want to be with you more than anything, Giovanni. Tonight really showed me that trying to stay away from you wasn't going to work. And I hated that I put you and everyone else in danger because I was so confused."

"You're allowed. Marriage with someone like me is a big step. I know coming into my world can seem overwhelming, but I swear to you, baby, I'll take care of you. I'll be with you every step of the way."

"I want to keep working."

"In the club?"

"Maybe not there, but I like working."

"Have you considered a stable of horses? We could put riding trails in the park and you could take kids out occasionally, kids with disabilities who might not be able to ride otherwise. The world is open to you, Sasha. Once we're married, if you want to quit the club, whatever dream you have, you can do."

"I never thought of something like that here in Chicago. You're amazing. Horses actually are very good for therapy. I had been taking classes before my parents' accident with the idea of using horses for therapy, but then I stopped just short of my degree when they were killed and Sandlin was injured. You must be psychic."

He wasn't about to tell her the investigators, both teams, had been digging up everything they could on her once he showed real interest. "Say you'll marry me immediately, and then we have to get some sleep." He was one to take advantage when he knew he had it.

She laughed softly. "You have a one-track mind."

"Is there a reason you're hesitating?"

"Everyone is going to think I'm pregnant."

His cock jerked. She laughed. "Oh my God, you're hoping I'm pregnant."

"Then you'll have to marry me."

"No one has to marry in this day and age. Women can cope with having a child without marriage."

He smacked her ass hard. "You are deliberately making me suffer. Admit it."

She laughed again, her body squirming over his, rubbing deliciously over his growing cock. "Absolutely I am. Yes, I'll marry you, because if I don't say yes, we'll never get any sleep."

"We'll get sleep," he said and rolled her to her side. "Because I'm going to make sure your mouth is so stuffed full you can't talk anymore now that I've got your promise."

She laughed softly, and slid her body down just enough in the bed that when he turned on his side, she could slide his cock into the hot haven of her mouth.

# CHAPTER EIGHTEEN

"The rifle was registered to Aaron," Stefano said, reaching across the table to pull the bowl of pasta to him. "He was arrested and taken into custody this afternoon."

Sasha gasped and looked up at Giovanni. His face was absolutely blank. He could have been carved from stone. She put her hand on his arm. It felt like a block of marble, not real flesh and blood. "I'm sorry, I know you didn't want it to be him."

"It isn't him." Giovanni's voice held absolute conviction. "No way would he ever use that rifle and then drop it. It wasn't his. His friend was a sharpshooter. They went through boot camp together and deployed together. His friend was killed in a shootout when they were on a routine patrol. Aaron hauled his body back and that rifle. The widow gave Aaron the rifle. She kept his tags and the flag. Aaron might have used a different rifle to try to kill me, but not that one. He showed it to me and told me it was the only rifle he kept in his house."

There was silence while his brothers and sisters all let that sink in. Taviano handed Stefano the spaghetti sauce. It was Taviano's recipe, and Sasha thought it could win awards.

"He has no alibi for any of the times something happened," Stefano continued very calmly. "He claimed in each case, he'd either been alone asleep or he'd been alone in his home gym training."

"It isn't him," Giovanni said stubbornly.

"If not Aaron," Vittorio said, "then who?"

"And why?" Emmanuelle asked. "None of this makes sense, especially if it isn't Aaron. Who is targeting Sasha and you? Even Sandlin?"

"Sasha, are you very certain you have no enemies? Sandlin? Could the driver of the other vehicle blame him and want the two of you dead?" Ricco asked.

She gave it some thought. She hadn't lived a fast-lane lifestyle. "My life was easy and uncomplicated. I worked on the ranch, went to school and barrel raced. I didn't leave a string of broken hearts behind me. I grew up with the boys there. We were more like brother and sister than sweethearts. I swear, there isn't anything I did that could have prompted this kind of retaliation."

"Sandlin?" Stefano prompted, heaping pasta and spaghetti sauce on Francesca's plate.

"Stop." Francesca caught his arm. "That's too much."

"No, it isn't." His voice brooked no argument.

Instantly, all eyes were on Francesca. She moved closer to her husband. "I can't possibly eat that much, and all of you stop staring at me."

"You're *so* pregnant," Emmanuelle said. "Aren't you?"

"It's too early to get excited," Francesca protested. "I've lost two already. The doctor says there's no reason, but I didn't want anyone to know because it's so horrible when I don't carry . . ." Her eyes filled with tears.

"That's why it was so much easier to say she hadn't gotten pregnant," Stefano said. "Or," he corrected, "to imply it. She's edging toward the three-month mark. She lost the others at six weeks so I think we're past the crisis point."

"Maybe she should be lying down," Vittorio said.

"I'm for that," Ricco agreed. "Stefano, shouldn't she be on bed rest?"

Francesca groaned. "None of you start. You know Stefano's bad enough. I'm not going on bed rest unless the doctor says it's necessary. Which he hasn't."

"Yeah, well, not all doctors are bright," Taviano said.

"Some of them pay no real attention to their patients. We should make this decision, not the doctor who probably can't remember her name."

Sasha nearly stuffed her napkin in her mouth to keep from laughing. They were all insane. She was very glad she wasn't Francesca. Stefano was bad enough, but if all the brothers were going to have an opinion on the pregnancy, it was going to be a very long nine months.

"The doctor knows her name," Stefano assured. "He's being paid to care for Francesca, day or night, at home. He's one of the best in his field."

Sasha was fairly certain that translated into being the very best. Her eyes met Francesca's, and the two women smiled and shook their heads at the same time.

"What do you think about bed rest?" Vittorio asked Stefano. His tone implied all kinds of things—the doctor was crazy and Vittorio's woman would already be lounging in a bed.

Sasha raised her eyebrow at Giovanni. He had to see Vittorio wasn't as laid-back as they all thought him to be. He might be their diplomat, but she suspected he could be the diplomat because he was in control at all times. He was that disciplined.

"I believed bed rest was needed," Stefano conceded, "but Dr. Hanson convinced me that there was an entire set of new problems with bed rest. So far, she's had a little spotting, but that's cleared up and the baby is growing at the correct pace. He doesn't see any complications so far."

"What about with Francesca? Does he say she can carry without risk to her?" Vittorio asked. Again, his tone implied that would have been his first question to the doctor, and if there was a risk, his woman wouldn't be pregnant.

Sasha rolled her eyes, and Mariko hid a smile. Francesca hissed out a breath of exasperation. "Francesca is right here, Vittorio. You could ask me."

"You wouldn't tell me the truth, or at least you'd softsoap it. What did the doctor say, Stefano?"

Francesca half-heartedly threw a piece of sourdough bread at Vittorio. He picked it out of the air without even looking her way.

"He said we would evaluate more as she gets further along. So far, there are no complications or dangers to her."

"I'm very sorry about the two losses," Sasha said to both parents. "That must have been so difficult on both of you, especially since you didn't tell anyone." She couldn't help remembering that Giovanni had told her how cruel Eloisa had been to Francesca. Of course, she had no way of knowing Francesca had suffered two miscarriages. It was no wonder Stefano wanted to protect his wife from his mother. She couldn't imagine how painful that must have been for both when they wanted children so badly.

"Thank you," Stefano said, reaching out to take Francesca's hand. "Getting back to the subject at hand, we were talking about this thing with Aaron and whether or not the attacks could be coming from something in your past."

Sasha shook her head as she finished chewing another bite of spaghetti. She really had to watch her weight if she was going to eat Taviano's cooking. It was that good. "Definitely not me. My life has been pretty unremarkable. Well . . ." she hedged. "Until I met Giovanni."

She couldn't help looking at him. They'd spent two days in his house, worshiping each other's body, sleeping and eating and starting the cycle all over again. Sometimes they skipped eating and sometimes they skipped sleeping. She hadn't tired of him. Or them. Not for a moment. Just looking at him brought those memories into her mind. All the images. The ways he'd taken her. The things he'd introduced her to, all of which she'd loved, even those she'd been a little intimidated by.

This morning, she'd surprised him by insisting he lie still while she had her wicked way with him, and she'd even used rope to tie his hands so he couldn't move. He moved. He wasn't a man easily kept down, especially when his body was hard and hot and very ready. Sasha blushed when their eyes met. He knew what she was thinking. That moment he'd flipped her over. The way he'd taken charge. Of course, she'd primed him. She knew at some point, if she kept teasing him, it was going to happen. The blush became a full body blush.

"What about Sandlin?" Stefano prompted.

Everyone was looking at her. Grinning. Her color deepened. "Well, he was very popular with the ladies, and he dated a lot. He was never engaged or even with one girl exclusively, at least not since high school. I don't think it could be that. He had friends and very rarely got into arguments. Sandlin wasn't like that."

"The accident?" Ricco prompted. "Could someone blame him? You said he was driving."

She took a deep breath, hating to think about that night. The call. The hospital. The sheriff trying to talk to her, to keep her calm when she wanted to go to her parents. Her brother. It had been a terrible nightmare. She pushed that aside and tried to remember the other family.

"The woman was drunk. Horribly drunk. She had children. I remember them being there. They weren't crying. I was. I was sobbing so loud and I couldn't stop. I'm pretty certain I was so loud no one in the hospital could possibly have been sleeping that night. The two of them, both boys, teens, I think, just stood there against the wall, their father telling me over and over how sorry he was. His wife walked away without so much as a broken bone."

"We've already checked into the family," Taviano said. "The report is, the woman is still a drunk, so much so that I doubt she could orchestrate any of this. The man moved away with his two sons and they live in Oregon now. They seem happy. We're still keeping a close eye, but again, nothing adds up there."

"That leads us back to Aaron," Emmanuelle said. "I'm with Giovanni. I don't think it's him. I think it's too much, all that evidence piling up against him."

"Let's look at this another way," Mariko said suddenly.

"If all this evidence against Aaron was manufactured, his credit card actually stolen to purchase bomb materials, the picture of Sasha stolen from his phone, the rifle that he had to have kept safe in his home, all of that kind of adds up to the fact that whoever is doing this is very close to him."

Giovanni's head jerked up. "Mariko, I want to kiss you right now."

"Well don't," Ricco all but growled.

Laughter spilled around the table. Giovanni nearly crushed Sasha to him. He set her back in her chair and blew a kiss across the table at Mariko in defiance of his brother.

"It's so fucking obvious now that you point it out. I wasn't looking at that. To beat the shit out of Raimondo, he has to be a pro. What the hell was wrong with me? Aaron's friends are all in the same profession. What if this isn't about Sasha, Sandlin or me? What if this is about Aaron?"

There was a stunned silence. They had been so focused on Giovanni and Sasha that they hadn't considered that at all.

"Aaron lived on the streets for years. He fought his way to the top. He's disciplined and goal oriented. He would mow down anyone in his path trying to stop him. He had to have stepped on other mixed martial arts fighters' careers. He defeated a number of really good fighters to get where he is. Any one of them could be an enemy."

Giovanni sounded almost relieved, and Sasha put one hand on his thigh under the table in order to comfort him. She knew how he felt about Aaron. She knew he'd been hurt. He really didn't want to think that his friend would orchestrate everything that had happened, including the fire that could have swept through multiple buildings, destroying livelihoods.

Giovanni smiled at her and put his hand over hers, pressing her palm deeper into the heated muscle of his thigh. "We've got to find this bastard and stop him."

"Should we call Vinci and ask him to represent Aaron?" Taviano asked.

Stefano shook his head. "It's actually better if Aaron is locked up. We don't know for certain there is someone else, but let's assume there is for now. Whoever is trying to frame him can't very well do anything else while he's in jail or the frame won't work. Everyone is safe for the moment. We can concentrate on figuring out who he is and set up a con. That's when we'll pull Aaron out."

"Who would have motivation?" Sasha asked. The heat from Giovanni's thigh nearly scorched her palm right through the material of his slacks. She began to rub her hand up and down his thigh.

"Any of the fighters he defeated on his way to the title," Emmanuelle said.

"Aaron told Sasha I competed with him for women."

"What the fuck?" Stefano snapped. "I should go pay that little asshole a visit. Teach him a lesson about lying to one of our women. We fuck up enough on our own without having that kind of shit spread around."

The fact that Stefano was so outraged made Sasha realize that none of Giovanni's brothers would compete for women and then drop them. It wouldn't happen. She had believed Giovanni, but it was nice to know none of the others would, either.

"The point is, if he said that, did he do it? If he did and won, would the woman be angry with him? Would the loser? What if the woman was someone the loser really wanted?" Emmanuelle asked.

"If the loser really wanted a woman, would he risk her on a bet?" Vittorio asked. "He didn't want her that bad if it happened and he deserved to lose her."

"What about Meredith Benson?"

Everyone at the table turned to look at Sasha. She'd expected it, but she still blushed. "I'm not jealous just because Giovanni kissed her . . ."

"I didn't kiss her," he denied, just like she knew he would. "She kissed me."

"Is there a difference?" She widened her eyes at him.

"There will be a discussion at home about this."

A frisson of excitement crept down her spine and her sex clenched. Her fingers bit into his thigh and crept closer to his cock. She was very happy to think about what kind of discussion they'd be having once they got home.

"I'm just saying, the woman set it up so the paparazzi would take pictures of her planting one on my helpless man for an imagined slight, perhaps she's mental enough to go to all the trouble of framing a friend of his." Even to herself it sounded a little lame. It sounded much better when she was thinking about it.

"I already asked the investigators to check her out," Stefano said. "She has an alibi for every single night, but someone paid that worm to attack Giovanni and you at the club, so maybe she paid someone to do all this. I just don't think she's that stupid."

Sasha didn't feel so much like a jealous woman. She really wasn't concerned about the most beautiful woman in Hollywood. Who would be?

Giovanni leaned close. "Stop it," he whispered. He opened her fingers and pressed her palm over his thigh. She hadn't even realized she'd closed her fist.

"Just so you're all aware, in the middle of this fucked-up mess, Sasha has agreed to marry me immediately. We've already gotten the license, and we'll be negotiating with Goodman today to get married in his facility so Sandlin can be with us. We thought taking him out of his environment would be upsetting to him. The doc noticed that if he's forced out onto the grounds and away from the sitting room or his own room, he becomes agitated."

Sasha looked down at her nearly empty plate. She didn't want to think too much about what that meant. She knew the doctor had been trying to prepare her to lose her brother, but she'd insisted on denial. She was still in denial. If he could only live three years, then she wanted every minute of those three years. She planned to ask the doctor about a private nurse and Sandlin living with her. First, she had to ask Giovanni, but she knew his answer. When it came to caring for family, his answer would always be yes.

Stefano sent her a smile. A legitimate, real smile. The one he generally reserved for Francesca. "When? It has to be very small, to be held there. We'll have to do the reception at the hotel so the community can come. I don't want to be the one to tell Signora Moretti that she isn't invited to Giovanni's wedding."

Another round of laughter went up. Sasha loved being with Giovanni's family. When they were alone together, they seemed to handle everything easily. The fact that someone had tried to burn down businesses and kill her or Giovanni—very sobering subjects that they all contributed to—but then they'd go into laughter. She loved that.

"By right away," Emmanuelle ventured, "do you mean in a month?"

Giovanni nearly spewed coffee across the table. He glared at his sister. "I spent all night tormenting her until she agreed to *immediately*."

Sasha smirked. "But you didn't negotiate exactly what *immediately* meant. A month, when it comes to a wedding, is definitely immediately."

He glared at her and she wanted to laugh. "I'm fully aware you liked your torture a little too much, baby, so I'll be upping the game tonight. When you agreed to 'immediately' that meant in the next couple of days."

The women gasped. Emmanuelle shook her head. Mariko smiled and shook hers as if she thought all men were crazy. Francesca gave her brother-in-law a stern look. "No one can put a wedding together in a couple of days. The dress. The cake. The flowers. We have to have the place decorated."

"To get the best planner can take months," Emmanuelle said.

"Baby, you want to marry me as soon as possible, don't you?" His voice was pure wickedness.

"Yes." She could barely get it out. Her lungs felt raw

with the need for air. How could a woman love a man so much so fast? She would do anything for him. He wanted to marry her immediately because of Sandlin. He might want to tie her to him, but more, he wanted to make absolutely certain that her brother would be well enough to attend the wedding and enjoy it.

"Don't agree to anything," Emmanuelle said. "He's going to pull out all stops to get his way. My brothers think they can boss everyone. You have to stand strong, Sasha. Your wedding day is your day."

"It's *our* day," Giovanni corrected. "The two of us, baby." He brought her hand to his mouth and kissed her open palm. Right in the center, sending little darts of fire racing straight to her heart. Little arrows. There was no way to tell him how wonderful he was. No way to show him. This wasn't for Giovanni no matter how much he said it was. Her heart ached with love. Her heart hurt with it. Giovanni and Sandlin, her two men.

"They'll do *anything*," Emmanuelle continued. "You just have to hold out."

"You promised to be my wife immediately, Sasha," Giovanni said. He was using the voice. His tone was sinful. Beautiful. "Immediately."

Sasha nodded. She heard the love in it. There was no speaking. No way to speak. If she tried, she'd burst into tears, and maybe she still would. Her beloved Sandlin. Her brother. She fought so hard to keep him. To make his life everything it could be. She would have sacrificed anything for him. Somehow, by some miracle, she found a man who loved her enough to want to do the same thing.

Francesca put her hands over her face. "I don't know how we're going to be able to do this, but I guess . . ." She trailed off, looking at Emmanuelle.

Emmanuelle groaned, threw her hands into the air and shook her head. "You're so whipped, Sasha. That man is going to walk all over you just the way Stefano walks on Francesca and Ricco walks on Mariko."

"Do I walk on you?" Stefano asked Francesca, his voice genuinely confused.

Another round of laughter erupted. Sasha was happy the spotlight was off her and on Francesca and Stefano. She knew if Giovanni said one more word to her she would burst into tears. She was good at keeping her emotions in check, but her eyes burned and her chest hurt so badly she could barely breathe. She needed to be alone to find a way to pull her wild emotions back in check. It was silly to be so emotional, but she'd just seen her man put his love into action, doing it for her. Something huge. The lump in her throat was enormous, so much so that she could barely breathe.

"If you'll excuse me for a minute?" Immediately the men stood, which always embarrassed her. She gave them a little salute and hurried away.

Luckily, she knew her way around since spending the night in Stefano's penthouse. She made her way down the hall to the other wing where Giovanni had shared a bedroom with her. She stood for a moment in front of the mirror, staring at her flushed face. Her hair was down. She wore a long skirt and a peasant blouse. The feel of the material was softer than anything she'd ever known. Where Lucia found such treasures she had no idea, but she loved nearly everything in the boutique and was grateful it hadn't burned along with her apartment and the deli.

The door opened and Giovanni slipped through. He closed it after him. "Are you all right, baby? What's wrong? If you really don't want to get married immediately, I won't railroad you into it."

That was it. The sound of his voice. That gentle, tender, sweet caring that could bring her to her knees. She burst into a storm of tears. Wild. Unrestrained. She wept for her dead parents and the boy who had been her brother, always there with her. Always looking out for her. Teaching her how to ride, how to rope. Sandlin.

She covered her face and wept. The sound of her sobs

filled the room, and it was enough. Her sorrow could have filled the entire penthouse had Giovanni not closed the door behind him. He crossed the room and took her into his arms. She kept her hands over her face, but pushed her face into his chest. His arms locked around her and he put his head on hers.

Sasha wasn't certain how long he held her, but she found herself in his lap where he sat on the edge of the bed. When she could finally get herself under control, he was rubbing her back, rocking her gently and murmuring how much he loved her and everything was going to be all right.

"I'm sorry." She whispered it. "I couldn't help it. I think I had a breakdown, like a complete and utter meltdown. I swear, Giovanni, it was like a tsunami. I was afraid I wouldn't make it out of the room before I completely went to pieces. You're insisting on marrying me immediately because of Sandlin, aren't you?" She forced herself to get her head out of his chest so she could look up at him.

His eyes moved over her face. She knew she was a mess, but it didn't seem to matter to him. He still looked at her as if she was his entire world. "I want to make certain Sandlin has the chance to be a big part of our wedding and then our marriage. He's your family, and that makes him mine."

Her fingers curled into his shirt and with her free hand she thumped his shoulder. Not hard, just a strike and then another. Protesting the truth. "You're doing it because you talked to the doctor, and Sandlin's going to die, isn't he?"

Giovanni took a breath. She felt it right through her. As if they were sharing the same skin, the same muscles and bones. He breathed and so did she. "He did, didn't he?"

"We're all going to die someday, Sasha. We can only live our lives the best way we can. I believe in family." He gestured toward the dining room where his brothers and sisters were. "I love them. I try to enjoy every minute I have with them. I think they all operate the same way. We live life large because we know it can be over in the blink of an eye. I had a younger brother. Ettore. All of us loved him. He was really amazing, Sasha. We learned from his death that we can't always have those we love with us every day. So, when we're together, we make certain to love one another, enjoy one another. Be in those moments. Right there. Right here and now. I want to do that with Sandlin."

She took a deep breath, hoping he felt it the way she did when he had breathed for the two of them. "I love you so much. I understand what you're saying. I do. And I'm so sorry about your brother, I didn't know."

His hand stroked caresses down her hair. "I love you, baby. I love everything about you. We're going to include Sandlin in what we have. My family wants to meet him. They'll visit him as well if he likes them and is comfortable."

"I've been thinking about asking the doctor if he thinks it would be good for Sandlin to live with me. With us. We could hire a private nurse. I'm willing to work extra hours to pay for it."

"Baby, that was one of the first things I asked. I told him about the house and grounds. The gardens. I even said if he thought it would be better for Sandlin to go back to Wyoming, we would do that. He said Sandlin was far better off where he is. He'd be confused and at this stage, his world has shrunk . . ."

"But that's just it. If he was with me, he could get better. I could talk to him more, remind him more." She knew she was fighting a losing battle. That terrible pressure in her chest told her she needed to face the truth. "They could try to operate one more time." That was sheer desperation and she knew it.

"You know he said that would kill him on the operating table." His arms tightened around her. "I'm so sorry, baby, but we'll make his life so good while he's still with us. You'll be free to spend more time with him. He'll like that. I've already talked to Stefano about getting the library more current. We can get him the books you think he'll love."

She pressed her face tightly against his neck. "I don't want to lose him."

"I know. We're reaching out to other doctors, the leaders in this field, and gathering all the information we can, just in case there's something his doctor has missed." She heard the determination in his voice.

She knew there wasn't, she'd spent the last two months researching. Still, she hoped. She took a deep breath to fight back the tears threatening again. She had Giovanni, and he was willing to fight for her brother with her. To give him the best life possible, no matter what that took. "Thank you. Just . . . Thank you. I don't know what I'd do without you, Giovanni."

"You probably wouldn't have a madman burning down your apartment."

She sat up straight. "If this person is really targeting Aaron, and not you, maybe it was the picture that Aaron took of me that was the catalyst. That was his opportunity to start his campaign against Aaron. Then Aaron played right into it by sending me flowers. If he talked to his friends about me, about having the picture . . ." She trailed off, frowning. "Would he do that?"

"If he was competing with someone. It's possible. Men play sophomoric games. You caught me when I was telling the finer points of my game to you. And look at John Darby. He goes to extremes, but his frat boys definitely have games they play at college and with him. I know that Aaron can't be faithful, he never stayed with a woman long."

"Or maybe it was because he was in competition with someone else and the moment he got the girl, he didn't want her anymore," Sasha said. "Giovanni, I know you're going to think I'm crazy, but sometimes I just know things. I feel this is exactly what Aaron was doing and whoever he plays his little game with is the one that is framing him."

Giovanni's hands went around her waist and he gently lifted her off him. "Let's get you washed up."

She stood shakily on her feet, absorbing the feeling, savoring the way she felt loved by him. She needed him more than ever, when she never had felt like a needy woman. "I must be a mess. When I cry, I get all red and splotchy."

"You're beautiful, baby. But I'm not a big fan of you crying. That breaks my heart, and I feel like I have to go slay a few dragons."

She couldn't help but laugh. Giovanni made everything better. Everything. Even the truth about Sandlin. He was right, she needed to be happy with whatever time she had left with him.

As she washed up in the bathroom, Giovanni stood beside her, as if they'd been doing such things for years. It felt comfortable. He met her gaze in the mirror.

"I'm going to talk to Aaron."

She shook her head. "Whoever this man is, he'll be looking for that. If he sees you talking to Aaron, he'll be afraid you're figuring it out. Right now, everyone is safe . . ."

"Only if we're right."

"We can still take precautions."

Giovanni caught her to him and lowered his mouth to hers. His kiss was wild. So hot it scorched her. So sweet it sent her heart tumbling over a cliff. "You look beautiful."

"I don't have more makeup. They're going to see the real me."

"I love the real you."

Holding hands, they walked back to the others, who had retreated from the dining room to the great room where they had after-dinner drinks in their hands.

Stefano looked up. His gaze slid over Sasha, clearly seeing too much. His gaze moved to Giovanni, and something passed between them. She realized Stefano had been concerned about her. They all had. A part of her was embarrassed that she'd broken down over the realization that Giovanni knew Sandlin's time was limited and he wanted to include him in the wedding—in his family. This one. The one that was so accepting of her.

"We've been throwing out the idea that Sid Larsen or Chesney Reynolds was involved, but looking over the reports, it appears as if both have alibis," Stefano said.

"Sasha thinks I shouldn't be seen talking to Aaron," Giovanni told his family after explaining her theory. "But the only way to find out if he regularly competed with someone for a woman is to ask him."

"She's right," Stefano said. "Right now, if this man is trying to frame Aaron, he thinks his job is done. He can't attack anyone else, not without blowing everything he's put in motion. He's handed the cops their arrest and conviction. He isn't going to think that our family might champion him. If you suddenly show up at the jail, visiting Aaron, that's going to make this man crazy. He might very well retaliate. In fact, most likely he'll be worried enough to strike at you, Sasha *and* Sandlin."

"One of the others has to talk to him," Sasha said. "Unseen. I know they can do it. You said so. If that's the case, someone else has to visit him when no cameras can catch them, caution Aaron not to tell a single soul about the visit and then ask him."

Stefano shook his head. "It's too risky. That's not what we do, Sasha. When we come out of the shadows, anyone who has seen us doesn't survive. How would we explain to Aaron how we got there? We can never appear anything but normal."

Sasha and Francesca burst out laughing. The others stared at one another as if confused.

"Tell us what the joke is," Giovanni prompted.

"There's nothing normal about any of you. No one thinks that," Francesca said. "The first time I ever saw Stefano, I thought he was a member of the mafia, and a very mean one at that. He scared me to death."

Stefano flashed her a smirk. "I still scare you to death." He looked very pleased at the idea.

Francesca laughed and snuggled closer to him. "You keep telling yourself that, babe."

"She's on to you," Emmanuelle said. "No more bossing her around, especially now that she's with child. I love how that sounds, Francesca. You're with child. Are you planning on telling Eloisa?"

Stefano threaded his fingers through Francesca's. "Not for a while. Francesca needs to feel secure that she's going to carry this child with no more complications. I'm not quite ready to forgive Eloisa the things she said to my wife behind my back. We don't keep things from each other, and she should have known that. What she says to Francesca, I want her to say to my face."

A little shiver went down Sasha's spine. She would never want to be on the wrong side of Stefano, especially if it had to do with Francesca. He obviously loved her very much. Francesca was completely comfortable with her husband. His scary demeanor didn't affect her in the least. Sasha realized she'd gotten that way with Giovanni. She knew with absolute certainty that he'd never hurt her, and he would fight for her whenever it was needed.

"What about the wedding?" Vittorio asked. "Will Eloisa be going to that?"

Sasha's first thought was *hell* no. But she was Giovanni's mother. She saw them all looking at one another and then at her. Giovanni's arm circled her waist and he pulled her against his chest, so her back was to his front. His arm locked just under her breasts. She didn't like being so exposed. Her face still felt swollen and tight from crying so much.

Sasha couldn't help it, she reached up to shield her face, trying to pull her hair subtly to cover her. Giovanni's mouth was instantly against her ear. "Baby, you're so beautiful, you take my breath away. Don't be embarrassed because you love someone and were emotional. That's amazing. You're amazing."

She leaned her head against his chest and reached back with one arm to circle his neck. The action lifted her breasts and pushed her bottom tightly against him. At once his teeth tugged at her earlobe, and she wished they were home together. She loved their home. She loved him. She wanted all this to be over so she didn't have to worry night and day.

"What do you think, Sasha?" Mariko asked. "Would you mind Eloisa coming to your wedding?"

"She's much better once you're actually married. Prior to marriage, she views you as a threat to the family, but after," Francesca said, "you *are* family."

"She still says things that are difficult to take," Sasha said. "You've been her family for a while now yet she thought nothing of coming in and making you feel bad."

"She didn't know I had two miscarriages," Francesca pointed out.

Stefano made a sound like a growling panther. "Baby, you're the most forgiving person on this planet. Eloisa needs her head examined, and if she ever speaks to you or any one of my sisters, new or not, like that again, she is going to be officially banished."

Francesca gasped. "You can't do that, Stefano."

"Watch me, Francesca." His voice was harder than ever. "I'm not putting up with it. She isn't mellowing. She's getting worse. What happens when she starts talking to our children that way? Or taking them out for her kind of training sessions? She learns now that she can't behave that way, or she goes."

Sasha believed him. Every word that came out of his mouth was a decree. "If I invite her to the wedding, is there a way to keep her from Sandlin? I can handle anything she says to me . . ." She paused and looked up at Giovanni. "As long as you realize I can get ugly. I dealt with bulls and grew up surrounded by cowboys dealing with bulls. I don't like being pushed around and usually push back hard. As long as Giovanni's all right with that, I won't have a problem, but Sandlin's too sweet." She hated the way her voice broke.

Giovanni's arm tightened and he dropped his chin to the top of her head. "Baby, you can say whatever shit is warranted if Eloisa is ugly to you. As for Sandlin, we'll tell her if she wants to come, the requirement will be that she has to stay away from your brother."

"Then we should invite her. She's your mother, and I don't want to start off on the wrong foot."

Taviano snorted. "Everyone is on the wrong foot with Eloisa, Sasha. Francesca has been the sweetest being on the face of the planet, and our lovely mother is ugly every time the two get together."

"She has problems, Taviano," Francesca excused.

"Then she's had them for years," Stefano said. "Since I was born." He downed his bourbon and held out his glass to his brother to fill.

Vittorio took the glass and crossed the room to the crystal decanter. He glanced back at his younger brother. "Eloisa has been down on Nicoletta since the start. Does she know that she's a rider?"

"I don't know. I don't even care," Taviano snapped. "The fact that she knows what an ugly life Nicoletta has had but she has no sympathy whatsoever for her is enough for me."

"She has no compassion or mercy in her," Vittorio agreed, handing the glass back to his oldest brother.

"I'll go talk to Aaron," Emmanuelle said. "I can get in without being seen, give him an explanation he would believe and ask him the questions."

Giovanni shook his head. "Thanks, Emme, I love you for it, but if Aaron is playing bullshit competition games with his male friends, he won't tell you. It has to be a man."

"He sent me chocolates." Sasha turned her head to look up at Giovanni as realization swept over her, but the position was awkward. She stepped away from him, commanding the room. "James. James Corlege, Aaron's friend. After the incident in the club, Aaron sent me flowers with an apology."

"I remember," Emmanuelle said. "He did it in person. I thought it was so sweet that he wanted to pick them out himself."

"That same day, I received chocolates with a letter of

apology from James. One sent flowers, the other chocolates. Were they trying to one-up each other?"

Giovanni snapped his fingers. "You also received handpicked flowers. From your stalker. What do we have on them? I know their names were on the list for the investigators."

"I have the files on them. It seems Rigina and Rosina spent some time looking into them," Stefano said, flipping open one and handing the other to Vittorio.

"James is the up-and-coming fighter in Aaron's weight division. He can't compete with Aaron," Giovanni said. "He can't get the title away from him."

Sasha's breath caught in her throat. Could this all be about a division title? Not anything to do with her or Giovanni? "A fight title?"

There was silence in the room while they all gave that some thought. Stefano shook his head, frustrated. "I'm looking at the dates of each incident. Corlege has a solid alibi for two of the incidents. The other times he claimed he was sleeping."

"Same with Tom Mariland," Vittorio said. "He was seen by other fighters at the gym on two of the dates."

"So, our suspects all have alibis. That leaves us with Aaron," Giovanni said. "I still don't buy it, but I'm beginning to think I could be wrong."

"All of us have alibis when you're guilty as hell," Emmanuelle pointed out. "They aren't riders, so none of them move through shadows, but maybe they have another way and we're just not figuring it out yet."

# CHAPTER NINETEEN

The weekend was crazy. More people were jammed into the club than ever before, pushing the number to full capacity with people standing in a very long line outside, hoping for a chance to come in. The extremely famous DJ inside, working her magic with the music, kept the dance party going hour after hour. Sasha worked the upper tier, not once looking at Giovanni. The tabloids were full of their broken engagement, all due to Giovanni's roving eye and his tryst with Meredith Benson.

Meredith was there, the paparazzi shooting her photograph over and over. Word was, she was a pariah in Hollywood and the one project she'd been about to work on had been yanked out from under her, due, the papers said, to the fact that she refused to come to work two mornings in a row. That was standard Meredith diva behavior, but her numerous absences, causing delays to the film, cost her dearly.

There was no way for her to fight the decision since they had plenty of evidence. Usually, it was too costly to bring in another actress when the film was a quarter of the way done, but in this case, another producer had funded the project. There was wild speculation who the producer was, but so far, the identity hadn't been uncovered.

She sent notes to the Ferraro table, but Giovanni didn't so much as turn around or deign to look her way. His brothers, as they came down the stairs to dance, didn't look at or acknowledge her, either. She was the center of attention with the flashing lights on her, but for the first time, she didn't seem to want the attention.

The MMA fighters arrived just after one, very pumped up after their bouts. James Corlege and Tom Mariland were the two big winners, and women flocked around them. The other fighters laughed and joked with them, cheering for them and buying them drinks. Sasha took the tray of drinks to their table and set them in front of the various fighters and their women. As she turned to go, Corlege caught her arm.

"I wanted to apologize for the way I acted the last time I saw you. I was upset over your engagement to Ferraro and I took it out on you in a very ugly way."

She gave him a small smile. "Thanks, I appreciate the apology. No worries." She turned away from him again.

Tom Mariland stepped in front of her, blocking her way. "I owe you an apology as well. Aaron was really upset about losing you to Ferraro, and he's a good friend of mine. James and I stayed up with him all night after the news of your engagement broke."

James nodded. "I thought we might have to take him to the hospital for alcohol poisoning."

Tom sighed. "He was so upset that we both thought you'd been in a relationship with him and had dumped him for Ferraro. It was only a couple of nights ago that he admitted he'd never been with you and, in fact, barely knew you. I felt like an idiot."

"It's okay, really."

"No, it's not. There was no excuse to talk to you that way," Corlege insisted.

"That picture he took of me, the one that ended up in the tabloids, did you know he had it?" She bit her lip and lowered her eyes. "Before it ended up all over the magazines?"

The men looked at each other.

She sighed. "I can see from your faces that Aaron shared it with you."

Tom nodded. "I'm sorry. It seems I'm always owing you

an apology." He sighed. "Aaron thought you were beautiful. He had dozens of pictures of you on his phone. He showed them to us. That's why I thought you two were a thing and you had cheated on him with Ferraro. But . . ." He hesitated. "He also liked to share his women. It was a thing. I think he's a bit of an exhibitionist."

Sasha had to turn her head away. Tom and James were painting Aaron with an entirely different brush than Giovanni had. Who was right? If it had been just Tom or just James, she would have thought one was lying, but both of them? As a rule she could hear lies, and she was hearing a mixture of truth and lies, but what was true and what was the lie? Did they have it wrong? Had Aaron been the one trying to kill her? If so, what could possibly be his reason?

"Sasha, if there's anything I can do for you, just let me know," Corlege persisted.

Another woman caught his arm and pulled on it in an effort to remove his hand from Sasha. She glared at Sasha. "Run along, honey. You're supposed to be serving drinks."

"Candy, don't talk to her like that," Corlege reprimanded, his voice harsh. He bunched his fist in the woman's hair.

Candy winced, turned red and, when Corlege returned to his seat, pulling her with him by her hair, she curled up at his feet. He held a glass of vodka and grapefruit to her mouth and she gulped it down, some spilling down the front of her. Several of the men laughed and turned to kiss the women sitting on their laps.

Disgusted, Sasha turned away. She made her way down to the bar where Alan looked her over. "You look tired, honey."

She glanced up the stairs to see Tom and James both watching her. Immediately she looked away, not wanting to see them anymore. "I'm all right, just need a little break. I've been at this for hours. How did Nancy ever work both tiers? It seems just when I serve a round of drinks to a table, they're already asking for more. One tier is all I can handle. Thank God, I don't have to work both."

"She didn't work both tiers unless her partner was ill," Alan corrected. He glanced at his watch. "Take your break. It's only a couple of minutes early. If you're back a couple of minutes early, it will even out."

"Thanks, I think I will." Being too close to Corlege and watching the way he treated the woman he'd brought with him turned her stomach. She was tired of seeing so many women debase themselves in order to try to marry money.

She went down the stairs and headed straight for the employee lounge. She'd just gotten her heels off and was sitting back, her head against the very comfortable back of the chair, when the click of heels told her she wasn't alone. Cautiously, she opened one eye. Meredith Benson stood over her, hands on her hips.

"Go away," Sasha said. "I mean it. Go away, or I'll call security and have your ass hauled out of here."

Meredith's breath hissed out of her like an angry cat's. "How dare you talk to me that way! Do you have any idea who I am?"

"You're the skank who had her tongue down Giovanni's throat for show."

"I came in here to tell you that he had nothing to do with it."

"I know that. You made a scene, kissing my man, making him look bad just because you're so vain you wanted to be the one to dump him. One doesn't get dumped if it's a one-night stand. Go away."

Meredith ground her teeth. "I'm trying to be nice and repair the damage I did."

"You're trying to get Giovanni to let you have your career back. That's the only reason you would follow me in here and tell the truth. Have you forgotten? Or don't you read the crap you contribute to? Giovanni and I are a thing of the past. I have absolutely no influence on him at all."

She shooed Meredith away. "Go. Maybe one of your many lovers will take you back after you dumped them for the publicity."

Meredith pulled her arm back to hurl the heavy glass she held in her hand at Sasha. A hand caught her wrist and yanked her backward. James Corlege took the glass from her hand as Sasha slowly sat up.

"Get out of here," Corlege advised.

Meredith backed out of the room, her face twisted with malice.

Sasha sighed. "Thanks. She doesn't like me. I'm not certain why, not when she's the one trying to screw things up between my supposed fiancé and me."

His eyebrow shot up. "Supposed fiancé? I saw the ring on your finger. Tabloids lie all the time, but that ring was real."

She shrugged. "My boss did me a favor. My brother was in a car accident and suffered a traumatic brain injury. I don't have a lot of money or clout. The Ferraros do. Giovanni was nice enough to offer to help. Being engaged made it easier to breach patient confidentiality. Being a Ferraro made it so much easier to get to the administrator's ear. Meredith actually did us a favor because we would have had to find a different way to break up."

He was silent a moment. "None of it was real? Not all those hot looks?"

She laughed. "I should have been an actress, right? No, none of it was real. The Ferraros are very loyal to anyone who works for them. They've been extraordinary with me. I was so worried about Sandlin, that's my brother, and they straightened things out. I can pay for the facility, but I couldn't get to the doctor and I needed to do that in order to understand why they hadn't scheduled another operation."

"You work too hard." He pulled her foot between his hands and began a foot massage.

It was intimate. Too intimate. It also felt good when her feet were screaming at her. She knew she should stop him.

Giovanni was going to have a fit, and James made her want to curl up and hide, but her feet hurt so bad, she didn't care.

"Isn't your girl going to get upset with you, James?" Deliberately she used his first name.

"She isn't my girl. She's a groupie. Women like fighters. She'll do me and then the same night crawl into someone else's bed."

Her stomach lurched. Wyoming wasn't that far away. Cattle ranches weren't the end of the world. She'd never considered herself sheltered. She always believed men were the ones doing very bad behavior and playing ugly games, but she was getting her eyes opened about the women who pursued fighters, the wealthy, athletes and diplomats. It was no wonder these men didn't have much respect for women. They had become conditioned to get anything they wanted. She let her breath out slowly, once again feeling that maybe she didn't belong there.

Still, she had a job to do. "I was so shocked to see on the news that Aaron had been arrested for starting the fire and stalking me. Have you been to see him?"

James frowned and shook his head. "It doesn't surprise me. The cops were by to interview all the fighters. Tom is his closest friend. He wasn't surprised, either. We knew he'd fixated on you after he got so drunk when he found out about the engagement."

His fingers moved over her bare feet until she wanted to groan in appreciation. The door opened and slammed closed behind Tom Mariland. He glared at James, his hands on his hips.

"What's going on in here?" he demanded, his gaze dropping to James's fingers stroking along her heels.

"Just giving the lady a foot massage, Tom. She's been working all evening in those high heels. We were talking about Aaron."

At once Tom crossed the room to sit down on the edge of the lounge Sasha was sitting in, forcing her to scoot over. "That's such a tragedy, Aaron going off the deep end like that," Tom agreed. "He was drinking too much, and I think it just got to him. I'd tell you he was a good guy, but I'm pretty certain I'm not going to convince you of that."

"You know, neither of you is supposed to be back here," Sasha said, uneasiness creeping into her voice, as if she didn't want to get into trouble. "How did you get back here? Security is everywhere tonight."

"They've got their hands full with drunks," James said. "I slipped a couple of guys some money to start an altercation. Just pushing and shoving a bit on the floor."

Tom nodded. "It isn't that difficult."

Sasha was very uncomfortable being so close to Tom, especially with her feet in James's hands. "Aaron burned down my apartment with everything in it"—she continued their earlier conversation—"so, no, I don't think you're going to convince me Aaron's a good guy. Worse, he could have really hurt my brother by setting off charges in the ceiling of the place where he's getting care."

The door swung open again, this time slamming shut so hard the crash was louder than the music. Tom jumped to his feet. James swung around to face the threat, and Sasha jerked her feet out of his hands as Giovanni stalked in. Anger darkened her fiancé's face. He wasn't acting. Yeah, the foot massage, as good as it felt, probably wasn't the best idea.

"What the fuck, Corlege? Keep your fuckin' hands to yourself."

Corlege stood up slowly, straightening to his full height. Sasha could see the muscles rippling in his body. He looked coolly confident. If he knew that Aaron trained with Giovanni, he clearly hadn't bothered to assess his fighting skills.

"She doesn't belong to you."

"The hell she doesn't."

"Giovanni." Someone had to be the voice of reason. "He knows you were just being sweet to me for my brother's sake."

Giovanni's dark eyes swept over her, and she pressed her

lips together very tightly. He wasn't going to hear the voice of reason. He was angry. More than angry. Giovanni in this mood was actually a little terrifying. She had never seen this side of him.

Tom moved, trying to circle around to the side of Giovanni, and her heart plunged. He would weigh in on Corlege's side. Both men were MMA champions. She knew Giovanni could take one of them, but both coming at him at the same time?

"You have no right to be in here. It's an employee lounge and it says so right on the door. Get the fuck out." Giovanni's glide to the side of the room with the least furniture was almost imperceptible. It took him closer to James but put distance between Tom and him. At least she didn't have to worry that he wasn't aware of Tom as an added threat.

"What do you plan to do? Call security so you can hide behind them the way you always do? I suppose that makes you feel like a big man, to call your security force to deal with real men who fight their own fights."

"James," Sasha cautioned, hoping that concentrating on the enemy might get better results. "You don't want to get banned from the club." It was totally the wrong thing to say, and as soon as the words left her mouth, she knew she had just amped up the trash-talking. Taking a breath, she moved her feet to the floor. If Giovanni was going to have to fight James, he wasn't going to be fighting Tom at the same time.

"Right, because that would be the chickenshit thing he would do," James taunted.

"Do you think I need security guards to wipe up the floor with your ass?"

Sasha looked up at the camera, silently begging one of his brothers to come help. She knew they had to be watching. She wanted to scream at them to get in there. For all they knew, one of the two men had a gun with him. She didn't know which of the two was guilty of framing Aaron, but she was sure one of them had. Whichever it was, he was bound to be willing to kill Giovanni.

James rolled his shoulders. Out of the corner of her eye, she saw Tom echo his movements. Giovanni was perfectly still, but he looked casual, like a lazy tiger regarding two cubs challenging him for territory—or a woman.

"This is silly. James, Tom, you have to go back upstairs before everyone does something they can't take back." She tried again.

"Baby, you go on upstairs," Giovanni prodded. "Get back to work."

That wasn't happening. She wasn't leaving him alone with a possible madman—one already proven willing to use bombs, fire and bullets to get his way. Giovanni was ruining their entire plan—or he had another one she just didn't know about.

James launched himself at Giovanni with a series of kicks. Giovanni blocked every one of them, his fist slamming down again and again on James's legs as the MMA fighter tried using his famous forward snap kick and equally lethal roundhouse kick to drive his opponent toward Tom. Giovanni didn't give ground at all. He stood, loose-limbed, his feet under his shoulders, elbows tucked in until he lashed out with a block. He was strong, and when he hit, it was as if he was dropping a hammer down. James was limping a little as he backed off.

"Holy shit, you really do hit that hard. I thought the first time you clocked me it was me being drunk thinking you hit like that."

It was obvious to Sasha that James was trying to keep Giovanni's attention centered on him so Tom could move in. Tom hurled himself into the air, both feet driving at Giovanni from the side. Simultaneously, James did the same. Giovanni didn't move. Sasha did. She threw her high heel right at Tom's face. She'd spent her entire life on a ranch, and when she needed to hit something, she did it. The high heel slammed into his face hard, throwing him off-balance because he saw the missile coming at him at the last minute and tried to deflect it.

She shouldn't have worried. Giovanni blocked both men's attacks, again striking hard with a closed fist, slamming it on exposed thighs to give them a dead leg. Tom dropped out of the air to hit the ground on his butt. James staggered back. Tom kept moving, this time going for Sasha, sweeping her legs out from under her. She hit the floor hard. Tom was on her in a second, punching toward her face.

The first blow hit the floor as she rolled. The second hit the back of her shoulder. He never got a third shot in. Giovanni stomped him hard, kicked him in the ribs and flipped him over with a third and fourth kick before James could get near him.

James got in one shot as Giovanni was turning toward him, but then it was over, Giovanni moving with blurring speed, hands and feet pounding until both men lay on the floor bleeding. Sasha dragged herself back to the chair and threw herself into it.

"What is wrong with you, woman?" Giovanni demanded.

"I was helping. They weren't fighting fair."

"Neither were you," Tom groused. "What the fuck did you hit me with? A tank?" He spat blood.

"It was a shoe, you moron," Sasha said. "I think you broke my shoulder."

Giovanni's hands were there, gently moving over her, checking for damage. "What the hell was this about, James? You knew Aaron trained with me. You can't take him. If I can beat the shit out of him, it would stand to reason that you can't take me." He indicated Tom with his chin. "Did you tell Tom about Aaron sparring with me?"

"Aaron couldn't quit bragging about it," Tom said, spitting more blood. He pressed his hand to his mouth and glared at Sasha. "That was always his trouble. He talked so much trash, he didn't know when to quit."

"Big fuckin' deal, sparring with a Ferraro," James added. "Never did a day's work in your life. Walk around all badass carrying a gun and looking dangerous? You think that's going to impress us? Not likely. Aaron was an idiot."

"He got all the women," Sasha said. "I thought he was so hot when he was in that ring."

Giovanni glared at her. She fluttered her lashes at him.

"He got shit," Tom said. "Women were all over us."

"He told me you competed for women," Sasha said, "and he *always* won. I have to admit, I can see why. He just walked up the stairs and you could see all that power. He bragged he took every woman from you."

James swore. "Fuckin' liar. I won my share of the bets."

"I did, too," Tom said. "Aaron ran his mouth but he lied all the time to make himself look good. The bet on you was fifty thousand dollars. He needed the money, so he had to get Ferraro out of the way." His gaze shifted just for a moment to James.

"You bet fifty thousand dollars that you could date me?"

James climbed slowly to his feet. "We don't date, we fuck 'em and then drop 'em. That's the bet."

She nodded. "I see. He shared that picture of me with both of you, didn't he? And you all three made the bet."

"Of course he did. To give us an incentive to work harder." James laughed. "Then Ferraro snapped you up and killed the plan. All along, it was just a ruse."

"What do you mean?" Tom asked.

"She wasn't really engaged to him. It was so he could help her straighten things out at Hendrick Center."

Tom scowled. "You've got to be kidding. The brain-dead patients." He stood up and staggered to the door.

Sasha started to protest, furious that Tom would talk about the patients at the Center that way, but Giovanni put a hand on her arm and shook his head. They watched the door close after them, and then she glared at her fiancé.

"Why didn't you let me tell them off?" Fury made her voice tremble, but it was at the two fighters, not Giovanni.

"We were already skating on thin ice, baby." He caught her chin and examined her face for bruises.

"I don't understand."

"When you told him we weren't really engaged, you never mentioned the Center's name. You said your brother had a traumatic brain injury. Anyone who didn't have a family member or friend in the facility wouldn't know about the facility. And Tom wasn't present for the conversation. He referred to the patients as 'brain-dead.' It's both of them. Together."

Stefano and Taviano entered the room, both obviously overhearing the last thing Giovanni said. They'd been watching and listening from the control room.

Stefano indicated the door that led between the lounge and the hall where the two men had disappeared. "That's why their alibis checked out. When one was doing something, the other was seen. Once we went back and looked at anyone who would benefit from Aaron being out of the way, we concentrated on both Corlege and Mariland. Mariland is a firebug. He has a sealed record of starting multiple fires as a child. He went into the Army. They didn't look at his sealed records, because they couldn't. He also is very good at explosives."

"And Corlege?" Giovanni asked.

"Corlege is a very sick man. He likes to hurt women. He's had three relationships where his partner has ended up in the hospital," Taviano said.

"Sheesh." She rolled her eyes. "It's funny that Tom is the one who hit me when Corlege probably wishes he could have."

"Which is why none of us wanted you here in the first place, Sasha," Stefano said. "You could have really been hurt."

"You needed me to help carry out this plan. I told you I'd be all right." She couldn't help the smugness in her voice.

"He got his hands on you." Giovanni glared at her. "You let him touch your feet."

"I was getting information, and you burst in here like a crazy person," she protested, feeling slightly guilty. "There wasn't supposed to be hitting. In any case, I needed a foot massage."

"You want a fuckin' foot massage, Sasha, you get it from your man, not the ones we suspect of trying to kill you."

"That's my cue to leave. I have to go back to work." She rolled her shoulder experimentally. It hurt, but not nearly as bad as it had when Tom hit her. More likely, he'd grazed her when she was rolling.

"You aren't going back to work. We already have another server working the second tier, and Nancy shifted to the top one. You're going to take it easy right here and then go home with me."

She started to protest, looked around at the set features and then shrugged. "Fine." She didn't feel all that good anyway. Her shoulder *did* hurt, but she wasn't about to mention that and get another lecture. "Why didn't they just kill Aaron? They didn't mind in the least killing me. Or Giovanni. Why the elaborate plan?"

"Best guess," Stefano said, "jealousy. They wanted his title and wanted Aaron to see them in the winner's seat. Or at least James did. He seemed to be the leader between the two of them. They both wanted to win the competitions for the groupies. They probably got talking over a bottle of booze one night, sat around talking smack about Aaron and then thought up ways to actually get rid of him. The more they talked, the more elaborate the plan and the better it sounded. We've seen it before."

"We know all this, but can we get enough evidence to convict them?" Sasha asked.

The three men looked at one another. It was Giovanni who spoke. Gently. "Baby. We just have to get Aaron off. That shouldn't be difficult now that we know where to look."

"I don't understand. The cops are going to want to arrest them."

"They'll try," Stefano agreed. "Let's go home. My woman is waiting for me. And for all you observant shadow riders, not one of you noticed she wasn't drinking alcohol when we came to the club dancing. I bet her that you'd notice and I lost that bet."

Giovanni and Taviano both looked at their brother like he'd lost his mind.

"She used to drink Moscow mules and cosmopolitans, but for the last few months, it's been water. Or sparkling water. Maybe you haven't been paying attention." Stefano gave them his mean look. "There is very little Francesca does that I don't notice."

Giovanni nudged Sasha. "Pay attention, baby. I follow in Stefano's footsteps when it comes to my woman. I notice everything."

She thought about giving him a smart-ass answer, but she remained silent. She really wanted to go home and soak in that fabulous tub in the master suite.

Giovanni glanced at Stefano. "Will you be inviting our New York cousins to come for my wedding?"

"Of course."

"Perfect. I can't wait to see them. Come on, baby, let's go home." He knelt down to slip her heels back on her feet. His hands brushed her ankles as he did up the straps. "Who knew you were so good with a shoe?"

"I have many talents." She sent him a small smile.

"One of them is not staying out of trouble when your man is fighting."

"In my defense," she said, "I didn't know he was *that* good."

Taviano choked. Stefano turned away, clearing his throat. Giovanni stood up slowly. "I've been keeping count of all your little indiscretions," he warned. "I believe in punishments."

She laughed. "I'll be looking forward to that." Her

smile faded and she took his hand to allow him to pull her up. "You do know it goes both ways, right?"

Giovanni wrapped his arm around her. "Not sure what you mean, woman."

"I'm very good with ropes. Hog-tying is something of a specialty. Torturing is second nature." She leaned into him, and he put his head down so her lips were against his ear. "I'm very, very good with my mouth."

He laughed as they walked down the hall to the private entrance and exit for the Ferraro family. Once in the parking lot, he handed her gently into the car. "Your shoulder is going to be black and blue. I wanted to beat the crap out of Tom."

"Um . . . babe? I think you did. I think both of them are going to wake up very sore tomorrow."

"They'll be celebrating tonight, thinking they put one over on Aaron. You played your part beautifully, Sasha. I will say, I didn't expect them to follow you into the break room. We had it set up to watch over you at their table, but this was so much better. Especially when they attacked me."

"Do you have someone watching them?"

He nodded as he slid onto the seat beside her. "Ricco is following James, and Mariko is following Tom. If they're together, which we hope, they'll talk. They won't be able to help but brag. That's just another nail in the coffin. We'll be able to provide that to the investigators along with everything else we've got on them. There's going to be plenty of proof."

"And Aaron?"

"He'll have to stay in jail a little longer. Just until after we're married."

"That long?" She put her head on his shoulder and closed her eyes against the stream of lights.

"Baby, we're getting married in two days."

She couldn't help but smile at the reprimand in his voice. Of course, she knew when they were getting married. "Aren't you a little afraid for Mariko and Ricco? If one or both get caught, I'm sure Tom or James won't have a problem shooting them."

"They'll never come out of the shadows. In any case, even if they did, they're too well trained and far too fast. Ricco is the fastest of all of us."

It surprised her that Giovanni would name his brother faster, but she realized none of the Ferraro brothers ever bragged. They teased one another, but they didn't brag out of the family circle or in it. They were arrogant, but it came from a place of complete confidence.

"He's really that much faster than you?" She'd just seen Giovanni in action, and if he was fast enough to take on two mixed martial arts fighters, then Ricco had to be insanely fast.

"Yes. And he never, never gets turned around in a city."

"I didn't think about that happening," she admitted. She reached down to rub at her aching ankle. Her feet were still painful.

Immediately, Giovanni lifted her feet into his lap and undid the tiny buckles on the thin straps. He dropped the shoes onto the floor and began to massage her feet. His fingers were strong and they moved into her sore muscles, a deep pressure, until she wanted to cry with relief.

"That feels so good, honey," she admitted. "I should have stopped James, but my feet hurt so bad I was shameless."

"You were," he agreed, but he didn't stop. "We'll talk about that more when we get home."

"Are we going to talk about how your skanky actress with the roving tongue managed to slip through security and get into the employee lounge when we get home as well?"

"Don't try diversion. It won't work. Meredith isn't *my* actress, and you can handle ten actresses like her with one hand tied behind your back. If we stopped her and not the other two, it would have possibly given away the fact that we were letting them slip through on purpose."

She was a bit mollified that he believed she could handle Meredith so easily.

"We're also going to talk about how you didn't exit the room when you were supposed to, *before* the fighting started. I gave you enough time, but you didn't take it. Worse, you threw your shoe at Tom so he'd come at you. Those MMA fighters could break your jaw with one punch."

"I'm scrappy and fast. I had to be, working with cattle and horses."

He sent her a look that said he wasn't happy with her and she was going to hear about it so she thought it prudent to change the subject. She glanced at the front seat where Enzo drove and Emilio sat on the passenger side. "You said Ricco never loses his way. How do people get turned around in the shadows?"

"You're moving very fast, the speed is insane. Especially narrow shadows. Some tubes are like slick rails. Everything is blurred because you're moving so fast. The neighborhoods are unfamiliar. I know my way around Chicago, but I usually work in San Francisco, Los Angeles or New York. I've even worked overseas. Ricco trained in Japan. All of us trained in Europe or Asia. Sometimes, both."

"Your life is fascinating."

The car stopped, and Emilio opened the door for them. Giovanni slipped out first and then reached for her. Gathering her into his arms, he cradled her close to his chest. Sasha put her arms around his neck and leaned into him. Inhaling his scent. He smelled like home to her now. He carried her as if she weighed no more than a feather. As if she was a princess. She knew he carried her because her feet hurt. He was like that, paying attention to every detail.

He carried her through the house, right to the master suite. She loved the way the house was set up, and she'd already been adding her own touches here and there. She would be bringing treasures she had put in storage—thankfully—things that had belonged to her parents and brother. For now, it was little things, like arranging flowers in large vases and scattering them around the house. Her mother had loved flowers. She grew them in the garden and then cut them for the house. Sasha had always thought it was a little silly since the flowers were right outside, but now she really wanted to surround herself with the things that reminded her of her mother, and she wanted her own garden.

Giovanni deposited her in the armchair right in front of the fireplace and went on through to the bath to fill the square, oversized tub. She picked up the remote and started the flames so they flickered and threw out dancing shadows. Putting her head back she looked around the room with its high ceilings and beautiful appointments. She had never thought that she might be living in luxury. She still had a difficult time coming to terms with it. She wasn't certain she would ever actually do so.

"Baby?"

She turned her head almost lazily. Her man stood in the doorway, watching her. She smiled at him, the feeling of love so strong her heart felt shaky with it. "Right here, Giovanni. I don't know if I can move."

"You don't have to. I'll undress you and get you in the bath. The hot water will help."

"It's strange to think that someone would try to kill us. Both of us. Not because we did anything to them, but because they wanted to hurt someone else. That kind of thinking eludes me. Do you think we've got it wrong? I mean, really, that's so bizarre."

"Unfortunately, people kill for all kinds of reasons, Sasha. They hurt each other and steal from each other. I've always found the useless robberies to be the thing I find hard to understand. Killing for five bucks. Or a candy bar. How does a person do that?" He shrugged. "I don't want you thinking about it anymore. We're home and we're safe. I know your brother is because I just checked on him. We've tightened security there and no one is going to get near him."

"Thank you." She flashed him a small grin. "I was just sitting here thinking I could never get used to this, but that right there, being able to make a phone call and have someone actually talk to you and reassure you that Sandlin was in his room and sound asleep, an actual person reassuring you at this time of night, that I could get used to."

He laughed. "I suppose I'm spoiled. I would expect it. In fact, if someone didn't get their ass in gear and tell me immediately, I might get them fired. I've had that since I was very young."

"You were spoiled." She stretched lazily.

He walked over to her, and she watched him come, his muscles moving beneath his tight shirt, his dark features so beautiful to her. He scooped her out of the chair and took her into the bathroom. It was every bit as luxurious as the bedroom. The fireplace in there was lit as well. Flames flickered, licking at the logs.

Sasha kept her eyes on Giovanni's face as he slowly pulled her club uniform off and tossed it aside. He kissed her. Slowly. So hot. Perfect. Taking her breath and her heart at the same time. His hands moved over her body, gentle. Tender even. All the while she could feel possession in his touch. He helped her into the large tub and then inspected her shoulder carefully. He pressed a warm cloth over the spot that was throbbing. "I added some salts into the water. They should help. Scoot down until your shoulder is underwater. I'll put a pillow behind your head."

She did so and then he joined her, pulling her feet into his lap. "I've got to wash that man's touch off your skin."

"It really bothered you, didn't it?"

"I don't want anyone touching you. Family hugs. There will be kissing on the cheek. But no one else. I don't share what's mine." He looked around the room. "All this, Sasha. It doesn't mean anything without you. Nothing I have in my life means anything without you. I live hard. The things I have to do are sometimes very difficult. I do them because it's my duty, but I've never had what I needed to make it all worthwhile until I found you."

She heard the sincerity in every word. No one had ever made her feel so wanted—or needed. "I'm not going anywhere."

"I worry you will. I practically railroaded you."

She laughed. She couldn't help it. "Honey, I'm not someone who can be railroaded. I'm here with you because I want to be with you. I'll always choose you. I had one moment of freaking out, and after I realized it wasn't about you at all, or even your world, although no sane person wants to be in your world, I knew I wanted to be with you. I was losing my mind over things I had no control over, like someone trying to kill us. It was convenient to think it was about you or how you live, but it wasn't. I'm ashamed I even had that moment."

She knew he would dismiss it, and he did, with a single wave of his hand and the best foot massage of her life. After, he made love to her, so tenderly he stole her soul along with her heart. He woke her in the middle of the night and delivered her "punishment," which just so happened to be the hottest thing she'd ever experienced, and their erotic tango turned so wild she was certain it might take weeks to recover. It was morning when she woke him for his "punishment."

# CHAPTER TWENTY

"I tried to get bail posted for Aaron," Tom Mariland said. "I don't know why I couldn't make it happen. I tried three bondsmen. All said the same thing, they couldn't get him out until Monday. There's no way we can take out all the Ferraros at this wedding and get away with it."

"We can get away with it," James Corlege said. "We just can't blame it on Aaron." He paced across the room, his hand beating a little tattoo rhythm on his thigh. "Fucking bitch lied to me, said her engagement to that moron wasn't real and all the time she planned a wedding behind my back. I hate them. I hate her most of all."

Tom gave a snort of laughter. "You sound like the bitch belonged to you."

"She would have if Giovanni moneybags Ferraro hadn't enticed her away. Women are so easily led by their tits straight to the money. Dangle cash and they'll spread their legs and do whatever a man wants." James turned and smashed his fist into the wall. "At least Aaron's going down for the fire and the stalking. Getting Marita to screw the bastard and get his condom out of the trash for us was a stroke of genius. There is no way Aaron can explain how his sperm was all over Sasha's underwear when they find it's his DNA."

He began pacing again. "There has to be a way, Tom. All the Ferraros together. Sasha. Her brother. We could take them out with an explosion. Something going wrong with their heating system." He tapped his thigh over and over. "I hate them all. They walk around thinking they're all so superior to the rest of us."

Tom shrugged. "A good fire after the explosion. I like fire. It's beautiful and deadly, greedy for anything in its path. I like watching it eat people alive."

James turned and faced the other man. "You're so good at using fire. Maybe you're right. I should listen to you, Tom," he flattered the man. "How would we do that? Start a fire in a place that big so they couldn't get out?"

Deliberately he pulled out a chair and sank into it, leaning toward the other fighter as if eager to learn from him. Tom preened, just as James knew he would. Tom would have to die, of course, he knew too much, but he would have one last use. If he could be the instrument of death to the Ferraros, it would be James's finest coup. His revenge on the fucking rich. He'd been getting rid of his enemies since he was fifteen when he'd killed his rival, leaving his body in a manhole. It hadn't been discovered for months. He'd relived that first kill over and over.

Over the years, he'd been very careful to make certain others were blamed for a death or he made it look as if it was an accident. He'd made the mistake of beating the hell out of his first wife instead of letting her go, watching her and then killing her later when no one would suspect him. She'd taken money from his wallet with the intention of leaving him. He didn't put up with that shit. If she wanted his money, she had ways of earning it. He gave her lots of opportunities, she was just lazy.

Tom droned on and he tuned him out, thinking of his second wife. She'd been a fun one, willing to do anything he wanted, so eager to please him. He'd loved that about her. Then he'd lost a major fight, and she'd had the balls to tell him he drank too much the night before. He'd beat the fuck out of her. She'd left him, and he actually missed her. If he could have, he would have found a way to get her back, but she wouldn't even take his calls.

His last girlfriend had been a joke. He beat the shit out of her on a regular basis, but she liked it. She wanted him beating her so that wasn't any fun. Then, when he split up with her, she wanted to press charges against him. He visited her in the middle of the night and let her know he could have cut her throat and would if she didn't drop the charges. Poof. No charges.

He'd watched Sasha for some time when she was first hired and working the main floor. She was really beautiful and had the kind of figure he preferred. He decided she would be wife three. He'd made the mistake of telling Aaron. Aaron bet him that she would fall for him because he was the better fighter.

Aaron brought Tom in on the bet to make things interesting. That was what he always said, he liked to make things interesting. James wanted to kill the fuck, but that wasn't good enough. He wouldn't suffer enough. And now, Sasha, marrying Giovanni Ferraro, needed to suffer, too. They all did. Every damned one of them.

He'd liked his little game though. It was fun. If he could have, he would have fucked with them a lot more. He thought of them as puppets dancing on his strings. He sighed. The fun had to end sometime, and if he could pull this off, killing every Ferraro, Sasha and her brain-dead brother, all in one final blow, it would be such a thing of beauty.

He leaned back in his chair. Tom had seated himself across the table from him, drawing something on a piece of paper. Tom sat up straight, still talking, but something shimmered in the shadows behind him, distracting James from hearing him. His eyes were deceiving him.

Tom's head was in the shadows, and for a moment a man seemed to step out of the shadows to stand behind him. He wore a pin-striped suit, just like the Ferraro brothers. This one was beautiful. James liked nice clothes. The suit was dark charcoal with the thinnest stripes. The shirt beneath the vest and jacket was lighter charcoal. The tie was a dark charcoal to match the suit.

The man caught Tom's head in his hands. At the same time, James felt hands on his head. The man in the shadows snapped Tom's neck and murmured, "Justice is served." Then James's world went black.

Sasha came to Giovanni on the arm of Stefano. Sandlin couldn't walk her down the aisle, but he was there, standing between Vittorio and Taviano. She couldn't help shooting him a quick glance as she walked past him to her man. Sandlin beamed at her, clearly happy, and that brought her own happiness up a notch.

She noticed the cousins from New York there, all three brothers, handsome in their pin-striped suits. Their suits were dark charcoal with thin lighter charcoal stripes, while Giovanni and his brothers wore gray with black stripes. All of them looked so handsome. Giovanni took her breath away, just that look on his face. Stefano placed her hand in his brother's and leaned in to brush a kiss on her cheek before taking his place beside Francesca.

"You're the most beautiful woman I've ever seen," Giovanni whispered. "Thank you for being mine."

She couldn't speak, afraid she'd cry and ruin the makeup Emmanuelle had spent hours on. Emmanuelle had worked hard to pull the wedding off. Of course, money talked, and she'd gotten the planner she wanted. Strangely, Eloisa worked with her, putting together the reception for those at the Hendrick Center as well as the town reception. That was the bigger reception, the one at the hotel where the people the Ferraros had known most of their lives would be guests.

She heard the preacher speaking and then Giovanni was looking into her eyes and she found herself falling like she did when he looked at her like that. She answered in the affirmative when he asked her, just as Giovanni had. His voice had been firm. Hers trembled. She still meant every word, as if the vow was sealed into blood and bone. She would be his. He would be hers. She truly felt as if they'd been born for each other.

Then Giovanni was kissing her, and everyone receded. There was only him. That mouth of his could always command her. Always make her laugh. She was lost there with him until Stefano started the clapping that pulled them back from the edge of that cliff they always seemed to fall over.

Giovanni danced for the third time with his wife. They didn't have too much more time before they would have to leave, but she was having so much fun and he liked watching her have fun. He kept his eye on her brother. Sandlin moved through the crowd a few times and then he retreated, going to his new favorite spot.

His favorite couch had been moved into the larger common room and put in a quiet corner where there was still plenty of light for him to read. He was on the couch now, but he was smiling sweetly like he did, a genuine Sandlin smile—and it was Eloisa beside him. Her body was turned toward Sandlin, her posture and position indicating she was open to him and enjoying the conversation, which made no sense to Giovanni.

His mother abhorred weakness. She had always been hard on Ettore because he'd been born with weaker lungs and had respiratory problems. No amount of her driving him could cure his problem. She'd acted as if she despised him from the time he was born, yet here she sat next to Sandlin acting like what might be considered actually human. On the one hand he was grateful, but on the other, he found himself angry with her that she couldn't have treated her own son with as much compassion.

Henry, the man who oversaw their fleet of vehicles, was dressed in a suit and seated beside Eloisa. His body posture screamed protective. All three were eating small slices of wedding cake and drinking punch. Giovanni had never seen his mother drink punch. She preferred very fine wine or champagne.

"We're going to have to leave, Sasha," Giovanni said, reluctantly. "Emmanuelle has been signaling frantically for the last ten minutes. It's one thing to be fashionably late to our wedding reception, it's something altogether different not to show up at all."

"This is our wedding reception," she pointed out.

Sasha was gorgeous in her wedding gown. It was Emmanuelle who had found the perfect dress for her. The silk slip was a nude, fitted silhouette that clung to every curve. Over the slip was the designer's contrasting translucent signature elements. Scattered into the embroidery were sequins that shimmered when she walked or moved. The sequins glimmered down the long sleeves and around the neck and tracked down the dress and across the trailing fishtail hem. It was breathtaking. The designer was one of Emmanuelle's favorites.

He knew, because Emmanuelle had told him, that once he was alone with Sasha, he had only to undo a couple of hooks and the silk slip would fall around her ankles, leaving her in the translucent embroidered outer layer. Giovanni couldn't help thinking about that as she'd walked down the aisle toward him and as he'd whirled her around the dance floor. It kept him in a constant state of arousal, which he wasn't certain he would survive until they got home.

He glanced over to Nicoletta. Taviano had leaned down and was whispering to her. She shook her head. A look of impatience crossed his face. He took her hand and pulled her up, gathering her to him for a dance. The two moved across the dance floor in perfect rhythm, but Nicoletta was holding herself—or trying to hold herself—away from his brother.

Giovanni led Sasha to the small couch where Sandlin sat with Eloisa and Henry. "We're going to have to go. We promised Goodman we wouldn't be here more than three hours total. He felt it would be too disruptive to the patients."

"He's getting paid far more than he should have," Eloisa snapped. "He can wait."

"No, Eloisa, he really can't," Giovanni said, exasperated. "He did us a favor, and the crews still have to clean up. That's more time disrupting the patients. You can see that Sandlin is tired."

Eloisa smiled at Sandlin. "I suppose you need to rest now, don't you?"

He nodded. "It was nice to meet you."

"I enjoyed meeting you as well." She stood up, hands on her hips, glaring at her son. "You neglected to tell me that Sasha was capable of producing riders. I noticed her brother's shadow and made certain my shadow connected with his. I was shocked at the strength there, and even more shocked when he recognized my shadow. She comes from a very strong family. Have you looked into her background?"

"Eloisa, Sasha is standing right here. At any time, you could have asked her. Of course, I know her background. I asked her and she told me. Had you waited to be introduced that morning at Stefano's, I'm certain you would have seen her shadow at some point."

She ignored that. "I suppose she must be pregnant. All the gossip columns are speculating. Public relations reps have been asking repeatedly for an answer. I do wish you could have waited, Giovanni, and been just a little more responsible."

"Oh, for heaven's sake," Sasha snapped and whirled away. "I've had enough. Are we going, or what?" Ignoring Eloisa and Giovanni, she reached for her brother's hands. "Sandlin, thank you for coming to my wedding. I'll be back in a few days. Giovanni and I are going on a honeymoon. When I get back, I'll show you pictures and tell you all about it."

Sandlin nodded. "I'd like that. And you can read to me."

"Of course, I'll read to you. I always do, don't I?" She kissed first one cheek and then the other.

Sandlin nodded again. "Yes, you do."

"Emmanuelle said she would come to read to you when I'm gone. You remember Emmanuelle, right?" She pointed out her sister-in-law, whirling around on the floor with a man she didn't recognize.

"Is she good at it, like you?" Sandlin hadn't even looked toward the dance floor.

"Yes, very good," Sasha assured her brother.

"Okay then. You can go with Giovanni." He sounded as if he was giving her a great concession.

Sasha laughed, kissed him again and took her husband's hand.

"Why don't you like him?" Signora Moretti asked Nicoletta as Taviano walked past the table where they sat with Lucia and Amo.

"Like who?" Nicoletta asked, frowning.

"Oh, stop that, girl," Agnese Moretti scolded. "You're not very good at covering your expressions. I've been working with you for a long time now and I can tell when you don't like someone. The Ferraros are paying for your education, they make it clear that you're under their protection and they're giving you lessons in self-defense, which I don't agree a young girl should be doing. Not until you're older. Instead of appreciating them, you make it clear you don't want anything to do with the family."

"That's not true, Signora Moretti," Nicoletta denied.

"Of course it is," Agnese persisted. "My understanding is that Stefano served with your father, and when your parents were killed, he brought you here. Isn't that true? Did the family do something to offend you? Take you from another relative you preferred?"

A small shudder went through Nicoletta's body and she stood abruptly, as if the fight-or-flight response had kicked in. At once, the members of the Ferraro family turned their heads.

It was Vittorio who got there first. He held out his hand to the girl. "Dance with me." There was pure command in his voice, but his touch was gentle as he pulled her into his body and swung them onto the dance floor.

He was quiet for a few moments, holding her close as if absorbing whatever it was that had upset her. When she quieted, he allowed space between them. "Is she prying? Upsetting you? You have only to ask and we'll find you another tutor."

Nicoletta moistened her bottom lip with her tongue. "No. Signora Moretti has been really good to me. She takes getting used to, but she really brought my studies up and helped me finish the grades I needed fast in order to graduate. She makes every subject easy to understand. I'm going to graduate in another week or so." She paused. "I like the training in the gym your family has given me. I hope to continue that."

"You'll have more time once you finish school," Vittorio pointed out.

"Yes. I told Lucia and Amo I would stay, but I want to pay them rent. I'm working at the restaurant now, and once I'm full-time, I'll be able to pay them."

"Nicoletta, you know Stefano pays for your rent and clothes. If we could have taken you in ourselves, we would have, but Lucia and Amo were far better equipped. Still, you're part of our family."

She shook her head and almost pulled out of his arms. He just tightened his hold and locked his arm like a bar across her back. "Settle down. Don't you think it's time you got over the fact that we know about your past? You're punishing our family because we got you out of a horrendous situation."

"Is that what you call it? A horrendous situation?" There was a cross between a sneer and a sob in her voice. "I call it something else. Maybe you've never lived in hell, Vittorio. Maybe you've never had to hide from others how ashamed you are. How dirty."

His hand caught her chin and yanked her head up so her eyes were forced to meet his. "Don't you *ever* let me hear you call yourself that. Never. It is so far from the truth, I want to put you over my knee and paddle that right out of you. Don't let something like that into your brain. *They* did that. Not you. You're bright and beautiful and so far above them they wanted to break you. They wanted to bring you down into the muck with them. They can't take that you shine, and you do. You are not dirty. That is not you, Nicoletta."

She stared into his eyes for a long time and then she swallowed. Nodded. The music ended and instead of Vittorio taking her back to the table where Signora Moretti watched over her with Lucia and Amo, he took her over to Stefano. Stefano immediately whirled her into his arms. Stefano intimidated her. There was no other word for it. She realized, now that she was eighteen, the Ferraro family wasn't going to back off. They were determined that she stay in their territory where they could look out for her.

Giovanni lifted his hand as he guided Sasha around them. "Save me a dance, Nicoletta."

Sasha smiled at the girl. "She's really beautiful, Giovanni."

"She is. She doesn't realize it. She's hell on wheels in the training hall. You should see that girl move. She's fast. She doesn't realize that, either, because Emmanuelle and Mariko, the two working with her right now, have trained all of their lives, but all of us are astounded. Her reflexes are incredible."

"Why aren't any of you men training her?"

His woman sounded a little snippy, as if she was going to take him to task because, at the moment, they were leaving Nicoletta's self-defense training to the females. "She's very leery around us, sweetheart. We'll be training her eventually, but right now, she's more apt to show up if she's working with Emme or Mariko. We'd have to put our hands on her and she's not ready for that. In any case, Mariko has developed a very good relationship with her, and we want to encourage that. You can see she's very intimidated by us. She doesn't like us touching her, or even standing too close."

"She likes him."

Giovanni's head came up sharply. "Likes who?" Because that "who" was going to have his head removed if he was making a move on Nicoletta.

"Taviano. Sheesh, Giovanni, you're kind of a hothead."

He threw back his head and laughed. "Baby. You're just beginning to notice? Why aren't you intimidated?"

"Because I'm better with a rope than you are. I think I proved that the other night."

He rested his lips against her ear. His tongue did a brief foray, and he felt the answering shiver of her body. "*Dio*, but I love you," he whispered.

Benito Petrov danced past them with Angelina Laconi in his arms. Petrov owned the pizzeria with his son, Tito. A widower, no one thought he would ever date again, but it looked to Giovanni as if he was very comfortable with Angelina, although she was several years younger.

"You aren't even going to protest the rope thing?"

"Because it's too absurd to bother protesting. You just brought it up because Mariko told you about that rope thing Ricco does with her that totally turns her on."

She pulled back and scowled up at him. "What rope thing? Mariko told you about a rope thing your brother does?"

"Mariko would never talk to me. I thought she talked to you." He pretended to give it some thought. "Where did I hear about that technique?"

She burst out laughing, just as he knew she would. He loved that sound. He knew he wanted to hear it for the rest of his life.

"You made that up."

"I did," he admitted and then put his mouth over her ear

again. "But you're thinking about it, and your panties are damp for me, aren't they?"

"Silly man. My panties are always damp for you, haven't you figured that out yet?"

He wanted to get her home. He *needed* to get her home. He turned his head and stiffened. In the doorway of the hotel ballroom, Valentino Saldi stood framed. He wore a suit, and his shoulders nearly touched from one side of the frame to the other. He paused there, his gaze sweeping around the dance floor and tables until he found what he was looking for.

Emmanuelle. Giovanni nearly stopped dancing right in the middle of the song. He caught sight of Ricco dancing with Nicoletta. They had decided to take turns, making that first declaration to her that she was part of their family. Each one would dance with her at least once. Giovanni included. She was Taviano's. He'd made that clear. No matter whether she was or wasn't, they'd brought her into the family and it was time she accepted it.

Valentino walked across the floor, weaving in and out of the people. Everyone liked him. He was a good man, no matter that he was part of the Saldi organization. His family owned the meat company, and he often delivered their products himself. The Ferraros were convinced he did it in order to see Emmanuelle more, but he was always friendly with everyone. Still, there was an aura of danger about him and everyone knew he was a Saldi.

His cousin and bodyguard, Dario, paced behind him, also in a suit. For just one moment, his gaze shifted to follow Nicoletta around the dance floor and then he was all business, and Giovanni wasn't certain he actually saw that momentary breach.

Emmanuelle stood to one side of the room, talking with Signora Vitale. His sister turned her head slowly just before Valentino reached her side. He held out his hand to her. Giovanni willed his sister to walk away. She didn't. She just stood very still. Frozen like a statue. Valentino was the one to step forward. He pulled Emmanuelle into his arms and brushed a kiss onto her forehead.

She jerked her head away, said something to him. Giovanni knew that look. She was angry. Hurt. More hurt than angry. "Baby," he said softly. "I have to help Emme."

"Of course." They hurried over to the couple. He'd been dancing them closer and closer so it wasn't far.

"Emmanuelle. You promised me this dance." Giovanni took her right out of Valentino's arms and turned his sister into his chest so she could hide her face.

Emmanuelle went with him as he guided her across the room. He just held her, feeling the tremors running through her. He didn't talk. There wasn't anything to say, and he wasn't going to put her on the spot. No one could pry anything out of her if she didn't want to share, and so far, she hadn't said a word to any of them about Valentino, or why she was so upset with him.

Valentino immediately held out his arms to the bride. He expected her to turn him down, but she smiled at him and let him take her out among the whirling couples. He kept his eye on Emmanuelle, making certain to stay close enough that when the music ended, he would be able to claim her again.

"You're very brave to come here when you hurt that girl," Sasha said. "Her brothers would very much like to teach you a few hard lessons."

He was a little shocked that she spoke to him at all. "I'm sorry. I read the papers so I know your name is Sasha, but we haven't been formally introduced. I'm Valentino Saldi. My friends call me Val. I had to crash your wedding reception, which I'm very aware is terrible manners. And I'm also aware her brothers would like to throw me into the nearest river and drown me. Dario, my bodyguard, knows it, too. She won't take my calls."

"Emmanuelle isn't nearly as tough as everyone thinks she is," Sasha said. "Nor has she had the easiest time. I don't know why you keep pursuing her when you make her so miserable. It doesn't make any sense."

"It doesn't? Why does any man pursue a woman?"

Sasha recalled the conversation at the Ferraro table half said in jest. "Sex?"

"For any man," Valentino agreed. "But to risk one's life, it has to be more than sex."

She agreed with that assessment. "That's the general consensus. But some men do like the adrenaline rush, and what a feat it would be to defeat your rivals by going after their sister."

"I wasn't aware we were rivals."

Sasha shrugged. She felt very protective over Emmanuelle. "How many times have you broken up with Emme and then gone after her again?"

"Emmanuelle does the breaking up. I have never sent her home. She goes back again and again. I'm unsure why. When I ask her, she just cries and leaves me. I've tried to live without her. I've tried dating other women. God help me, I even tried fucking another woman. That was a disaster in more ways than one." He sighed, his eyes on the woman in Giovanni's arms. "I do know that if she does what she says she's going to do, there's going to be bloodshed, and she needs to know that up front."

"What do you mean? You wouldn't dare hurt her."

Valentino stopped on the dance floor, looking down into her face. For the first time a shiver went down her spine and she was a little afraid of him. "I would kill any man who threatened her or touched her. Never her. Never Emmanuelle."

Thankfully, the music ended, and Valentino took her hand and gave her back to Giovanni. When Emmanuelle tried to turn away, he caught her wrist. "You're dancing with me, Emme."

Sasha saw Emmanuelle take a deep breath and then she turned back to him. "There isn't anything to say. I don't want to keep doing this."

"You have to hear me out."

She shook her head. "I *saw* you, Val. With my own eyes. I saw you." Tears filled her eyes and she looked to Giovanni. "I need you to get me out of here."

There it was. His sister never asked for help, and she was asking. Giovanni gently took her hand out of Val's. "Excuse me, Sasha. I'll be right back." He strode away, his arm around Emmanuelle. He took her out of the ballroom.

Sasha followed Valentino and Dario at a distance because they were trailing after Giovanni and Emmanuelle. Giovanni went straight to Stefano's private elevator, put in the code and kissed the top of his sister's head. He stood there like a silent sentinel until the doors closed and then he turned toward Valentino.

"You're a good man, Val," he said. "But she means it. No is no in my world."

Sasha knew it really wasn't. No, to the Ferraros, meant "try harder." She wasn't certain that Giovanni really understood that they had a double standard.

Valentino shook his head. "She's hurt, Giovanni. You know she loves me. You know she belongs with me."

"The sad truth is," Giovanni said, "she can't ever be with you. I don't know what happened, but you're going to have to respect her refusal. This isn't like the ten times before. This time she's adamant. I've never seen her refuse to dance with you. Nor has she ever asked for our help in dealing with you. Not ever. Leave her alone, Val, and let her heal."

He held out his arm, and Sasha moved quickly under his shoulder, her arm around his waist. The two of them faced the bodyguard and Valentino, who shook his head and turned to walk away.

"Val?" Giovanni called.

He turned back.

"I'm really sorry."

Val nodded and walked toward the front of the hotel.

"You really do like him. I thought there was some feud and you were all ready to do him in for some reason other than Emmanuelle." She rubbed his chest over his heart because she felt his hurt for the other man.

"The feud between our families goes way back, well over a hundred years. The Saldis are a crime family. That's the bottom line. Valentino stands to inherit it all. He's the prince in that family. He was born into it and brought up in it. Emmanuelle can't go there. She's expected to carry out her duty. She has to have children, riders."

"She can't be happy? Your family wants to turn her into Eloisa?"

"Why would you think Eloisa wasn't happy in her marriage?"

She rolled her eyes. "Anyone can see she wasn't happy. She didn't want children. Her family forced her to be someone she wasn't. That's what is going to happen to Emmanuelle."

Giovanni stood there for a long time staring at the elevator, his arms around her. Tight. "That's true, but I didn't realize others could see it so easily in Eloisa. I'm going to talk to Stefano and the others about this. I've never thought of it this way. Never. She isn't going to be another Eloisa."

"Having said that . . ." Sasha backpedaled a bit. "Valentino really hurt her. Whatever he did, she isn't going to forgive."

Giovanni let out his breath. "Believe me, baby, that's a good thing. Our family would never accept him, and his would never accept her." He nuzzled the top of her head. "Let's go home."

"I thought we'd never get home tonight."

At last. Giovanni carried Sasha over the threshold. He kept the age-old tradition to ward off bad luck. They'd had enough of that and he wasn't taking chances. He set her in the large chair in the great room, turned on the fireplace with the remote, added music and closed all the drapes. Sasha started to remove her shoes.

"Don't, Sasha. Not yet." He removed his jacket and loosened his tie as she slowly straightened. "I want another dance with you, baby. Are you too tired?"

She shook her head and stood up. "It was a beautiful day and I don't want it to be over. I did drink a little too much champagne though."

"That's good. I wouldn't mind a little drunken sex with you." He pulled her close and reached behind her to find the little hooks holding the nude-colored slip under the beautiful transparent layer of sequined embroidery. The silk slithered down her body, leaving her in only a pair of nude lace panties that were little more than a strip.

Sasha laughed and stepped out of the slip. "Did you know about that little trick the entire time?"

"Of course."

He pulled her into his arms and began to guide her in a series of intricate steps that kept her hips pressed tightly against his. He loved the way her body felt against his. Through the transparent material, her skin felt like silk, sliding over him. His cock grew hard. Hungry. He slid his hands down the curve of her spine, found that indentation where her back met the rounded curves of her buttocks. His hands moved lower, found her cheeks. Firm. Soft. He kneaded, massaged. He loved that she savored his touch.

She threw her head back, pressing her breasts into him. Her nipples pierced the delicate fabric, rubbing along his shirt. He wanted to feel them against his skin.

"Take my shirt off." He stopped right in the middle of the room.

Firelight played over her body, over her skin, so that she glowed. She reached up immediately and began to slip each button out of its hole. She undid the cuff links, and he slipped them into his pocket. After opening the cuffs, she dropped her hand and rubbed over his hard length. Then she pushed the shirt from his shoulders. Giovanni slipped out of it.

"Now my shoes."

She crouched low without hesitation and undid the laces so he could step out of the shoes. One hand resting on her shoulder, he lifted his foot so she could take off his sock. He did the same with the other side but was very careful of the spot where her shoulder might still be sore. He reached for her, helping her to her feet.

"I love how you look right now," he said as she unzipped his trousers. "Our wedding night, dressed just for your husband."

"I have a few more surprises," she confessed. "I actually went shopping."

Her blush intrigued him. She liked sex. She was adventurous. He couldn't imagine what she'd purchased that had her blushing. His cock jerked hard as she pulled his clothes down his legs so he could step out of them.

He caught her hand and tugged until she was on the other side of the long couch. Very slowly he pulled up the long translucent sheath that covered her body. When she stood only in her high heels, garters and stockings with that tiny strip of lace for panties, he stepped back to look at her.

"Do you have any idea how much time I spend thinking about ways to take you?" He turned his finger in a circle, indicating for her to turn around.

She did so. His heart clenched. His cock throbbed and pushed harder against his stomach. Even his balls reacted, feeling tight and hot. He loved the way that little strip of cloth disappeared between her two cheeks. It had to go, but it was hot. He caught at it and jerked, knowing the action forced the strip to rub against her clit.

She caught the back of the couch with both hands and gripped hard, a little cry of pleasure escaping. Giovanni couldn't wait another minute. He shoved with his foot until her feet were wide apart. Catching the nape of her neck he pushed her head down so she was bent over the back of the couch. He waited, holding her there, admiring the way she looked.

"I don't want you to move, baby. Stay just like that for me."

A little groan escaped. "You want to play."

"I always want to play."

He rubbed her cheek and then his hand went lower. Found hot liquid. His. He tasted her. Savored her. Devoured her. Spent time painting his name on her with that hot liquid. All the while she pleaded and begged for him to take her. His fingers went deep. His tongue. He drew that honey out of her and striped her with it. When she made that little keening sound that drove him crazy, he took her, plunging deep, holding nothing back, taking her the way he'd always wanted to. She was his woman, his private miracle, and he was going to love her until the end of his days and beyond.

She screamed out her orgasms, one after another until he couldn't wait one more second. He flew with her, soaring, his body shaking with the strength of his release. It took some time to recover enough to step back and help her out of her shoes, garters and stockings. He left them on the great room floor and carried his bride to their bed.

To his astonishment, there were a few items lying on the bed. He hadn't bought them so he was fairly certain his woman had. He put her down right on the edge and picked up the nearest little toy. "Baby. Do you have any idea what this is for?"

She nodded, watching him carefully.

"You ever tried this before?"

She shook her head.

Heat swept through him. Joy. He was so damned lucky to have found her. He carefully examined each toy. Three had remote controls. For him. He loved that idea.

"My wedding presents?"

She nodded, looking a little shy. "You like to play. I wanted you to know that I was willing to play with you, however you wanted to."

There was a pair of handcuffs, fur-lined, but she had realized he wasn't that into bondage. Her comfort was too important to him and he couldn't relax enough if she was in bonds. He worried that she might not tell him if she was hurting. But maybe if the cuffs were fur-lined and not tight . . . The rest of it though . . . He looked at the toys. She was willing to play whenever and however he wanted.

*Dio.* His cock was already rising. Apparently just the thought of what he was going to do with those toys was working on him. He wasn't going to wait until later. "It's going to be a very long night, Sasha." Warning her seemed a good idea.

"I've been thinking about this from the moment I bought everything. I'm hoping the night is long. I love you, Giovanni Ferraro."

"I'm so in love with you, Sasha Ferraro." He didn't know how he got this lucky but he was going to cherish her forever. His woman.

Keep reading for an excerpt from
the next Carpathian novel by Christine Feehan

## DARK SENTINEL

Coming September 2018 from Piatkus

Contemplating allowing himself to die made Andor Katona feel a coward. He had never believed that sitting out in the open, waiting to meet the dawn and have the sun fry him was an act of nobility. He—and a very few others—had always believed it to be an act of cowardice. Yet here he was, deliberating whether or not to give himself permission to die. The sun wasn't close, but the loss of blood and near-fatal wounds he'd sustained battling so many vampires at one time had weakened him.

The human vampire hunters hadn't recognized him as a hunter and had attacked while he'd left his body an empty shell so he could try to heal those wounds. A stake close to the heart—they'd missed—hadn't felt so good. They really weren't very good at their self-appointed task. They'd torn open his chest and more blood had spilled onto the battle ground. He'd never thought he'd die in a country far from home—killed by a trio of bumbling humans—but dying seemed a good alternative to continuing a life of battle in an endless gray void.

The three men, Carter, Barnaby and Shorty, huddled together a distance from him, casting him terrified and hate-filled glances. They were trying to convince themselves they'd done it right and he was dying. Of course, they'd expected him to die immediately and now wondered why he hadn't and what they should do about it. He could have told them they'd need another stake and a much better impaling technique if they wanted him to die. Did he really have to instruct others on how to kill him? That was ridiculous.

Sighing, he tried weighing the pros and cons of dying in order to make a rational decision. He'd lived too long. Far too long. He'd killed too often—so much so that there was little left of his soul. He'd lived with honor, but there had to be a time when one could let go with honor. It was past his time. He'd known that for well over a century. He'd searched the world over for his lifemate, the woman holding the other half of his soul, the light to his darkness. She didn't exist. It was that simple. She didn't exist.

Carpathian males lost all emotion and the ability to see in color after two hundred years. Some lost it earlier. They had to exist on memories, and after so many centuries, even those faded. They retained their battle skills—honed them nightly—but as time passed, all those long endless years, even the memories of family and friends faded away. He lived his life far from humans most of the time, working in the night to keep them safe.

Vampires were Carpathians who had given up their honor in order to feel again. There was a rush when one killed while feeding. Adrenaline-laced blood could produce a high. Vampires craved the high, and they terrorized their victims before killing them. Andor had hunted them on nearly every continent. As time passed, the centuries coming and going, the whispers of temptation to turn increased. For a few hundred years, those whispers sustained him, even if he knew the promise was empty. Eventually, even that was lost to him. Then he lived in a gray world of . . . nothing.

He entered the monastery high in the remote Carpathian Mountains, a place where a very few ancients locked themselves away from the world when they were deemed too dangerous to hunt and kill, and they didn't believe in giving themselves to the dawn. Every kill increased the danger of turning and he had lived too long, and knew too much to be a vampire. Few hunters would ever be able to defeat him, yet here he was, nearly done in by a trio of inept, bumbling human assassins.

He had entered the monastery, taking the vow to be honorable in waiting for his lifemate. Of course, the situation had been made worse by secreting themselves in a place where there was no hope of finding the one woman who could restore emotions and color into their lives—but they had known that. They accepted the truth, their women were no longer in the same world with them.

The whispers of his would-be killers grew annoying. Really annoying. His head was swimming, making it difficult to think. He lay looking up at the sky. Stars were out, but they appeared as blurred lights, nothing more. Their light was a dull gray, just as the moon was. He looked down at the blood seeping out of his body, pooling around him from more than a dozen wounds, and that didn't count the stake. The blood was a darker gray. An ugly mess. How had he gotten here, so far from his homeland and the monastery where he'd placed himself so he wouldn't give in to the nothingness that surrounded him?

Hope had come to the monks, so they'd scattered, looking once again for the women who might save their souls. When the world was too changed and too vast and they realized once more they didn't fit and there was little hope, they answered the call of their fellow monk and followed him to the United States. The vampires had grown powerful and Carpathians were behind in the ways of the new world. It had been an effort to catch up, when before he had always found it easy to learn newer, more modern things. That had led him to this moment—considering that he'd outlived his time.

Everything was different. He was forced to live in close proximity to humans and to hide who and what he was. Women were different. They no longer were satisfied having a man care for them. He had no idea what to do with a modern woman. Contemplating his demise seemed so much wiser than trying to understand the reasoning of a present-day woman.

It was difficult to think, although the night was beautiful. The humans kept talking, whispering together, sending anxious looks his way. He wanted them to be quiet and considered silencing them so he could continue to contemplate, but it was finally dawning on them that maybe they should have studied anatomy a little better before deciding on their profession.

Carter ended up drawing the short straw. The others sent him over to figure out what had gone wrong. He was shaking, trembling from head to foot as he approached, clearly terrified of the man they had tried to murder. Sweat poured off the assassin and he wiped it away with the back of his hand as he drew near.

He loomed over Andor, the stink of fanaticism reeking from his pores, his features twisted into a mask of hatred and determination. Andor wasn't quite ready to make up his mind about death. He lifted his hand to push enough air at the man to send him flying backward when a woman rushed out of the darkness and attacked.

The moon was full, scattering beams of light over the battleground. There was no evidence of the vampires he'd killed because he'd disposed of them properly. He wasn't getting a minute of peace any time soon, not even with a stake sticking out of him and his blood everywhere, not with his supposed savior in the form of a little whirlwind of fury attacking his three would-be assassins. He was going to have to rescue her. That meant living longer. He didn't like having his mind made up for him.

She moved with incredible speed, an avenging angel, her long hair flying, her hiking boots crunching rock, dirt and the lightning-scorched grass beneath her feet. She bashed Carter with what appeared to be a sauce pot, whirling like a tornado and striking him again. She went under his punch, blocking it upward with one arm that sounded and must have felt like a blow as she clobbered him right in the face with the pot. Carter staggered backward and then hit the ground.

Andor closed his eyes briefly, thinking perhaps he was seeing an illusion. What woman would attack three men with a sauce pot when they'd just staked someone? He sighed again and thought about how much blood he was going to lose when he sat up and yanked out the stake. It would leave a good-sized hole in his chest. On the other hand, he could leave it in . . .

"Don't you move," she hissed, not looking at him, but one slender hand came back behind her, palm toward him in the universal signal to stop.

He went still. Utterly still. Frozen. His lungs felt raw, burning for air. It wasn't possible. It couldn't be. More than a thousand years. An endless void. His eyes hurt so bad he had to close them, a dangerous thing to do when she was certain to be attacked.

The other two men, who hadn't the courage of Carter, had backed a distance from him, just in case Carter did whatever he was considering to remedy the situation—in other words, trying to kill Andor again—and they thought themselves safe. Both men might not want anything to do with the big man on the ground, but a woman armed with a sauce pot was an entirely different matter. They separated and circled around, edging up on either side of her while she was busy smacking Carter with the pot.

"What is *wrong* with you people?" She was furious, emphasizing each word with a bang of the pot on Carter. "Are you crazy? That's a human being you're murdering."

Andor had been lying in a puddle of his own blood, contemplating death, surrounded by a gray world. Everything was gray, or shades of it. The ground. The blood. The trees. The moon overhead. Even his three would-be assassins. He had no real emotion, feeling detached and completely removed from what was happening to him. The world changed in the blink of an eye. His burning eyes, his lungs that refused to obey his commands. Everything so raw he could barely comprehend what was happening.

Color burst behind his eyes. Vivid. Brilliant. Terrible. In spite of the night, he could see the green in the trees and the shrubs. Varying shades. His blood appeared red, a bright shade of crimson. He made out colors on the three men, blues and true blacks. The moon caught the woman right in its spotlight, the beams illuminating her.

Andor's breath caught in his throat. Her hair was the color of chestnuts, dark brown with reddish and golden undertones making the thick mass gleam in the moonbeams. Her eyes were large and very green and she had a mouth that he could fixate on when he'd never obsessed or fixated on anything in his very long existence.

The vivid colors were disorienting when he already was in a weakened state. His stomach knotted. Churned. He felt as if he had vertigo. He needed to sit up. To protect her. The colors flashed through his mind, swirling into a nightmare of soundless chaos. At the same time, emotions poured in, feelings he couldn't sort through fast enough to make sense of or process.

Carter was on the ground cowering as Shorty reached for the woman. She whirled around and bonked him over the head. "Do you have *any* idea how hard it is for me to meditate when you're *murdering* someone?" She glared at Andor over her shoulder. "And you. Lying there, deciding whether or not you've had enough of life? What is *wrong* with you? Life is to be cherished. Not thrown away."

Shorty tried another misguided attempt to punch her. She hit his hand with the pot so hard even Andor winced at the sound. Shorty howled and stepped back, regarding her warily.

"I'm on a journey seeking personal enlightenment and you are disturbing my aura of love." The pot hit Barnaby on his shoulder hard enough that he covered up and turned sideways to avoid another swipe. He'd made the mistake of trying to sneak up on her from the other side.

"I'm on a path of nonviolence so that my life can be an example to the world of what it would be like living in a better place. Peace . . ." She smashed the pot against the side of Barnaby's head as he went at her again and then kicked the side of his knee hard enough to send him to the ground. "Love." She turned toward Shorty and began to advance on him menacingly. "Embracing nature."

Shorty grinned at her and shook his head. "You're a nut."

"Maybe, but you're a murderer." She ducked a punch and bashed his arm, blocking it smoothly with the pot while she stepped in and punched his jaw. Hard.

Andor could see Shorty's head snap back. She had quite a punch but he was going to have to do something before the murderous pack got serious about going after his woman. He forced his body to move. It wasn't easy with a stake protruding from his chest, right beneath his heart. When he moved, blood leaked out around the wood. It hurt like hell and he had to cut off his ability to feel pain if he was going to actually move.

"*Don't.*" Her voice hissed out at him, a clear command. Annoyed.

No one in his lifetime had ever used a tone like that on him. *He* gave the orders, not a woman, and certainly not a human. Worse. A human woman.

"Don't you move. I'll get to you in a minute." She turned her head to look at him over her shoulder and her eyes widened in horror. "Oh. My. God." Her sauce pot lowered and she half turned toward him.

He waved his hand toward Shorty, who was coming up behind her fast. Shorty stumbled and fell, almost at her feet, drawing her attention. She smashed the pot over his head. She became a little fury, rushing Barnaby again.

"Why would you do that to another human being?" There was a little sob in her voice, as if just seeing the cruelty of the stake in Andor's chest hurt her as well. "I'm supposed to be learning to live without anger and you're *torturing* and brutally murdering another man. How can I possibly be okay with that? If this is some kind of test, I'm failing. You're making me fail." She kicked Barnaby in the chest hard. Her forward snap kick was powerful and it sent the assassin flying back so far, he hit a tree and slid to the ground.

"He's not human," Carter shouted. "That's a vampire."

She stopped in her tracks. "You're all crazy. He's a man." For the first time, wariness had crept in.

Maybe she finally realized she was out in the middle of nowhere with three madmen who had staked another man. Andor could only hope.

"There's no such things as vampires."

The three men got shakily to their feet and then fanned out, surrounding her. "We saw him. He called down lightning. Look at the scorch marks on the grass," Carter said.

"They're right, in that there are such creatures as vampires," Andor said calmly. He managed to sit all the way up, both hands supporting the stake. He was weaker than he realized. Maybe he really wasn't going to make it out of this one. He'd lost far too much blood. "They're also wrong. I'm not a vampire. I was hunting them. They saw the tail end of the fight." He had no idea why he was bothering to explain. He had never explained his actions in his life.

"Don't listen to him," Shorty said. "Cover your ears. Vampires can beguile you."

"Beguile me?" She sounded as if she thought Shorty was insane. Her gaze shifted to Andor and she paled. "For God's sake, lie back down now."

Her skin looked beautiful in the moonlight. His eyes on hers, Andor reached up to grasp the thick stake protruding from his chest. Her eyes widened. She shook her head, dropped the sauce pot and ran toward him.

"No. Don't pull that out."

Shorty tried to grab her as she ran past him. The thought of one of these men putting their hands on her brought out something in Andor he hadn't known was lurking beneath the surface. It exploded out of him, a roar of pure rage. It came with the force of a volcano, welling up from somewhere deep and threatening to annihilate everything in its path.

"Do not touch her." It was a decree. A command. Nothing less.

The mandate froze all three men. She made it past them and was on her knees at his side, her face a mask of worry as she touched the stake.

"Don't move." She jumped back up, pulled a cell phone from her jeans and began frantically trying to get it to work. She kept putting her arm up into the air, waving her phone around and moving from one place to another.

"What are you doing?"

"I need to find just one bar. Just one. We're down in this valley and I can't get service to call in rescue." She pushed past Shorty and then stopped. Froze. Very slowly she turned her head to look at the man. He wasn't moving. He stood, one arm outstretched but he was looking the other way. Not at her. "Um." She backed away from Shorty. "What's wrong with you?" She looked at the other two men. Neither so much as blinked. She backed up even more. "Something's wrong with them." She turned very slowly to look at Andor.

He could smell her fear. It was beginning to dawn on her that no human being could live with a stake the size of the one he had in his chest. Now the men claiming he was a vampire weren't able to move. They looked like statues carved of stone. He considered leaving them like that, but it would raise questions in the human world and he couldn't have that. Not now, when there seemed to be a real war brewing between vampires and Carpathians. More than that, he needed blood if he was going to survive this time, and the three could supply it. He *had* to survive now. There was no other choice.

"I need your help," he said quietly.

She shook her head, but she took several steps toward

him. "I'm not good with blood. I need to call someone . . ." Her voice was faint this time.

"There isn't time. If you don't do as I ask, I *will* die and you will have risked your life for nothing. Thank you for that, by the way." He kept very calm, hoping she would follow his lead.

"When I say I'm not good with blood, I mean I could faint."

"I'll deal with the blood. You just do what I tell you and we'll get through this."

She looked from the three men frozen like statues back to him. Her gaze dropped to the pooling blood. "You're bleeding from more than the stake."

"I told you, before they came, I was engaged in a battle." Hands covering the gaping wound in his belly, because he could see she really might faint, he had no choice but to lie back. Sun scorch his weakness. She was afraid now, he could see it in her expression and feel it in her mind. He was doing his best to keep her from reading his thoughts. She was clearly telepathic. She had knowledge of his consideration to end his life and she wouldn't have that if she wasn't reading him. Keeping her out of his mind took effort.

"Okay." She moved cautiously toward him, her sauce pot held like a weapon. "I wasn't kidding when I said I don't do well around blood."

For the first time, he caught a note of shame. Of guilt. He didn't like it. He liked her annoyed. He liked her fighting. He liked her confident. That jarring note put knots in his gut and gave him a need to gather her close and comfort her. It was also getting more difficult to block the pain in his chest. He wanted to grasp the stake and pull it out, but he needed her to have everything ready for him.

"You're going to need to pack my wounds with fresh soil. It can't be burnt. If there's scorch marks on the ground or grass, it can't be used." He closed his eyes. He could feel the beads of blood dotting his forehead and running down his face. When she saw that up close, she might really faint and then he'd have no one to help. It was too late to send out a call.

"What's your name?" At least, if he was going to die, he'd go knowing the name of the woman who had come to save him.

"Lorraine. Lorraine Peters." He heard her take a deep breath. She was that close. "And you're not going to die. We can do this. Are you certain about the soil?" She was already scooping dirt into her sauce pot. "It's very unsanitary."

"My body responds to the soil. To the earth. When you have enough, bring it to me." He wanted to see her face, but he was afraid if he opened his eyes and looked at her, she would be the last thing he saw. He would take that vision with him to the next life, instead of enjoying time with her after waiting for so many centuries.

Her body jerked hard and Andor realized he was drifting. She might have caught some of his thoughts.

"I am sliding in and out of consciousness and having odd dreams. I think these men put weird thoughts in my head." It was the best he could do and it seemed to work. She was breathing again. Not even, but still, he hadn't lost her yet. He tried to keep air moving in and out of his lungs.

"I'm sorry I'm such a baby about blood." She knelt beside him. "I just don't see how I'm going to be of help to you. This stake . . ." She trailed off. There were tears in her voice. Misery.

She wasn't worried about him being a vampire. She wasn't thinking about the three men standing behind her as still as statues. She was thinking she was an utter failure as a human being because she couldn't look at the blood seeping around the stake or dripping from any number of wounds he couldn't heal.

"Bring the soil up close to me. I need to mix saliva with it." He hoped she'd be so intrigued she'd forget about the blood. A sense of urgency was beginning to take hold. He knew he was slipping away. Too much blood loss.

"Um . . ."

"Andor. My name is Andor Katona."

"You've lost so much blood. You need a transfusion."

She was still catching partial thoughts, but didn't realize it. He had to be careful, but it was impossible when he was trying to keep himself alive. Ordinarily, he would open the earth, shut down and try to allow the soil to heal him, but he was too far gone and he knew it now. Anxiety gripped him. After centuries of hunting her, he found her, and he was slipping away inch by inch, or pint by pint of blood loss.

"I can spit," she offered.

There was a note of hesitancy like she thought he was a lunatic and she was simply indulging him because she was certain he was going to die. He was beginning to think he might.

"Let me." He didn't know if her saliva was powerful enough to help with healing. His saliva contained a healing agent as well as a numbing one.

He scooped a handful of the soil, mixed it with his saliva and pressed it into one of the gaping wounds in his belly where a vampire had tried to eviscerate him. Now that she had something to do besides faint at the sight of him covered in blood, she concentrated on helping him pack his wounds.

Andor closed his eyes and tried to conserve his strength. As an ancient, he had built up tremendous power and control. He had never considered that three humans—not very bright ones at that—might bring him down.

"Don't." She whispered the command. "Tell me what to do next."

"I need blood. I've lost too much. Pack the soil around the stake. I can't take it out until I have a transfusion."

"I'll give you my blood," she said, her voice trembling. "But I'm afraid I really will pass out. Just tell me what to do."

He was *starving*. Every cell in his body craved blood. Was it safe to take her blood? He would have to stop before he took too much from her and he didn't know if he still had that kind of control. He had to rely on her. If she was weak, she couldn't help him. On the other hand, if he was going to release one of the human males from their frozen state, he would need to be stronger to keep them under his power.

He could feel two of his teeth growing sharp. Lengthening. He breathed deep and kept his head turned from hers. "I can help you through it if you let me. I'm telepathic as well. You know we have shields, barricades in our minds, so to speak. Trust me enough to let me make it easier for you. I don't have much more time."

There was a small silence. He lifted his lashes just enough to see her chewing at her full lower lip with small white teeth. She nodded. "Yes. But hurry. I'm already feeling dizzy. I'm trying not to look but it's nearly impossible. And my hands are covered in . . ."

"I'll take care of it." He reached for her mind immediately. There was no sense in waiting. She was either going to let down her barriers and he was going to live, or she wouldn't and he wasn't going to make it.

He reached for her hand, and just that act sent pain crashing through him, driving the air from his lungs in a brutal rush of agony. Her skin was soft, like silk. His thumb brushed over her pulse, where it beat so frantically. She was afraid of him. Of giving her blood. Of fainting and making a fool of herself. Her phobia of blood made her feel foolish and weak. She detested it and tried very hard to overcome it.

He forced himself to stop reading her and took complete control, using the last of his strength to take over her mind. He was very lucky in that she had taken down her shields herself, giving her trust to him when he had yet to earn it. He didn't delve deeper into her mind to find out why. He sank his teeth into her wrist.

Her blood burst into his mouth like bubbles of the finest champagne. Nothing had ever tasted so exquisite. So perfect. He knew he would always be obsessed, would always crave her taste. He savored every drop, feeling his cells reach for the nourishment, soaking it up, desperate to replace what was lost.

For the first time that he could remember, Andor had to fight himself for discipline. For control. He didn't want to stop. He *never* wanted to stop. He was desperate for blood. Her blood. Very gently he swept his tongue over the two holes in her wrist and turned his head toward the three would-be assassins.

Shorty came to life, one slow inch at a time. His body jerked and he took a step toward the Carpathian. Terror was written on the man's face. Andor ignored it. He didn't want to waste his strength on calming the man; after all, he'd helped drive a stake through Andor's chest.

The moment Shorty got to him and knelt obediently, presenting his neck, Andor sank his teeth deep. The blood was good. Not tainted with alcohol or drugs. He took as much as he dared and then sent the man back to his campsite after wiping his memories. He planted an encounter with wild animals, something that would definitely spook him, and make him uneasy enough to want to break camp and go home.

He brought Barnaby close next, instructing him to kneel beside him and grasp the stake with both hands. Andor took the remainder of the soil, mixed it with his saliva, took a deep breath and told the human to remove the stake. Nothing in his long life had ever hurt as much as it did when that stake was driven into his chest. It hurt nearly as much when it was removed.

Blood welled up and he shoved the soil deep into the hole, gritting his teeth, grinding them together to keep from striking out at the helpless man. More blood spilled around the wound, soaking into the dirt. He couldn't breathe for a moment. Or think. He just lay there, gasping, staring at Lorraine's beautiful face, telling himself she was worth everything that he had endured, including this.

His vows to her were carved into his back—tattooed

there in the old primitive method, the ink made by the monks in the monastery. They had to scar the skin deliberately with each poke from an array of needles. He had the vows in Carpathian going down his back. He'd meant every single word.

*Olen wäkeva kuntankért. Olen wäkeva pita belső kulymet. Olen wäkeva—félért ku vigyázak. Hängemért.*

He had other tattoos, but none meant as much to him. The code he lived by was scarred forever into his back. He was Carpathian and it took a lot to leave a scar. He had suffered to put those words into his skin, but they needed to be there—for her. The code was simple.

*Staying strong for our people. Staying strong to keep the demon inside. Staying strong for her. Only her.*

Those last two words of his code—his vow—said everything. Every wound he had suffered in battle, every time he had to kill an old friend or relative, every night that he rose and endured the gray void, was for her. Now he knew her name. Lorraine. He loved the sound of it. He loved the look of her and her grit. She had courage, even if she needed to temper it a bit with wisdom.

While he took Barnaby's blood, he thought of the monastery and those long, endless years without hope. They spent nights practicing their battle skills and then working on their tattooing techniques. All of those residing in the monastery had become brothers—although they knew they might have to kill the other. The difference was—it would be an honorable way to die.

He sent Barnaby on his way with the same memory of wild animals getting too near their camp. He planted a memory of them all running in different directions and then one by one making their way back to camp with the idea of breaking it down and heading to their homes. They no longer sought to hunt and kill vampires, nor did they believe in them.

Now that he was a little stronger, he directed Carter, the one who had actually driven the stake into his chest, to start digging into the soil. Andor knew he couldn't move. He was too heavy for Lorraine to help him get out of the sun. He had to get into the ground, had to have Lorraine pitch her tent right over the top of him.

Carter couldn't dig very deep without tools. He used Lorraine's sauce pot. He dug right next to Andor so the Carpathian could shift his body enough to slide into the shallow depression. It was no more than a foot deep, but it was long enough and wide enough for his body, which was saying something. He wasn't a small man.

He forced Carter to help him and then took his blood before sending him on his way with the same memories as Barnaby and Shorty. It was the best that he could do. Just that small movement had him leaking blood. He needed time to let the soil rejuvenate him enough to gather the strength to begin healing himself. Carpathians as old as he was were incredibly strong. He could overcome this, he just needed a little luck on his side and Lorraine.

He released her mind and she blinked at him, still kneeling, but now he was about a foot from her in the depression. He should have had Carter dig it deeper, but he couldn't take the time. He attempted a smile at her, going for reassurance, but just looking at her hurt nearly as much as the hole in his chest.

On her, the colors appeared even more vivid. Her hair, with the moon shining down on it, was a beautiful mix of hues. Her skin was nearly translucent she was so pale. He knew that was from him taking her blood.

"Are you feeling all right?"

She blinked several times, calling his attention to the sweep of thick, long lashes. "Where's the stake? How did you get it out?" On her knees, she shuffled closer to him and let out a little feminine gasp that caught him somewhere deep when she saw the hole in his chest packed with soil. It wasn't a small hole. It hadn't been a small stake.

"I didn't want you to have to deal with it. I do need your help. I'm weak. Really weak."

She looked beyond him and then turned around fast, clearly looking for the three men.

"They left. Ran."

"Cowards, but I'm glad they're gone. Still, having them where I could see them made me happier because now I have to worry they might come back to try to kill us."

"They ran out of here and I planted a suggestion, one that, if it takes, means they won't even remember us."

"You're an extremely strong telepath," she said. "And I can't believe you're still alive, but we need to call for help. Get a helicopter to get you out of here. I'm going to have to hike up to the top of the mountain and see if I can get cell service."

He shook his head. "Are you camping with a tent?"

"Of course." Her fingers brushed at the stubble on his face. She had a little frown as she rubbed at something along his jaw, determined to remove it. He was certain it was a bloodstain. Her gaze studiously avoided any other part of his body where the wounds had bled, leaving wet, red stains behind.

"How long will it take you to break down your camp and bring everything here?"

She frowned at him. "Not long at all. I camp a lot, but seriously, Andor, I'm not good at taking care of injured people and you don't seem to realize how bad off you are. We need a helicopter."

"My body doesn't respond to regular medicine."

"Does it respond to a surgeon repairing holes in your body? That gash in your stomach was horrendous. And that stake . . ." She trailed off, going even paler if that was possible.

"No, I told you, although you're trying hard to make me human. I hunt vampires. My body makeup is different. I know you thought I was going to die and you humored me by allowing me to put soil in my wounds, but the earth really has healing properties." Sun scorch him, he was exhausted. "Please. I'm asking for your help. Get your things and come back. Wild animals will find me and I'm helpless."

She regarded him with a small frown. "I didn't think about the animals, but you're right. I have no idea what to do." She sank back onto her heels. "If I leave you to hike up the mountain, you could really be in danger. If I stay, seriously, Andor, you could die. You should already be dead."

He was beginning to really fall for that frown, or maybe he was just light-headed from the pain. Keeping it at bay was becoming difficult in spite of the infusion of blood. He was still leaking far too much, and right now, blood was at a premium. He had been careful not to leave the three vampire assassins too weak. He wanted them out of the area.

"Just hurry and get your camping things."

"The scent of blood will draw wildlife. There are bears and coyotes in these mountains. For all I know, there could be wolves, but I don't think so. I can't leave you alone."

"You have to. We need your tent. I can't be out in the sun. Not even for a few minutes. You have to cover me with your tent and the soil through the daytime. I'll sleep and hope the soil starts the healing process." It was going to be a long process at the rate he was going.

He knew the moment he'd won. Her face changed from worry and indecision to determination. "It's going to take about twenty minutes. I'm not that far from here, but it is a little bit of a hike." She was already on her feet, anxious to go now that they had a plan.

"Lorraine, thank you for not asking questions and arguing."

"What would be the use? I can't leave you, and I can't raise anyone from down here in this valley. You're either going to live or die, and you're the strongest person I've ever met, so I'm betting you're going to live."

He hoped she was right. He didn't feel very strong. In fact, he just wanted to close his eyes and let the night take him for a little while. Just to give himself a few minutes where he didn't have to block the pain. It was taking so much strength. He was trying to slow the steady leaking of blood. Once she was back with the tent and had set everything up, he could take more of her blood, but he needed her fit, not weak.

"I'll need water," he reminded as she started to turn away.

"I have plenty and there's a stream not too far from here. I have a filtration system." She was backing away, her eyes moving over his torn body for the first time since he'd been in her mind. She swallowed hard and shook her head again. "I'll be back in a few, hang on."

Andor watched her go. She seemed to take his strength with her. His lungs continued to burn for air, telling him he needed to shut down soon. There was too much damage to his body. He had destroyed seven vampires. Two were very close to being master vampires. They'd lived long enough that he should have run across them, but he seldom remembered names or even faces of the undead.

He closed his eyes. She would come back, although she really detested the sight of blood. He read the revulsion and the way it made her ill. Her stomach churned and she'd fought not to be sick. She really had to work not to faint. It was a testimony to her courage and tenacity that she'd stuck around to help him.

She was his lifemate. He knew she was, yet he was so wounded he couldn't bind them together, he didn't dare. That meant she could still walk away from him and he'd be more dangerous than ever. He could only hope that he had read her correctly and she was everything he believed her to be. She was coming back. She had to, if he had any chance at all of surviving.

piatkus